LINCOLN'S ANGEL

The Rebecca Pomroy Story

a biographical novel by

DL FOWLER

To contact DL Fowler
visit http://DLFowler.com/contact-us

Printed in the United States of America
Harbor Hill Publishing
Gig Harbor, WA

Library of Congress Control Number: 2023922105

ISBN-13: 979-8-9889640-2-5 (hardcover)
ISBN-13: 979-8-9889640-3-2 (paperback)
ISBN-13: 979-8-9889640-4-9 (epub)

CONTENTS

To those who sacrifice so others can know healing

Deep affliction has only made them stronger—
Charles Dickens, *Oliver Twist*

CHAPTER ONE

No sooner than folks thought winter had sighed her last hoary breath, she huffed right back in—landing a blow more riotous, more ruinous than a howling tempest.

Fourteen-year-old Rebecca rose early on that bitter Boston morning in March of 1832. It wasn't that she had to worry one of her sisters or her brother would budge ahead of her to run an errand to the upholsterer's shop on Dock Square. None of them champed at the bit to face the angry storm that churned off New England's coastline. They were content to remain cocooned in their quilts.

Mama slipped a copper token into a sack of worsted wool drapery she had finished hemming the night before. She winked at her youngest daughter and whispered, "Spend it on yourself, but say nothing about it to William or your sisters."

Rebecca nodded but the coin wouldn't be the only secret she'd be keeping. Nothing would deter her. Not frozen rain dinging her cheeks or a hostile north wind knifing through her woolen coat and layered garments all the way to the bone. Not even consequences for disobeying Mama's strict orders to avoid lower Ann Street's squalor. From the first time she tagged along with Papa to that notorious district, she had borne witness to his charity toward destitute souls. He ingrained in her the notion that every life was precious, regardless of station. During her sea-captain papa's long absences, she had begun to follow in his footsteps, extending hope to indigent mothers of every kind and color and to the tykes that clung to their tattered skirts. It mattered, not, whether Mama, or anyone else, approved.

A drunken sailor vomited epithets and vulgarities at snowflakes lapping his face as Rebecca reached lower Ann Street. She imagined he had just stumbled—or been tossed—out of one of many brothels in the neighborhood. As she approached, he leaned against the post of a broken gaslamp and leered at her. She angled across the street, only to have him let out a loud whistle and thrust his pelvis at her like an eager cur.

At the next corner, a ring of street-urchins malingered in front of a jilt shop, begging for alms. A passerby, presumably a merchant on his way to open his Faneuil Market shop, stopped to offer a few pennies. One boy snatched the man's coin purse and tossed it to a second boy who dodged into a tavern. The pickpocket's mark slipped and tumbled on the slick sidewalk, spoiling any chance he might have had at recovering his purse.

Rebecca clutched her bundle closer and walked more briskly toward Dock Square. Papa taught her not only to be charitable, but to be careful. He cautioned, wherever need abounded, desperation lurked.

After dropping off Mama's piecework, she visited several merchants who were opening their shops in nearby Faneuil Market. They gave her donations of combs, soaps, second-hand clothes and boots, old blankets, and morsels of food. She had made rounds of the market so many times with Papa that she learned his plea by heart—

> *My soul is tortured by the sight of them. I find it impossible to turn a deaf ear to those childish voices, their harsh discords make every nerve in my body shudder with pity.*

She repeated Papa's words with compassion and humility on that day, just as he had taught her, and the merchants did not disappoint. When her rounds of the market were finished, she carried her bounty through frigid lower Ann Street, leading a parade of children and their mothers to an alley near North Square. She huddled the children close to her in a passageway between two tall buildings, sheltering them from the elements. She did not balk at their smudged faces, grimy hands, sour breath, or threadbare, musty clothing. She read nursery rhymes as their mothers rummaged through sacks filled with necessities she had gathered.

Little Ryan nestled into her lap and clutched her thumb as she read. The boy's chubby hand reminded her of Samuel, her eighteen-month-old brother who succumbed to measles and joined the choir of angels three years prior. She paused her reading and pressed her tongue to the roof of her mouth, intent on holding it there until the memory dissolved. But that memory was not alone.

Another memory, as hazy as a marine fog, slipped through a seam in her mind—an earlier brother also named Samuel. Dark voices and somber sounds. Rebecca shuddered. Mama's woeful moans and Papa's muted groan. Thud, thump——clods of loamy soil plopped atop a Lilliputian pine box that had been lowered with ropes to the bottom of a shadowy hole, dug in dank earth. Her older sisters had recounted stories of laying flowers in Copps Hill Burying Ground at an infant's grave—another Samuel from a time before Rebecca understood that death had teeth, and it bit—some to kill, others to wound. Both interred Samuels bore Papa's Christian name.

Rebecca found Ryan's mother when she finished reading. She whispered encouragement in the woman's ear and pressed Mama's copper coin into her hands.

Before slogging home, Rebecca stopped at the dock where she had bid Papa goodbye as he departed on his most recent voyage. She stood in silence, braced against a swirl of glacial onshore gusts, and anchored to the very spot where she had lingered as his ship disappeared into the horizon. Brackish wafts filled her nostrils as she gazed past billows of iron-grey ocean that heaved and fell, heaved and fell, all the way to a black wall where everything became the same, or perhaps nothing at all.

Alabaster-breasted gulls broadcast incessant shrills, hovering and swooping near shore before soaring off like stringless kites—their dark wingtips conflating with edges of mounting storm clouds. She wished the gulls could pierce the veil beyond which she could not see and spirit Papa home.

Her hopes bore fruit later on that stormy March day. After she returned from her errand on Dock Square, Captain Samuel Holliday docked his crippled ship at Aspinwall's mast yard—a quarter mile from the Holliday family home, a brick cottage behind Ellis Cook's upper Ann Street grocery.

The fierce storm that was hammering the coast of late had forced Papa's schooner leagues off course on the return voyage from Europe. The ship's masthead sustained damage. During the last few days of sailing, the crew feared they might not make it back to Boston Harbor. Rebecca imagined it was Papa's aplomb and steady hand that had disquieted their alarm.

✳ ✳ ✳

Papa patted Rebecca's head the next morning after breakfast. He could make her troubles fade with a hearty laugh. She imagined that by speaking a single word he often gentled the storms that roiled and tossed about his sturdy wooden ship.

"Come," Papa said. "Off to Atwood's for oysters. Your mother has promised to make stew for supper. And on the way, I must check on Mr. Aspinwall's repairs."

Eight-year-old William asked if he could go see Papa's ship.

Mama didn't so much as peek away from the pot she was tending over the kitchen fire. "Not you, William. You have firewood to bring in or we shall all freeze to death."

Papa added, "No one goes aboard except crew until the mast is repaired."

Mama called out to Papa as he led their youngest daughter outside. "You shall be avoiding lower Ann Street on your way to Atwood's."

"She shall be safe enough walking with me," he answered.

A curtain of downy snowflakes drifted across their path and pillowed their footsteps. The biting cold no longer mattered to Rebecca as she basked in Papa's presence. Like a faithful pup, she followed him anywhere he would take her when he returned from endless voyages across the churning seas between Boston and Europe.

Rebecca waited on the wharf at Aspinwall's mast yard while Papa went aboard his ship to talk with the repair crew. Soon after he boarded, rows of frothy swells rocked his sleek schooner. It strained against its moorings. A flag, whipped by the wind, drew her gaze to the masthead and to a man who hugged the main pillar as it swayed to and fro. She ducked her head as a salty blast stung her eyes.

In the next instant, the man shouted from the upper reaches, "Watch out below!"

She looked up. The masthead had shivered from the mainmast. Its girth and length grew more menacing as it plunged toward the deck. Her focus flicked from Papa to the freefalling timber, from the timber to Papa, and again to the timber.

A scream stalled in her throat.

A resounding thud. Screeching gulls. Panicked groans. Yelps and yowls erupted on the ship's deck. An outburst of seamen's words, the kind that raised Mama's hackles anytime Papa used them. Rebecca strained to pick out Papa's timbre in the chorus of panic.

No cacophony of sounds could hide his voice from her. Not the chaos of Dock Square, the bedlam of merchant seamen loading and offloading cargo on the docks, nor the ruckus of whalers or fishermen emptying their holds. During Papa's long sea voyages, she often listened for him in thunderclaps, pelting rain, and howling gales. In her nightly dreams, she peered into blackness, in search of him.

A seeming eternity passed before a large man started down the gangway.

A wiry workman angled past him and began running the instant his feet touched the wood-planked wharf.

The large man continued down the gangway and stopped in front of her.

She peered around him. "I'm waiting for Papa."

"It's nasty out here," he said. "Let's go into the office and wait by the stove." His hollow eyes and grim tone struck panic in the deepest corners of her soul. Her mind teemed with questions her tongue dreaded asking.

The man offered his hand. She clung to it as she glanced over her shoulder, craning her neck to keep Papa's ship in sight. Several men appeared at the top of the gangway. Each held an edge or corner of a patchwork quilt—a makeshift litter. An arm dangled at one side. A boot hung over the end. Smudges of blood on a sailor's coat.

She called out, "Papa?"

A knot tightened in Rebecca's stomach. She flashed hot and cold. The edges of her mind caved like a molten candle folding in on itself and extinguishing its flame. Her legs gave way. She tumbled to the ground.

* * *

After Rebecca awoke on a cot in Mr. Aspinwall's office, she rose and followed one of Papa's friends outside—her jaw clenched. The horrific scene took root in her memory. She plodded beside the man, until they arrived at the Holliday family home.

On hearing the grim news of Papa's accident, Mama and her eldest, Susanna, scrambled through gritty slush and muck to the three-story, weathered boarding house on Charter Street where the widows Pearson and Brydia—midwives both—tended to him. Men from the ship had rushed him there straight from Aspinwall's.

Rebecca crouched in a dark corner of the upper Ann Street cottage, her knees drawn to her chest. She would not believe Papa could be gone. Sisters Sarah and Dorcas huddled a few feet away, sobbing on a settee Papa had scavenged from an abandoned brig. William clung to Dorcas's elbow, his gaze never wandering from Rebecca, his favorite sister.

Susanna returned within an hour. Her voice pitched as she gave the news, "Papa is dead."

William leapt from the settee and flung himself into Rebecca's arms. She stiffened. The room teetered. Images reeled in her mind—the cascading masthead, the bloody coat, the arm dangling, the boot.

From that dreadful day, March 29, 1832, high places filled her with foreboding.

❋ ❋ ❋

Papa had not been long in the ground before the family coffers ran almost dry and the cupboards approached empty. Rebecca could no longer afford the time to make rounds of lower Ann Street, offering relief to destitute families and entertaining the children. She and her three sisters worked long hours alongside Mama, competing for pennies against a host of other women in the same predicament.

Piecework wages that Mama and her daughters earned from sewing draperies, slipcovers, and the like were scarcely enough to make ends meet. The upholsterer on

Dock Square who employed them aggravated their poverty by dithering when wages came due. Even when they succeeded in collecting whatever sums were owed them, Susanna had nothing to share of her part. She and her carpenter apprentice husband struggled to keep their own household with a young daughter and infant son. But the other three girls turned over all their wages to Mama.

William struggled to find any work at all, and Mama would not hear of him begging for alms on street corners. When he did so behind her back, he slipped the pittance he collected into the tin cup that held the family's meager savings. His cheeks warmed any time Mama announced her previous counting must have been wrong.

Hunger would have compounded their misery, were it not for the generous widow Cook, who took charge of the grocery business after her husband's sudden death.

*** * ***

Mama carried an armful of root vegetables and a bag of flour into the cottage a year after Papa's death. She ignored the girls who sat in front of the hearth, fast about their sewing. She spread out the meager rations Mrs. Cook had doled out to her on the rough-hewn table, gripped the back of an idle chair, and released a soft quavering moan.

Sarah, wispy at almost eighteen, and hardy Dorcas, a year younger, dropped their work and rushed to Mama's side. Rebecca kept her head down and continued sewing.

Mama straightened and muttered, "We shall persevere."

"Yes," Dorcas said. "We surely shall."

Rebecca brought herself to her feet and joined them. "What do you mean?" she asked.

"Mrs. Cook," Mama answered. "She has found a new husband and is giving up the grocery. So, empty stomachs will not be our only problem. Anyone who purchases the grocery will become our landlord and will surely raise our rent. What shall we do for a roof over our heads? We cannot afford to pay any increase."

Dorcas elbowed Rebecca as she reassured the others, "Then we must seek more work and sew all the faster."

Rebecca sat in bed later that evening, reading by candlelight. Her throat pinched as she sounded out each word in her mind. She and her sisters never enjoyed the privilege of formal schooling, though Papa taught them the rudiments of reading whenever he was home from sea, just as his father had done with him back in his native England. The volumes of *The History of Tom Jones a Foundling* were Papa's prized possessions. He allowed his daughters to begin reading the first volume when they were twelve years old, the later ones were reserved for a time when they were more mature. Rebecca had hoped to read to him from it the night he .... Echoes of grief traced the contour of her face, depositing tangy drips at the corners of her mouth. She wanted to prove how earnestly she had practiced while he was away.

Her chin quivered as she inhaled the earthy aroma of the book's leather binding. She craved Papa's strong arms, his baritone notes, and mischievous laugh. She longed for the scent of sea that clung to his wool coat. Memories which once warmed her like embers aglow on the hearth had become daggers slashing at her heart.

A crack of thunder touched off a storm in her mind. Rogue memories rained down in torrents. Falling mastheads, sailors scurrying past, their boots red as blood. William. She awakened with a start, panting, gasping. Why was William in her dream? She scanned the room.

The others were asleep.

As her heart and mind settled, her thoughts lit on nine-year-old William, on whom had fallen the responsibility of carrying the Holliday name into posterity. William had taken on work at Aspinwall's dock for the few pennies a day paid to urchin boys who toiled at the meanest tasks. Rebecca begged him to find employment elsewhere, fearing calamity might befall him.

✳ ✳ ✳

William learned from his first day on the docks to strap muslin bands around the knuckles of both hands before scraping barnacles off the hull of a ship. He paused on a chilly November day to tighten the knot on his left hand— biting down with his teeth on one end of the strap and gripping the other end with his right hand.

A tall, weathered-faced stranger approached.

"Hello," the man said. "Looks like rough work."

A crisp onshore gust nipped William's cheek. "Not as rough as those seas get." He continued scraping.

"That's some excitement for a boy your age, sailing across a vast ocean. How old are you?"

"Almost twelve."

"That so?" the stranger said. "I was about your age when I first went to sea."

William let the barnacles be and wiped his hands on a coarse rag. "I've not been. But Papa had."

"Your papa's a sailor?"

"He was a captain, but a masthead fell and killed him. Over a year ago, right on this wharf."

The stranger removed his hat. "I'm truly sorry. My name is Father Taylor. Men around here call me the Mariners' Apostle. You may have heard of me."

"Heard of you? Everyone who works these docks knows who you are. You're from that new church, the Seamen's Bethel. I ain't much for religion, anymore, but Mama is. She's staunch Baptist."

"I would like to offer my assistance to your family. Where can I find your mother?"

"Don't know if she'd be interested, but you can try. We live in a cottage on upper Ann Street behind Mr. Cook's old grocery. The grocery's not there anymore." William turned back to his work.

Later that afternoon, Rebecca answered a rap on the cottage door to find Father Taylor at the stoop. After he introduced himself, she asked, "Are you from the new brick church down on North Square?"

"Yes."

"I watched your church being built," she said. "Part way, I mean. I stopped when men started working on the tower. I got dizzy watching them."

Father Taylor's gabled church took up half of a city block near the Black Sea district of lower Ann Street. It was seven bays deep and four bays across, with a one-and-a-half story center tower, all atop a raised basement.

"Invite the parson in," Mama called out from inside the cottage. "We cannot afford to heat the whole out of doors."

Father Taylor stepped inside and found Mama and her girls wrapped in shawls and blankets as they worked. Only a remnant of ash remained in the hearth. He thought better of shedding his coat.

Mama introduced her daughters and asked, "What can a brood of destitute girls do for you? We are scratching to survive."

"I should be the one offering help," Father Taylor replied,

"We are not too proud to accept charity." Mama stiffened. "Even from a Methodist."

"If you have children at your church," Rebecca said, "I can read to them in return for your kindness. It would be good practice for me."

"Yes, miss. In fact, Mother Taylor and I have our own litter of sea pups. They love reading." He looked to Mama for approval.

"So long as she keeps up with her share of the sewing and you do not lead her astray into your Methodist persuasion." Mama added, "We are staunch Baptists."

Rebecca took Father Taylor's acceptance of her offer as a sign. Maybe, help did come from on high. She could return to lower Ann Street and the destitute children and their mothers who struggled there to survive. In turn for her service, God would surely reward her family and spare them from further affliction.

Rebecca traded her nighttime reading for afternoon story times with the children at the Seamen's Bethel. Mornings continued to find her in a sewing circle with her sisters and Mama. Piecework not finished during the day was carried over into the night, sometimes into the early morning hours, under candlelight. Every noon time Mama took great care inspecting and counting Rebecca's work before she left for the Seamen's Bethel. Then she would shake her head and wave her daughter out the door. Rebecca endured her mother's scrutiny. All were aware that many hands make light work, but they could not deny Father Taylor's aid had been a godsend.

As word of Rebecca's work at the Bethel spread, many of the mothers and urchins from lower Ann Street followed her there. After a few months, Father Taylor recruited her to solicit alms from local merchants to finance the increased costs of serving growing numbers of sailors' families. To prevent her new responsibilities at the Bethel from taking away time from her sewing duties, she rose another hour earlier each morning and stitched at a fevered pitch until the others woke. Any sleep she might be giving up would likely cut short the night terrors which had begun to visit her with increasing frequency.

CHAPTER TWO

A young man sparked Rebecca's curiosity a few months before she turned nineteen. Her harried days—consumed by work at the Bethel and keeping up with piecework and chores at home—left only narrow windows of opportunity to indulge in social pastimes. Staying busy helped her keep a tight lid on the stew of emotions that simmered inside her. It didn't take much to trigger memories of Papa's tragedy and the foreboding that accompanied them. It had taken four years to build walls strong enough and high enough to hold the memories at bay and to keep interlopers from scaling them to peek inside. The last thing she needed was an outsider prying into her well-guarded sensibilities.

Nonetheless, something about the dark-haired stranger attracted her. Maybe it was his shyness. Or was it modesty? That wasn't something someone could decipher just by appearances. He required closer inspection.

She had been soliciting alms on behalf of the Seamen's Bethel when she first saw the young man in bustling Faneuil Market. She smiled and offered him a timid wave, but, to her dismay, he darted off and disappeared into the crowd.

She glimpsed him again the next day, weaving through the crowd.

Maybe he's trying to avoid me. I'm not that unattractive. Am I? Afterall, I'm still unmarried. Fine. I have no illusions of finding a dashing prince and living happily ever after. That only happens in fairytales. So what, if he finds my less than ample breasts off-putting.

She tucked a rogue strand of auburn hair behind her ear.

The young man zigged when he should have zagged.

She blocked his path. "Hello. I'm soliciting donations for Father Taylor's Bethel. He gives aid to distressed families of sailors."

The young man wheezed. "I must go. Please excuse..."

"Are you a merchant?"

He nodded.

"May I call on you at your shop?" she asked.

"Yes. Tomorrow." His words whistled, not through his teeth but from somewhere in his chest. "27 Dock Square."

"In the afternoon?"

"Yes. Don't mean to be rude. Must go." He hunched as he plodded off.

※ ※ ※

The next afternoon, Rebecca stood outside Dock Square No. 27, debating with herself over whether to go inside. The street teemed with boisterous vendors, barking hawkers, and horses snorting as they strained against collars that tethered them to overloaded carts. She couldn't fathom a reason she should give the young man the time of day. The arguments in her head volleyed back and forth like hails of musket fire from the ranks of Patriots and redcoats.

He needs to learn some manners ... no, he will only make excuses for his rude behavior ... scolding him would be a waste of effort ... yes, rude ... that's the appropriate word.

The word 'rude' had hung in his wake as he retreated from their previous day's encounter. She turned to leave then stopped herself.

Am I being too hasty? Maybe he had been late for an appointment with a customer.

She turned back to the shop and stared at the door handle. Still, she thought, he could have been more polite.

When the push and tug in her head abated, she marched across the threshold, triggering a bell mounted on the door. Momentarily, the young man passed through the curtain that shielded the work area from the front of the store. He hesitated at the sight of her, then summoned his shopkeeper's smile. "Good day, miss. How may I be of service today?"

"You might begin by offering an apology for rebuffing me so rudely yesterday."

"Please, I do apologize. I wasn't being rude. It was my asthmatic condition. A coughing spell was about to beset me."

"I see," she said.

"My name is Daniel. Daniel Pomroy."

"Hello Daniel. I am Rebecca Holliday." She glanced around. "You keep a tidy shop."

"It's a humble upholstery and I am a mere apprentice. Most of the work is done in the shop behind the curtain. Sails for ships. Bedding and mattresses for finer homes. Not much to offer for the public."

"I see."

"I hope to own the place once the current proprietor retires."

"Speaking of your employer, may I speak with him about donating to Father Taylor's Bethel?"

"I'm afraid he's out for the afternoon."

"What about you? Even a pittance would help."

Daniel averted her eyes. "I would gladly contribute were my wages not so meager and my obligations so steep. I support not only myself but also my widowed mother."

"You are to be commended for being a conscientious son," she said. "I suppose we have something in common. My mother is widowed. My three sisters and I, as well as our younger brother, work hard to help keep a roof over our heads and food on the table."

"Yet you raise donations for a worthy charity."

"I am glad you think it worthy." She hesitated. "Do you have brothers or sisters?"

"I carry the burden alone. Mother's health prevents her from finding employment."

"I shall not bother you in that case. God bless you and your mother."

Daniel rubbed the back of his neck. "Would it be forward of me to ask if I may see you again?"

She suppressed a budding smile as an unexpected warmth brushed her cheeks. "I have little time for leisure."

"I imagine, if you had such time," he said, "you could find more worthy company."

"You could come by the Bethel some afternoon and listen to me read to the children."

He stuffed his hands in his apron pockets. "I would like that."

The bell rang, announcing a customer's arrival.

"I shall leave you to your business," she said.

She stopped at the textile shop on the corner of Ann Street on her way to Father Taylor's Bethel and bought fabric to make a wedding gift for her sister. Dorcas would be marrying a Chelsea farmer, Minot Derby, only two days before the fourth anniversary of Papa's death. Rebecca hoped the celebration would take everyone's minds off the pang of grief that grew more intense upon the approach of March 29 each year. Having a successful farmer in the family might also ease their destitution.

✳ ✳ ✳

Acrimony greeted Rebecca when she returned home later that afternoon from her reading session with children at the Bethel. Mama shrilled, "We are not taking in that mangy cur. We don't need another mouth to feed."

Sarah and Dorcas stood behind William—he cuddled a whimpering lump of fur.

Rebecca pleaded, "Mama."

"What's a poor widow to do once all her girls are married off, and she's left with a useless boy and his helpless dog?"

Rebecca edged over to William and petted the pup. "I'm sure—"

Mama cut her off. "And you're one to talk. When these two are off making their own nests, I will have just half a daughter's efforts to help me keep up with all this sewing."

"But—" Rebecca started.

Mama waved her off and stirred the pot of potato soup hanging over glowing coals.

Rebecca turned to her sisters and mimed a question, pleading for an explanation.

With her back still to her children, Mama said, "Congratulate Sarah. The last of your sisters is getting married."

Rebecca pursed her lips to hide her excitement.

Dorcas explained, "Charles Yendell is courting our sister."

"You mean," Rebecca asked, "that handsome young grocer down the street?"

Sarah beamed. "We're to marry in September."

"If you're done celebrating," Mama grumbled, "you can set the table for supper. And William, put that stinky mutt outside to find its own provision."

William shuffled toward the door. As he passed Rebecca, he mumbled, "I'm moving across the river to

Chelsea after Dorcas is married. Minot says he could use another farmhand."

As William went outside, Rebecca slipped past Mama, scanning the kitchen for scraps. She stuffed what she could find into her apron pockets and joined him on the front stoop. She sidled up to him then jerked away. "He does stink."

He muttered, "I know why Papa spent so much time at sea."

"You're being too harsh. She hasn't been the same since Papa ..."

"I miss him, too, but I don't take it out on poor, orphaned creatures."

Rebecca stroked the pup. "Mama bears the weight of the world. The thing she fears most is all of us growing up and leaving her alone."

"I cannot be who she wants me to be." He set his jaw.

"We all fret over you working on the docks. You might follow in Papa's footsteps. Too closely."

"You can stop worrying," he said. "I'll soon be breaking my back as a farmhand."

* * *

Daniel creaked open the door to a classroom in the basement of Father Taylor's Bethel where Rebecca read to the children. She glanced up but didn't let her gaze linger. In the back of her mind, she hoped she had not displayed too much pleasure over his visit.

He edged forward and took a seat on the floor with the children.

After she finished the session, she eyed Daniel as the children filed out. She tousled the hair of several of the boys and gave the girls pats on their heads. When the last of the children were out of earshot she said, "You came."

"You read very well," he said. "You were fortunate to attend school. Not many girls have that privilege." He sputtered. "That is changing, of course."

"I did not attend any school. It wasn't something my family could afford."

"How did you learn to read so well?"

She held up the volume of *Tom Jones*. "Papa taught me before ... before he was killed."

"I am sorry," he said. "How old were you?"

"Three months before I turned fifteen."

Daniel lowered his head. "My father's heart gave out. I was five. He and his partner owned The Feather Shop at the corner of Dock Square."

"I visited that store yesterday." She canted her head to one side. "When did you learn upholstering?"

"His partner, Mr. Simpson, let me help in his workroom behind the store. I am grateful for his mentorship, and he recommended me to apprentice for my current employer. That was three years ago. I was eighteen. Now I am acquiring a respectable trade."

"You started late," she said. "Many boys are already finished apprenticing by sixteen."

"I was a slow learner. Sick a lot."

"Do you still miss your father?" she asked.

"I have been able to soldier on. But yes, and my mother still grieves deeply. It is possibly the reason she is not well most of the time."

Rebecca fell silent. Memories of Mama's explosion the prior evening needled her.

"I should be going," he said.

"Please come back any time. If you'd like, you can read. I'm sure the boys will be inspired, and the girls will be charmed."

He smiled. "Very well. I will look forward to seeing you. Soon."

✵ ✵ ✵

As romance blossomed between Rebecca and Daniel over the next few months, she shortened her donation collection rounds and carried her piecework to the Dock

Square shop to sew alongside her new beau. One Saturday afternoon in late July she pushed a needle so hard through a thick fold of fabric that the point broke off in her thumb. She yelped.

Daniel dropped his work and clasped her hands in both of his as he examined the slim margin by which the needle shaft protruded above the skin. He retrieved a razor from his apron pocket. "I must make a small cut," he said. "There is not enough of the needle to grip with my pliers."

"Don't worry," she replied as she squeezed back tears. "I shan't wilt from the pain or the sight of a little blood."

Daniel made a small incision at one side of the stub and nudged the tips of the pliers into the cut. After he failed on a couple of attempts at removing it, Rebecca snatched the pliers out of his hand.

"You are being too dainty," she insisted.

Before Daniel could lodge an objection, she plucked out the broken needle point. He did not miss the chance, however, to address a modest bloom of blood rising from her wound. He took her hand and raised it to his mouth. They locked eyes for a second before a smile unfolded on her lips. He took her expression for an invitation and kissed her thumb. When she didn't object, he prolonged the kiss.

Her cheeks warmed. "My," she said. "That was forward."

"I am sorry," Daniel said. "I thought ..."

She leaned towards him and kissed his cheek. "It is good to know you kiss so tenderly."

"Why don't we take a stroll?" he said.

As they neared the waterfront during their stroll, Rebecca nudged him, trying to steer him away from the wharf.

"What's the matter?" he asked.

"I don't care to be around the docks," she answered.

"You have no problem going to the Bethel or lower Ann Street."

"I just don't want to. Besides, those places are not on the docks."

Daniel scanned the waterfront, searching for a cause for her apprehension. He spotted a large group of Black Bostonians gathered at the foot of a gangway of an idle cargo ship and gestured toward the scene. "Are they the problem?"

"No," she replied. "It isn't that."

The thought of approaching the wharf unlatched a door in Rebecca's mind. Painful memories began leaking out. She fought to corral them, shove them back where they belonged. Where they could do no harm.

Daniel took her hand. "Come," he said.

His firm grip grounded her, gave her a measure of hope the memories would stay locked away, at least for the moment. She followed him.

Fine hairs rose on the back of Rebecca's neck as they lingered on the fringe of the assembly. The air was electric with tension.

A deputy sheriff started down the gangplank of the ship, followed by two colored women and a stern-faced white gentleman. Cheers erupted as all four stepped onto the dock and waded into the crowd.

Daniel asked a bystander what the commotion meant. The man said two run-away slaves had been confined on the ship by petition of their former master from down south. An attorney went aboard with the sheriff to serve a writ, and they must have succeeded in winning the women's release.

"Good for him," Daniel said.

Rebecca squeezed his hand and echoed his sentiment. "Yes. Good for him, and God bless those poor women."

"If that is the case," the man continued, "Chief Justice Shaw will decide their fate at a hearing tomorrow morning."

Rebecca pressed Daniel to escort her so she could witness the proceedings.

"I had to nudge you to go see what was going on," Daniel replied. "Now you want to get involved in something that is not our business."

She looked askance at him. "'He prayeth best, who loveth best, all things both great and small, for the dear God who loveth us made and loveth all.'"

"I don't understand."

"The poet who wrote those lines was an Englishman—one of Papa's favorites. The poem is called *The Rime of the Ancient Mariner*."

"But what does that have to do with two Negro women appearing in court?"

"According to Papa, the point of the poem is that all creatures deserve our blessing in equal measure."

"Because God blessed us first," he added.

"Mr. Pomroy." She poked him in the side. "It seems that you have been listening to Father Taylor's sermons."

"His humor holds my attention," Daniel replied. "He once told a story about a preacher friend on the prairie who dabbled in politics. Father Taylor said his friend's political opponent stood nearly six-and-a half-feet tall and was so angular that if you dropped a plummet from the center of his head it would cut him three times before it touched his feet."

Rebecca laughed. "I remember that story. I believe the preacher's adversary wasn't old enough to raise whiskers on his chin and was reputed to be an infidel. His name was Link-something. Like a long link of sausage. It was good that a man of God came out on top among the voters."

"Yes, and the prairie preacher was Cartwright, as in the right cart won the race."

Rebecca's eyes gleamed as she gazed into his. "I believe you are beginning to grow on me."

* * *

Rebecca and Daniel met at the Seamen's Bethel the next morning and proceeded to the courthouse—a three-story sandstone building covering a narrow block of Court Street. Daniel read Rebecca's unease as they approached the jittery throng of mostly Negro women who waited outside.

"Do you want to go through with this?" he asked.

She nodded. "We're here. We might as well go in."

Daniel led her along the margins of the crowd and up the courthouse steps. They took refuge behind two massive columns at one side of the colonnade. He draped an arm over her shoulder the moment the doors opened and guided her up a flight of stairs to the second-story courtroom, where they found a seat at the rear of the chamber. The press of Black humanity that followed in their wake spilled forward and filled every row. The chamber was abuzz until two colored women entered, led by a deputy sheriff.

At nine o'clock, Chief Justice Shaw ascended the imposing dais and seated himself. He rapped the gavel and called the court into session before reading his opinion without fanfare. "The question before the court," he said, "simply put, is did the captain of the brig *Chickasaw* have the right to convert his vessel into a prison? It is my studied opinion that no such right exists and that the women were unlawfully detained. The prisoners must be discharged from all further detention."

The slaveholder's agent stood and inquired whether he needed a new warrant to arrest the women under the Fugitive Slave Law. While the question was being laid before the court, a constable was accosted by spectators as he made a beeline for the chamber's entryway.

Someone yelled, "He's gonna bar the door. They ain't gonna let them go free."

An overflow crowd that had gathered in the corridor outside the chamber, straining to hear the proceedings, charged in and demanded justice.

Rebecca and Daniel hunkered in their seats.

Judge Shaw slammed down his gavel and shouted, "Order!"

A loud voice from among the spectators rang out, "Go! Go! Get them women outta here."

A husky old colored woman crossed the low railing that separated the audience from the litigants. She threw her arms around a constable who had been guarding the detainees and wrestled him to the floor.

Dozens more breached the railing and surrounded the two runaways.

A loud chant filled the courtroom. "Don't stop! Don't stop!"

The swarm of spectators swept the two women through the judge's private passageway near the dais.

When the judge bolted from the bench, Daniel grabbed Rebecca's arm and exhorted her to follow. They dashed up a side aisle to the near-empty vestibule and down the stairway to the main floor. As soon as they reached the street, a carriage sped past, raising cheers from a throng of onlookers.

Rebecca and Daniel didn't stop long enough to ask who was in the carriage but ran as fast as their feet would carry them down Court Street, not stopping to catch their breath until they passed the Old State House. Daniel doubled over, his lungs burning, each breath whistling in his chest.

She put her hand on his back. "Are you going to be all right? What can I do to help?"

He glanced up at her, his hands gripping his knees. "I am fine," he gasped.

She stared back toward the courthouse. "I hope that carriage was racing those two women to their freedom. They crave liberty like everyone else, but there is a line drawn in the soil, beyond which that right is denied. A line drawn not by God but by greed and cruelty. It is my sincere prayer that they never again be made to cross over to the wrong side of that line."

Daniel straightened, drawing breath. "The same greed is all around. Corrupt men in every city build empires on the backs of the poor, regardless of their color."

"Since Boston is my home," she said, "it is here that I shall combat them. Whenever I walk the length of Ann Street, my soul is tortured by the sight of friendless, destitute, and degraded children—every kind and color—malingering, unsheltered, exposed to every blight and degree of vice."

He flinched at a sharp pain in his lungs. "I wish you would not immerse yourself in such depravity, no matter how charitable your intentions."

"It is impossible to turn a deaf ear to the cries of helpless children and the pleas of their poor mothers."

"Do you plan to feed and shelter all of the city's wretched souls? By yourself? You cannot just pick up any urchin and take her home like she was a stray dog."

"I have never suggested such, but if needs be, I shall. Before Papa died, I imagined it my destiny to gather small children and distract them from their misery. Reading to them, playing games, gathering flowers." She sighed. "I nearly became one of them. As Father Taylor sometimes says, 'there but by the grace of God go I.'"

"You've just one set of hands," he pleaded. "And you work them to the bone as it is."

"Those two women today were not alone." She crossed her arms. "Hundreds gathered to help in their hour of despair, but someone was at the head, setting the scene in motion. It shall be my purpose to ease suffering wherever I find it and to encourage others to do likewise."

"Have you considered the costs?" he asked. "Not only in money, but in exposing yourself to danger and all sorts of diseases that spread among the poor."

"Do you think anyone of those people at the courthouse gave heed to the risk they were taking?"

"Rebecca Holliday, you are like no other girl I have ever known."

"I am no girl, but a young woman, likely to become an old maid."

"A woman you very well are, but someday an old maid?" He shook his head. "Impossible."

"You think I shall be under some man's thumb?" She scrunched up her nose.

"A man would be a fool to imagine himself as your head. Your foot soldier is more likely."

"There is no appeal in having a drudge for a husband. An ally would be more to my taste."

"I believe you are on to something." He smiled. "We were in fact allies of a sort this very morning at the courthouse. Were we not?"

Rebecca's mind drifted back to recent moments when her cheeks warmed at the thought of him. "Daniel Pomroy, that almost sounded like a marriage proposal."

"I shall have to improve upon it if it sounded only almost." He took her hand. "Would you have me for a husband?"

She tilted her head. "I could imagine the possibility."

"Then I shall work to convince you beyond all doubt."

✳ ✳ ✳

Rebecca dipped-dabbed the spoon in her soup at supper that evening, eager to tell Sarah about Daniel's proposal. It was not something she wanted to discuss in Mama's presence, though—not yet.

"Something wrong with the soup, dear?" Mama asked.

"No ..." Rebecca toyed with a lock of hair dangling beside her face.

"I know it's only potato soup," Mama replied. "I had to go sparingly on the salt."

Sarah reached across the table and patted Mama's hand. "My darling Charles will gladly offer some salt from his grocery. I shall ask him tomorrow. He's taking me on a picnic."

Mama regarded Rebecca. "How about you? When are you going to find some handsome beau to marry and leave your mama high and dry to fend for herself?"

"Mama," Sarah huffed. "Our husbands will—"

Rebecca interrupted. "Of course, they will."

"Humph." Mama sneered "You're one to talk. You only have time for that Methodist preacher and his street urchins. No man will put up with a wife who neglects her family to save the world."

"I'll have you know," Rebecca pushed back from the table. "This very afternoon I received a marriage proposal." Her face reddened.

Sarah set aside her soup spoon. "Daniel proposed? Did you say yes?"

"I said I would consider the matter." She drew her lips into a tight line.

"There you have it." Mama snatched her napkin and tossed it down on the table. "You'll be down at that upholstery shop sewing for your husband, and I'll be left with these stacks of piecework and no one to help. My fingers are already gnarled from stitching day and night."

"I would make time for both. I can give up some of my time at the Bethel."

"Oh, now you can give up time at that place." Mama leered at her. "For a husband. But you would not do that for your poor mother."

Sarah folded her arms. "Mama, that's unfair."

Mama stood and muttered, "I am not the villain," then stomped off to her bedroom, gnashing her teeth.

Sarah turned to Rebecca. "Well?"

"Well, what?"

"Are you?"

Rebecca sank back in her chair. "I have yet to make up my mind."

"Why not? He's a fine fellow with a secure future."

"I need time to think on it. Marriage has not been on the top of my mind."

"You seem quite smitten with one another. Surely, the topic has come up before now."

"It has been hinted at, I suppose, but other matters have consumed my attention."

"It's time you set those matters aside to give Daniel's proposal every consideration, before you lose him. Unless you do not truly love him."

CHAPTER THREE

Rebecca and Daniel sewed side-by-side at the upholstery shop on a searing late August day. Sarah's words rang in her ears—unless you do not truly love him.

"Am I wrong in saying Mama is being unreasonable?" Rebecca asked. "Shouldn't she want her daughters to marry and live happy lives?"

Daniel paused his stitching. "It has only been five years since your father's passing. Your mother still grieves. My mother has mourned for more than fifteen."

She shrugged. "We all mourn."

"Your mother fears she shall wind up abandoned and alone once Sarah marries and you decide to take the leap."

"We shall never abandon her." She cast a sideways glance at Daniel. "We will be there for her, just not under the same roof."

"Marriage adds new obligations with no increase in the number of each day's hours." Daniel took her hand. "How would you make room in your heart for a husband alongside your other passions?"

"When the time comes, I will find a way."

"I asked for your hand in marriage. Am I to take it that your answer is no?"

"That is not at all what I meant."

Daniel released her hand and returned to his stitching. "If we were to marry, what would you give up to make time for us?"

"Do we not spend a great deal of time together now?" She angled her head into his line of vision.

"But the obligations of marriage may demand more," Daniel replied. "What will you do once we have children? Who will you neglect? Your mother? Your husband? Will you resent me when you are no longer able to help destitute mothers and children?"

"Are you saying you will not be my ally? My partner?"

"I am more than your ally and partner. I only ask what we will do when obstacles impede us."

"We shall press on with our best efforts."

"Rebecca, darling, I must know. Do you love me above all else?"

She bit her lip and stared into his eyes.

"I suppose in your hesitation I have all the answer I need."

She cupped his face. "I only paused to search my heart. To be certain my answer is true. That there is no hidden reservation buried within me."

"What did you find?"

"Only that I love you above all else and I cannot bear the thought of losing you."

"Lose me?" He snickered. "If you take me as your husband, you shall never get rid of me."

"You cannot promise that. Papa had dreams for our family. Dreams that died when he ...." She hung her head. "I cannot shake the memory of that masthead crashing down on Papa. Even though Reverend Knowles said at Papa's burial that I should 'lift up my eyes to the hills from whence cometh my help,' my head spins when I look up high. A foreboding comes over me whenever I approach the docks."

"Now and then," Daniel replied, "I am awakened in the night by the memory of my father's death. I found mother on the floor, sobbing over his body. His eyes bulged, and his mouth gaped open, as if staring into the mouth of death. For many years, the first thing I did each morning was to go to my mother's bedside to be sure she was still there. She would always assure me that even in death, she would not abandon me. Over time, the pain of losing my father has not gone away, but it has dulled."

"My mind plays tricks on me," Rebecca said. "Sometimes I cannot tell whether my alarm is real or if I am simply reliving memories of the horrible day Papa died." Rebecca pressed her palms to her forehead.

"Maybe," Daniel said, "we can help each other learn not to fear things that only exist in our memories."

"We can do that," she said. "And we can do something else, together. When I was a child, I wanted to follow in Papa's footsteps, helping destitute mothers and their tykes. After he died, I resolved to honor him by carrying on the work he taught me. I hope by doing so, God will spare me and my family from any more grief."

"Does God make such bargains?"

"Do I have anywhere else to turn?"

Daniel leaned into her and whispered. "If I make an oath this very day to protect you from all calamities, shall you marry me?"

"It is beyond your power to keep such a promise." She took a step back and gazed into his eyes. "Yes! I shall marry you." She smiled. "Soon after Sarah and Charles are wed next month." She wrapped her arms around him.

"Weeks afterward, not months," he said.

"Days, if you wish. I do not want to distract from their celebration."

* * *

Sarah and Charles exchanged marriage vows on the second of September. Ten days later, Rebecca clung to Daniel's arm as they ascended the stairs to the tenement on Temple Street where he lived with his widowed mother, Clarissa.

He whispered, "I will do all I can to make you feel safe in your new home, even if it is on the third floor."

"Your love gives me strength," Rebecca replied.

Reverend Baron Stow, pastor of the Baldwin Place Second Baptist Church where Rebecca was baptized in her youth, officiated over their wedding in the tenement's parlor. Rebecca's sisters and their husbands were present, as were Mama, William, and Clarissa and her sisters, Prudence and Hannah.

Rebecca awoke the next morning in her new home, now shared by four—the newlyweds and both of their mothers. When Daniel and Clarissa invited Mama to move in, she wasted no time extricating herself from the burden of rent on the Ann Street cottage. She slept in a makeshift bed in the parlor, shoved against a window that looked down on dusty Temple Street.

Daniel had dry-coughed and rasped during the night. Once or twice, he sat straight up and strained to catch his breath. As morning light filtered into the flat, he slept at last, and Rebecca slipped out of bed. She passed through the curtain that partitioned their sleeping area from the parlor where Mama continued to snore, as she had all night.

Rebecca joined Clarissa at the coal stove where she stood waiting for steam to billow from the kettle.

"Breathing in the vapors helps my boy," Clarissa said.

"Does he suffer like this most nights?" Rebecca asked.

"More and more frequently."

"Is there no better relief?"

"Daniel's Aunt Prudence sometimes brings thorn-apple leaves. We burn them in a small copper bowl, and he takes in the smoke." Clarissa gave in to a fit of coughing.

Rebecca plucked the hissing kettle off the stove and held it under her mother-in-law's nose. "Here. Breathe in. Do you have these spells often?"

"I am afraid you shall have your hands full, caring for two near invalids under this roof," Clarissa said. "If Prudence's constitution were stronger, we could rely on her to come help."

"I shall be your nurse, if you like," Rebecca said.

"I don't want to be a burden," Clarissa replied.

"You would not be a burden. We are family, now."

While Rebecca waited for her new husband to stir, she wrote in her journal, a habit Father Taylor's wife helped her establish when they first met. It pained her to think she might have to give up her work among the street urchins if caring for loved ones became too demanding.

Mama woke within the hour and padded to the kitchen, grumbling about her restless sleep and achy body.

The first thing Rebecca noticed was Mama's flushed face. She put her hand to her mother's forehead. "My," she said. "You're feverish."

"I'm exhausted, is all," Mama replied. "The excitement of the past weeks has taken its toll."

Rebecca put her arm around Mama and guided her back to bed. "Let's get you some more rest or I shall have three near invalids to be nurse to."

When Daniel began coughing and wheezing behind the curtain, Rebecca took him a cup of tea, hoping to calm his fits. He inhaled the steam—his breath shrilled in his chest.

"I hear your Aunt Prudence has a remedy that helps," she said.

He sipped the tea and nodded.

"I understand she lives on West Castle Street. What is her house number?"

"Twenty-six."

Rebecca caressed his cheek. "I'll hurry back."

Half an hour later, Aunt Prudence's wan countenance betrayed her fragile health when she answered the door.

Rebecca described Daniel's condition, and Aunt Prudence responded, "Another one of his episodes. Let me make myself more presentable and gather a few necessaries. Keeping those two in passible health can seem daunting. Not to worry. I shall teach you everything I have learned over the years from a parade of doctors coming and going in this house, if you are a willing student."

"More than willing," Rebecca replied.

Fifteen minutes into their trek back to Clarissa's Temple Street apartment, Aunt Prudence pressed a hand to her chest and groaned. Rebecca clutched the old woman's elbow. "What's the matter?"

Aunt Prudence waved off the question. "Just flutters. Nothing worrisome."

"Do you feel ill?"

"I'll be fine. Just need to catch my breath."

"We shall take it slow the rest of the way," Rebecca replied.

Aunt Prudence winced as they resumed their walk. She paused again and coughed into her kerchief before they turned onto Temple Street. "My sister tells me you have a penchant for mingling with the poor waifs and their mothers along Ann Street. I consider it my duty to caution you. Your husband's health is vulnerable. Consider carefully whether it is wise for you to continue your work among that sickly lot. There is no telling what diseases you might unwittingly carry back into your new home.

CHAPTER FOUR

A wave of nausea swept over Rebecca, a year into her marriage, as she tended a simmering pot of porridge at the Temple Street apartment. "This too shall pass," her sisters kept assuring her. Dorcas was a couple of months further along carrying her second child, and Susanna was expecting her third. Rebecca clung to that promise until the queasiness ebbed.

She began pouring tea when Daniel's footfalls echoed from the sparingly veiled bed to the kitchen. He sidled up to her from behind and wrapped his arms around her. "It confounds me," he said, "how you are able to find the energy to do all you do."

"Someone's in a good mood this morning," Rebecca replied as she turned and offered him the steaming cup.

"I had a good sleep for a change," he replied.

"I hope your meeting at the upholstery goes well this morning." She gave him a peck on the cheek.

"The owner did give me reason for hope when we closed the shop yesterday evening."

"Take care," she said. "Your fits come from tiring yourself and letting yourself become anxious."

"I feel well enough I may even walk today." Daniel said.

"Oh no, you won't." She dug into her apron pocket. "Here's money from last week's piecework. Take the omnibus and save your strength."

"I am fine," he said. "Besides, you are the one who deserves to be pampered."

"I am not pampering. I am saying what is best for you."

"So, you are practicing for motherhood. That is a good thing. Nonetheless, I shall walk whenever I feel up to it."

* * *

Daniel did not head to the shop that morning. Instead, he walked about a mile in the opposite direction to an address on Vernon Place—a single-block, dead-end stub off Charter Street. His destination was a three-story home a short distance north of the upper Ann Street cottage where Rebecca had lived most of her childhood. Though Vernon Place had once been the address of grand homes passed down through generations of prominent Boston families, the residences had been converted into tenements. A grocery and six units—including one that was vacant—occupied the old house Daniel had his sights on.

Before meeting with the estate agent, Daniel watched a handful of children playing in the street. The scene evoked a wistful smile. Indeed, he mused, this would be an idyllic place for all the future Pomroy children to call home. On seeing the empty ground-floor flat, he signed the rental contract and laid down the money for the first month's rent. They could move in the next day if they wanted.

By the time Daniel finished the half-hour long trek back to Temple Street, his lungs burned like white-hot coals. He braced against the doorjamb to catch his breath, wanting to greet everyone with a bright smile, not flush-faced.

While Daniel collected himself on the stoop outside, Rebecca recovered from another wave of nausea. She bent over a bucket she kept near at hand, spit out the water she had swished in her mouth, and wiped the back of her neck before returning to a pile of dirty laundry.

Mama addled up to her and reached for the bedclothes Rebecca had begun dipping into the washtub. "Here. Let me do that."

"Shouldn't you be—."

"Shush," Mama replied. "I am not an invalid. I'm feeling fine today." She guided Rebecca to a chair. "Let's get you off your feet and put something in your stomach to settle it."

Before Rebecca found a comfortable position in the chair, Daniel pushed open the door.

Clarissa turned to him. Her eyes widened. "What are you doing home so early? Are you unwell?"

"Pray tell us you were not let go," Mama said.

Rebecca buried her head in her hands. "Tell me it isn't so."

Daniel laughed. "I bear good tidings. I have been made a junior partner. That means less physically taxing work and an increase in wages."

Rebecca leapt from her chair and embraced him.

Clarissa clapped her hands. "My son. I never doubted this day would come."

"That's not all," Daniel said, holding Rebecca in his arms. "I learned of my promotion yesterday and kept it a secret so I could surprise you this morning. I have just now returned from renting a flat up on Vernon Place."

Rebecca pulled back. "How are we going to afford that?"

"What of Prudence?" Clarissa crossed her arms. "I will not abandon my sister. She has always been there for us."

"She will not be neglected," Rebecca said. "I will continue to call on her twice weekly or more."

"As shall I," Daniel said.

"See to it that you do," Clarissa replied. "With her weak heart, you won't find her traipsing up to Vernon Place to deliver your leaves."

"Are you certain we can afford the lease?" Rebecca asked. "I don't understand why we must move, especially so far away."

"It does not cost any more than we are paying now," Daniel replied. "This morning, children were playing happily in the street. It's a wholesome neighborhood, closer to Sarah and Dorcas and to Sunday services—removed from the depravity that's spreading up from the docks."

"I would love to be near Sarah so I could give her more of my attention," Rebecca said. "And being closer to the Chelsea ferry means we could visit Dorcas and William more often. It does seem a practical enough decision."

"What of Susanna and her brood?" Mama asked.

"Considering how little time they have for the lot of us," Daniel replied, "I doubt we'll see any less of them."

Mama held her tongue.

"And you are absolutely certain we can afford it?" Rebecca repeated.

"Yes," Daniel answered. "And the landlord said a young woman is looking to board with us in exchange for housework and nursery care. He will vouch for her."

Rebecca hugged Daniel. "What a lovely surprise."

✳ ✳ ✳

Rebecca—her belly plump as a mature watermelon—waddled home six months later through springtime mud and slush, carrying a bundle of thornapple leaves. Her visits to Aunt Prudence had become more frequent of late. Daniel's weak lungs had been further battered by severe winter weather, leaving it to her to make almost daily three-mile treks afoot. What had been a forty-five-minute jaunt, one way, took more than an hour in her condition.

Acute cramping set in as she approached the vicinity of the Baldwin Place Second Baptist Church, a scant quarter of a mile short of home. The Holliday family sought consolation at the church after Papa's death—and kept seeking it as time passed, though with eroding confidence.

It was not a place she would choose for childbirth, but it happened to be along the safest and most direct route from Aunt Prudence. She would have much preferred seeking help at the Seamen's Bethel. If she still had such a thing as a spiritual home, it was the Bethel, but it was several blocks out of the way—too long of a detour once severe cramps began clamping her abdomen with each step.

During a momentary reprieve from the labor pangs, she took a deep breath, let it out slowly, and edged closer to the Baldwin Place church. At the foot of the church steps, another wave of contractions struck. She hunched and expelled her breath in short bursts. When the latest cramps subsided, she kept her head lowered, making sure of her footing, as she ascended the steps and pushed through the door.

Once inside, she called out for help.

Reverend Stow—the pastor who had officiated at her wedding and her sisters' weddings—turned in the pew near the front of the church where he had been lost in prayer. At the sight of her, he leapt and hastened to help. "What should I do?" he asked.

"It's coming," Rebecca answered, holding her belly. Warm fluid leaked down her thighs. "Can you help me home?"

"My dear child," he sputtered. "Should I call for a midwife?"

"No!" She grunted.

"Why are you not lying in at home? Please tell me you have made arrangements, in case—"

"There's no time." She groaned. A new round of deep spasms left her near breathless. She hunched forward, gripping the back of a pew. "Is there no one who can help?"

"Tell me what to do."

"I must go home. Mama knows what to do. She's had five of her own and delivered all of this child's cousins."

"Of course. Of course. I'll get my carriage. Sit here." He helped her into the pew and hurried down the aisle, disappearing through a door behind the pulpit.

Images flooded Rebecca's mind—biblical Jacob, wrestling an angel, a ladder reaching to heaven. She peeked at the empty cross hung above the altar, the symbol that inspired hope during her innocence. A symbol of victory for some who were troubled, bereaved, downtrodden, or persecuted. But no longer for her.

A touch of vertigo accompanied a restless kick in her womb. The time of trial was upon her. She must survive. If she succumbed, there would be no one to care for Daniel. She refused to so much as glance again at the cross. Besides, it was empty. Empty like Papa's chair at supper when he was away at sea. A chair that remained vacant for years thereafter.

No, she reminded herself. Don't look for help where there is none.

The cramps subsided by the time she boarded Reverend Stow's carriage. Nonetheless, as they bounded through pothole after pothole along the way home, she feared the next bump in the road would jar the baby out.

On their arrival at the Vernon Place tenement, Mama drew upon a reservoir of latent energy to take command of necessary arrangements. She put Rebecca straight to bed, prepared a lancet in case it would be needed, and took a count of clean sheets.

Clarissa took Daniel. "Above all else," she said, "stay out of the way. It's best if you make yourself scarce. Go to Aunt Prudence's house and wait. We'll send someone to collect you once the baby arrives. In the meantime, ready yourself for praying. As often as not, prayer becomes our only ally in these matters."

Daniel pitched back on his heels. "Why? Is something wrong? Rebecca? The baby?"

"There is no cause for alarm," Clarissa said. "But childbirth can be a delicate matter. I am sure all shall go well."

The door to the flat had barely shut behind Daniel when Rebecca let out a low moan. Pain rolled through her like sea swells pushed by a racing storm, each wave greater than the last. Her moans swelled into groans that exploded into screams.

Julia, the young woman boarder, applied cool towels to Rebecca's forehead. Clarissa held her daughter-in-law's hand and offered calm encouragements. Mama crouched between Rebecca's thighs and kept a hand pressed on the expectant mother's abdomen. With each contraction, Mama responded with the command, "Push!"

Rebecca sat upright the best she could, crunched forward, and grunted. Burning and tingling in her flesh—stretched near to its limits—multiplied her anxiety. After each push, Mama slid her fingers into the birth canal to assess the baby's progress.

As daylight faded, the contractions stalled, though the intervals of pain persisted. The baby was not moving. The burning and tingling Rebecca had experienced gave way to a warm oozing between her legs. Her pulse raced.

Mama pulled her bloody fingers from the birth canal. She glanced at Clarissa and mimed the word lancet.

Clarissa passed the bloodletting instrument into Mama's hand, shielding the three-inch steel tip from Rebecca's view.

Mama and Clarissa whispered fervent prayers.

"Is my baby okay?" Rebecca wailed.

Mama replied, "Everything is going to be fine. There appears to be a little blockage, but I shall have no problem getting it fixed. I might also be able to relieve some of your pain."

Mama took a clean towel from Julia and held it under the baby's head. She slid the lancet into the birth canal and pricked gently. Blood spurted and gushed between Rebecca's legs.

Rebecca jerked. "What is happening?"

"Nothing to worry about," Mama replied.

"Don't let my baby die," Rebecca pleaded.

"I have not lost one yet. Nor have I lost a mother." She stanched the ebbing flow with the towel and announced, "You can start pushing again."

The contractions resumed, by shorter intervals. Along with them, the stabbing pains and pressure grew more intense. She pushed hard, and the pain spread, becoming sharper and deeper. It garroted her breath. Her groans yielded to grunts. She bit down, pushing harder. Her teeth bore into her lip. A ripping, slicing, burning raced through her. Her face was slick with sweat.

Mama's eyes widened as the baby's head crowned. She urged Rebecca to push with all her strength.

The soft cries and whimper of a baby boy came an hour later, displacing all pain, sweat, and wailing. Rebecca—overcome by the miracle of life—was oblivious to the sight of Mama cleaning up the residue of her labor. Clarissa and Julia cleaned and swaddled the newborn before laying him at Rebecca's breast. His soft skin against her bosom was all the relief she needed.

Daniel's anxiety had nibbled, gnawed, and made a meal of his patience at Aunt Prudence's home, until she sent him to fetch the carriage. They arrived at the Vernon Place tenement moments before his son's birth. When he took the boy into his arms, he swelled with pride. He had spent his entire life ruing the sickly body he had been saddled with. Of late, he fretted his flagging health might snuff out any chances of providing a family with a secure future. His small efforts of packing a basket of snacks to spare expense of purchasing lunch or walking to avoid the cost of the omnibus seemed paltry.

As he took the boy in his arms, he resolved to preserve his own health and prolong his life in any way possible, for his new son's sake. He would lay a foundation and build a legacy to leave behind after a long and fruitful life.

Aunt Prudence's eyes dewed at the sight of her new grandnephew. "Does the little one have a name?" she asked.

Daniel whispered, "George."

Prudence furrowed her brow. She could not think of anyone among the Farrington line who might be the namesake for a boy named George.

* * *

The afterglow of George's birth became a faint glimmer as Rebecca faced the harder realities of motherhood. Multiple breast feedings, double laundry duty, and her baby's colic encroached on her already careworn days.

Although Daniel's health had shown signs of promise over the course of two summers, the intervening winter took its toll. Dense, muggy air and frigid temperatures pummeled his fragile lungs, erasing tiny steps forward and sending him backwards by leaps and bounds. Clarissa's and Aunt Prudence's constitutions continued to erode, and Mama's condition ascended peaks and meandered valleys. Caring for all of them, on top of sewing to supplement Daniel's income when he was unable to work, consumed Rebecca from early morning until late into the evening.

Sleep did not come easy for Rebecca. Daniel's incessant hacking formed a dissonant chorus with little George's wailing that exacerbated her sleeplessness. What sleep she did manage was often charged with night-terrors.

Her burdensome days melded into challenging weeks and snaked into cheerless months, like a parade of mourners trudging to the tempo of a funeral dirge. On top of it all, Rebecca resigned herself to the death of her youthful ambitions, dreams not merely postponed but carried off to molder in forgotten ground.

Memories of her younger years became laced with guilt. She failed Father and Mother Taylor when she gave up her responsibilities at the Bethel. The indigent families of lower Ann Street paid a price, through no fault of their own. Little Ryan, who had held a special place in her heart, was one of the many she abandoned. After Papa's death when she had continued to read to families huddled around her in an alley across from the Seamen's Bethel, Ryan was always the first to claim a place on her lap or next to her. She learned he had been born aboard a ship—one of many that departed Ireland carrying families desperate to escape famine and persecution. Ryan's older sister died during the crossing, as did his father who left behind a wife and two tykes to fend for themselves. Still, there were times she could imagine the boy's hand nested in her own and the thrum of his heartbeat against her breast.

CHAPTER FIVE

ebecca caressed Sarah's forearm on a November afternoon, two and a half years after George's birth. A few feet away, Mama railed at William.

"How can you refuse to make peace with your Maker?" Mama demanded. "Especially when poor Sarah lies near death."

William leaned back on his heels, his jaw tightening. "I will make peace with God when he ceases warring against this family."

Rebecca turned to her brother. "This is not the time or place for arguing."

"I need fresh air," William muttered as he stormed out of the home where Sarah and Charles had harbored hopes of raising a family after many fruitless years of marriage.

During those years, Sarah became an aunt several times, and jealousy deepened with the arrival of each niece or nephew. She had borne the bitter pill of barrenness as if it were leprosy. Sarah's melancholy deepened two autumns after Rebecca gave birth to George, when Rebecca announced she was in the family way for a second time. Sarah spiraled further downward two months after Rebecca's news, when a little one began to grow in her own womb, and thoughts percolated in her mind that giving birth could carry a death sentence for child or mother or both.

The storm surges in her heart ebbed the following September with the safe arrival of a son, Charles, Jr. Rebecca's Willie was born only weeks earlier in July.

Charles Yendell fixed his gaze on his dying wife who lay unmindful of the exchange between Mama and William. He took his two-month-old son from the nanny and cradled him in his arms as he hummed a lullaby.

Sarah stirred at the sound of her son's whimpers. She mumbled to Rebecca. "I must say good-bye to my boy."

Charles laid their son on Sarah's breast. She murmured to the baby and kissed him. When Sarah's head wobbled, the nanny collected the little one and carried him to his cradle.

Lumps had appeared on Sarah's neck the week after she gave birth. Over the next several days, she woke nightly, soaked in sweat. Coughing fits set in shortly afterwards.

Rebecca rarely left Sarah's bedside after the doctor pronounced her condition grave. The only times she was away were when she returned home for short nights of sleep or when she visited Aunt Prudence with questions about the affliction doctors called scrofula. Prudence possessed a wealth of knowledge, but she could not teach Rebecca how to bury her horror at the sight of cheese-like pus that erupted from lesions on Sarah's neck. Nor could Prudence offer a remedy for the hollowness Rebecca would experience when she clasped Sarah's hand, knowing the final breath could come at any moment.

William never returned that evening, but the others— Mama, Susanna, Dorcas, and Rebecca joined Charles in saying goodbye. They stood whimpering and moaning while Sarah's mouth remained agape, like a hatchling awaiting morsels from a mother's beak. Though when she pecked at the air, it was as if she hoped to retrieve wisps of breath that had escaped through her lips. Those miniscule signs of life eventually ceased, and the reality of her death crushed everyone, especially Rebecca who had labored so hard to keep a flicker of life from dying out.

Once shock gave way to resignation, Rebecca went to Charles, Jr's., cradle, kissed him, and said a prayer for him and for all his days to come—especially for the times he would struggle to make sense of a world that robbed him of his mother at such a tender age. Her reflections turned to her two sisters still living and to their children. She whispered each of their names—Susanna and Dorcas, Susan, George, Rebecca, Minot, Jr., and William.

Rebecca said goodnight to Charles and started home, her mind as dull as the fog covering that November night. The only images she could conjure were of her sons. George reminded her of herself—cautious, serious, contemplative. As best as anyone could read, Willie, though still a suckling baby, would turn out to become much like his grandfather, embracing adventure everywhere and in everything.

As she trod the last few blocks, the cocoon of resilience she had spun around her heart began to unravel. She had been helpless to save Sarah's life. Now Charles, Jr., lay motherless in his crib. The ache in the eyes of every motherless child is the same, regardless of class.

When she arrived home, Daniel and George sat cross-legged on the floor. George clung to the mast of a toy ship.

That simple toy opened a door in Rebecca's mind. Images of the day Papa died spilled out. The cascading masthead, the dangling boot, the bloody coat. "Tell me you did not take them to the docks," she yelled.

The color drained from Daniel's face.

"You know I don't want them around the docks." She scanned the room. "Where's Willie?"

Daniel stood. "If you haven't woken him, he's asleep in his crib."

Rebecca snatched the toy from George's hands and started for the bedroom to check on Willie.

"Rebecca," Daniel said softly.

She ignored his plea.

Later, after nursing Willie and kissing George goodnight, Rebecca joined Daniel in bed and began weeping, her back to him. He turned toward her. When she didn't recoil, he nestled closer. "There are no mastheads. Everyone is safe."

"Charles, Jr., isn't safe," she murmured.

"His father will keep him safe."

"Why would a loving God cut a beautiful life so short? How could he rob a mere baby of his doting mother?"

"God's ways are mysterious," Daniel replied.

She sat up. "I have entertained that answer more times than I care to remember." Tears blurred her vision. She blinked them away. "It brings me no consolation."

"I did not take them to the docks," Daniel said. "We were at a shop in the market. George lit up at the sight of that toy boat."

She turned to him. "I wish I could escape the foreboding that comes over me every time I am reminded of Papa's ship."

"You're still grieving, and I was insensitive." He cupped her cheek. "These past months have been hard on you, but you are a remarkable woman, a loving mother and devoted sister."

She kissed the palm of his hand. "You are the sweetest husband and father." She curled into him and sobbed.

✳ ✳ ✳

Temperatures plunged to nearly twenty degrees on the third Friday night in January, two months after Sarah's death. Pillows of downy snow turned into a glacial crust, and Rebecca clung to Daniel's arm to avoid careening to the sidewalk.

"We should return home," she coaxed, "where we can warm ourselves by the hearth."

"I know how much it means for you to see Mr. Dickens steam into port," Daniel replied.

"I wanted to prove," she said, "that I could visit the docks without memories of Papa flooding back. But in this weather?"

"I can manage," Daniel replied. "But if you're not up to it..."

"What I am truly looking forward to is getting a close-up view of Mr. Dickens at Father Taylor's Bethel. The newspapers say Father Taylor is the only preacher Mr. Dickens covets hearing while in America."

The bone-dry artic wind agitated Daniel into spasmodic coughing. "Hopefully ..." he strained to draw a breath "... the weather will be better then."

Before she could respond, his feet slipped on the ice. Only her strong grip on his arm saved him from landing in a heap.

"If we are not more sensible today," she teased, "we shall likely be too infirm next Sunday to be at the service Mr. Dickens is expected to attend." She steadied him on his feet. "Father Taylor has kindly arranged for a carriage to drive us there."

"If that's what you wish."

"Father Taylor said Mr. Waldo Emerson will be in the service also. My brother will not forgive me if we fail to meet his Unitarian idol and make a detailed report on our encounter."

A coughing spasm prevented Daniel from offering a reply, but he didn't need to. Rebecca had already made up her mind to turn back towards home.

✳ ✳ ✳

A week later, temperatures moderated to above forty degrees, and pilgrims, intent on catching glimpses of the English author, packed into every block near the Seamen's Bethel. Rebecca and Daniel huddled under a wool blanket as Father Taylor's carriage slopped through slush. Her fingers caressed the quarter-leather bindings of the *Oliver Twist* volumes Daniel's Aunt Prudence had given her.

Father Taylor's wife and their two youngest daughters, Mary Ellen and Eliza, greeted Rebecca and Daniel on their arrival. Eliza, the younger of the two girls held her one-year-old brother, Eddie. Mrs. Taylor's smile waned as the couple disembarked. "I had hoped you would bring those two boys," Mother Taylor said.

"We thought it best to leave them home," Rebecca replied.

"My husband will be disappointed. We especially hoped to meet the little one. He must be nearly four months old by now."

"Almost seven months," Rebecca said, "and George soon will turn three years old."

"And how are your mothers?"

"I am afraid Daniel's mother has grown quite frail, and Mama has her good days and bad days."

"I can imagine how consuming it must be, keeping up a home and raising two children while nursing a sickly household. In any event, we are overjoyed the two of you could come."

"Not only does Rebecca have her hands full with the lot of us," Daniel said, "but in the autumn just passed, she gave every waking hour to attend to a sister who succumbed to a gruesome illness."

Mother Taylor took Rebecca's hand. "Word of your loss has reached us. Please accept our deepest condolences. You are an angel who shall remain in our constant prayers. Now, my husband insists you join him in his study for a brief greeting before service."

In the study, Rebecca's focus landed on Father Taylor. She had rarely seen him since George was born, and the image that greeted her caught her by surprise. His weathered features had always betrayed a hard early life, but as he stood before her, even deeper lines marked his leathered brow. He gave the appearance of a man well over sixty, though she knew him to be hardly past fifty.

Father Taylor glanced past the four men he held in conversation, and his face brightened. "Rebecca. Thank God, you have come."

"How could we have said no to your invitation?" she replied. "I'm sorry it's been so long. There has been so much ..."

"My dear Rebecca, I was so distressed to get word of your sister's passing. I regret not calling on you and your family. I know how dearly you loved her."

She swallowed a lump in her throat. "When Mother Taylor sent condolences, she explained you were away on your travels."

"It is difficult to know God's purpose in tragedy," Father Taylor added. "But I assure you, she is now at peace, and He who created all things has His hand constantly on those she loved."

"I will try to find comfort in your words." She wanted to tell him what was roiling inside her—how impotent she felt and how much she feared failing as a mother, wife, and daughter, like she failed to subdue the awful disease that consumed Sarah, like the way she froze on the wharf, helpless, as she watched that masthead fall and crush Papa's skull—and especially how she lets a powerful sense of foreboding disarm her whenever she is reminded of that day. But it was not the proper occasion for baring one's soul.

Father Taylor replied, "Do not hesitate to call on me when you need a friend." He turned to the others. "Speaking of friends, let me introduce some of mine."

Each of the men appeared to be nearly the same age as her Daniel. The shortest introduced himself as Mr. Longfellow. Two of the others she recognized immediately. Mr. Sumner's courtly bearing and tall, broad-shouldered frame were legendary throughout

Boston, and Mr. Emerson's image appeared frequently about town on handbills.

Emerson took her hand. "Father Taylor tells us how much he misses your help with the children here." He offered a handshake to Daniel and feigned a scowl. "I take it you are the young rogue who has stolen her affections and now occupies all of her time."

"I am happy to be the guilty party, though were it up to me, she would have plenty of time to give to the Bethel." Daniel stifled a cough. "Unfortunately, she married into a sickly lot."

While Rebecca's focus shifted to the fourth man in the group, Emerson continued, "I suppose your Baptist family may hold an unfavorable opinion of me."

Father Taylor interrupted. "It is true, Waldo, that Rebecca's mother is a staunch Baptist. Even so, she acquiesced to her daughter assisting at a Methodist mission. But your liberal proclivities surely transgress the dear woman's bounds of religious tolerance. That said, I don't believe my dear friend came here at her mother's behest to scrutinize your beliefs. By the looks of the books in her hands, she came to meet Mr. Dickens."

Emerson laughed.

Dickens took her hand and pressed it to his lips. "My pleasure, Mrs. Pomroy."

She blushed. "The pleasure is mine, sir."

Dickens freed one of the volumes from Rebecca's grasp and inspected it. "Your New York publishing houses have printed reasonable, though unauthorized, editions of my novel. From what Father Taylor tells me about your work with impoverished children, you could have told Twist's story as well as I have done, maybe better."

"That's hardly possible," she replied. "I have not received a proper education."

"Do not sell yourself short. I am told you are among the most literate young women I may ever meet in America. So, what is your favorite part of the story?"

"There is no singular part, aside from the resolution of its main principle. I see in Master Oliver many of the children I have known and nurtured on Boston's streets and here at the Bethel. My hope ..." she glanced at Father Taylor, "... my prayer for each is that they can have a bright future, just like young Oliver was blessed with in the end. I miss reading to them, bringing some measure of hope to their lives through books, or at least offering a temporary escape from their misery ... introducing them to new worlds. But as my husband has said, duty calls me otherwise."

"Indeed," Dickens said. "I am happy my story has plucked a chord in you."

"Sir—"

"Please. Call me Boz."

Her pulse raced. "Mr. Boz, could I be so bold as to ask you to sign my volumes."

"It would be my honor." He took a quill from Father Taylor's desk and wrote an inscription in each book.

After Dickens signed the volumes, Mother Taylor escorted Rebecca and Daniel to a reserved front pew on one side of the tightly packed sanctuary. Sailors crammed into the center section, and the public at large filled the sides and balconies.

Years before, when Rebecca attended services regularly, she stole glances at the large mural behind the pulpit, ten or twelve feet high—a stormy sea, high-rolling waves, an old wooden ship bent over and driving through a gale in great peril. It was meant to inspire the sailors, but it triggered memories in her that she did not care to relive.

There was a part of the painting she could never bring herself to so much as peek at. An old salt described it to her—an angel hovering at the top of the scene with outstretched arms, casting down a golden anchor bigger than itself, to aid the ship. He said the angel was too slight to be of any help, and the flimsy line tied to the anchor would break under the weight of the ship. How apropos, she thought. She tried to put herself in the place of little Ryan. Or in the place of a mother escaping famine in Europe, crossing the vast, gray Atlantic, losing a child or husband to disease, and landing on the streets of Boston's Black Sea of poverty.

She acknowledged that her own trials paled in comparison to those faced by the street children and their families. She could not imagine weathering such storms. She was too weak. She barely handled the troubles she had been dealt so far.

Daniel whispered to Rebecca as they waited for the service to begin. "You miss it, don't you?"

Rebecca squeezed his hand. "I do."

"Do you begrudge me for insisting—"

"No. My time with those dear souls was a season I cherish, but you and our sons are more precious to me than life itself."

✳ ✳ ✳

Mid-April hosted a few breezy, balmy days and Daniel's health remained stable—the perfect recipe for a family picnic—until Daniel began crafting a kite out of tissue paper and basswood. The door to a chamber in Rebecca's mind opened a crack, and dark memories slipped out.

While the four of them sat on a blanket on the broad lawn of Boston Common, she assessed the kite. Daniel had decorated it with a hand-painted design, accented by three-year-old George's scribbles and baby Willie's handprints. She strained to smile at it as it rested on the ground while Daniel called out images formed by clouds floating overhead. When George asked what formations she saw in the sky, she answered without looking, "George Washington's head."

"Where?" George demanded.

She pointed to the sky behind him, her eyes still cast downward, and said, "Oh, I guess it's gone now."

Daniel tousled George's hair. "I must find a portrait of our first president for you to hang in our home. Next time you can find it without help. You and General Washington share the same Christian name." He reached for the kite. "Let's give this beauty a try."

George jumped to his feet and yelled, "Yay!"

Daniel rose and offered Rebecca a hand up.

"Sorry," she said. "I'm feeling a bit shaky. Willie and I can watch from here."

"Yes, I suppose so," he said. "You weren't even looking at the clouds, were you?"

"No." Guilt pricked her conscience as she glanced at George. "I'm a little unwell and didn't want to make a fuss over it."

"Should we go home?" he asked.

"No, I'm sure whatever it is will pass. I don't want to spoil the afternoon. We seldom take time to frolic."

She watched as Daniel instructed George on the fine points of launching, flying, and reeling in the kite. She recalled kite flying when she was a girl—Papa and Mama, Susanna, Dorcas, Sarah, William who was no bigger than Willie. Sarah would imitate the kites as they sailed in the sky, dancing and darting as if she flew in the same variegated wind currents that carried the kites aloft. Rebecca's throat tightened whenever George waved at her in the distance and when he jumped up and down with amazement when his Pa landed the kite safely only a few feet from where she sat.

Her eyes misted. Ten years had passed since that masthead fell, crushing Papa. The line between the past and present sometimes became so blurred, she could not tell the difference between them. Reality told her one thing, but memories still fooled her into believing danger lurked overhead, about to descend on someone she loved—like the Angel of Death swooping down and stealing Sarah away. Warring against memories drained her energy.

While she held Willie, and Daniel packed up the picnic fixings, George became distracted by the sight of toy boats sailing on the pond. Some were simple hulls with a pinewood dowel for a mast and tiny, triangular cuts of cloth for sails. But one seized her attention. A duplicate of Papa's three-masted schooner, its scale burgeoning larger and larger as it invaded her mind. She began shaking. Daniel collected Willie from her arms and drew her close.

As she hung onto him, he whispered, "Memories are illusions, only echoes from the past with no power of their own. They are no longer real. Until you can see that, you will miss out on whatever moments of happiness come our way."

George was too consumed by awe over the miniature schooner to notice his mother's distress.

* * *

Weeks after her episode at the family picnic, Rebecca called on Father Taylor at the Bethel. "I fret over my brother," she said. "He is now eighteen years old, and with Papa gone, he has no good model to pattern his life after."

"I believe William has a good heart. Just keep watch on him and pray that he doesn't turn down a wrong path, believing it to be a good one." Father Taylor picked up a news clipping from his desk and waved it in front of her. "My friend Reverend Cartwright, a prairie preacher, sent me this article about a speech he listened to on temperance. The well-intended young man who gave the speech, named Lincoln, is a long drink of water whom Reverend Cartwright called out as an infidel during an election several years ago. Nevertheless, this Lincoln fellow went about making a name for himself in local politics. Never mind his intentions, he is deceived. His modern views on how to address the imbiber play right into the devil's hand. It is easy for a young man to follow a way that sounds right, though that road can lead to destruction. Do what you can to keep your brother on the right path."

"I will do my best," she said.

Father Taylor cocked his head. "William is not the reason you've come to see me, though. You already keep an eye on him, and your sister and her husband do also. Hopefully you pray, as well."

She kneaded her hands. "I am weary."

"What makes you so weary?" he asked.

She hesitated, biting her lip. "The calamities that have befallen those I love. What if Daniel's health keeps getting worse. What if he .... I can't lose him."

"I cannot promise that life will be without its trials. I can only promise that the Almighty is greater than sickness and death. He is able to subdue grief."

"Why? Why must we endure such pain?"

"Why we must endure is one of the great mysteries of life, but how we endure is simple—by trusting in God and His Grace."

"I cannot do that," she replied.

"Examine yourself more deeply. The fact that you are here, asking questions, is proof that you can."

CHAPTER SIX

Daniel blotted fresh ink from an entry in his personal ledger as he sat at his writing desk in a small parlor off the entryway. Rebecca had taken their sons and nephew, Charles, Jr., to lay flowers at Sarah's grave—her sister now two years gone. Melancholy always hung over her for days after her pilgrimages to the cemetery where Papa and her sister were laid to rest.

He took a deep breath, pressed his fingers together in the form of a steeple, and savored the slight margin by which his deposits, at last, exceeded his debts—success garnered despite his battle against persistent asthmatic flareups. His achievement was even more remarkable considering the financial setbacks small merchants and working-class men suffered in the half-dozen years since the Panic of '37.

Commotion at the front door drew Daniel's attention. The voices belonged to neither Rebecca nor the children. He closed his ledger and remained seated. Seven years of marriage had taught him to stay out of the feud between Rebecca's brother and Mama.

William's tone was firm. "I am not here to argue."

"I'm not arguing," Mama replied. "I am pleading with you to return to your faith."

"If by faith you mean your Calvinist doctrine, I understand it to say that my salvation was sealed when I was a boy, and it cannot be undone."

Before Mama replied, Rebecca pushed open the front door and the three boys rushed to William, each throwing their arms around one of his legs.

"William?" Rebecca said.

Mama stepped back from the others. She glowered at Rebecca. "And you are to blame. Dipping your toes into Methodism. Look at your boys." Mama gestured toward her three grandsons. "Your brother and his Unitarian—"

"Universalist," William interjected.

"His infidel friends will surely lead these innocents right to the brink of damnation."

"Mama!" Rebecca scolded.

Mama turned and shuffled down the hall to look in on Clarissa who had been bedridden for weeks.

William gripped his sister's elbow. "Let her be. I should not have come unannounced."

"You shouldn't provoke her. Her health is bad enough as it is," Rebecca said. "Why did you come?"

"I came to settle my account with Daniel." William handed her an envelope.

Rebecca stared at the envelope.

Mama shrieked from down the hallway. "Oh God! Come! Someone come."

Rebecca ran toward her. Daniel bolted from the parlor and followed close on her heels.

Mama stood in the doorway of Clarissa's room, her hand over her mouth. Rebecca peeked past her mother at Clarissa who lay in bed gasping. Daniel angled around the others to his mother's bedside.

Rebecca shouted. "William. Fetch the doctor. Then go collect Aunt Prudence."

Clarissa's chest clattered with each shallow inhale and exhale. The moment Daniel had always feared was upon him. She had been the constant in his life since he was a boy, since the day his father's heart ceased working. She became the sun governing his days and the moon guarding his nights. He clutched her hand and moaned.

Rebecca gasped. Her husband's grief overwhelmed her while their two sons tugged at her apron.

By the time the doctor arrived, the rattle in Clarissa's lungs gave way to sporadic whistling—her breaths thin and far apart. The atmosphere in the room grew heavy.

Rebecca massaged her mother-in-law's arm.

Daniel rocked back and forth in a chair next to her, holding his mother's hand and whimpering.

When William and Aunt Prudence appeared at the threshold of the bedroom a little more than an hour later, Clarissa's eyelids flittered, and she struggled to sit up. Her arm trembled as she extended it toward her sister, and she gave up a smile before sinking back into the bed. Her last breath was but a wisp.

Daniel hardened himself soon after Clarissa's soul passed into eternity. His tear ducts remained dry on that first sleepless night as he lay beside Rebecca, not wanting to awaken the next morning in a house where, for the first time in his life, his mother was not.

Rebecca slept fitfully that night, worrying over her husband. She tossed and turned in their bed, warding off nightmares laced with eleven-year-old memories—memories she struggled to tame and keep stuffed away in her mind's vault. Though she kept pushing them back, they rolled out faster and faster until she awoke.

She rose while the moon still flooded the night sky, threw coal on the few surviving embers, pumped the bellows to revive a flame, and put a kettle on the stove for heating water to make tea. She must rise above her trepidations and set her mind on her husband.

Daniel gritted his teeth as he dressed at daybreak to leave for work. His temple ached a twinge when Rebecca asked why he was leaving early and without breakfast.

"Your boss will not complain if you are late," she said.

"Yes," he replied, his voice flat. "I suppose he would not. But I must make up for the time I will miss to arrange for my mother's burial."

He maintained a flinty veneer as he plodded through an early morning mist along Ann Street, passing indigents and urchins who loitered under streetlamps. His jaw tightened as intemperate sailors stumbled and staggered out of brothels, inns, and taverns in the notorious Black Sea neighborhood near Dock Square.

His workbench at the back of the store, secluded behind a curtain, became his refuge, except when the shopkeeper's bell announced a customer's arrival. An obligatory smile obscured his anguish as he addressed their needs courteously, precisely without being curt. Once they left, he returned to his workbench and busied his hands and mind until the next interruption. He worked into the evening, staying well past supper hour, having worked the entire day without thinking to eat. At home he ignored entreaties from his two sons—George, who tried his best to hide the sting of his father's aloofness, and Willie, who wore his wounds openly.

After picking at his supper in silence, Daniel sat at his writing desk and inhaled wisps from a bowl of smoldering thorn-apple leaves. He poured over his personal ledger with full knowledge there had been no change in his accounts except for William's repayment of his loan. The exercise was a defense against idleness and a diversion from conversation—until Rebecca stood next to him.

"Is the asthma giving you trouble tonight?" she asked.

He waved at the trail of smoke rising from the leaves. "Maybe a little. I am not one to take chances."

She clutched a volume of Dickens' *Twist.* "Let me read to you. It might settle your mind."

"I am increasingly confident," he said, "we shall soon be able to buy our own place. I have my sights set on Chelsea, a region of rapid growth and economic vitality."

"I don't think Mama will agree to move across the river. She will miss her friends at the church."

"She can find new friends. Nothing, no one is permanent."

"We can talk when you're ready," she said. "But if you don't want to read, at least come to bed."

"In a while." He turned a page in his ledger.

Hours later, he joined her in bed, but for the entire night his vacant stare remained fixed on the ceiling. Without a wink of sleep, he rose before sunrise and repeated the prior day's ritual.

On the third day, he buried his mother, and on returning home, he collapsed onto the bed. Exhaustion conquered his dread of waking without his mother under the same roof.

After the children were asleep, Rebecca crawled into bed beside him. She watched him sleep as trifles of moonlight peek-a-booed into the room. His anguished expression took on the form of a ghoulish thespian mask.

He woke early to find Rebecca staring at him, her cheeks streaked with telltale signs she had wept during the night. His lips twitched. Sorrow percolated near the surface of his pretense. He blinked and rose from bed.

"Come back to bed," she said. "You should rest. I shall make tea."

"I am rested well enough."

"Please."

"I am needed at the shop." He began to dress.

"I am concerned for you."

He drew a raspy breath and clutched his chest, hoping to forestall a spasm.

"See what I mean," she said.

"It's this old house. Too damn drafty. No wonder I am all the time sickly." He shuffled off to the kitchen.

Rebecca sat, sullen, at a table near the kitchen fire after Daniel left for work.

Mama joined her and asked, "How is Daniel today?"

"I don't know how to comfort him."

"Be patient. Men prefer to suffer in silence."

"I fear there is more to it than that." Rebecca folded her hands on the table.

CHAPTER SEVEN

William dropped off piecework for Rebecca from a Chelsea upholsterer in late December, saving her a trip across the river. Billows of slate-black clouds churned on the horizon, and he hoped to finish the day's errands so he could return to the farm before the storm pushed inland.

Mama cornered him in the entryway as he was on his way out. "Who is this Eunice girl?" she asked.

"She's a Peirce," William replied. "Minot and Dorcas's neighbors. We are to be married after the new year by Reverend Streeter at his Universalist Church."

"So, it will not be a Christian union," she spat back.

"We will be wed in the sight of God and in the presence of people who love us."

Mama crossed her arms. "I love you, but I shall not be attending."

"That is your choice, not ours. But remember, as the good book says, 'they shall eat the fruit of their own way.'"

Daniel leapt from his chair in the entryway parlor where he had lingered to avoid the fray he knew would erupt. It was little more than a year since his mother passed, and his grief was still raw. The persistent arguing between William and Mama finally wore his patience to a nub. He could not fathom how a mother and son could be at each other's throats incessantly. It was as if each relished wounding the other. He often told Rebecca,

"When one of those two dies, the other will be saddled with a load of regret." He scurried past them as he threw on a coat and bolted from the tenement.

Icy crystals swirled in Daniel's path as he trudged down Ann Street toward the docks. Melancholy settled over him—and with it came the same haze that kept rolling through his thoughts since his mother died. He walked on, impervious to the approaching nor'easter, unconscious of any purpose or destination.

His mental fog lifted when the ferry—which he had absentmindedly boarded—jolted on its arrival across the river. A wintry gust chafed his face. He crimped his eyes shut—what possessed me?

The briny shore sucked his boots into its greedy maw when he alighted on the Chelsea side. Planks, a few yards away, gave him secure purchase and led to Broadway Street, a rough-hewn thoroughfare that ran through the village center. Andrew Haskell—a Chelsea resident who operated a business near Boston's Dock Square and whom Daniel had known for many years—often spoke of John Low's store a short distance up Broadway.

Frigid air stung Daniel's lungs as he stepped onto the planks. Spangles of snow nipped his brow. He drew his scarf tight over his mouth and nose as he considered turning back, deferring until spring. But other notions pushed him forward—I am becoming too feeble to work and provide for my family. My body is wasting from disease. When I fail to raise my member, to give Rebecca healthy seed, I see the disappointment in her eyes. I shall not leave her and our sons without a legacy. I must do whatever it takes to assure they have a permanent home. The monies are there to do it now. Strike while the iron is hot.

Daniel lumbered for twenty minutes with snow swallowing his shoe tops then gripping his ankles. He wheezed and coughed—his lungs caving like crushed tins. When he found John Low's store on the corner of

Broadway and Cross Streets, he was doubled over, like he had caught a sandbag with his chest and curled himself around it. Low ushered him to a chair by the iron stove and poured him a mug of steaming tea.

Daniel could not muster breath enough to speak.

Low patted him on the back. "Take your time. Sip your tea."

✳ ✳ ✳

Rebecca paced the kitchen, wringing her hands. Night had fallen, and gusty winds had burgeoned into a howling gale. No Daniel. She told herself, he promised he would not abandon me.

Mama added more wood to the fire.

"This is not like him," Rebecca murmured.

Mama asked, "Could he have gone to the shop and decided to hunker down until the storm passes?"

"He left so abruptly," Rebecca replied. "Said nothing. What if something happened?"

"Your Daniel is not one to take chances."

"I do not fret about him inviting trouble, but there's a reason folks call the lower part of Ann Street the Black Sea. It's where trouble finds you." In her heart Rebecca was shaking her fist at the Almighty. Why must you test us so?

Mama hung a kettle over the fire. "I'll fix some tea. It will calm your nerves."

"When he returns, I shall put down my foot. No more shall he walk to work. It's the omnibus from now on. Or if needs be, we shall purchase a carriage and horse of our own."

Rebecca collapsed in a chair and three-year-old Willie crawled into her lap, whining. "Pa gone?" he asked. "Like Grandpa?"

The question echoed in her mind—Like grandpa? Rebecca rued all those times Mama filled the boys' heads with stories about their grandfather's exploits at sea. She stroked Willie's hair. "He will return soon."

Five-year-old George played on the floor with his toy boat. Without looking up, he said, "I hope Pa doesn't get too cold out in the snow."

"He is by a warm fire," Rebecca replied. "And missing his family."

"How do you know?" George asked.

Rebecca started to answer but was interrupted by William returning, his coat caked with snow.

"William?" she said.

Mama answered George's question. "Your Pa is a clever man. Come. Let me ready the two of you for bed." She picked up Willie and took George's hand.

Rebecca kissed her sons good night and warned Mama, "No grandpa stories tonight." She turned to William as Mama retreated to the boys' bedroom.

"I thought you were on your way back to the farm." Rebecca said.

"The ferry stopped running. The storm makes crossing too dangerous. Do you mind if I stay the night?"

"You can sleep with the boys."

"I'll relieve Mama."

"But—"

"I know." He grinned. "No grandpa stories."

When Mama returned from bedding down the boys, she sat next to Rebecca. "We can take turns waiting up for him if you want."

"I cannot imagine sleeping until I know." Rebecca replied.

"He's fine. He probably took the omnibus down to the shop, and he has the good sense not to walk back in weather such as this. Especially after dark."

"More likely, he hoofed it rather than giving in and catching the omnibus." Rebecca scrunched up her nose. "But why did he leave in the first place?"

"I do not know," Mama answered. "I was engaged with William at the time. If Daniel said something, I missed hearing it."

"Engaged? You mean bickering—as usual."

"I grieve for your brother's soul and for the little souls he may someday bring into the world."

"Have you considered that your incessant criticism might drive him further away?" Rebecca glared at her mother.

Mama scowled as she retreated to her bed.

Rebecca, on the verge of crying, shouted as her mother tramped off. "Do you ever consider how your haranguing affects the rest of us who live under this roof?"

* * *

John Low turned his sleigh off the main road, nearly four miles from his store, and his team of horses drew it through unmarked snow toward a farmhouse. Fifty acres of good soil lay behind the house. Beyond that, another twenty acres of bog butted against Rumney Marsh.

Minot Derby's hounds broke out into rounds of barking, prompting him to leave his chair by the fire and peer out a window. He squinted through a gap in the curtains. A flicker of light, a lantern dimmed by a veil of snow, dithered up the drive.

Dorcas huddled the children to herd them off to bed. "Who would be calling on a night like this?"

Minot shrugged. "I hope William had the good sense to stay in the city." He pulled on his coat, picked up a lantern, and stepped onto the porch.

Daniel had succumbed to a spasm of coughing in the carriage by the time it pulled to a stop in front of the farmhouse. His attempt to greet Minot on the porch devolved into chaotic sputtering and hacking. Minot draped his coat over Daniel and waved in gratitude to Low.

Once inside, Daniel slumped into Minot's chair by the hearth. When his coughing subsided, he detected tiny splotches of blood on his kerchief. He tucked the kerchief away, hoping he had been discreet enough and had not tipped off Dorcas or Minot to how serious his illness had become.

When Dorcas served tea, Daniel took the cup in his hands and found a measure of relief by breathing in its vapors. Hope I'm not imposing. Storm surprised me."

"Not at all," Minot said, scratching his head. "Is everything right at home?"

Dorcas stiffened.

"All ... are well," Daniel answered in halting phrases. "Only planned to be away ... few hours. Came for quick look. Thinking of buying. Chelsea." He assessed their drawn expressions. "Want to give Rebecca ... children ... permanent home. Chelsea's good."

Minot and Dorcas looked at each other, as they floundered for the right words.

"Hope ... it's happy news," Daniel added.

"We're surprised," Dorcas said. "That is all."

"It is very good news," Minot replied. "But how are you? Your health ..."

"The coughing." Daniel shook his head. "Timing wasn't wise. I apologize. Should have forewarned. Planned to return home before. Low drove me. Looked at some areas. Storm worsened. Ferry wouldn't run ... this weather."

"Did you find some good prospects?" Minot asked.

"Yes. Three-story house. Near Low's store. Space for boarders ... extra income."

"That would be nice," Dorcas said. "My sister and nephews only three miles away, and no ferry to contend with." She straightened her apron. "What does Mama say about leaving her neighborhood?"

"Haven't talked with Rebecca. Anxious for safety these days. Crime gone bad to worse ... migrants ... fleeing Ireland ... famine ... by tens of thousands. Penniless. No skills. Orphaned children. Robbing to survive. Parents dead … during crossing. And sailors. From every part of the world."

"The riot," Minot added, "a couple of years ago on lower Ann Street showed how bad things will get. Authorities should have dealt more severely with that mob of riotous Negroes."

Dorcas spoke up. "The sailors who started the affair should have been dealt with. And the other white sailors who joined them."

"How were our sailors to blame?" Minot countered.

"The Negro boarders," Dorcas replied, "were peaceably biding their time in front of the place where they live. There was no call for those sailors to shove them off the sidewalk. They could have stepped into the empty street to pass. It was an even greater disgrace that a band of white sailors from across the street joined in ransacking the Negro house."

"I apologize," Daniel said. "Didn't mean to provoke an argument."

"It is not your fault," Dorcas replied. "Minot is the one who should apologize. We have been around and around on this subject since we first heard news of the riot. He needles me in front of company. Isn't that right dear?"

"If I offended," Minot said, "I am sorry. More importantly, we are happy to help you and Rebecca in any way we can."

"Thank you," Daniel replied. "Money's no problem. Mama needs … gentle nudge. Wish she and William … could make peace."

"They will have to," Dorcas said. "Especially, when William and Eunice have children."

"At least," Minot said, "let me speak with a friend who knows the real estate in this region."

Daniel's hacking cough persisted through the night, leaving him more fatigued at dawn than he was when the household retired the previous night. He shuffled into the kitchen, relieved at the absence of fresh blood splotches on his kerchief.

Dorcas offered him a steaming mug of tea. "I do not know which was louder during the night, the storm or your croup."

"Winter has never been my friend." Daniel sipped his tea.

"Minot and the hands are out surveying storm damage."

"I should help," Daniel said.

"You should stay out of nasty weather."

"Is William back?" he asked.

"I think anyone with sense stayed put until Mother Nature settled herself."

"Do you think your mother will come around and accept William's Universalist inclinations?"

Dorcas drew a long breath. "It seems William would do well to be more considerate of Mama's sensibilities."

"What do you know about his betrothed?"

"Eunice? He could do far worse," she replied. "She's kind, diligent, patient, and not bad to look at."

Daniel choked on his tea.

Dorcas laughed.

"Is his fascination with Universalism her doing?" he asked.

"Heavens no. That fetish is all his. Her folks are no keener on the idea than Mama."

"I shall ride the earliest ferry sailing back to Boston. I cannot imagine the anguish I have put on Rebecca."

"She does not become angry without cause," Dorcas replied. "Though doubtless, by now you have tried her patience as no one has ever done."

⁂ ⁂ ⁂

Although the storm had calmed during the night, Rebecca did not. She sat in an armchair in the family parlor until daybreak, nodding a few times, but never falling asleep. Her anger swelled and waned and swelled again as she rehearsed what she would say when Daniel walked through the door, hopefully healthy and safe.

William kissed the top of her head and asked if she wanted him to check the Dock Square shop before he returned to the farm. She said she would go to the shop herself on the omnibus if Daniel failed to return by noon.

No sooner than William had left, Daniel eased open the door to the flat. He hoped Rebecca would still be sleeping and that he could slip into bed without waking her.

"Where have you been?" Rebecca blurted, still seated in the armchair.

"House hunting. In Chelsea."

"House hunting? Why in heaven's name?"

Daniel tried to stutter a reply.

She held up her hand. "What is wrong with you lately?"

"I can explain," he said.

"I feared something had happened to you. Some horrible accident in that wretched storm. I thought I had lost you."

His hacking returned.

She rose from the chair and folded her arms around him, drawing him close. "Promise me you will do nothing of this sort again."

"I find it so hard to sleep in this drafty old house."

George and Willie rushed out of their bedroom and threw their arms around Daniel.

"Pa, you came home," George shouted.

Willie wept as he clung to his father.

Mama stood, glaring at Daniel from the bedroom doorway, her arms folded.

CHAPTER EIGHT

Mama's absence surprised no one, when William and Eunice exchanged vows at the First Universalist Church in Boston on February 27, 1845. Her bitterness still had not abated a year later when Eunice gave birth to a new Holliday grandchild.

William's pain left no room for reconciliation six months afterwards when his child's weak lungs filled, snuffing out the breath of life. His resentment multiplied the following April as he sat at Eunice's bedside, his chin pressed to his chest.

Rebecca leaned forward from her seat on the opposite side of the bed. She continued to dab her sister-in-law's forehead. She spurned the doctor's grim prognosis that Eunice would soon be lost in death. She worked all the harder to make her sister-in-law comfortable, to ply her with water and cover her with cold, wet towels. She clung to the hope that she would not be made to relive the heartache of watching Eunice's six-month-old child suffer in death, of losing Clarissa, Sarah, and Papa. The doctor urged her to pray, but Rebecca knew better.

No help ever came from above.

William and Rebecca held Eunice's hands in her final moments on earth. He thanked her for devoting herself to his wife's care. Her heart ached—not only for his grief but also from fear over what might become of him. Despair and bitterness had robbed him of his appetite for life.

Guilt needled Rebecca as she stood at Eunice's graveside—*everything is my fault. I reneged on my bargain with the Almighty—to be a blessing to the poor souls of lower Ann Street and to the children of the Bethel. I blocked Mama's overture of peace toward William.*

Days before Eunice died, Rebecca told Mama that any olive branch would be too little, too late and would be as welcome as salt rubbed in an open wound.

In return for Rebecca's rebellion, she believed God had visited affliction upon those she loved and grief upon those left behind.

After the last mourners offered their condolences, William embraced Rebecca and whispered, "Good-bye."

"Can we see you home?" she asked.

He shook his head. "I'm not going home. Everything is packed. I'm going west."

"Now?" Her mouth gaped.

"There is nothing more for me here." His voice cracked.

"That is not true. You have Susanna, Dorcas, and me. You have nephews and nieces. What about Mama? We will all miss you."

"Mama." He scoffed.

"She wants to make amends," Rebecca pleaded. "She's ready to do that now."

"Maybe she's ready, but I am not."

Rebecca clenched her jaw. "Religion. You both claim that is the problem. But no. Pride. Pride on both of your parts is the reason you throw the rest of us aside."

"I am not throwing anyone aside. I need to put some distance between ..." he indicated the graves where he had buried his wife and child, "... all of this and me. I need to find something to live for."

Her eyes misted. "You will write, won't you?"

"When I'm settled."

"I don't know how many more I can lose ..." She wrapped her arms around him and sobbed.

✳ ✳ ✳

Melancholy fettered Rebecca two months after William's departure as she trudged to Seamen's Bethel through muddy streets, wrought by an early June storm. Excuses to turn back flooded her mind, yet she persisted.

She asked Father Taylor, as they sat side-by-side in the chapel, "Which of all the religions in the world would have given my Papa entrance into heaven?"

"I had a few encounters with your father," he replied. "He struck me as an honest, earnest man, well respected on the docks. Loved by his sailors. He could not abide intemperance, but on most matters, if a man were to set his feet in the right direction, he stood ready to forgive."

"Does God truly honor only one religion?"

Taylor stroked his chin. "Religions are not of God's making. He sees each man's heart."

"Papa had a good heart." Rebecca sniffled. "I miss him."

"You have had a rough go in your young life. I was deeply saddened by the news that your sister-in-law recently passed into her Savior's arms."

"I thought I should never get over losing Papa. I have not, but I am no longer certain for whom I mourn ... there have been more than my heart can bear."

"Those who are gone don't need our sympathies," Father Taylor replied.

Her voice quavered. "You mean those who are dead."

"Have you heard anything from William?"

She shook her head, and neither of them spoke for a time until Rebecca broke the silence. "If God did not make religions, what good are they?"

"I suppose," he said, "they keep us searching for Him until we discover He has been with us all the time."

"If He is here, why does He not relieve our pain? Why? Why does He let Daniel continue to suffer? Why does He not make people get along—make them stop arguing about whose religion is greater than the rest?"

"I would be a liar if I denied asking myself those same questions day after day. Some of my Methodist brethren say I am too intolerant of intemperance, yet too accepting of slavery and of my Unitarian friends. My Unitarian friends shake their heads, claiming we Methodists make too much a circus of our worship. More time is spent plucking splinters out of another's eyes than tending to the log that hinders our own sight."

"Who among you is right?" she asked.

He replied, "Whenever I discover myself stuck in the quagmire of self-righteousness, I turn to the simple wisdom of God's Word—'what doth the Lord require of thee, but to do justly, and to love mercy, and to walk humbly with thy God?' We all too often forget that we sail under different flags, but with the same Commander."

"You speak of mercy, but all I know of God is his punishment. Humility, you say. How much lower must I be bent?" she asked. "I pray each wave of affliction will be the last. Then comes another, stronger storm." A tremor rose in her throat. "I fret over my husband. For five years since Willie's birth, I have been unable to conceive. He blames himself and is overcome with embarrassment. He no longer shows interest in marital pleasures. His health continues to worsen. I cannot bear the thought of losing him."

Taylor asked, "Does Daniel have good friends who are able to lift his spirits? Cheerful company and physical exertion work wonders for a man's constitution."

"He struggles just to keep up with the demands of his employment. He has little time or vigor for friends."

"Let me introduce you to someone who I believe can help your husband. It is providential that he is visiting here at the Bethel this very moment."

"Does this man love children and songs and poetry?" she asked.

"Yes," Father Taylor replied. "He has several children of his own for whom he composes original songs and poems. His name is Porter Dyer, but we call him our Psalmist. I should mention that he is a Congregational minister who serves as a city missionary on the docks. When it comes to serving seamen, he may claim to man the main sail, and I the jib, but we both have the same object—to catch the wind."

"He sounds like he would be a perfect friend for my Daniel."

"I'm glad you think so." Father Taylor cocked his head. "Now let me ask you something. What shall we do about Rebecca?"

"I think you have given me what I need—a reason for hope. Perhaps it does work to seek help from on high."

On her walk home, Rebecca decided to put Father Taylor's inspiration to the test. She lifted her chin as she passed the Old North Church and stole a peek at the steeple. As she tracked its skyward reach, strength drained from her legs. Buildings around her appeared to rock. She fell to her knees, panting. A foreboding shrouded her. She shut her eyes.

The masthead. Help doesn't come from on high—memories do.

Her mind went blank.

Her pulse and breath settled after a few minutes, and the shadowy dimness lifted. She rose, regained her equilibrium, and continued home.

✳ ✳ ✳

Rebecca prodded Daniel on the subject of Porter Dyer for weeks, approaching him from every angle with one line of reasoning after another. He resisted her every entreaty, claiming he had no need of a friend called the Psalmist. He repeated his disinterest in early July before leaving for the omnibus to the shop. Later that same morning, Porter Dyer walked through the entrance to 27 Dock Square and invited Daniel to Atwood's for a midday repast.

"A tempting offer," Daniel said. "But who's going to watch the shop?"

Porter shoved his hands into his pockets. "Shall I fetch a basket of oysters for us to share?"

"Oysters are a treat I rarely have an opportunity to enjoy. My wife is not fond of them. Nor of anything that lives in the sea. She will walk blocks out of her way to avoid passing Atwood's."

Porter returned a short while later with smoked oysters and fried potatoes. As they sat at a worktable behind the curtain, he said, "I understand you enjoy poetry."

"Ah," Daniel replied. "She has been plotting to turn us into fast friends."

Porter grinned. "Who do you idolize among the great poets?"

"I enjoy anything by Keats. I regard all of his works with reverence."

"That's a fascinating choice. Any verses in particular?"

Daniel cleared his throat.

> *A thing of beauty is a joy forever:*
> *Its loveliness increases; it will never*
> *Pass into nothingness; but still will keep*
> *A bower quiet for us, and a sleep*
> *Full of sweet dreams, and health, and quiet*
> *breathing.*

Porter clapped. "Bravo. A bold selection. *Endymion* was not the critics' favorite."

"Not being a scholar, I judge only by the emotion it stirs in me. And you? What works do you admire?"

"I do not put myself in the same class as Keats," Porter replied. "But I fancy myself as something of an amateur poet."

"Have you written some lines?"

"I write mainly for my children, though someday, perhaps, I may publish some of them in journals or as a collection."

Daniel sat back in his chair. "Go ahead and try something out on me."

"Mind you, this piece is not refined, as of yet."

"I'm listening," Daniel said.

Porter recited—

> *I love in Winter's eve to sit beside the genial stove*
> *And take upon my willing knees the children of my love*
> *And tell my private history for thirty years and more*
> *To ears which listen eagerly to things unheard before*
> *To see their bright teeth glisten as I mention something queer*
> *Or how their young eyes sparkle as my story wakes a tear.*

Daniel applauded. "Ahhh. A father's love has never been so eloquently captured. You are indeed a poet."

Their shared passion for children and poetry fostered a daily lunchtime ritual and fueled a steadfast bond. However, Porter's announcement on a temperate, cloudy September day, only two months after their friendship began, shocked Daniel into gloomy silence. He stared away.

"I am not calling an end to our friendship," Porter said, breaking the silence.

Daniel collected his thoughts. "When do you start?"

"The end of the month."

"How long have you known?"

"The Norfolk Conference invited me to preach there a couple of weeks ago. I apparently was not awful. On Sunday past, they officially called me to serve as pastor for one year."

Daniel shook his head. "Hingham?"

"A two-hour ferry ride."

"How often will you be back?"

"Often. And I will write you."

"What will happen after a year?"

"That remains to be seen. If I do well, a church here in Boston could call me."

Daniel smiled. "I am sure you will do well, and the good people of Hingham will not let you go. Rebecca and I can bring the boys down for an occasional holiday."

Porter rocked back in his chair. "You would all be most welcome."

"Congratulations on a well-deserved honor. Your friendship has lifted my spirits more than you know."

✻ ✻ ✻

Rebecca stared out the window into the bowels of a nasty storm in late February of the following year. The burn from a wave of nausea remained in her throat. It had been weeks since her last flow. If that were not evidence enough, memories of the family way she had previously navigated left no room for doubt—a third Pomroy offspring was growing in her womb. She wanted to dance, like Dorcas would do at the farm when rain came after a long drought.

Certainly, Daniel would dance with her when he returned home from work. He had spoken often of how badly he wanted a daughter of his own after a visit the previous November by Porter and his wife, Esther. They brought their four children with them, and Daniel's eyes lit brighter than they had in years when he bounced their one-year-old Mary on his knee. Since that visit, Daniel had worn a constant smile on his face.

The unseasonably fair weather that had stretched from the prior October into the heart of February had helped both his constitution and his attitude. His ability to raise his member returned, and apparently his seed was healthy. Time would tell whether his wish for a daughter was granted.

From the moment he learned of Rebecca's condition, he redoubled his efforts at saving enough money to buy a proper home. Julia, the young woman who lived with them rent-free in exchange for minding the boys, was replaced by a paid boarder. He once more eschewed taking the omnibus and skipped midday lunch breaks. He allowed himself only one distraction from work. Each day he walked the three-mile loop to and from Aunt Prudence's home to check on his ailing aunt before returning home from the upholstery shop.

During a freak snowstorm in the middle of April, Daniel slogged home through mud after visiting Aunt Prudence. He clutched his back along the way, and his lungs strained for whatever breath his labored gasps could collect. By the time he arrived home, his lungs—aflame from overexertion—erupted into spasms.

Rebecca rushed to greet him as she envisioned another calamity crashing down on them. "I am putting my foot down," she said. "You shall ride the omnibus from now on and you will eat your midday meal. No more taking chances with your health."

He offered no rebuttal as he shuffled toward the family parlor where he collapsed into a chair by the hearth. She retrieved a sprig of thorn-apple leaves, lit them in the copper bowl, and placed them on the table beside his chair. He inhaled the smoke until the coughing subsided then went to bed. During the night he woke several times with a start, laboring to catch his breath.

The next morning, as Daniel prepared to leave for the upholstery shop Rebecca said, "I do not want you working such long hours. Bring home as much sewing as you can, and I will help you keep up on your work as I watch the boys and tend to Mama's health."

"I am not helpless," he contended.

"No, but you shall work yourself into an early grave."

"I suppose next you will want me to stop calling on Aunt Prudence."

"Not entirely. Once or twice a week should suffice."

He shrugged as he trudged out the door.

* * *

When Daniel returned home that evening, he took Rebecca's hand. "Mr. Fenno, Jr., Minot's real estate agent friend, visited the shop this afternoon. He wants to show us a home across the river, a short distance from the ferry landing. The boys should come with us."

"What of Mama?"

"Mama can still live with us."

"And Aunt Prudence?"

"She has Aunt Hannah," he replied. "They can look after each other well enough, now that they share the same home."

"But Hannah's health is no better than her sister's."

"I shall call on them each afternoon," Daniel replied.

"Did we not agree this morning that you needed to visit less frequently? Besides, I don't understand why it is so urgent for us to leave the city."

"You do not see what I witness every day. This city's darkness and depravity are snaking up Ann Street. It is only a matter of time before it engulfs us and our children." He laid his hand on her belly, and she covered his hand with her own.

"What about Susanna and her brood?" Rebecca asked.

"They are always traipsing off to her husband's people in New Hampshire. Chelsea isn't far out of their way. They can visit Mama and us whenever they go up there."

Rebecca scrunched her nose. "Who's going to be here for Sarah's young one?"

"You mean on the rare occasion his father chooses to be sociable? We can take the new steam ferry across to see them, whenever Charles makes himself available."

"And your work?" she asked.

"An omnibus has begun regular routes between Winnisimmet Square on the Chelsea side of the river and

Faneuil Market. I shall yield to your insistence that I begin riding it to and from the shop."

"Very well. Since the matter has such a grip on your mind, the boys and I will go with you once the weather settles. We should see fairer days soon."

A tic worked upward in his chest. He turned away from Rebecca and reached for the copper bowl of smoldering thorn-apple leaves. A coughing spasm took hold, refusing to submit. Too little smoke, too late.

Her heart pinched as she prepared a cup of tea, hoping it might abate the cough as he sipped.

✳ ✳ ✳

The affliction Rebecca fretted would come next did not involve Daniel's health. She covered her face with her hands, weeks later, when the doctor explained consumption was laying waste to Mama's body. Scenes of Sarah's battle against the same disease preyed on her mind. It mattered little that the doctor assured her Mama's life could be extended several more years with proper treatment. He added that moving her away from the coast to a drier inland climate would help.

Rebecca reminded Mama that, on various occasions, Dorcas had invited her to settle in with them at the farm. Mama always objected, not wanting to move away from familiar surroundings. Rebecca encouraged her to reconsider, given the doctor's recommendation. Mama countered that she was heartbroken to be rejected by her youngest daughter—did not the Good Book say, 'honor thy father and thy mother?'

Rebecca began to second-guess herself. Mama was right. Instead of unshouldering herself of responsibility to care for her mother, she should be looking on high for help and healing. She recalled her decision to give up serving the Bethel children and the indigent families of lower Ann Street. Had that choice been the source of the family's afflictions?

Rebecca hoped to strike a compromise by advancing the timeline for moving to Chelsea. Mama rebuffed her. When the doctor chimed in, insisting the Derby's farm, though only a few miles farther inland would be a better choice, Mama acceded to his recommendation. She continued to complain she felt unwelcome living in Rebecca's home as she set about packing for her move across the river.

* * *

The rift between mother and daughter did not deter Rebecca and her young family from searching for a new home on the Chelsea side of the river several months later. As the steam ferry passed ships at anchor in Boston Harbor, seven-year-old Willie asked, "Did Grandpapa sail to England on one of those?"

Daniel pushed Willie's cap down over his eyes. "Your grandfather's ship was much smaller and not as sturdy."

Willie adjusted his cap. "I want to sail a big ship someday."

George screwed up his face as he peered at his mother. "Did you see it when he died?"

A shiver trilled up Rebecca's spine. Memories of the plummeting masthead still haunted her even a decade-and-a-half after her father's death. She leaned into Daniel and whispered, "I will miss the city, but am happy to pack up our boys and remove them from the allure of those wretched docks."

Daniel drew a labored breath. He told himself, at last, the roof over our heads will belong to us. We shall never again fear being cast out onto the streets if we cannot afford rent. He gazed teary-eyed at Rebecca and the boys as he imagined a day, likely soon, when he would be laid up in a bed, useless as a breadwinner.

"I am eager," Rebecca said, "to see how Mama is faring now that she is settled in with Dorcas and Minot."

Daniel feigned a smirk. "The real question is, how are Minot and Dorcas faring?"

She laughed. "Nonetheless, I will feel much better being closer to her."

John Fenno, Jr., met the Pomroys at the ferry landing and drove them to a nearby neighborhood. The plush carriage interior exceeded any luxury previously known to the boys. Willie waved to everyone they passed on the street while George sat erect, unsmiling, with his hands folded in his lap.

Fenno pulled the carriage to a stop in front of a three-story wood-frame house—No. 140 Chestnut Street.

"I believe this is similar to one Mr. Low showed me a few years ago," Daniel said as he helped Rebecca down from the carriage.

Worry lines rippled across Rebecca's brow. She tugged at Daniel's elbow. "This is certainly beyond our means."

"This isn't Boston." Daniel grinned.

Rebecca surveyed the exterior of the house, careful to gaze no higher than the first-floor windows. She made mental notes—narrow, wood-frame, wood siding, vacant land on either side for a garden. She wondered if it was true that by merely crossing a river, one's money could buy so much more.

"Don't deliberate long," Fenno said. "With the new omnibus service starting, Boston investors will snatch up homes and vacant lots. Come inside and look around."

Rebecca peered to her left as they stood in the entryway, assessing a spacious room. Fenno answered her unspoken question. "That could be a formal dining room, and to your right is a small parlor. The family parlor and kitchen are down the hall."

"Do each of the tenants have a separate entry?" Rebecca asked.

"No," Daniel replied. "The entire house will be ours."

"What shall we do with so much space?"

"If that little one you're carrying is a girl," Daniel replied, "she can have a room of her own when she's older."

Fenno added, "Any rooms you do not require can be let out to boarders."

"Can we make do living on the ground floor?" she asked.

"If you prefer," Fenno replied. "This floor has two bedrooms."

"We cannot afford such a place," she demurred.

"Mrs. Pomroy," Fenno said. "The price is $1,800, and terms are available. Did I mention the Methodist and Congregational churches and a school are short walks away?"

As they toured the rest of the ground floor, Rebecca became more at ease with the idea of resettling her little family in Chelsea. She drew the line, though, when it came to accompanying George and Willie as they explored the upstairs and attic. Instead, she and Daniel stepped outside where Rebecca picked out the perfect patch for a vegetable garden.

When the boys returned, bubbling with laughter, Daniel took Rebecca's hand. "What do you say, dear?"

She gnawed at her lip before answering. "Daniel, I trust your judgment. Whatever you think is fine with me."

"Since that be the case," Daniel turned to Fenno, "is it possible to consummate the purchase today?"

Fenno retrieved a packet of documents from his valise and sat on the front stoop, flanked by Daniel and Rebecca. He filled in blanks on two identical copies of the pre-printed document and presented them for signature. "My office will inform you once the documents are approved."

✳ ✳ ✳

Rebecca clung to Daniel's arm two weeks later as they returned to their new Chestnut Street home. They had attended a political meeting in Chelsea's Independence Hall, featuring Illinois Congressman Abraham Lincoln. According to Rebecca, the only thing flatter than the few blocks between the meeting place and home was Mr. Lincoln's coarse humor.

As they crossed the street from the auditorium to Winnisimmet Park, Rebecca said, "At least, when Father Taylor sprinkles his sermons with crude stories, it is for a moral purpose. He hopes to convince sailors that there is a dear price to pay for intemperance and depravity."

"But this fellow is not a preacher," Daniel replied. "To say nothing of the fact that he's from the fringes of civilization. We should not expect him to appreciate our sophisticated eastern sensibilities."

"If General Zachary Taylor wants northern votes to put him in the President's House," Rebecca said, "he should send a more appropriate surrogate—someone whose name people know, someone whom they respect. Father Taylor has spoken of Mr. Lincoln, but not in a flattering way. The Congressman is wrongheaded about how to free the imbiber from the bottle. Until today, I have known nothing else of what he stands for and I remain unimpressed." She winced as the baby kicked inside her.

"Whom would you suggest?" Daniel cocked his head.

"A true abolitionist, a man who has more to say than, General Taylor is not as evil as the other slaveholder who opposes him. Someone such as our own Mr. Sumner, who would have advocated for allowing Black children to attend the same schools as white children or other matters of substance.

Daniel laughed. "I cannot debate with you on that point. And beyond being a bona fide enemy of the slave power, Mr. Sumner's gestures are not so awkward, and the tenor of his voice is far easier on the ears."

Rebecca leaned into Daniel moments later when they were midway through the park. "Can we sit for a moment?" she asked. "Something has me all aswoon."

Daniel cupped her forehead. "You're clammy and a bit pale. Let's sit here."

A woman approached with four girls following in her wake. "Do you need help?" the woman asked. "We live only a block away. I'm Phemie. These are my daughters. My husband is the local gilder—Mr. Cushing."

"I shall be fine," Rebecca said.

"We are the Pomroys from over on Chestnut Street," Daniel replied. "Daniel and Rebecca."

"How close are you to giving birth?" Phemie asked.

"Another few weeks." Rebecca flinched at the baby's movement in her womb.

"Is it your first?"

"No, we have two boys," Daniel said. "They've gone home ahead of us. We've come from the meeting hall."

"It's a warm afternoon," Phemie said. "I'm certain everything will be fine when you've rested a few minutes and drink some water." She sent Almira, her eldest daughter, to fetch water for Rebecca.

Once Rebecca was back on her feet, Phemie offered to help in any way she might be needed during Rebecca's remaining days of pregnancy. She also recommended her neighbor, Mrs. Currier, if Rebecca had not yet secured the services of a midwife.

Rebecca and Daniel proceeded home after thanking Phemie and her daughters for their assistance. When they arrived at their stoop, Rebecca hesitated.

"Is something the matter?" Daniel asked.

"I have been thinking on our new friend's suggestion about a midwife. Do you think Mama would be offended?"

"I try to avoid making judgments about your mother," he replied.

"If this child comes quickly, I will feel more at ease if help was only a couple of blocks away, rather than all the way out in the country."

"We should consider your needs first."

Rebecca sighed. "I hope she can be made to see it that way."

* * *

Daniel paced in the family parlor a couple of months later, on a cool, cloudy November afternoon. He had not stopped his lumbering march since the midwife arrived, despite swollen legs and feet that hobbled him, like a ship lugging an anchor over a rocky shoal. Mrs. Currier tended to Rebecca in the large bedroom at the end of the long hallway, with Phemie and twelve-year-old Almira serving as her assistants.

Rebecca's grunting and shrieking stopped after a couple of hours, giving way to tiny whimpers that stopped Daniel in his tracks.

He barreled into the bedroom.

Rebecca sat halfway up in bed, flushed but smiling. She cooed, "We have our girl, just like we hoped."

"Shall I take the news to George and Willie?" Daniel asked.

"They won't be pleased to have a sister instead of a little brother," Rebecca replied.

"Be that as it may, I should tell them their mother is well."

Daniel crossed the street and walked a couple of doors down to the Bagnall house where the boys had remained during the birthing hours.

George glowered when his father spoke the word sister.

Mrs. Bagnall delighted in the news and asked, "Have you decided on a name?"

"Clara Jane," Daniel replied. "My mother's name was Clarissa."

"I have some little girl's things to pass on to her," Mrs. Bagnall added. "I may need them back, though."

Young Wilbur Bagnall, Willie's constant playmate added, "Sisters aren't so bad." He glanced at his sister,

Emma. "Except when they make sour faces while I play piano."

"Yeah," echoed Willie. "Little sisters don't bully, either."

"I don't bully you," George sputtered.

"Sisters can be pests," Emma said. Then she stuck out her tongue.

"All right, children," Mrs. Bagnall said. "That is enough."

Daniel thanked her for tending to the boys and led them home to meet Clara Jane.

CHAPTER NINE

Six-month-old Clara Jane's tiny hands kneaded and swatted at her mother's bosom. When the infant's demands remained unmet, her plaintive whimpers broke into screaming outrage.

"Excuse me, Dr. Forsyth," Rebecca said to the customer in the confectionery shop she had opened in the large room across the entryway from the small parlor.

"It is not the little one's fault," Dr. Forsyth replied as he inspected the array of toffees, caramels, lollipops, and hard candies on display. "Believe me, I have witnessed worse behavior in the waiting room at my clinic."

Rebecca had set up the shop to replace a portion of Daniel's wages after he became bedridden and unable to work due to the large quantity of fluids that had built up in his body. The shop was Aunt Prudence's inspiration. She even loaned the money for purchasing inventory, fixtures, and specialized confectionery supplies for the kitchen.

Rebecca had taken several other measures to keep her family from sinking into poverty. She took on additional piecework from a second Chelsea upholsterer, as well as two more on Dock Square. Rent from a boarder—a young tanner with a wife and two children—also helped fill the gap. In addition to assuming the role of breadwinner for her family, Rebecca shouldered the sole responsibility for looking after Aunt Prudence and Aunt Hannah.

After Clara Jane's tantrum continued for a bit longer, Rebecca turned to Amelia Bell—a widow in her sixties who received room and board in exchange for helping in the shop and minding the children, when needed. "Will you kindly assist Dr. Forsyth while I tend to the little one?"

"That won't be necessary," the doctor said. "These treats are tantalizing, but I should keep to my task of seeing to your husband's health. My hope is that we can curb the buildup of fluids, lest we find ourselves wrestling with dropsy—a far more severe matter."

✳ ✳ ✳

Daniel's body expelled a large quantity of fluids a couple of months later, and the swelling receded. Andrew Haskell—a founder of Chelsea's benevolence committee and one of the Dock Square merchants—came to his aide and arranged new employment for him at an upholstery shop near Chestnut Street. The upholsterer agreed to hire Daniel, with reservations over his asthmatic condition and lingering shortness of breath. His wages were substantially reduced compared to what he had made as a junior partner in Boston.

When Daniel was not overcome with fatigue or constrained by his new employment, he relieved Rebecca from making calls on Aunt Prudence and Aunt Hannah. On one occasion, he leaned against the doorjamb at 26 West Castle Street, gasping as he waited for someone to answer his knock. He considered giving up but allowed them another moment. The door opened at last but only a crack. Hannah peered through the gap.

"Oh, it's you," she said as she opened the door wider. "Rebecca tells us you have been quite ill."

"I am much improved." He edged past her, wheezing.

Hannah followed him down the hall. "If she's awake, she'll be delighted to see you. Poor thing spends all of her time sleeping these days."

They paused in the doorway to the bedroom. Prudence lay propped up with a pile of pillows, her mouth hanging open as she took short, shallow breaths.

"Shall we disturb her?" Daniel asked.

"She probably won't notice."

They stood at Prudence's bedside after tiptoeing in.

"She is all puffed up," Daniel whispered.

Prudence blinked. "That's not the only part of me that's bloated."

Hannah tried to explain. "Her ankles and feet are—"

"Like pâte à choux," Prudence barked. She clutched her chest.

Hannah whispered, "Doctor says the general swelling is likely a sign of dropsy. Her heart could be failing. We'd best let her rest. I am thinking a little Grecian foxglove might do her some good."

Hannah clung to Daniel's arm as they retreated down the hallway to the parlor. She sniffed in short breaths.

"How are you faring?" he asked.

"Oh, I'm managing."

"Has the doctor examined you?" Daniel asked.

"Last week when Rebecca was here, the doctor came," Hannah said. "He treated Prudence with leeches and gave me a dosage of arsenicum."

"I shall ask Rebecca what the doctor had to say."

✳ ✳ ✳

While Daniel was visiting his aunts in Boston, Phemie Cushing stopped in at the confectionery shop. She was joined by her daughters—twelve-year-old Almira, seven-year-old Annie, six-year-old Hannah, and five-year-old Eliza. A son, fifteen-year-old Frank, accompanied them.

Rebecca gestured to the glass case where she kept the choicest candies and offered them samples. "Take what you like," she said. "I cannot make enough goodies to thank your family for the help you've been."

Phemie opened her coin purse. "Your cheerfulness is reward enough. We have been so worried about you and your family. Please allow me to pay."

"I insist," Rebecca said. "Your daughters remind me of my own nieces."

Eliza held up a bell that had been laying on the counter. "What is this for, Mrs. Pomroy?" she asked.

"You may call me Auntie Pomroy. I would like that. As for the bell, Mr. Pomroy plans to attach it to the door so it will ring when customers come into the shop, in case I am in my kitchen or doing other chores."

"If you don't mind, I can take care of that right now," Frank offered.

"That's kind of you, but unnecessary," Rebecca said.

"Go ahead and let him hang it," Phemie replied.

Rebecca retrieved a toolbox from behind the counter and smiled as she handed it to Frank. "If you insist."

✳ ✳ ✳

George and Willie jumped from Uncle Minot's wagon on their arrival at the Derbys' farmhouse for a long-promised Independence Day celebration in the country. Rebecca climbed down and inhaled the July air, laden with the aromas of cut hay and freshly turned earth. The three-mile ride from dank Chelsea to the sunbaked inland fields had brightened her perspective. It also made breathing less toilsome for Daniel.

Mama sat on the porch, holding Susanna's one-year-old Tommy. Her cheery smile caught Rebecca off guard.

"Let me have that precious little girl," Mama said as she coaxed Clara Jane to join cousin Tommy in grandma's lap.

Rebecca understood the universal urge of mothers to huddle their broods under their wings. For her, it blossomed when George turned ten, more than halfway along his journey toward becoming a man. Willie would follow close behind. A few years more and Clara Jane would take her turn as a mother.

Dorcas stepped onto the porch carrying a letter pressed to her chest. "This came yesterday," Dorcas said. "It's good news. Very good news."

Rebecca unfolded the letter. Four years of anxiety melted away as she read it. Tears of relief welled behind her eyes. William had written, finally. He was in California ... boarding with a druggist named Sason from Massachusetts ... panning for gold. The letter probably accounted for a large portion of the turnabout in Mama's demeanor. But there was more. Rebecca surveyed the brood that had flocked onto the porch after her family's arrival—her two remaining sisters flanked by their families. Not only was Mama's only son safe and well, she also basked in the collective affections of ten of her eleven living grandchildren swarming around her.

The only gloom among them hovered over Susanna and Thomas, who had recently returned from burying Thomas's father in New Hampshire. Susanna wore black. Thomas signified his grief with a black armband.

Susanna spoke up. "Thomas and I have some news of our own. He has inherited his father's farm. Though it is small by some folks' standards, we have decided to resettle there and make as good a go of it as we can."

The color drained from Mama's face. She rocked forward. Her two small grandchildren spilled out of her lap. Rebecca knelt in front of them and reached out to brace the little ones from hitting the hardwood surface. Mama's limp body tumbled into her.

Thomas and Minot came to Rebecca's aid and together they carried Mama to her bed. By the time the doctor arrived, though stricken with fever, Mama had recovered enough to sit up and take a sip of water. The radiance that had greeted Rebecca on her arrival was eclipsed by a careworn countenance—as if her mother had aged decades in only a couple of hours.

The doctor speculated the fever would break if she remained undisturbed and consumed a large quantity of water. Instead, coughing spasms plagued her day and night, her appetite waned, she nagged and picked and complained at every turn. Bad days outnumbered good days by an unhealthy margin, and on bad days she was often too fatigued to make her own way outdoors to the privy. During the nights, her urine conflated with night sweats to drench her gown and bedclothes.

By harvest time, Dorcas came to her wits end as Mama's sole caretaker and called on Rebecca for help. Rebecca began making twice weekly visits to the farm to aid in Mama's care.

After changing Mama's bedpans and mattresses, cleaning up her vomit, and bathing and dressing her, Rebecca helped with the laundry for everyone at the farm and gave Dorcas a hand in the kitchen as they prepared meals for the family and farmhands. All the while she held her tongue while inundated with gripes and complaints.

When she returned home there was little left of her. Nonetheless, she gave every ounce of her remaining energy, and then some, to her husband's precarious health, to stitching piecework, to her boarders and confectionery customers, to an unweaned daughter, and to two rambunctious sons underfoot, on top of continuing her frequent trips to Boston to look in on Daniel's aunts.

* * *

Daniel began to rally as the harvest wound down, even as Rebecca's nerves wrenched tighter and tighter. She hoped his progress might be sustainable but remained skeptical. One key factor in his improvement may have been the news that Porter and his wife Esther were in Chelsea and would call on them. Nevertheless, the Dyers' visit would be short and the grave purpose that occasioned it weighed on them—the local Congregational minister and his wife had buried two children of their own in a two-week span.

Daniel embraced Porter instantly as his Psalmist friend crossed the threshold into his home. "It is a delight to see you," Daniel said, "regardless of the circumstances."

"I am equally happy to be in your home," Porter replied.

After the four went through to the family parlor, Rebecca said, "I cannot comprehend what Reverend Langworthy and his wife are going through. It must be a bitter trial to bury one's children when they are still babes with a lifetime of possibilities ahead."

"All these years after losing our own little Henry," Esther said, "we continue to miss him. Yes, we have other children, but still ..." She dabbed her tears.

Rebecca laid her hand on Esther's. "I was only a child when I lost Papa. Daniel suffered the same. I still endure moments of profound sadness, but if I lost one of my little ones, I'm not sure I could carry on."

Porter pinched his brow. "I was truly overwhelmed by Reverend Langworthy's confession during worship today. After laying his two-year-old daughter and five-year-old son in the ground, losing both of them a mere seventeen days apart, he stood before his own flock and said, 'What a miserable comforter I must have been when you were passing through unimaginable sorrows. I see now, I knew nothing about pain and heartbreak.'"

"How does one muster such faith?" Daniel asked.

Porter shook his head. "There is no arrogance, no self-indulgence about the man. He is utterly humble. I suppose the secret to faith lies somewhere in that."

Rebecca stood. "I apologize. I must have lost my manners. I shall make tea. I have biscuits as well."

"May I help?" Esther asked.

"Thank you, but everything is prepared. You sit with the men. Daniel is hoping Porter brought some new poems to share."

Rebecca hurried out of the parlor and stood in the kitchen, pressing the heels of her hands to her temples. The hazy image of a child laid out in a coffin flashed through her mind. She took a deep breath to compose herself.

When she returned to the parlor, they spent the afternoon reminiscing about their friendship while Amelia Bell managed the Pomroy children. Try as she may to be attentive during the conversation, Rebecca's mind wandered to the child in the coffin, flitted to her own children, back to Daniel, Porter, Esther, and their conversation.

CHAPTER TEN

Rebecca offered Prudence fifty dollars during a visit before Christmas. It was money they had saved over the course of several months—a partial payment for the loan Prudence made to Daniel to start the confectionery shop. Prudence refused the payment and insisted she bring Daniel to see her as soon as possible.

"We are planning to come Christmas Eve. Will that be soon enough?" Rebecca asked.

"I suppose that will suffice. However, tomorrow is never guaranteed, especially at my age and in my state." Prudence winced and pressed her hand to her chest.

Rebecca returned Christmas Eve with Daniel, along with ten-year-old George, eight-year-old Willie, and one-year-old Clara Jane. While Aunt Hannah doted on the children, Prudence called Daniel and Rebecca to her bedside. She gathered her thoughts and panted them out in urgent spurts. She had made changes to her will. She bequeathed Daniel the promissory note in the amount of three-hundred-and-four dollars she laid against him for the loan to start the confectionery shop. The bequest carried the condition that he deposit fifty dollars in an account for the sole use and benefit of his son George. She also set aside fifty dollars of her estate in an account to be held for Willie until he attained the age of twenty-one.

As Rebecca collected her family to leave, Prudence gave her an elaborately wrapped package. "A small thank you for all the comfort you have brought us. You may open it now or on Christmas morning."

"Open it now," the boys clamored.

Rebecca's breath caught in her throat as she unwrapped a copy of Dickens's *The Haunted Man.*

Prudence rasped, "I thought you might like this one to go along with your *Twist* volumes." Then she motioned for Daniel to come close. "I presume there is a decent livery near where you live."

Daniel nodded affirmatively.

"Take my carriage and use it tomorrow when you go for Christmas dinner at the Derbys' farm." Her voice had grown thin. "In fact, you might as well keep it for a time to make your coming and going a bit easier. Be sure to stable the horse overnight. It might die from the cold if it doesn't have proper shelter."

An overnight meringue of snow on Christmas morning took Daniel's and the children's minds off the numbing cold. Rebecca's anxieties were not so easily assuaged, though. Her visits to the farm became less frequent after the harvest when Dorcas no longer required her help, and Rebecca fretted over the state her mother might be in when they arrived. Then again, regardless of Mama's frame of mind at any given moment, she could always spiral down and spoil an otherwise festive occasion.

On their arrival at the farm, Rebecca hung back with Clara Jane as Daniel secured the carriage, and the boys bounded up the porch stairs and into the farmhouse. Laughter and cheerful chatter greeted the boys' entrance, with Mama's spirited voice breaking through the rest. Rebecca's anxiety melted away and a smile budded on her face. She passed off Clara Jane to Daniel and reached into the carriage to collect the confectionaries they brought to sweeten the day. She followed Daniel inside with her hands full.

"Bring that little one to me," Mama cooed from her chair by the hearth. "I do not see nearly enough of her."

Rebecca rolled her eyes without losing her smile. "I suppose we could all move in, and it still wouldn't be enough."

Mama chuckled. "No, it would not. I can never have enough of these little ones."

"Then you won't mind," Rebecca said, "if I leave them with you and Dorcas for a few days. Prudence is failing fast, and I worry the burden is too much for poor Hannah."

"Oh dear," Mama replied. "I do wish I could go see them before..."

Rebecca leaned and kissed Mama. "I wish so, too. But you would catch your death in this weather."

Frigid temperatures, icy rain, and heavy snow hammered Boston after Rebecca and her family returned from the Christmas gathering at the Derbys' farm. Daniel relapsed and spent a week during the height of the storms dragging himself out of bed to the outdoor privy, expelling as much excess fluid as his body would yield. Rebecca returned one day from calling on Prudence to find him shivering and barefoot on the back stoop, wrapped in urine-soaked bedclothes. Amelia Bell, who tended the confectionery shop in Rebecca's absence, had not seen him slip out of the house.

As Rebecca helped him inside, he murmured clipped phrases through his chattering teeth, "Couldn't hold ... great gush ... all wet." She bathed him, put him into fresh clothes, and settled him in a dry bed in the small parlor off the entryway before sheltering Aunt Prudence's horse.

A stable boy stopped her before she was able to pull inside the livery. "Boss say you have to pay what you owes."

She climbed down and marched into the barn.

The stable boy called after her, "He busy."

Rebecca waited outside the office while Andrew Haskell stood in the doorway discussing business with the livery owner. When Haskell turned to leave, he exchanged nods with her.

Haskell was only a few steps past her when she raised her voice to the owner. "You cannot give some grace to an afflicted family in weather like this?"

"I have to feed my young ones, too," the owner shouted in reply.

Haskell turned back and stood next to her. He glared at the owner, "What is this about, Mrs. Pomroy?"

She explained her plight—two elderly, sickly aunts in Boston, her husband deathly ill and out of work, sparse sales in the confectionery shop to begin the new year, three children to feed and care for. "He demands I pay our debt now or he will let the horse die in the cold. The horse isn't even ours. We have it on loan."

Haskell pulled out his purse and said to the livery owner, "How much does this dear woman owe?"

"It is not your debt to pay," he replied.

"Never mind," Haskell said. "Add the amount to my account. It better be a fair amount."

"But ..." the owner stuttered.

"Shall we take our business elsewhere?" Haskell asked. "Wait, I have a better idea. The other directors of the bank and I should treat you the same as you treat Mrs. Pomroy. And don't give me any yarns about your poor family. I happen to know you are a derelict old bachelor."

The livery owner called out to his stable boy, "Tend to Mrs. Pomory's horse and carriage."

Rebecca sat at Prudence's bedside three days after the livery incident, caressing the elderly woman's hand. A doctor sat on the other side of the bed. Fluids bloated every nook of Prudence's body. As the end neared, her panting eased, and her thin breaths came in intervals two or so minutes apart. Chest spasms followed.

Prudence clung to the last fragile fibers of life for several hours, until her final breath rushed out of her body.

The doctor rose and reached over, testing for signs of a pulse. Resignation registered on his face, giving Rebecca the only cue she needed. A flood of tears spilled out.

Hannah lay in bed down the hall, her ankles and feet too swollen to amble down the hall to her sister's side.

*   *   *

Seventeen-year-old Bill Haskell kept watch several days later, waiting for the Pomroy family's return from burying their aunt. His mother, Ann, stationed him at her parlor window across the street to alert her of their arrival. Icy crystals, strewn like jewels over Chestnut Street, glistened under the winter sun and held him entranced. When the crunch of carriage wheels and the clomp of hoofs broke his reverie, he called out, "Ma. They're back."

Ann Haskell collected the meal she had prepared for her neighbors. She and her husband, Micajah, were all too familiar with affliction. Their sickly son, Francis, died recently, days short of his fifth birthday. Another son, Edward, had succumbed in infancy. They had buried parents and siblings, as well. They suffered the stain of bankruptcy that dogged Micajah for ten years, straining their bond with Ann's older brothers—Andrew and William—who were both leading citizens of the town and also her husband's younger cousins.

Despite adversity, Micajah rallied and attained business success as a shoemaker. Most importantly, unlike cousins Andrew and William whose heads were turned by Unitarianism, Micajah remained faithful to the gospel. He served the Congregational Church as Superintendent of Sabbath School.

Ann's breath fogged in the cold as she and her housekeeper carried baskets of food across Chestnut Street to the Pomroy's front door. After Rebecca welcomed them inside, Ann expressed her family's condolences and offered to take charge of Rebecca's children and look in on Daniel whenever a need arose. Ann had older children, two hired household help, and an elderly boarder at her beck and call. "May I offer you a word of advice before I leave?" Ann asked.

Rebecca shrugged.

"It is natural in times of loss to become angry with God. Do not let your anger take root. Take it from someone who has gone down that road—if you harbor ill will toward the Almighty, it will fester like an unhealed wound."

Rebecca drew her arms tight across her chest, staring in silence before she replied. "What I wish to be over is my husband's illness. It has plagued him since childhood, and though there have been seasons of reprieve when we thought the misery was at last over, each time it has assaulted him anew with greater vengeance." She pinched the bridge of her nose. "I am so weary."

"There, there," Ann said. "Look to God in Heaven for strength."

"No. No," Rebecca replied, shaking her head. "When he took Papa from me, I vowed never again to look for help from above."

"Then I will be your intercessor," Ann replied, "and petition God daily for you and your family."

✳ ✳ ✳

Aunt Hannah slumped in a cushioned armchair next to her bed at the West Castle Street house a few weeks after her sister's burial. Her face and neck swollen like rising yeast buns.

Rebecca turned to strip the bed of linens that had become spoiled with yellowish-brown stains. The acrid odor assaulted Rebecca's nostrils. "Will you be comfortable sitting there for a bit? I should take your mattress outside to air. I can bring in the one from Prudence's bed."

Hannah whispered, "You are an angel."

"No," Rebecca demurred. "Angels come from above. You shall never find me joining in such high company."

"You cared for both my sisters and now me, even when we couldn't lift ourselves out of bed to go to the privy," Hannah said. "We agreed our Daniel married an angel."

Rebecca dragged the soiled mattress and linens outside and returned to make a fresh bed for Hannah and bathe her. The progress of the disease presented itself as Rebecca removed Hannah's nightshirt. The puffiness in her ankles and feet that kept her in bed the day Prudence died, had pushed all the way up her calves, thighs, and torso. The swelling in every part of her body matched that of her neck and jowls.

Once Rebecca settled her into bed, Hannah panted and put her hand to her chest. The next breath came hard. She murmured, "Go be with Daniel and your children. They need you more than an old, dying woman."

"They are under Mrs. Bell's competent care. You are the one who needs me most, right now."

"I shall make do with my housekeeper," Aunt Hannah insisted. "Now, go and leave me to die in peace."

"Should you die without a loved one by your side, I would not live in peace. Now, can I get you anything before I clean your mattress?"

"I'll be fine, dear. Thank you."

Rebecca returned often over the next weeks, each time finding Hannah all the more contentious and sometimes delusional. In one of her lucid moments, Hannah gave Rebecca money to purchase a new mattress. She burbled as if speaking underwater, "St. Peter won't think kindly if I try to ride to glory in this old, borrowed chariot."

Daniel assumed responsibility for crafting the mattress—a labor of love Rebecca could not deny him. His design called for the highest quality fabric, which he would sew himself, and he planned to fill it with the best goose down. He had determined that neither the scarcity of materials nor his ill health would deter him. Nonetheless, goose down could not be had at any price, and the dropsy landed him bedridden in early March. So, Rebecca finished the mattress herself, though not as elegantly as Daniel had planned.

On the day Rebecca tied off the last stitch in the new mattress, she loaded it into Prudence's carriage on a brisk morning for the drive to West Castle Street.

Hannah's dour housekeeper sniffled as she met Rebecca at the door.

"She's gone," the housekeeper said.

"Gone? Where? Who?"

"An angel took her soul where all dead folk go."

Rebecca ran to Hannah's bedside. The old woman lay still, her hands across her chest. The doctor was closing his bag.

"How long?" Rebecca asked, her heart sinking in her chest.

"She went peacefully in her sleep during the night," the doctor replied. "The housekeeper found her like this when she arrived this morning. Not the slightest hint of agitation that I could detect."

Rebecca leaned forward to kiss Hannah's forehead. Salty dewdrops leaked from the corners of her eyes onto Hannah's cheeks. "I'm sorry," she whispered. "I should have been here to hold your hand."

The doctor shook his head. "You did all anyone could expect."

"She shouldn't have been alone," she murmured.

"That is not always a matter left in our hands."

"But I held the others' hands. My sister and sister-in-law. Hannah's sisters. All but Papa. He was the only one until Hannah. I wasn't here. I could have, should have...."

Rebecca's eyes ached as she returned home. News of Hannah's death would devastate Daniel, even though it was not unexpected. She was his mother's only remaining family, and his own mortality would stare him in the face. The mattress, the disappointment of being unable to finish it, had been a bitter enough pill for him.

When Rebecca arrived at the Chestnut Street house and peeked into the small parlor off the entryway, Daniel wasn't in his sickbed. She proceeded down the hallway and as she approached the kitchen, a woman's sobbing caught her off guard. Amelia Bell wept into a threadbare towel as she sat across from Daniel at a table. While Rebecca stood only steps away, Amelia murmured, "I know you folks have been set upon by plenty of affliction. Honestly, I think you don't know the half of what it is like."

"What do you mean we don't know what affliction is like?" Rebecca muttered.

Amelia sat up straight.

Daniel answered for her. "She is all alone in a foreign place. Famine and disease have claimed most of her relatives back home in Ireland. Now she has received word that her remaining son is dead. His widow and four children are penniless and without food, having no way to pay for passage abroad."

Amelia sniffled. "I don't mean to say your family has not known tragedy, but you still have a home, a husband, three beautiful children, and more. I have nothing. My husband, all of my children, my brothers, sisters, and my cousins are gone. What little family I have left there—a cousin's wife and her children—may not survive long. Famine and disease have ravaged my beloved Ireland."

Rebecca slumped into a chair at the table. Three years earlier, Father Taylor served as chaplain aboard the frigate Macedonian on a relief mission to Ireland. He returned with stories that broke her heart. The ship—loaded with hundreds of barrels of pork, beans, thousands of bags of flour, corn and cornmeal—sailed out of New York Harbor after lengthy delays caused by religious and social bigotry. Father Taylor told of horrific suffering he witnessed while among the Irish people. A small portion of that mass of desperate souls, who could not otherwise have afforded passage to America, were placed aboard the frigate and brought to Boston. They dreamed of new, better lives, only to discover new and better did not often mean good. Father Taylor assured her that what she witnessed on lower Ann Street paled in comparison to the misery he encountered abroad.

The childish voices and harsh discords of Boston's lower Ann Street echoed in Rebecca's mind—they resounded with the weight of unkept promises.

Rebecca took Daniel's hand. "How can we help?"

"We have a little put away," he replied. "At least it would be a start."

"I will call on Father Taylor about arranging for the family's passage and speak with our neighbors. I'm certain they will help."

Amelia's despair was washed away by tears of joy as she expressed her gratitude before going upstairs to put the children to bed. When Amelia was out of earshot, Rebecca gave Daniel the news of Hannah's passing. His shoulders drooped and his body began to shake as he wept. She went to his side, leaned close and kissed his cheek, then cradled him as he grieved.

✳ ✳ ✳

Daniel's health took a turn for the better in early May after Hannah's burial, but gloom continued to hang over Rebecca's mood. He hoped a visit to the Dyers in Hingham would lift her spirits. Although her melancholy persisted through most of the train passage from Boston, her disposition grew sunnier and she budded a smile as the passing countryside became more serene.

The moment they arrived in Hingham, the Dyers' six-year-old daughter, Helen, took charge of Clara Jane. E.P., Jr,, the same age as eleven-year-old George, whisked the

Pomroys' sons off in search of adventure. While Daniel and Porter spent the remainder of the afternoon diving into the deep waters of Keats's poetry, Rebecca and Esther enjoyed a respite from being tethered to the responsibilities of motherhood.

The two men emerged from the parlor when summoned for dinner, and Porter suggested they all attend a lecture later that evening by the Baptist abolitionist, William Lloyd Garrison. Rebecca replied, "I wish not to spoil the rare freedom this visit has afforded me. Don't get me wrong. I am as opposed to slavery as anyone, and I shall not deprive Daniel of the opportunity to see the great man. But for my part, I think once Esther and I put the children to bed, the two of us should sit here for the remainder of the evening, sipping tea, and conversing, undisturbed."

Esther concurred.

The trip to Hingham proved an apt prelude to the ensuing months. Rebecca found relaxation working in the garden alongside Willie. She enlisted Clara Jane as her assistant in the confectionery shop, helping her make candies and offering samples to customers. She opened a portal into George's mind and heart as she helped him with reading assignments from the public school. All were things she lamented having no time to enjoy while nursing Daniel through his past seasons of ill health as she attended to four elderly kin.

She deepened her bond with Ann Haskell who introduced her to the ladies of the Congregational church. Whether hosting a sewing circle in her family parlor, or sipping tea with neighbors, Rebecca widened her circle of friends. Even if she could not bring herself to trust in help from on high, she warmed to the notion of keeping company with those who did.

Daniel kept fluids from rising in his body the entire summer. He found the energy to introduce a selection of fancy goods into the confectionery shop's inventory.

Through his correspondence with Porter and with Rebecca's encouragement, he took a keener interest in the anti-slavery cause after the Fugitive Slave Act of 1850 passed Congress in early September.

New Englanders had sheltered hundreds of escapees from bondage and abetted their flight into Canada since before the nation's founding. The new fugitive slave law required them to capture and return runaways to slaveholders in the south. Protest rallies sprang up all over Massachusetts, including one in Boston.

Temperate weather greeted Daniel on the morning of October 5 as he boarded the ten o'clock morning omnibus for Boston. Porter caught an early train to Boston from Hingham, and the two friends met at Atwood's around noon. Hours later, they joined a throng of thousands at Faneuil Hall to hear speakers rail against the new law.

When Daniel returned home the next morning he told Rebecca, "The entire time I was there, I thought of how thrilled you would have been were you with us."

"I am certain," Rebecca said, "the orators were more eloquent than that prairie congressman who was in town a couple of years ago canvassing for General Taylor's presidential campaign. I forget his name."

"I believe the congressman's name was Lincoln. But there was no such equivocation by the speakers last evening. Each one was forthright and resolute in his opposition to the slave power. The most passionate address was brought by the former slave Douglass."

"From all the talk about him," Rebecca said, "I would have expected no less."

"He challenged us to treat any slave hunter the same way our forefathers handled King George's redcoats. There are some four hundred to six hundred escaped slaves in Boston whose lives are threatened by this iniquitous new law. According to Douglass, we should prepare to see the streets of Boston flowing with blood in defense of liberty to all."

"I do so wish I had been there." Rebecca took Daniel's hand. "What you describe reminds me of the day we witnessed those two Negro women gaining their freedom at the expense of a slave hunter. Maybe if there are more such meetings we can go together and stand shoulder to shoulder in defense of our colored neighbors."

"We shall be allies in their defense," he said. "Just as we pledged in younger years."

Rebecca recalled her decision to bring Porter and Esther Dyer into their lives, and a rare burst of pride stirred in her. Daniel had a friend who sparked his passions—first poetry then a cause greater than himself. Her hope was restored that her husband could enjoy good health and a long life.

Daniel continued, "The meeting organizers pledged aid, cooperation, and relief to fugitive slaves as well as other colored inhabitants of the city. They decried the new fugitive slave law and declared, 'Our moral sense revolts against it. We believe this law to be the height of injustice and inhumanity.'"

Rebecca furrowed her brow. "I wonder what ever became of Mr. Lincoln?"

"I suppose his star burned out," Daniel replied. "As has been the case for so many of the fence-sitters on the slave issue.

* * *

The shopkeeper's bell rang a few days later, alerting Rebecca to a customer's arrival. She straightened her apron and hastened from the kitchen to the shop. Ann Haskell stood before her, hunched over and gasping. Ann caught her breath and blurted, "My husband has not stopped coughing for days. He's wasting away. I've tried everything. Nothing works."

"Is there a fever?" Rebecca asked.

"Slight, if any. But his head aches, terribly."

"Let me fetch some of Daniel's thorn-apple leaves. They always seem to relieve his spasms."

Rebecca returned with a few of the leaves and the copper dish. "Let the leaves smolder in this dish and have Micajah breathe in the smoke and vapors. Let me know if they help."

Ann sent one of her children to Rebecca the next morning to report that Micajah's fever had intensified, and his coughing continued unabated. He now complained of stomach aches. "Ma says to ask if you have some of Dr. Townsend's Sarsaparilla."

"No," she replied. "But wait. I do have Dr. Sappington's pills."

Rebecca fetched the pills and rushed across the street to the Haskell home.

Ann sat at her husband's bedside, her shoulders drooped. "I have tried these already," she said. "I had hoped you might have a more current remedy."

"Have you called for Dr. Forsyth?" Rebecca asked.

Ann stared at her husband. "He is so miserly. He would have apoplexy over such an expense. Will you stay with him so I can go see if any of the druggists have a stronger cure? I am afraid to leave him alone."

Rebecca nodded. "Of course."

While Ann was away, Micajah's nose dripped a thin line of blood to the corner of his mouth. Rebecca dabbed the blood then applied cold towels to his head and chest.

Micajah's condition deteriorated for several more days. By the time Dr. Forsyth was called, a delirium-inducing fever raged, and tiny rosy dots covered his chest. The doctor applied leeches and resorted to lancing veins in his arm to let out more of the tainted blood. He administered higher quantities of Quinine over the following week, without success. After a general feebleness set in, the rash turned splotchy and spread over his torso. Higher and higher doses of calomel became the only defense against the typhoid fever that ravaged him. Despite the doctor's efforts, Micajah's body intensified its rebellion against the fever—rattled breathing, diarrhea, vomiting, hallucination, seizures.

Rebecca wrapped her arms around Ann and held her close as the disease snuffed out Micajah's life.

CHAPTER ELEVEN

A woman who resembled someone from Rebecca's past visited the confectionery shop in early December, a few months after Micajah's passing—the third to die under Rebecca's care that year. The new fancy goods the woman perused were Daniel's inspiration. He convinced Rebecca they would draw more customers into the shop.

As for the woman, Rebecca often teetered on approaching her when their paths crossed around town but wasn't certain enough to do so.

"Hello," the woman said. "I have seen you about, but until now, I did not recall how we know each other. We once attended the same church in Boston. Reverend Stow was our pastor."

"I suspected something of the kind," Rebecca said. "Reverend Stow married Daniel and me at Baldwin Place Baptist Church fifteen years ago."

"My husband and I were married at the same church," the woman said, "by Reverend Knowles. A few years later, I was baptized by Reverend Stow."

"You were one of the Rileys, right?" Rebecca asked. "Amelia Jane?"

"Everyone calls me Jane. I married the portrait artist, Charles Hubbard. His studio is around the corner on Malden."

Rebecca smoothed her apron. "I understand your husband is a celebrated painter. I love the piece that hangs in his studio window."

"It is beautiful. He titled it *The Falls at Nashua, New Hampshire*. It's his favorite and I doubt he will ever bring himself to sell it."

Rebecca gestured to a display of fancy goods. "Is there something in particular you are looking for?"

"Trinkets for our children's Christmas stockings." Jane paused. "Do you have children?"

"The youngest is napping," Rebecca replied. "She's two-years-old. Her brothers are ten and twelve."

"My three youngest are close in age to your sons."

"It sounds like we have much in common." Rebecca indicated a tray of caramels and lollipops. "Children always enjoy sweets."

"Often too much," Jane replied. She pointed to a shelf behind Rebecca. "I think the girls might like those tortoiseshell combs."

As Rebecca showed her the combs, Jane asked, "What are your children's names?"

"The oldest is George."

"He wouldn't by chance be a handsome dark-haired boy, quite serious, studious?"

Rebecca laughed. "That sounds like him."

"And his brother, he's Willie. Am I right?"

Rebecca wrinkled her brow. "They haven't been causing trouble, have they?"

"Heavens no. They are delightful. Your Willie is a charmer."

"They are already friends with yours? What are their names?"

"Your George," Jane replied, "Is quite chummy with my Charles. Two peas in a pod. They tend to ignore Willie, but my girls—Elizabeth and Florence, especially Flo—adore him."

"That sounds like Willie." Rebecca tilted her head. "Do they spend a great deal of time in your home?"

"Don't let that concern you. They are always welcome."

"And yours are welcome here," Rebecca replied. "It's just that sometimes ... sometimes my husband is unwell."

"My girls have told me so. They say underneath Willie's charm, he sometimes broods and says he worries about his father."

Rebecca grimaced. "Daniel finds it difficult to get out of bed of late. Without his income, I must take up the slack by sewing for Mr. Clough's upholstery and tending store on my own. We can no longer afford to hire help."

Jane Hubbard paid for her purchases and said, "If you would allow, Charles and I can help you. You have a wonderful shop. We shall spread the word among our friends, and if you would like, I am certain he would allow you to hang one of his paintings as an attraction."

"You are kind."

"Think nothing of it. After all, it seems we are somewhat old friends." Jane turned to leave and spotted Almira Cushing waiting in the entryway. Jane glanced back at Rebecca. "Speaking of friends, have you met Almira?"

"Yes," Rebecca replied. "She and her family were among the first friends we made when we moved here."

"And a lovely family they are," Jane said. "Mr. Cushing does the gild work on many of my husband's frames, and young Frank is quite the handyman."

"Jane, thank you for stopping in," Rebecca said as she turned her attention to Almira. "And what can I do for you, young lady?"

"I came to offer my help. I heard you have lost Mrs. Bell."

"Unfortunately, business has not been good enough to pay help, and we needed to rent out her room for extra income."

"I am happy to help out in the shop," Almira said. "I can also help with Clara Jane, and you don't need to pay me."

"That's generous." A hint of a smile pulled at Rebecca's lips. "Fortunately, we are not at the point of needing charity, as of yet."

"If you are willing to teach me to make candy, that would be pay enough."

Rebecca assessed Almira. "How old are you, dear?" she asked.

"I will soon be fifteen, and with three younger sisters, I have experience tending children."

"My goodness. I am sometimes taken aback at how fast time passes. It seems like only yesterday when you were only twelve."

"I have grown up in those few years."

Rebecca adjusted her apron. "I can see that. I accept your offer. Thank you."

✳ ✳ ✳

Clara Jane retreated to Almira's side behind the counter a few weeks after Jane Hubbard's visit. The young mother who entered the shop with two children was not a familiar face, and Clara tended to be shy around strangers. Almira plucked two sugar candies from a tray and guided Clara Jane around the counter, encouraging her to offer them to the children.

"We have both confectioneries and fancy goods," Almira said.

Rebecca entered the shop, carrying a tray of lemon drops, fresh from the kitchen.

"This is Mrs. Pomroy, the owner," Almira said.

The woman smiled at Rebecca. "A friend told me about this place. I am Anna Loud. We live a few doors down the street from the Bagnalls. Mr. Bagnall is my husband's business partner. I believe your Willie and one of the Bagnall boys are chums."

"Wilbur is here often," Rebecca replied. "Especially now that his mother is bedridden."

"Such a pity," Anna said. "What if the worst happens through her time of trial? How will Mr. Bagnall manage on his own with all those children? We pray often for the family."

"I send over a meal at least once each week," Rebecca said, "and give the little ones treats whenever they're over. Now, is there something in particular I can show you?"

"Those peppermints and lemon drops are calling me."

"They are quite popular," Rebecca said. "Let me put some in a bag for you. They will be my treat. If you like them, the price is quite reasonable."

As Rebecca counted out six of each, Anna said, "We attend the Methodist church nearby. My husband is a Trustee, as is Mr. Bagnall. I understand you are friends with their daughter-in-law, Elmyra. She has told us you are acquainted with Father Taylor of the Seamen's Bethel."

Rebecca handed her the bag. "Yes, Elmyra stops by often for tea and we have drawn close. I imagine she has told you that when I was a girl, I read stories to children at the Bethel, including Father Taylor's daughters."

"Indeed, she has told us so. My husband and I saw Father Taylor preach at the Eastham camp meetings. He must have been exciting to work for."

Rebecca laughed. "He certainly is the most colorful preacher I have ever seen. He was like an uncle to me, after my own papa died."

Anna pulled some coins from her pocket. "Here, let me pay for these. I know from my husband's business how precious every penny is."

"That is not necessary," Rebecca replied.

"I insist," Anna said, holding out a palm full of pennies.

"I appreciate it very much." Rebecca reached out and accepted the coins.

⁎ ⁎ ⁎

As summer pushed aside spring, Rebecca tapped into her meager rainy-day fund and rented a carriage from the local livery to drive Daniel and the children out to the country. She hoped the fresh, drier air at the Derbys' farm would bring Daniel relief from a resurgence of coughing spasms.

Minot and Dorcas's seven-year-old Sarah whisked Clara Jane off to the pasture as soon as they arrived to see the horses, cows, goats, and sheep. George and Willie ran off to make mischief with their cousins, Minot, Jr., and William—the latter named after his mother's brother whom he could recall only vaguely, as was also the case with Rebecca's Willie.

During a round of hide-and-seek, when Willie found his pa napping on the porch in the rocking chair, he lost interest in the game. He stood at the bottom step, unfazed by his father's labored snoring as he took in the vision of his father at rest. Then he settled at Pa's feet and clutched an ankle as if to hold him back from death.

Rebecca witnessed the poignant scene as she peeked out to check on Daniel. Her mind was invaded by images of Mama working her fingers to the bone, sewing to make ends meet after Papa died. She attempted to compose herself as she returned to the kitchen to help Dorcas prepare dinner, but there was no hiding the anguish that chipped away at her spirit. Her reddened eyes and slumped shoulders betrayed her grief. Dorcas hugged her, and Rebecca again broke into sobs.

Dorcas whispered, "I wish I could promise all will be well and have you hold me to it."

"I just don't know how ..."

"If it's money, I can talk with Minot. Last year's harvest was lean, but this year, God willing, it will be good."

"I appreciate your offer, but you have done so much already. We're behind on our purchases for the store, and the livery begrudges me every time I go to rent a carriage and horse. I will just have to ask for more time to pay our debts. I hate troubling Dr. Forsyth over what we owe him. He has already been so patient."

"Minot and I will help however we can."

As dusk settled over the farm a short time later, Minot came in from the fields and sat on the porch with Daniel.

"You must be glad to be out of your old haunts in Boston," Minot said.

"I have never regretted moving across the river," Daniel replied. "Even for a moment."

"It must have been some scene this past spring," Minot continued. "A hundred constables cracking down on all that crime and decadence—dozens of arrests in only a couple of days. How do you fit two-hundred brothels on one city street? Plus, gambling dens and saloons. That's the neighborhood where our wives grew up."

"It keeps spreading," Daniel said. "And nothing can be done about it. Who knows what will happen? Rebecca overheard women in her shop saying their husbands think all of Chelsea as far north as Cary Farm will soon be row upon row of houses."

"And the depraved element of all stripes," Minot replied, "especially the Irish and the Catholics—the very ones decent folks from Boston hope to escape—will cling to their coattails as they cross the river. I can assure you this, you'll never find me selling out to those Boston land barons. All I need to be happy is the smell of fresh turned soil by day and the contentment of my family around the hearth at night. Fresh air and hard work are the secrets to a long life."

Daniel tottered to his feet, coughing. "There's a bit of a chill in the air. I best head in."

Instead of sitting by the hearth, Daniel went straight to bed without supper. He rose the next morning after everyone had eaten breakfast and gone about their days—Minot out on the back twenty acres repairing fences, Dorcas in the kitchen preparing the mid-day meal, the children off playing in the fields, Rebecca running an errand to an upholsterer's shop in Chelsea to deliver piecework she finished during the early morning hours.

Minot's refrain, 'hard work is the secret to a long life,' gnawed at Daniel. He ambled out to the barn and mucked stalls for a short time. His ankles and feet soon began to drag like anchors trawled over an ocean floor. As he continued, his chest bound up and he labored at drawing deep breaths. George and Minot, Jr., found him lying unconscious in a pile of hay. They raced into the house.

Rebecca and Dorcas hurried to Daniel's aid, and with the help of the two boys, carried him back to bed.

When he woke, Rebecca scolded, "What on Earth were you about?"

"I'm tired of being dead weight," he muttered.

'Dead weight,' she thought. His words cut deep. Despair washed over her. He has relapsed ... his health ... his spirit.

The swelling in Daniel's legs receded after a few days of bed rest and Rebecca drove the family home. His melancholy cast a pall over the entire family. Rebecca rummaged through memories in search of moments when his illness was not all consuming. There were only a few scattered over a long trail of afflictions and misery. By the time Rebecca pulled the rented carriage to a stop in front of their home, her throat was raw from revisiting her bounty of sorrows.

She braced for the abuse the livery owner would level at her. He had lent out the carriage for only a single night's fee.

CHAPTER TWELVE

On a Sunday afternoon in late September—three years after Daniel's collapse at the Derby farm— Ann Haskell rushed across the street, nearly breathless, to tell Rebecca, "Esther and Porter. Their little Franklin is gone."

Rebecca wept as she repeated the message to Daniel.

His chin quivered. Six-month-old Franklin was the Dyers' eighth child and the second they would bury.

"We must go to them if you are strong enough," Rebecca murmured. "Ann will see to the children while we are away."

Daniel insisted he could manage the trip, so they caught an afternoon train and found lodging in Hingham where they refreshed themselves and donned mourning attire before calling on Porter and Esther.

Rebecca battled melancholy as they arrived at their friends' home. But what they found inside was not the solemn, mournful scene they expected. Instead, visitors spoke encouragement, and their countenances bore witness to discordant emotions. A few offered somber condolences, many spoke of victory. A handful proclaimed celebration.

Daniel and Rebecca angled through the cramped home until they found Porter and Esther who greeted them with warm embraces and tender smiles. "It is an unexpected blessing that you have come in our hour of bereavement," Esther said.

"I cannot fathom what you are going through," Rebecca replied. "You must be devastated. My heart goes out to you."

Daniel added, "You have our deepest sympathies."

"He was sickly since birth," Porter said. "We are relieved he is no longer suffering."

"Still," Rebecca replied, "if he had lived, he may have outgrown his infirmities and ..."

"He rests safely in the arms of his Heavenly Father," Esther replied. "That gives us reason to celebrate."

"I find comfort in Holy Scripture," Porter said. "'Better is he ... which hath not yet been, who hath not seen the evil work that is done under the sun.'"

A knot twisted in Rebecca's stomach. She could not imagine herself saying such a thing if she lost one of her own.

Daniel's shoulders sagged, his stamina waning, as he told Porter, "Your faith has always been an inspiration. You are my rock."

Porter smiled. "I have told you before, Daniel. Do not make men into idols. We shall always fail each other in some way. The truth is, I am barely hanging on."

Rebecca held back what she was inclined to say—it is not only men who fail us.

"Do not misunderstand," Porter added. "We mourn, indeed. We miss him terribly. But our grief is tempered by hope—hope in future glory."

"Tell us about your little ones," Esther said. "Clara Jane. She must be, what, five?"

"She's the apple of her father's eye," Rebecca replied. "And she's so proud to be her mother's little helper in the shop."

"And the boys?" Porter asked.

"George talks of attending Harvard College one day," Daniel said.

Rebecca detected Daniel's voice thinning from fatigue. She took a firm grip on his arm and whispered in his ear, "How are you doing?"

Daniel nodded and continued answering Porter. "Willie may become another Keats, except we hope he will not mimic the poet's sickliness."

"I keep telling him," Rebecca said, "not to set his sights too high, lest he be disappointed. The loftier the perch, the greater the fall."

"Esther and I have missed you," Porter said. "We shall come up to visit again on some happier occasion."

"By the way, how is your mother's health?" Esther asked.

"She is much the same as she has been for some time. Not getting better and not getting worse."

"We continue to pray for her," Porter said.

"Yes, we pray, too," Rebecca replied. The presumption that God answered some people's prayers while ignoring the pleas of others rankled her.

Daniel leaned into Rebecca. "Come dear, I must sit for a bit."

"Thank you for coming," Porter said. Esther echoed his gratitude.

"It is an honor to be your friends. In good times and in bad," Daniel replied, his voice gravelly.

✳ ✳ ✳

As Rebecca and Almira Cushing were tidying the shop the following March, one of the Derbys' farmhands rushed through the door. "Come at once, Mrs. Pomroy," he insisted. "The missus said to come fetch you. It's Mr. Derby. It's bad. Really bad."

Rebecca yanked off her apron. "Almira," she said. "Take care of Clara Jane while I go see what I can do to help. If I don't return by supper, see to it that everyone is fed and let your mother know you may be staying the night. Tell her I've gone to the farm on an urgent matter."

She turned to George and Willie. "You two see to your father. If you need help, ask Mrs. Haskell."

She hesitated on her way out to the Derbys' carriage, then detoured into the small parlor where Daniel lay. She tiptoed to his bedside and whispered his name. He twitched but continued to sleep. She kissed his forehead and headed again for the front door.

When Rebecca arrived at the farm, Dorcas sat on the front porch, rocking and weeping.

"How's Minot?" she asked.

"He's gone." Dorcas wailed, shaking her head.

Rebecca knelt in front of her sister, clasping her hands. "Shh ... shh. What happened?"

Dorcas shrugged. "Doctor thinks apoplexy. He collapsed right here on the porch."

"Is the doctor still here?" Rebecca asked.

Dorcas shook her head. "No. He went to summon the undertaker."

"Can I see Minot?"

"He is laid out on a spare bed across from our bedroom."

Rebecca rose and went to the room where Minot lay.

Dorcas followed and stood beside her husband's body. "What shall I do?" she asked.

"We shall speak with the undertaker when he arrives. I can take Mama home with me. You don't need that burden right now."

"That would be a great relief," Dorcas said. "I wish William was here."

"Can one of your neighbors help you manage the farm for a while?"

"One of the Fennos?" Dorcas bit her lip.

"That should do," Rebecca said. "I will speak with John Fenno. He may know the right person. Someone in his family or the Peirces'."

"A Peirce would be good."

Rebecca took her sister's hand. "I shall stay the night. Daniel and the children are being looked after."

Mama's arrival in the Pomroy household the next day presented challenges. Daniel's sickroom was already set up in the parlor off the entryway, and Rebecca could not abide Clara Jane joining her brothers in their upstairs bedroom. Neither could she afford to ask the upstairs boarders to move out. In any event, Mama was in no condition to navigate stairs—hobbled as she was by swollen, painful knees and ankles.

Rebecca set up cots in the kitchen for herself and Clara Jane, and Mama took the large first-floor bedroom.

Curiosity, restrained by caution, kept Clara Jane anchored in the hallway outside the room she had shared with her mother before her grandmother arrived. George said their grandmother had lived with them once before— in Boston. Clara Jane said they had never lived in any house other than where they lived now. George told her, of course she thought that. She hadn't been born yet when they lived on Boston's north end.

Mama kept inviting Clara Jane to come closer, and over time she inched her way to the bed. It took weeks of cajoling for her to walk straight to her grandmother's bedside without invitation. Next, she would crawl into bed beside Mama for afternoon story times.

She was not allowed in Mama's room when Dr. Forsyth visited, which piqued her interest even more. She mustered the courage one day to stand at the bedroom door and strained to hear as she peeked through the keyhole. She wished she could unhear the words that reached her ears. She was sure Dr. Forsyth said he would make Mama bleed until the sickness went away.

As time passed, Clara Jane and her older brothers witnessed changes in their mother. Rebecca lulled about, slump shouldered, as if under a load she could barely support. She stopped smiling altogether. She rarely talked, and when they spoke to her or were rude to each other or to customers, she stared into the distance as if distracted by something no one else could see.

Their grandmother became a different person before their eyes, as well. She complained constantly of headaches as her body and mind withered under the curse of her disease. Her sweetness toward her grandchildren often exploded into rage without warning. Clara Jane said her grandmother was becoming the cod liver oil the doctor forced her to swallow.

✳ ✳ ✳

Wilbur Bagnall's mother had given birth to her fourth son the previous January and was back on her feet weeks later. Then in June, a couple of months after Mama moved in with Rebecca's family, Mrs. Bagnall was overcome with fatigue and coughing spells. Fever forced her to bed in late August, and the doctor decided her body was ravaged by consumption.

Wilbur became grief-stricken. He gave up his deepest passion—music. He quit playing the piano and stopped teaching Willie how to play. He shut his violin in its case and stowed it under his bed. He decided that death stalked his home, and his music wouldn't make the intruder go away. He would not leave his mother's bedside. He clung to her hand and refused to release it. He was determined to wrest her from the Reaper's grip when the time came for her to give in to death. When his spinster Aunt Mary, who had taken charge of the household during his mother's illness, demanded he act like a man and restrain his grief, he paid no heed.

Willie became inconsolable over the news that his closest friend's mother was dying from the same terrible disease that was ravaging Grandma. He asked Rebecca, "Why can't the doctor keep Wilbur's mother from dying?"

"The doctor," Rebecca said, "is doing everything he can to make her well."

"Is Grandma going to die?" he asked.

"Everyone dies," Rebecca replied. "Some when they are young, but certainly by the time they are very old."

"Is Pa going to die?" he asked, choking on the words.

"He will not die," she replied. "I shall see to it."

Willie raced across the street in late September when Wilbur's Aunt Mary began hanging black crepe on the windows and door. He bounded onto the porch and flung the door open, not bothering to knock.

Mr. Bagnall stood in the large living room gesturing and talking to a finely dressed man. Willie darted toward the staircase, but Mr. Bagnall caught hold of his collar. "Stop young man. Have some respect for my dead wife."

"I'm sorry, sir," Willie said. "Wilbur. Is he all right?"

"Wilbur is upstairs. He is too despondent for visitors."

"I want to see him. To know he is all right."

"Fine, but if he refuses you, leave him be. Do you hear? And walk."

Willie minded his steps as he climbed the stairs and knocked on Wilbur's bedroom door.

There was no answer.

"It's Willie. Are you all right?"

"No."

"Then let me in. I don't want you to be alone."

"You cannot bring her back," Wilbur protested.

"I know. But I can sit with you."

"Fine," Wilbur said.

They sat together for several hours in silence, except for their moans and whimpers.

❊ ❊ ❊

Two months after Mrs. Bagnall passed, Rebecca propped Mama's head with pillows to make breathing less of a chore. There was nothing other than laudanum induced sleep that could offer relief from the heaviness and burning in her lungs or the sting from lesions that covered her body.

Clara Jane often joined her mother's vigil by day, and Willie, who found sleep illusive under the strain of his grandma's impending death, spelled his mother a few hours each night. All agreed Mama should not die alone. Sometimes the question of George's absence from his grandmother's bedside would percolate to the surface during a conversation. Rebecca was quick to put the matter to rest, saying, "We all have different ways to protect ourselves from pain."

Rebecca held her mother's hand, bluish and cold. The old woman's mouth hung open, as if waiting for death to extract her last breath. The only signs of life were feeble nods of her head, like vain efforts to snag errant wisps of breath before they escaped.

Mama died of consumption three weeks before Christmas at the age of sixty-four years.

* * *

Seven-year-old Clara Jane whined, a year after her grandmother died. She complained she was hot and tired. Rebecca's patience was thread-bare, and she cautioned, "If you are too fatigued to finish your chores, you do not have enough energy to eat. You shall go to bed without supper."

Clara Jane made no complaint and put herself to bed, but she woke in the middle of the night, sweating and plagued by spasmodic coughing. Rebecca slipped out of bed to check on her. The girl's forehead was almost hot to the touch.

Rebecca collected some towels, soaked them in a pot with cold water, and draped Clara Jane's head and chest to subdue the fever. She retrieved the bottle of Dr. Sappington's fever remedy, propped up her daughter's head, and plied her with pills. Clara Jane's arms dangled like weathered mooring ropes hung from a ship's cleats.

The fever lessened by morning, though Clara's malaise continued, and her appetite had not returned to normal.

Rebecca assured herself that her daughter was on the mend. The medicine must have worked. Clara Jane was out of bed after several days, despite a lingering cough.

CHAPTER THIRTEEN

George finished public schooling in the spring of his seventeenth year. His hopes of matriculating at Harvard College evaporated—not because he lacked scholarly aptitude but due to his father's debility. He soon began working as a clerk at a grocery on Broadway at Fourth to help support the family.

"I do not understand," he said to his mother. "Why can I not keep some of my wages to spend as I please? My friends do."

"Their fathers can work to provide for their families," Rebecca replied. "But I am unable to make up for the loss of Pa's wages, all by myself. I cannot pay Dr. Forsyth, and shopkeepers must extend us credit. It is only through their goodwill that we are able to survive. Mind you. One day soon those shopkeepers will run out of patience, and we will be forced to sell our home."

"Why am I punished for his infirmity?" he asked.

"You think it is punishment to help put food on your family's table? You should be grateful you are able to work so that you and the rest of us can eat and have a roof over our heads."

George huffed as he headed to the front door.

Rebecca called after him. "Don't forget to bring home a few potatoes for supper."

He preferred she had said to bring home a fine roast from the butcher.

Later that morning, when Rebecca carried a bowl of the previous night's potato and carrot soup to Daniel in the small parlor, he wheezed a feeble, "Thank you."

She helped him sit up.

"How is our little angel, this morning?" he asked.

"I have not checked on her in the last hour, but she coughed all through the night. Neither of us got a wink of sleep."

"Is she eating?"

Rebecca shook her head, no.

"I wish I could get up and see her."

"You can when both of you are stronger. I just need to get her to eat something." Rebecca cupped his cheek. "The waters in you are rising again."

"And they always recede. You worry too much."

She leaned forward and kissed him then went to check on Clara Jane.

Willie sat at his sister's bedside reading to her—

> *But, O, my little ducky dear, how very prone to err!*
> *Poor little darling, dripping wet! how mother pities her!*
> *Dear little chick, how wet and cold! run, Jane, and light a fire,*
> *And mother'll kiss her darling babe, and then sit down and dry her."*
> *Now wherefore smiles that erring child with mischief in her eye?*

Clara's eyes were closed, but she wore a smile.

"That's one of Mr. Dyer's poems," Rebecca whispered.

"It's my favorite," Clara Jane murmured.

"I brought you some soup."

"I don't feel like eating," Clara Jane replied.

"You must, dear. You're so weak and are becoming so thin I am afraid you will blow away in the slightest breeze. What if Willie feeds you?"

Clara Jane winced as she sat up. "I suppose."

"As soon as you eat," Willie raised a spoonful of soup to his sister's lips, "I'm going to look for a job so I can help like George. You don't want to make me late, do you?"

"And where will you be looking for a job?" Rebecca asked.

"The docks."

"I will not allow it," Rebecca planted her hands on her hips. "Anywhere, except the docks."

"Ma, I want to be a sailor like your papa was."

"I said, no."

"Pa said I could."

"Your father is not well. You should be ashamed for taking advantage of him when he is so ill."

Willie lowered his head, his jaw clenched.

"The answer is no, and that is final." Rebecca turned and walked down the hall to the confectionery shop.

After Clara Jane's coughing persisted unabated, Rebecca sent for Dr. Forsyth.

The doctor listened to the girl's lungs, his eyes narrowing with each breath she took. "Any discomfort?" he asked.

Clara Jane put her hand to her chest. "Feels like little mice scratching inside me."

"In your lungs?"

She nodded.

After questioning both mother and daughter at length, Dr. Forsyth invited Rebecca to join him in the hallway where they could continue the conversation in private. Once alone he said, "Your mother suffered with consumption—"

Rebecca blanched. "Consumption?" Her voice cracked. "No! Not my little girl."

"I'm sorry," Dr. Forsyth said. "But we will do all we can to save her. Has anyone else in your family suffered from the same ailment?"

Rebecca's next breath stalled momentarily in her chest. "We lost my sister Sarah to the disease fifteen years ago."

"I would normally recommend outdoor exercise, once the weather warms." Dr. Forsyth hesitated. "And plenty of rest."

"We shall do anything we need to."

Dr. Forsyth ran his fingers through his hair. "Given your family history, we should act aggressively. In addition to keeping her warm in bed and feeding her a hardy diet, we shall begin a regimen of cod liver oil and inhaling turpentine. If there is no progress, we shall have to begin purging and drawing as much blood as she can tolerate. Call for me at once if she coughs up white phlegm or blood."

"Will she get better?" Rebecca asked.

"I shall not give you false hope. You know from your own experience that this disease is difficult to combat. The outcome can be dire. But we will do our best to overcome it. Above all," Dr. Forsyth said, "you must remain strong for everyone's sake."

Rebecca returned to Clara Jane's bedside to find her sobbing uncontrollably. An almost audible groan rose from the hollows of Rebecca's soul. She stroked her daughter's hair and whispered assurances to her, promising that all would be well. It would only be a matter of time.

✳ ✳ ✳

Snows came and went during the first half of December, but the dingy slush never washed away completely. Willie rushed home the week before Christmas to finish chores before supper. A stiff, icy onshore wind kicked up as he headed down the gangway of the ship he had spent the day readying for its maiden voyage. By the time he arrived home, his ears had turned numb from the frigid air. Once inside, he shook off the cold and went to the kitchen to warm himself by the stove.

"Go check on your sister," Rebecca said as she cut potatoes for a bare-bones soup.

Willie did not have to be asked twice to check on Clara Jane. She had gone from bad to worse—coughing up white phlegm and occasionally bloody sputum. She appeared gaunt, almost ghostly. Fear gripped him, thinking each time he saw her would be the last. He was never in the room when Dr. Forsyth visited her, but the stories she told about his treatments sent bile worming up his throat.

George arrived home shortly after Willie, and already, a new deluge of heavy snow was clogging the streets. "Temperature is falling fast, and the sidewalks are turning to ice," he said. "I almost lost my footing half-a-dozen times."

"George," Rebecca said. "Before you get out of your coat and boots, bring in enough coal and wood to last through this storm."

The storm waned overnight, but temperatures continued to plummet, and by morning the thermometer showed minus twelve degrees. The mercury hovered near zero for days.

Rebecca crawled under the quilt with Daniel each bitterly cold night, offering her body heat to keep him warm, while the boys and Clara Jane huddled in bed together. On Christmas Eve, gale force winds blew in from the ocean carrying dense, heavy snow. By Christmas Day, the town of Chelsea lay crippled under an icy, white blanket, and all New England was rumored to be paralyzed. Cities, towns, and villages became cut off, one from another, as roads and rail lines were rendered impassable.

Snows continued into the new year, mounting in drifts several feet high, blocking windows and entrances of homes and shuttering businesses. The numbing temperatures persisted. A thick layer of ice locked vessels of every kind and size in place where they were moored—runabouts, ferries, barges, ships—whether at anchor or in their docks.

Rebecca inventoried her stores of medicine, food, and fuel after the first week of January. Everything was in short supply. Her purse was empty as well. Neighbors, friends, and customers were shut up in their homes, and her sons' employment, even their past wages, were on hold. During a lull between storms, she left George and Willie in charge of Daniel and Clara Jane then ventured out to plead with whatever merchants she could find to extend further credit to keep her family alive.

An icy crust crunched under her boots as she pulled a makeshift sled and followed the path her sons shoveled for her earlier that morning. The sun, high in a stark blue sky, glistened off the crystalline snow. Any illusion of nature's beauty was lost on her as worries over her family and their survival consumed her focus.

She followed Malden Street to Broadway and turned the corner toward the grocery where George had clerked until the usual stream of shoppers abandoned the streets. Two men were loading crates into a sleigh. They climbed aboard, and the driver goaded his horses forward as Rebecca approached. When she arrived at the storefront, the proprietor was locking the door behind himself and hung a sign—Closed. She peered through the window. All the shelves were bare. She muttered under her breath, "The greed of some people knows no bounds—those with plenty hoard, those without suffer, and our cries fall on deaf ears."

She turned back down Broadway, heading for the nearest apothecary—she knew the druggist well. The sign on his door also read, Closed. She retraced her steps home, dragging the empty sled, and despite her wool scarf and mittens, her cheeks stung, and her hands prickled from the dry, freezing air.

Rebecca kept her head down, shielding her exposed face from the cold as she turned off Malden Street onto Chestnut. She had gone several yards toward home when she glimpsed a sleigh parked in the street. It resembled the one she had seen at the grocery, but if someone was calling on her, she was at a loss to figure out who it was.

Inside, she found Almira Cushing and the two men she had watched loading their sleigh outside the grocery. Rebecca had not recognized them out in the frigid weather, but they were Almira's older brothers, Francis and Frank.

"Almira," Rebecca said, "what brings you out in this weather?"

"Mother thought you might have some difficulty keeping your cupboards stocked in the storm. I hope you don't mind, but Eliza is in the kitchen putting things away."

Rebecca smiled. Tears welled in her. "That is so kind of you. Thank you. Thank you so much."

Almira held out a sack she had been holding. "Oh, here. We visited the druggist. He knew exactly what Dr. Forsyth had prescribed."

"You are an angel," Rebecca replied.

"Think nothing of it. Mother says, in times like this, neighbors should be watching out for each other. And if you need coal or the like, either Francis or Frank can bring some."

The Cushings' kindness could not have come at a better time. Days later, winds of hurricane proportion carrying several feet of additional snow battered the region. Howling winds ripped shingles off rooftops, tore shutters from their hinges, toppled church steeples, piled snow drifts ten to twenty feet high. Temperatures fell to catastrophic lows, approaching thirty degrees below zero. Roads and rails remained impassible, and the harbors were still frozen over. Even the river between Boston and Chelsea was a solid sheet of ice. Everything was in high demand and short supply. The entire engine of commerce seized up.

After the snows abated, freezing temperatures persisted. The air grew thin, light, and pristinely clear.

Dr. Forsyth visited after the worst of the weather cleared. Daniel's condition remained stable—shortness of breath and fatigue. Fluids in his legs, arms, and torso had swelled and ebbed over the previous weeks, like flood waters rising and falling when storms advance and retreat. Diuretic remedies—squill and cantharides—given to her by the Cushings helped.

Clara Jane's condition had worsened over the brutal winter. Chills, night sweats, nausea plagued her day and night. Her jaundiced skin hung loose around her ribs, neck, arms, legs, and feet. Her eyes receded deeper into their hollow sockets. The doctor told Rebecca to hope her daughter survived until summer, which she would need to be long and warm.

After the doctor left, Rebecca sent her sons on errands and withdrew to weep in private. *Why does God answer the prayers of others but not mine?*

Almira had been arranging candies in the display when she overheard George and Willie as they put on their coats to leave. She blanched. During the eight years she had been assisting in the shop and in the Pomroy household, her heart wrenched many times at witnessing Rebecca's despair. A frightening thought often preyed on her mind—to watch a child wasting away must be the worst trial a mother could face.

She went to check on Rebecca and found her hunched on the floor in the downstairs bedroom. She waited at the threshold as Rebecca mumbled unintelligible phrases.

A few moments passed before Rebecca composed herself and discovered Almira. "How long have you been standing there?"

"I didn't want to disturb you," Almira replied. "I thought you might be praying."

"Yes, though I probably did more complaining than praying."

"I wasn't listening. It wasn't my business."

"I think it's best," Rebecca said, "to close the shop for the day."

"Can I do anything for you?" Almira asked.

"The doctor has said transferring Clara Jane in June or July to Derbys' farm for fresh, drier air would be best. I don't know what more can be done." Rebecca wrung her hands. "How much must I lose before Heaven is done with me?"

"I cannot know the depth of your grief," Almira said. "I don't know what it means to fret over an ailing husband or lose a child."

CHAPTER FOURTEEN

pring came for no one because winter did not retreat fully until late May. Freezing temperatures, bone-biting rain, and sludgy snow prevailed right up to the threshold of summer, a season that did not arrive in time for Clara Jane.

From the middle of May, Clara Jane straddled two worlds—no longer part of life, still not reaped by death. In her final hours, she lay as a statue in repose, her pupils partially eclipsed by half-shuttered eyelids—her gaze other worldly.

Rebecca kissed her only daughter's cold forehead on the last day of May. Her tears spilled onto the girl's gaunt face. Rebecca lost her taste for life and rejected food and drink for a time after Clara Jane's soul took flight. Death would have been a welcome reprieve from the brokenness of her heart and soul.

Twenty-one-year-old Almira Cushing assimilated Rebecca's grief as she minded the shop during the slate-gray days of mourning. Her throat grew raw from drinking in the sorrow around her, even as she nursed her own heartache.

Almira stood at the graveside with more than two dozen mourners the day the young girl was laid away in the half-frozen ground. Clara Jane had become as much of a little sister to her as her own sisters. She would miss their hours together in the confectionery shop and in the kitchen. Clara Jane had grown before Almira's very eyes— from a toddler under her feet to a girl who could pull taffy without someone hovering over her. From being read to, to reading. Almira grieved for the doting father who had lost his little girl and for the distraught mother who watched the promising life snuffed out before the hoped-for young woman bloomed.

Esther and Porter Dyer visited after receiving word of Clara Jane's passing. Daniel begged to know how he could find faith in the wake of such a loss. Porter's message and efforts to raise their spirits fell flat. Rebecca held her tongue as Esther tried to console her—she could not bear hearing the words, God's will. She wanted nothing to do with a God who willed her little girl dead.

Father Taylor and his wife—their own grief still raw from the death of a cherished son-in-law—also called on Daniel and Rebecca. The Taylors' visit failed to pierce the pall of mourning that shrouded the Pomroy household.

Ann Haskell, Anna Loud, and Jane Hubbard reeled Rebecca back from the brink. As they helped her shutter the confectionery shop—keeping it open was a burden she could no longer bear, even with Almira's assistance— her neighbors' refrain became, "if you succumb to sorrow, who will look after Daniel and your boys?"

Once Rebecca's grief no longer anchored her in bed, she prepared a bowl of potato and carrot soup which she carried to Daniel. He lay teetering on the fringe of consciousness, his cheeks wet. She tested his forehead for fever, though she did not suspect that was the source of his dampness. He had sobbed the whole time she was in the kitchen absentmindedly stirring the pot of soup that needed no help other than the stove's heat.

"Are you awake?" she whispered.

He groaned.

"Here, let me help you sit," she said.

"Not hungry."

"You must eat. You must. I cannot bear to lose you."

"I want ... my ... Clara Jane." The words were barely audible through his sobs.

She set aside the bowl of soup and crawled into bed next to him, draping her arm across his chest and pulling him close. "Promise me you shall not leave me," she said.

They wept in each other's arms until Daniel drifted to sleep.

* * *

George returned home from work on a late summer evening the year after Clara Jane died and asked, "Why do our neighbors call us the afflicted family?"

"Who says we are?" Rebecca asked.

"Mrs. Loud was in the grocery today. She said she prays daily for our afflicted family."

"I suppose next time you should ask if she knows the perpetrator of our affliction," Rebecca replied. "If we knew their identity, we might be able to put an end to our suffering."

"It's because of Clara Jane, isn't it?"

"Not only Clara Jane," she replied. There was an uneven edge to her voice. "There's your father's constant sickness. Both he and I lost our fathers at a young age. Then there's my sister Sarah, your Uncle William's little one and wife, your grandmothers, Aunt Prudence, Aunt Hannah, Uncle Minot. Many families suffer losses. Our burden seems to fall unevenly on your mother's shoulders. As if I am punished."

He stared at the floor as if regretting the pain his question had inflicted. "When is supper?"

"It shall be ready when your brother is home from the docks."

"What if they keep him late?"

Willie dragged into the house before Rebecca could answer.

"Both of you hurry and get ready," she said.

"I'm not hungry," Willie replied. "I just want to go upstairs and rest. Eat without me."

"Are you sure?" Rebecca asked. "I even convinced your father to join us. We should eat together as a family. Your sister's death should have awakened all of us to the truth that we never know how much time we shall have each other. We should cherish every minute."

"I understand," Willie said. "But I do not feel at all well."

"Think of how long it has been since your father felt well enough to leave his sickroom for dinner," she said. "Do you imagine he feels any better than you?"

"I suppose not," Willie's shoulders sagged.

"Then go get ready. Both of you. I shall see your father to the table. Don't keep us waiting."

Willie opened the sack he used for carrying his lunch. "I picked up the post on my way home." He laid a letter addressed to Rebecca on the table and followed George upstairs.

She tore open the envelope and read her brother's single paragraph note.

Daniel ambled out of the small parlor and into the hallway in time to witness tears trail down her cheeks. "What is this about?" he asked.

Rebecca dabbed her eyes. "My brother has gotten married, and his wife is with child."

"Where does he write from? I take it that all is well," Daniel said.

She tucked the letter in her apron pocket. "He says they are well. He works on a farm in California. Come and sit while I bring dinner to the table. The boys will be down any moment."

George joined his father as Rebecca set out a pot of stew.

"Where is your brother?" she asked.

"He said his head aches so bad he can hardly see. He wrapped himself in a blanket and put himself to bed."

Willie woke the next morning, not well-rested and still complaining of a headache. "I don't want to miss work," he said.

Rebecca cupped his forehead. "Are you sure? You are a bit warm."

"Ma," he said. "Everything is warm when it's summer."

"Go, then. But don't overdo it."

Willie went to work but returned home before noon—coughing and feverish. Rebecca cast off her resistance to high places and followed him upstairs to put him to bed. As he changed into a fresh nightshirt, she noted his bedclothes from the previous night were still damp. He said he had woken in the wee hours in a sweat. She ran downstairs and sent George to fetch Dr. Forsyth.

When the doctor arrived, he furrowed his brow on hearing Rebecca describe Willie's symptoms.

"It is striking," Dr. Forsyth said, "that you have not acquired the same predisposition for this disease as the rest of your family. In Willie's case, the rapid progression troubles me. I will start with substantial dosages of Quinine. If there is no immediate relief, I shall apply leeches and resort to calomel."

Rebecca clenched her fists. "Are you telling me we shall lose Willie as well?"

"No. I am letting you know I shall attack this thing as aggressively as possible. In the meantime, force feed him if you must and see to it that he drinks plenty of clean water."

She shrieked. "It will be the same as it was with Clara Jane."

"Now there. Let's not get ahead of ourselves. In Willie's case we are attacking it at a much earlier stage. You were right to call for me when you did."

"I do not know how much more I can bear," she whimpered. "For twenty years I have devoted everything to caring for ailing loved ones and have enjoyed precious few joyful moments with my children. Now I am being robbed of them and of holding grandchildren in my old age."

Dr. Forsyth clasped her elbow. "My dear Mrs. Pomroy, no one has witnessed more of your tragic journey than I have. Please know I will do all in my power to spare you of more sorrow."

* * *

Daniel lay gravely ill downstairs in the small parlor in late March of the following year. Rebecca and George stood at Willie's bedside upstairs with Dr. Forsyth. The doctor lamented his best efforts to save Willie had proven insufficient.

Willie's voice had become faint, a gossamer of lightly knitted breaths. "I must say goodbye to Wilbur."

Rebecca choked back tears. "Dear sweet boy, I have not told you because I did not want to depress your spirits as you fought to heal."

"What is it?"

"Your friend is very ill. He cannot get out of bed, and it is not known if he will survive."

Willie's dull eyes filled with tears. His thin body trembled as he sobbed.

Dr. Forsyth gave him a dose of laudanum to induce sleep.

Willie's breathing turned shallow over the ensuing days. A chill fell over the room, and his face became painted with the purplish hue of death. Rebecca took one hand, and George took the other. They sat at his side, gripping his frail hands until, at a very late hour, his spirit departed.

Daniel was too feeble and dejected to be with Willie in his final hour or to attend his son's burial alongside Clara Jane in Woodlawn Cemetery.

* * *

Weeks after Willie passed, George braced his mother for a decision he had made with great anguish.

"I am a man, now. The man of the household. I shall take it as my responsibility to see that you and father are cared for and worry free."

"That is noble to say," Rebecca replied. "But how do you propose to take on such a great burden?"

"Mother, I know you shall object, but it is best for all of us that I take a job that pays much better than clerking at the grocery. It is the only way to gain the income our family requires."

"If you are about to say what I think," Rebecca said, "I will not abide it. I have lost enough already."

"You will not lose me, but it does require me to be away at times. For weeks or months."

"You shall not go to sea." She gritted her teeth.

"It is already arranged. I leave in three weeks."

She fell to her knees, wailing.

George took her hands and raised her up. She buried her face in his chest. "Mother," he said. "It is time you had some rest. Everything will be all right. I have asked Mrs. Loud and the widow Haskell to help you look after Pa, and I shall return before you know it."

While George was away, neighbors, friends, and other Chelsea folks gave Rebecca and Daniel their support. Ann Haskell, Anna Loud, and the new Mrs. Bagnall cooked meals and attended to Rebecca's shattered spirit. Ann's brother, Andrew Haskell, a founder of the Winnisimmet Benevolent Society, arranged for financial support. His wife, a member of the Ladies Union Relief Society delivered groceries weekly. During the Haskells' frequent calls, Andrew Haskell sat with Daniel and reminisced about Boston's Temple Street neighborhood and Daniel's early days in the upholstery business on Dock Square.

Jane Hubbard stopped in almost daily to fill in gaps that others missed and to trade stories with Rebecca about Reverend Stow and Boston's Baldwin Place Baptist

Church. Rebecca gave up a rare laugh when telling of the time she almost birthed George in a church pew while waiting for Reverend Stow to fetch his carriage.

Almira Cushing had not been as regular as the others in calling on Rebecca during George's absence. The reason became clear shortly before he returned from sea when Almira visited and introduced her new beau—eight years older than herself—a successful salesman named Solomon Fuller.

Rebecca greeted Mr. Fuller—she resisted calling him by his Christian name—with a raised eyebrow and invited Almira into the kitchen to help her prepare the tea service. Rebecca whispered to her as the kettle whistled, "I must confess, I would have cherished having you as my daughter-in-law. Do you love this man?"

Almira took Rebecca's hand. "I certainly do, and we are engaged to be married in a few months. Besides, George has never shown the slightest interest in me, nor I in him."

"Does Mr. Fuller love you?"

"His name is Solomon, and yes he does."

"Well then," Rebecca replied. "That is good enough for me."

"As for your George, I am sure one day he will bring home the daughter-in-law of your dreams."

Rebecca's face brightened. "As long as she is the girl of *his* dreams, I will be more than delighted."

George returned from sea two weeks late to find his mother melancholic and holed up in bed with drapes drawn. Fluids had begun to build up in his father at the rate of springtime floods. Daniel had not urinated for days, and his appetite was marginally better than Rebecca's.

To lift his mother's spirits, George promised not to return to sea until she and his father were restored to health. He asked if she wanted to visit Willie and Clara's graves only to have her sink back into bed and draw the quilt over her head.

As he left her bedside she said, "Willie's friend Wilbur has died. I hope they are together in Heaven."

Whenever George went to the small parlor to keep his father company, Daniel talked of seeing his angel children very soon. Daniel's attachment to Clara Jane and Willie, even more evident after their deaths, no longer stung George. Years of eroded affection—at least on George's part—had carved a valley between father and eldest son. Finally, George had moved on from disappointment to acceptance. He had begun to understand that it was disease and not alienation that had robbed him of the father he yearned for. With what little time they had left, he would no longer see the shadow of a man who languished in a small parlor off the entryway and inhaled smoke from thorn-apple leaves. He would see the man whose heart held more love than his body could carry.

In October, Daniel called for George to carry him out to the privy. They made it just in time for the urine to rush out of him, like a swollen river breaching a broken dam. He was able to walk back to bed with his son's assistance. A few hours later they repeated the same exercise, then after a few hours more they did so again, except on that occasion, Daniel walked back into the house under his own power. Daniel went outside to the privy the next morning without George's help, and instead of returning to bed, he walked into the kitchen.

"I haven't felt so well in my recent memory," he said, wearing a feeble grin. "I dispensed a full twenty pints in less than a day. I think I shall dance a jig."

George leapt from the chair where he had been sitting. "No. You shall do no such thing. But come with me. Mother can use some cheering up."

Daniel's rally should have been just the thing to pry Rebecca out of bed, but she was struck by the thought—

Willie and Clara Jane should have lived to see this day. She was immediately crestfallen.

Daniel laid his hand on George's shoulder. "Come son, I think I shall go back to bed."

By October's end, the fluids had resumed their surge in Daniel, gaining ground at a speed greater than any previous invasion. Dr. Forsyth drew on every weapon at his disposal to combat Daniel's dropsy—bloodletting, purgatives, cauterization, and Southey tubes—none of which he thought Rebecca should witness or even know of. He added larger than usual doses of mercury and arsenic. Once in a while, Dr. Forsyth entertained hope that some of his methods might be working. However, the new year brought persistent pain and pressure in Daniel's chest, squeezing the breath out of him. The doctor dug deeper into his bag for more remedies—none of which worked.

George took the initiative to invite Porter and Esther Dyer to visit at their earliest convenience. They arrived within a week, on a day when Daniel lay in his sickbed, his body puffed like an overstuffed down mattress. Daniel raised up half-sitting, and George helped Rebecca arrange pillows behind his father's back for support.

"I brought a poem for you," Porter said. He retrieved a scrap of paper from his vest pocket and read.

> *Yea, when this flesh and heart shall fail,*
> *And mortal life shall cease,*
> *I shall possess, within the veil,*
> *A life of joy and peace.*
> *The earth shall soon dissolve like snow,*
> *The sun forbear to shine;*
> *But God, who called me here below,*
> *Will be forever mine.*

Daniel's eyes lit up. "How I long for such release," he said.

Rebecca's eyes glistened with tears as she held Daniel's hand.

Not many days later, Father and Mother Taylor arrived. Their visit was short because Father Taylor was due to preach the next day. Daniel drifted in and out of shallow sleep while Rebecca made conversation with the Taylors. A smile curled Rebecca's lips when Father Taylor recounted his recent excursion west. He accompanied a group of orphans to Illinois where they were adopted into new homes.

"I do miss my times with the Bethel children," Rebecca said as scenes of lower Ann Street and the scruffy tykes rolled through her mind. She had to admit, not all memories were made of hoarfrost and timbers crashing down from above. Fond memories could be like embers warming a soul.

"I am heart-weary," Rebecca confessed.

"It is no wonder," Mother Taylor conceded, "with what you have been through the past two years. It is as if Satan has determined to sift you like wheat but be patient. When the enemy finishes, the Lord will renew you and rise you up, stronger than ever."

Rebecca thought back to the lines Porter had recited to Daniel days earlier. How Daniel confessed he yearned for release from this earthly vessel. She, too, was weary, depleted. She hoped she could be strong for him in his last hours. And strong for herself in the days after.

A few weeks into the New Year Daniel waxed nostalgic as he sat in his sickbed, bantering with Rebecca. He recalled a dozen years earlier when their love was young and yet untested. They witnessed two fugitive slaves fleeing a courthouse. Daniel pleaded with Rebecca to forgive him for derailing her youthful dreams, for stealing her away from lower Ann Street and its waifs and indigent mothers.

Rebecca demurred. He had not stolen her dreams. He gave her new ones. Nothing about the afflictions that had fallen on them had been his fault. She did not care to visit the question of who was to blame. She turned his attention in another direction—news of a shoemakers' strike in Lynn, Massachusetts, and the bravery of the strikers.

His eyes lit up and he raised both hands heavenward when she read to him from the newspaper. The strike had lit a fire under workers of all stripes throughout New England.

As she continued to read details from the news article, he sank back into his bed. A weak smile that he had been holding onto faded. Rebecca scrambled to revive it. "Do you remember?" she asked. "In our first months here in Chelsea, we endured an unremarkable speech by an awkward, melancholic, young Congressman Lincoln from the prairies. Now, it appears his star is rising. Some say he could be elected president."

Undeterred by his lack of response, she persisted. "He made quite a stir down in Connecticut, standing up for the likes of working men and women such as us." She held up a piece torn from the newspaper and waved it in front of his slumbering eyes. "Here's what he said. You'll like this. I am certain of it."

> *I am glad to know there is a system of labor where the laborer can strike if he wants to. I would to God such a system prevailed all over the world. Let us not be slandered or intimidated to turn from our duty. Eternal right makes might. Let us do our duty as we understand it!*

Rebecca's eyes watered as she caressed Daniel's cheek. "Even if your lips cannot tell me so, I know you cheer for those brave working men and women who are fighting for the right."

In the following weeks, Rebecca floundered in the valley of the shadow of his impending death. Waves of pain accompanied the swelling and tumefaction of his body, contorting his face. It was almost more than she could take.

Near the end of March, he lay in the small parlor, his mouth agape while death extracted the last breaths, as if drawing an anchor from the depths of his core, each link of the chain rippling across the purplish gunwale of his mouth. When his lungs expelled a final whoosh of breath, his long war against the surging floodwaters of unchecked dropsy ended.

Rebecca took his hand when he made his last gasp, but she could not sustain her grip. The mountain of grief piled up behind walls she erected in her heart over the years crashed down on her. She dropped to the floor like a discarded ragdoll and wailed. George gathered her up in his arms and carried her to bed then called for Charles White the undertaker.

Daniel was interred at Woodlawn Cemetery alongside his two children. The Taylors and the Dyers joined Rebecca, George, as well as Rebecca's sisters and their families at the burial. A host of neighbors and friends also attended. Rebecca's grief was so overwhelming she failed to take note of Almira's absence, despite the presence of the entire Cushing family.

George did notice, however, and asked Phemie Cushing what caused her daughter to stay away. Phemie explained that Almira had suffered nauseous spells over the past several days and was lying in until the doctor checked on her after the internment.

* * *

Rebecca remained in her bedroom over the following weeks, venturing out for trips to the privy only when she feared her bowels could rupture. She would have starved herself to death were it not for her friends Ann Haskins, Anna Loud, and Jane Hubbard who all but force fed her meals they had brought to keep her nourished.

Almira called on Rebecca in July with news that gleamed like a shard of light in the storm that hung over her mood. Almira was in the family way—already the child was quick in her womb, as if a butterfly was flapping its wings.

Rebecca's first instinct was to embrace Almira's joy over becoming a mother, but after several minutes her mind fixated on the words, "Better is he … which hath not yet been, who hath not seen the evil work that is done under the sun." They were words that consoled Porter Dyer on the death of his sickly son, but they evoked foreboding whenever Rebecca recalled them. Memories broke loose in her mind—Willie's fevers, Clara Jane's gaunt face, almost ghoulish eyes and her frail hand. The brief flare of delight died out and gloom churned right back in, settling over her countenance.

While his mother was fettered by melancholy, George made every effort to stave off creditors until a single option remained. He broached the notion with her of selling the house.

"My beautiful garden," she whimpered. "Willie and I worked so hard to make it …"

"Mother," George replied. "Your garden has turned to weeds."

"Who would do such a thing? Will we have no more beans? Poor Willie's beans." She sobbed.

"I shall clean up the garden," he said. "I must anyway if we are to have a chance at a good price."

"A good price?" she whined. "You cannot put a price on our little home—on hopes we once harbored for a bright future."

"Then I shall try to let it out. But if that venture is unsuccessful—"

"Let it out? To whom? Strangers?"

"To someone who will treat it with love and gentleness and pay a fair price. We shall require money to pay the creditors."

"Where shall we live? We must have someplace to live."

"Aunt Dorcas has invited us to live with her."

She waved her hand in the air. "I feel ill. I shall go to bed."

"About the house," George said.

"Do as you must." She went into her room and locked the door behind her.

Rebecca's friends persisted in their efforts to lift her spirits, even after she and George moved to the Derby farm. Each visited weekly through summer, winter, spring, and into the following summer. Dr. Forsyth called fortnightly.

Dorcas and George added their voices to the chorus of those encouraging her to persevere. Rebecca met their entreaties with indifference.

CHAPTER FIFTEEN

The days following Daniel's death melded into months until they became an entire year, each succeeding day a repeat of the former, as if the groundhog crawled from its burrow only to retreat inside, time and time again. Rebecca complained she had been singled out by God and stricken down, the justification for which she failed to understand—was it for not looking up to Him for help?

With all else lost, she imagined George afflicted, dying in agony, and leaving her utterly alone and penniless. If the Almighty had nothing more in store for her than suffering, she wished He would snuff out the last fading glimmer of her flame. As if to prove her point, she locked herself in her room for days at a time, neither eating nor drinking, giving the impression she had expired.

Rebecca's misery blocked out all of life around her, eclipsing the turmoil that engulfed every home, church, shop, farm, industry, and public square throughout the country. When Abraham Lincoln had been elected president the previous November she paid little attention, and when an avalanche of states began seceding from the Union all she could entertain was her own troubles. On the fateful morning when the bombardment of Fort Sumter plunged the nation into civil war, she ignored the consternation of her neighbors and showed not the slightest sign of interest.

Her malaise spiraled further downward in early July when George answered the president's call for volunteers. As he left for Boston to join up with his regiment, the 13th Massachusetts Infantry, he said, "Mother, this war is bigger than our small existence. It will determine your grandchildren's futures."

"Grandchildren," she huffed. "I have none and likely never will. Go. Give your life for all those other mothers' grandchildren."

"Then, think of the millions of African slaves who might see freedom if we prevail."

"God could free them in and instant, if he chose," she argued.

"I remember when you would have been proud to see your sons deliver those poor souls from bondage," he replied.

"Those days were for naught."

"You mean I am for naught." George clenched his jaw.

"Oh, no!" she exclaimed. "You are everything. You are all I have left."

He kissed his mother's cheek. "I shall return from this war and give you all the grandchildren you wish to have."

George had transacted a piece of business that momentarily lifted his mother's spirits a few days before he left to join his regiment. He convinced her to sign a rental agreement for the Chestnut Street house. She had to acknowledge the tenant was preferable to mere strangers. Almira's recently married brother, Frank, moved in with his bride, and their father took on the task of finding an acceptable buyer.

A few days after Frank moved into Rebecca's old house, Almira and little Georgy Fuller called on Rebecca at the Derbys' farm. When Rebecca held the little boy for the first time, images flashed through her mind—the times she held her own three little ones on the days each were born and many times over the years when she held them to her breast or in her lap. She recalled when they flew into her arms full of excitement or when she calmed them when they grew anxious. Then came images of the tykes on lower Ann Street who cuddled with her as she read to them, or laughed when they played, or marveled at finding a single flower sprouting between bricks on a sidewalk. She could not avoid the thought that the words "better is he which hath not yet been ..." could be replaced with "a child is born."

Almira watched Rebecca's eyes moisten and a smile breach her face as she held Georgy. "You have a chance for a new season of life," Almira told her. "You have George, and in time, you will have grandchildren. But family responsibilities need not consume you, nor should disappointment or grief fetter you. You are free to reclaim the dreams of your youth—to find new Olivers."

Rebecca stiffened. "New Olivers?"

"You have told me stories of the destitute, suffering souls that won your heart when you were a girl in Boston. How they were so much like the Oliver character in Mr. Dickens' novel."

"But Boston has changed so much," Rebecca protested.

"There are Olivers everywhere," Almira said. "You cannot find them here, nursing your own wounds."

"I would not know where to begin to look."

"I remember you once told me about something your brother, William, used to say, 'every wall is a gate.'"

Rebecca chuckled. "You don't miss a trick, do you? That is something he learned from listening to Mr. Waldo Emerson's lectures."

"Why beat your head against a wall, when time is better spent looking for the gate?"

The door to Rebecca's healing opened a crack. "I must look past death and embrace life."

"I can only imagine how hard it must be to have lost so much that you cherished," Almira said. "Even harder because of how deeply you have loved and sacrificed."

"My grief hangs on me like a yoke that I cannot seem to be free of."

"Look for a gate that will not let you carry it through to the other side."

Anna Loud called on Rebecca at the farm weeks after Almira's visit. "Have you decided about going with us to camp meeting?" Anna asked.

"Is it a Baptist affair? Or Methodist." Rebecca replied.

"Why, Methodist, of course."

"Oh, I suppose it wouldn't do to have someone in a Methodist camp who was raised as a Baptist."

"I have told you before, we Methodists are tolerant of others' beliefs, as long as they are Christian beliefs."

"I do not believe all Methodists are so welcoming. I recall many of your preachers making a great fuss over Father Taylor's openness to Unitarians and people of other faiths." Rebecca hesitated. "Do you suppose he will preach at your camp meeting?"

"I have not heard anyone mention him. But I am told his son-in-law, Reverend Barnes, will be preaching."

"A son-in-law?" Rebecca perked up. "Which one of the girls did he marry?"

"I cannot say as I know."

Rebecca rubbed her temples. "I doubt it was Nellie. I imagine her marrying an abolitionist lawyer. Maybe a doctor. Yes, an abolitionist lawyer and doctor. I could see Eliza marrying a preacher."

"If I told you Father Taylor will be preaching, would you come?"

"If you were telling the truth, I probably would." Rebecca offered a rare smile.

Anna grinned. "That's a start. At least I've gotten you to smile at the notion of going to camp meeting. Have you ever been to one?"

"No. I never have."

"Not even to hear Father Taylor?"

"I watched him preach every Sunday, before ..."

"Before what?"

"A sickly husband, invalid mothers and aunts, children."

"It would do you good to join us," Anna said. "Meet new people. Enjoy new scenery, the healing balm of the pine grove. The preaching might help you find a new purpose in life."

"I suppose it might do me some good. I haven't the energy to argue any longer with God."

"Warring with God is never a good idea," Anna replied. "Isn't it high time you surrendered and made peace?"

"If I am at war with God, it is not me who started it."

"No, but you have been much like Jacob in the scriptures—wrestling with an angel at the foot of heaven's ladder. Jacob was stricken, not out of anger or malice, but to fit him for a greater purpose."

✳ ✳ ✳

In late August on a sweltering Monday, Rebecca found herself clanking along the rails in a cramped Eastern Railroad car, surrounded by a host of Chelsea's Walnut Street Methodists. She was flanked by an elderly neighbor, Sally Slade—reverentially referred to as Sister Slade. Anna Loud and Sister Slade's daughter-in-law, Elmyra, occupied the seats facing her.

Elmyra Slade smiled at Rebecca, and Rebecca smiled back. While other neighbors, well intended as they were, became wearisome with their attention and advice, Elmyra's deeds and kindness were like tiny grains of sand. Unnoticed until, added together, they amounted to a coastline. During Daniel's long periods of bedridden confinement and heaps of soiled linens, Elmyra quietly helped with the laundry. When linens and quilts were soiled beyond redemption, she replaced them without fanfare. Rebecca could not recount all the ways Elmyra had been a friend. Guilt crept over Rebecca as she considered the debt she owed Elmyra—and the dearth of gratitude she had shown her.

Rebecca asked herself, have I been that way to everyone? Where was the Rebecca who had loved the blocks of lower Ann Street, who in the face of my own family's poverty had given so generously to others. Where was the Rebecca who vowed to follow in Papa's footsteps? Where was the Rebecca who brimmed with hope and charity for all, the Rebecca that existed before the parade of sickness and death? Maybe Daniel had been right years ago—memories are illusions, only echoes from the past with no power of their own. Only we can give them power—the power to enrich our lives or to destroy us.

Rebecca bit her lower lip as she pondered the question, what am I doing among such good people as these? Had not many of them also suffered? Was there ever a time Elmyra or Anna or any of the others aboard this train needed someone to smile at them, and I was too steeped in my own troubles?

That same day, a dozen locomotives pulled lines of loaded coaches along the iron rails from Boston to the Asbury Grove Camp Meeting in tiny Hamilton, Massachusetts. Rebecca was dressed exactly as Anna instructed—despite the late August heat, she wore three sets of undergarments and three ankle length dresses in layers. Most of the women on the train were attired likewise. The dress styles conformed to Methodist modesty, the layering helped minimize the weight of their trunks, making them easier to handle.

Mr. Slade, Sister Slade's husband, brought two ten-foot by ten-foot canvas tents—one for the four women and the other for himself and Mr. Bagnall. The Asbury Grove Camp Association provided for the rest of their needs, including meals and straw for mattresses and for covering the ground inside the tents.

At three o'clock that afternoon, after settling in at the campground, the others in Rebecca's party went down to

The Circle for the first preaching service. Rebecca remained alone in the tent, hobbled by fatigue and pricked by doubt as she stared at its stark, ashen walls. Her melancholy pressed down on her with greater and greater weight, until she feared it would choke life's breath out of her, just as Daniel's dropsy had suffocated him.

She forced herself to her feet and walked. Soon she meandered a path, stalked by her troubles, that snaked the perimeter of the campground, distancing herself from the cacophony of *The Circle*. She stayed apart from *The Circle* for the duration of the preaching service. As evening fell, she joined the delegation of Walnut Street Methodists for supper in one of the large society tents. She picked absent-mindedly at her food.

On Thursday afternoon when the hour of the preaching service approached, Rebecca continued to wallow. Swells of slate-grey clouds, mounting in the east, mirrored the oppression she suffered. Explosive claps of thunder, accompanied by violent gusts and driving rain, scattered the thousands who were gathered in *The Circle*. Trenches dug around the tents filled with water and threatened to overflow the straw-covered earthen floors. A retreating army of worshipers raced past the tent where Rebecca sat weary and alone.

The tent flap flew open in the wind, and a hunched, drenched, diminutive figure stumbled inside. Her face was obscured by a large, dripping-wet bonnet pulled down snug around her face. Rebecca leapt to her feet and helped secure the flap to shut out the storm. Her visitor turned out to be Sister Slade. Rebecca grabbed a woolen blanket from her bedding and wrapped it around the elderly woman.

"The others are running into town," Sister Slade reported as they sat together. "They hope to wait out the storm in the tiny hotel down the street."

"Why are you not with them?" Rebecca asked.

"At my age, I am more likely to be trampled by that horde of frightened Methodists than to be struck dead by lightning while sitting in this tent."

Rebecca laughed. "I feared you were an angel sent to shake me out of my misery."

"Do you mean to say you are dubious of angels?"

"Oh, I believe in angels." Rebecca replied. "It is God whom I distrust. I have been visited all too often by the angel of death stealing away loved ones. I have only my eldest son left, although this war will likely steal him away and leave me with nothing but gloom and no reason to go on living."

"In my long life, dear child," Sister Slade said, "I have experienced much that raises doubts. Those matters have been of man's making, not God's. Do not blame God for the disease and corruption mankind has inflicted on this world."

"But should not God intervene to protect us from evil?"

"If he be truly God," Sister Slade said, "there needs be mysteries that we mortals cannot understand. He sees all of eternity while we see only the speck of time to which we anchor ourselves."

"What good comes from serving such a God?"

Sister Slade took Rebecca's hand. "He gives us healing, my dear. As the wounds of affliction batter, bruise, and destroy our bodies, our souls are strengthened. That is why his Word tells us, 'Fear not them which kill the body, but are not able to kill the soul.' The soul is the inner part of us that lives forever. The body is temporary, only serving as a vessel for the soul while we walk this Earth."

"Both my body and soul have weathered all the bruising they can take," Rebecca said. "I am at the end of my rope. I must either find relief or die."

"Then pray for an iron spirit, which may bend in the fire but will not break."

"It seems that each time I pray, He answers with even greater affliction."

"If that be so, you should prepare for an even higher purpose than most."

"What more does God require of me?"

"Put all your faith on Him, who is watching over us like a mother hen over her brood. Tell him, Lord, do with me as you think best and give me strength to do your Will."

"I have done so." Rebecca replied. "More times than I can count."

"Has God finished with you yet, finished fitting you for his work, that is?"

"I suppose only He can answer that question."

"Then my dear, you should ask him," Sister Slade said. "As you do, incline your heart and mind toward doing what is right and good, toward loving all with mercy, and toward walking in humility."

"Do you think I find pleasure wallowing in grief, with no hope of relief? Oh, that my misery would fade, retreat like flood waters after a storm, and stop constantly knocking at my door. I have tried all that you say."

"None of us satisfy the Lord in our own strength."

"How, then?"

"By humbling ourselves," Sister Slade answered. "And entrusting our lives in God's hands. Instead of arguing with Him or finding fault with the path laid out before us, we must simply offer ourselves as instruments of his love and mercy."

"I suppose I have no other choice." Rebecca slumped in her seat.

"May I pray for you?" Sister Slade asked.

Midway through Sister Slade's prayer, the barrier between Rebecca's dark memories and stark reality became a mere gossamer, as fragile as cobwebs spun by tiny spiders. As the veil split open, she lifted her face toward Heaven and squeezed Sister Slade's hand.

Rebecca slept soundly that night for the first time in years, and when she awoke Sister Slade's words echoed in her mind, "pray for an iron spirit, which may bend in the fire but will not break." She dressed and hurried down to *The Circle* for the morning meeting, filled with new resolve. A great weight had been lifted from her shoulders. When the preaching was over and worshipers were invited to speak, Rebecca was the first to stand and tell of her newfound awareness of God's calling. From that moment, her appetite, strength, and spirits returned. On Saturday when the meetings concluded, she was loath to leave Asbury Grove.

CHAPTER SIXTEEN

Rebecca sat in Dorcas's kitchen near an open window on a mid-September morning, a couple of weeks after returning from Asbury Grove. A breath of summer wind, laden with scents of summer, lapped at the gingham curtain. Only days before, Rebecca celebrated the twenty-fifth anniversary of her marriage to Daniel with a rebirth of gratitude. She had been unable to rise from her bed the previous September—her first anniversary after losing the man she nursed and loved.

She was at last unfettered by burdens which had drained her soul almost to the point of death. Her experience at Asbury Grove grounded her in a new reality. After lifting her eyes to the Heavens while Sister Slade prayed, she opened herself to other campers who had faced and overcome grief. They all encouraged her to plant her feet firmly on the ground whenever old terrors pushed their way into her mind and to seek help from above. Over the ensuing days, the melancholy that had dogged her across endless seasons of affliction dissolved, like a marine fog chased away by an offshore breeze.

Rebecca savored the aroma of freshly brewed coffee as she took up the weekly *Chelsea Telegraph and Pioneer*. She consumed an account of the government's successes along North Carolina's Outer Banks. A Massachusetts man, General Benjamin Butler, commanded two New York regiments to victory. She skimmed past gossip about Mrs. Lincoln's shopping spree in New York City and fixed her attention on an announcement calling for women to serve as nurses in battlefield hospitals. She scrutinized each qualification and judged herself more than fitted for the task. Sister Slade's admonition during the storm at Asbury Grove came into finer focus, "if you ask for wisdom, He shall give it to you."

Rebecca tore the notice from the newspaper as Dorcas returned from the hen roost with a basket of eggs.

"Something caught your fancy?" Dorcas asked.

"You might say so." Rebecca tucked the newspaper item into her apron pocket.

"Keeping secrets?" Dorcas tilted her head.

"No. Only something I want to investigate before making a big fuss over it. It may turn out to be nothing at all."

"You won't see any theatrics from me. I'll leave that business to your other sister, and she's a good hundred miles away."

"If you must know, I think I have found new Olivers."

"Olivers?" Dorcas asked.

"Never mind. It's a long story." Rebecca pulled the snippet of newsprint from her pocket and gave it to Dorcas.

Dorcas studied it, glimpsed Rebecca, and returned her focus to the advertisement. She smiled. "I doubt there's another woman in the entire Republic as well prepared as you are for the task."

Rebecca smiled. "Can you ask one of your farmhands to ready a wagon? I'd like to go into town and ask Dr. Forsyth for his opinion."

Rebecca's pulse quickened when she pulled the wagon to a stop in front of Dr. Forsyth's office in her old neighborhood at the corner of Malden and Chestnut Streets. Her anxiety grew as she stepped down onto the sidewalk and strode through the doorway. Her heart was in her throat by the time she stood in front of him. She showed him the notice. "I can satisfy every requirement. What hinders my going? No earthly tie keeps me here now that my son, my only treasure still living, has gone to the battlefield, and my home has been sold."

Doctor Forsyth pinched his brow as he weighed his reply. Rebecca's jaw tightened in anticipation.

He cocked his head. "In your present state of health, you cannot endure the dreadful conditions you will find in those hospitals."

"But it is an opportunity to reclaim a youthful passion. To ease the burden of those in need. To be a healing balm to suffering souls. I want to be a mother to our wounded and dying soldiers."

"Before you bite off more than you can chew, you should speak with Mayor Fay. He has seen firsthand the carnage and arduous business you shall encounter. He is engaged with the Sanitary Commission."

Rebecca left the wagon parked in front of Dr. Forsyth's office and walked three blocks to city hall. Mayor Fay received her without hesitation. "Our entire city has worried over you," he said. "It is a most welcome sight to see you up and about."

"I am grateful for everyone's concern. Thank you for giving me a few moments of your time." She took mental note of the strain on his face. "I know you are quite burdened."

"I assure you, Mrs. Pomroy. My burdens are easy compared to your family's affliction. How can I be of service to you?"

After she stated her business, much as she had done with Dr. Forsyth, Mr. Fay explained, "I returned from the hospitals around Washington City last evening and fear a fragile woman like yourself would never be selected for such work. The sights I witnessed are unspeakable. And the meager rations—salt pork, meal, and low-quality beef—are barely palatable. As for living conditions, jail cells offer greater comforts."

"I shall trust God to supply my needs," she replied. "As a girl, I followed my father into some of the darkest corners of Boston, unafraid of danger that might befall us. We made it our mission to relieve the suffering of destitute children and their indigent mothers. Since my sister's death nineteen years ago, I have nursed a constant parade of sick loved ones. God sustained me as I held their hands when they crossed over into eternity. He has prepared me for this work."

He kneaded his brow. "I do not mean to discount your bravery in the face of tribulation, but in those hospitals, you will find your experiences magnified hundreds of times. Your nascent faith will be crushed by the misery you find. Truth be told, you won't be chosen. A thousand women have already entered their names in a register at the State House and they will be taken first."

"My mind is set." She held up the newspaper snippet. "This notice gives the name of Miss Dix who has charge over army nurses. I shall write her directly and let her decide."

"Do as you wish, Mrs. Pomroy. But for what it is worth, I think you must be a little insane."

She forced a smile and thanked Mayor Fay for his time. Before returning to the farm, she telegraphed Esther and Porter Dyer, saying she wished to call on them at their earliest convenience.

A couple of afternoons later, at twenty minutes before three o'clock the train carrying Rebecca to Hingham pulled out of Boston's Old Colony & Fall River depot. An hour and a half later, she fidgeted in the Dyers' carriage as it creaked along toward their home. Though she champed at the bit to know Porter and Esther's thoughts about her plan to become an army nurse, politeness dictated she entertain their questions about how she was getting on after George's enlistment.

"I have heard twice from George in the six weeks he has been in the war," Rebecca answered.

Their question obliged her to ask about the Dyer children. Esther crowed about Porter, Jr's., graduation from Amherst College and his employment as a teacher.

Rebecca apologized for not visiting when their youngest was born. That had been near the time Willie joined his sister in the grave, and over the ensuing months Daniel's eroding health drained her last stores of energy. The year and a half since his death had been a fog—until the Hamilton camp meeting.

Misgivings wormed into Rebecca's mind as she helped Esther prepare the evening meal. Mayor Fay's firsthand knowledge of the hospitals should not be disregarded, nor the one thousand names already in the register. The interloper in her head bored deeper into her thoughts while the family gathered around the supper table and Porter said grace. She worried Esther might raise the popular objection—a battlefield is no place for women.

Women were already ensconced in the war as nurses, and Mr. Fay's assessment of her was based on hearsay, town gossip about her frailty. Frailty? Rebecca could not recall being more invigorated. Her afflictions had not eroded her, they had steeled her. She was now ready to resume the work she had set out to do many years before on the street corners of lower Ann Street, in Father Taylor's Seamen's Bethel, and outside the courthouse where the two women, fugitives from slavery, had won their emancipation. Except now, her Olivers would be the boys and men—sick and injured soldiers—who fought to save the Union and stop the advance of slavery. When Porter finished his prayer, Rebecca stuck her hand in the pocket of her smock and pulled out the notice she had torn from the newspaper. As she unfolded it, Porter and Esther exchanged glances.

"I came to ask your advice," Rebecca said as she handed Porter the clipping. "I am desperate to send a letter to the woman in the notice, offering my services as a nurse for our boys."

Esther took Rebecca's hand. "I can think of no one better to care for our soldiers."

"Rebecca, are you certain?" Porter asked.

"Friends have warned about harsh conditions, meager rations, the perils of contracting diseases," she replied. "All of that I have passed through before."

"Yes," he said. "You have lived many times in the presence of death, with the young as well as the old and middled aged. But have you considered how it would be to hold the hand of a mere boy, as a surgeon saws off his mutilated, gangrened leg, knowing that for him, living might be a crueler fate than death?"

"I have not witnessed such, but I have dabbed the feverish brows of dying women tortured by the thought of leaving their little ones behind to the vagaries of a motherless childhood, as well as husbands whose last moments were flooded with guilt over leaving a widow and children rudderless to navigate the turbulence of life."

Porter thrummed his fingers on the table. "I can see you have given this much consideration, and that the Almighty has prepared you well for the task. Might I encourage you to sleep on it one more night, and in the morning when you are refreshed, we can talk again?"

Rebecca consented and after an evening of reminiscing, they retired for the night.

The next morning, their conversation continued over breakfast. Rebecca said, "I woke with these words on my tongue, 'What doth the Lord require of thee, but to do justly, and to love mercy, and to walk humbly with thy God?' I remain determined to give those poor boys the whole of me."

"I say go," Porter replied. "The Lord go with you."

Rebecca drew a deep breath. A burden had been lifted from her. "I shall write Miss Dix on my return home."

"No," Porter said. "Write it now, on the spot, and we shall post it this morning. Put the matter in Miss Dix's hands as well as God's. Let them make the choice."

Three days later, on Sunday morning, a telegraph messenger arrived at the Derbys' farm with an envelope addressed to Rebecca. Dorcas cringed as she accepted it. Newspaper reports of the Union Army's calamity, weeks earlier at the place they called Bull Run, had left the entire town on edge. Visions of George languishing in one of those field hospitals, or worse, filled her with dread. She doubted her sister could withstand another calamity, especially the loss of her only remaining child.

Rebecca joined her sister on the porch and flinched at the sight of the messenger taking his horse's reins and preparing to remount. Her throat tightened when Dorcas handed her the telegram. She opened it slowly. Her hands trembled.

> *Mrs. Pomroy:*
>
> *Application accepted. Report my house, c 14th and New York Ave, Washington City, Tuesday 24th instant.*
>
> *DL Dix, Supt Women Nurses Union Army*

"Is everything all right?" Dorcas asked.

"The most wonderful news." She bounced up and down as she waved the message.

"George is coming home?" Dorcas asked.

Rebecca showed her the telegram. "The Army has accepted me as a nurse."

They gripped each other's arms and jumped about, laughing and shrieking like schoolgirls.

Rebecca cut short her dancing and laughing, but her smile remained bright. "I should keep my promise to worship at the Congregational Church this morning. Ann Haskell is expecting me. It may be my only chance to bid my dear friend goodbye. Goodness. Everything is happening so fast. I have only today to prepare. When shall I pack?"

"Don't worry. I will gather your things while you're in church. Now, go get yourself fixed up and I shall have a horse and wagon readied." Dorcas shooed her into the house and started for the barn.

Rebecca approached Ann Haskell on the sidewalk outside the Congregational Church an hour later. Before either got in a word of greeting, Rebecca showed her the telegram from Miss Dix.

Ann held her hand to her mouth as she read. She asked, "You do intend to go?"

"Of course," Rebecca said.

"This is a matter for earnest prayer," Ann replied. "And celebration."

"There's little time for making a fuss," Rebecca said.

"Let me be the one to worry about that." Ann led her up the stairs, pausing in the doorway to whisper to a deacon.

As they headed down the aisle to the Haskell family pew, Rebecca said in hushed tones, "I should be back at the farm packing. I must be on the train tomorrow morning."

"You should give thanks to the Lord," Ann said. "This wonderful news is all His doing."

Pastor Plumb entered the pulpit a few moments later and greeted the congregation with an announcement. "I was informed just now that a friend of many, one who is among us here today and who has been severely tested and mightily prepared by God, is the first woman from our town to be accepted into service as an army nurse. There is no one better than Mrs. Rebecca Pomroy to bring healing and succor to the brave men and boys who sacrifice life and limb on behalf of our precious Union. Even now this good news is being carried to congregations throughout Chelsea so that they may join us in praying for our good sister. The deacons of our church will host a reception for Mrs. Pomroy at six o'clock this evening. Bring family and friends to wish her Godspeed."

Early the next morning, after a short night's sleep, Rebecca boarded the eight-and-a-half o'clock express train from Boston that was scheduled to arrive in New York City in the late afternoon. In New York she would catch a night train for the fifteen-hour journey to the nation's capital.

As the railcar lurched forward on the train's departure from Boston, she settled into a seat next to a window and waved goodbye to Dorcas. She sighed once the platform passed out of view. The life she and Daniel had built in Chelsea was gone. She was at the same time profoundly sad and teeming with anticipation.

CHAPTER SEVENTEEN

A matron greeted Rebecca Tuesday night at Miss Dix's office on the corner of Fourteenth Street and New York Avenue in Washington City. Threats of violence against the rails by secessionist sympathizers had caused delays as the train approached Baltimore. Rebecca was further detained by difficulties she encountered finding transportation from the train depot to the heart of the Capital. A single apple and one sandwich were the only nourishment she had packed for her odyssey. She had expected to find some form of refreshment on her arrival in the city, but none was available at such a late hour.

The matron apologized on behalf of Miss Dix, who was away on battlefields, delivering rations, supplies, and other necessaries to the wounded in field hospitals. The headquarters' entire food stores were needed for the soldiers, so Rebecca was offered water, but nothing to remedy her hunger. She was directed upstairs to a small room with a cot and woolen blanket.

Rebecca lay awake for a time with her stomach growling as she recalled the Godspeed wishes of Chelsea friends, both old and new. Her last thoughts before falling asleep were of Mayor Fay's tribute—

> *We have all suffered some, but none have lost*
> *so much and endured such depths of grief as*
> *our own Mrs. Pomroy. Now, having found new*

hope, she goes bearing the shield of faith, dressed in the breastplate of righteousness, and armed with the sword of truth to join the last remnant of her family on distant battlefields in service to God and country.

She resolved to merit his approbation.

She rose early the next morning, and finding Miss Dix still unavailable, she set out in search of something to eat. As she proceeded a couple of blocks west on New York Avenue and rounded the corner of a colossal granite building, the President's House stood in full view. Her stomach's nagging took a back seat to the spectacle. The president's residence evoked a memory from a dozen years earlier—the angular, shrill-voiced politician from Illinois whose speech she and Daniel had witnessed in Chelsea. In that day, Congressman Lincoln canvassed New England in support of slaveholder General Taylor's presidential aspiration. On this day, Mr. Lincoln was himself the president, leading the fight to keep slavery from rending the Union in two.

Hunger pangs soon reasserted themselves, pushing aside her memory. The question she and Daniel bandied about on that September afternoon so many years ago—whether Mr. Lincoln was abolitionist enough to suit New England voters—remained unresolved. She walked on, heading south as she passed along the front of the granite edifice. At the end of the building, with the President's House to her back, she turned east and encountered a stream of humanity, filing through the entrance of what she discovered was Willard's Hotel—a place where visitors and workers in the Capital gathered daily for breakfast.

She trailed the queue—men in mud-laden boots and grimy Union Blues with a few well-dressed civilians sprinkled in their midst. They snaked through Willard's lobby where the aromas of freshly baked bread and sizzling bacon beckoned them into an inner courtyard. In the center of the courtyard, battle-weary soldiers swarmed a crystal fountain and splashed water over their heads. An army of Negro bootblacks manned stations around the perimeter, cleaning and polishing boots.

Rebecca weaved her way through the courtyard and took a position near a doorway where servers passed in and out, carrying trays of food. Good fortune permitted her to prog a hot biscuit and two strips of bacon along with a mug of coffee.

When Rebecca returned to Miss Dix's headquarters, a tall, mannered, to some degree attractive woman stood in the lobby giving instructions to an aide.

"Mrs. Pomroy? the woman asked.

"Yes," Rebecca replied.

The woman nodded. "I am Miss Dix. We are happy you made it down from Boston on such short notice. Why don't you join me while I call on some of the city's hospitals? I shall show you some of the sights along the way."

"That would be kind of you."

Miss Dix directed her driver to take them down Pennsylvania Avenue toward the dome-less Capitol, allowing Rebecca to glimpse the place where the nation's laws were made. From the Capitol, the carriage looped back and clunked along on a dusty, rutted road. To one side of the road ran a slough laden with disease-infested sewage—a payload which, after coursing through the city's streets, would flow into the Potomac River.

Rebecca kept a kerchief over her nose and mouth as the carriage followed the roadway, passing Smithsonian Castle and a vast grassy area on the opposite side of the canal. A half-completed obelisk, intended as a monument to George Washington, stood like a massive granite stump at the center of the grassy field. Grazing livestock, large piles of offal picked at by feisty crows, rows of tents, and soldiers at drill surrounded the unfinished memorial. Miss Dix pointed out that the bowels of the obelisk served as a butchery and secure storage for the Army's meat supply. They crossed over the canal by way of a bridge and rattled over a broad dirt avenue south of the President's House.

Miss Dix said, "In your application, you said for many years you refused to look heavenward. What caused you to make such a resolution?"

"When I was not yet fifteen years old, I watched a masthead fall and crush my Papa as he stood on the deck of his ship."

"And you laid the blame on God."

"Yes." Rebecca stared down at her hands folded in her lap. "Never looking for help from above was my childish rebellion, and as afflictions came again and again throughout life and as they grew more severe with each new calamity, my soul shrank within me ... until I no longer had the desire to go on living."

"Yet you persevered."

"I have," Rebecca said. "The grief of losing so many I held dear has not disappeared, and likely never will. With help from on high, the pangs of memory have begun to retreat one wave at a time, like a receding tide sliding out to sea."

Miss Dix patted Rebecca's hand. "Memories are simply recollections of the past. Your past can only harm you if you allow it to eclipse the work laid out before you."

"My husband tried to help me understand that principle," Rebecca replied. "For many years, I remained blind to the work God was doing in the midst of my affliction. Now, my eyes are wide open."

"Good, because there is much more you will see, and little of it will be pleasant. I could not help but be impressed by how Providence seems to have prepared you," Miss Dix said. "From your letter I saw in you not only a tender-heartedness toward the dying and a familiarity with grief, but also a determination to plough ahead no matter how low you have been bent. That is a maturity I do not see in most women who apply for my corps. That impression is why I moved your application ahead of hundreds of others. Among the many who serve as nurses, my corps is special, so we are governed by stricter rules."

"I hope to prove worthy of your confidence."

Miss Dix smiled. "Your story reminds me of an incident in my own life. I had campaigned our Congress very hard for many years to set aside property to build an asylum for mentally ill women. It was to be the crowning achievement of my life. When the legislature appropriated the money that was needed, I declared, I have lifted up my eyes and my cup runneth over. But President Pierce vetoed the bill, and I succumbed to bitterness, nearly vowing to never look to God again for help."

"You said you nearly vowed. What stopped you?"

"I wondered myself, for a very long time," Miss Dix replied. "Eventually, the answer became clear—our past troubles prepare us for new challenges."

The carriage stopped at the three-story, brick Union Hotel in Georgetown. While they remained parked for a few moments, Miss Dix explained that, several months earlier, the government seized the hotel from secessionist sympathizers for use as a hospital and had displaced its residents.

As they entered the building, a confluence of stringent odors stalled Rebecca's breath. She observed the rows of hazy windows on opposing walls. "There's no ventilation. Why are all the windows shut?"

Miss Dix replied, "The soldiers on guard closed them as a caution against threatened rebel attacks."

"But the place is empty." Rebecca gestured around the nearly vacant space. "Where is everyone?"

"This is where new patients are brought to be evaluated before they're given beds wherever space allows. The surgeon is likely attending patients in the main ward, formerly the hotel's ballroom. There are more wards on the upstairs floors—set up in hallways and blocks of old guest rooms. After the battle a few months ago in Virginia near Manassas Creek, trains of ambulances flooded into the city carrying hundreds of wounded. Many of those boys are not here now—they survived, recovered enough to return to their regiments, or were mustered out. They've been replaced by others who've trickled in from field hospitals." She prompted Rebecca as she started to the opposite end of the lobby. "Come this way."

Rebecca kept her mouth and nose covered with her kerchief upon entering the main ward.

Miss Dix scoffed. "You'll get used to the stench soon enough. The dismissive attitude of doctors and male nurses may take longer to conquer. It is a rare one who regards us as anything more than maids to strip beds and empty chamber pots."

As they approached a lone surgeon standing at a patient's cot, Rebecca counted three female nurses for forty beds.

The doctor continued scribbling on a clipboard, even after they announced themselves.

Miss Dix scoffed at the lack of response from the surgeon.

He shifted his attention to a wounded soldier in the bed, and without glancing at Miss Dix he grumbled, "Can you not see I am occupied?"

"I came to inquire whether I can be of any help," Miss Dix replied.

"If by 'help' you mean, saddling me with another of your whiney female nurses, I can do without them. They are not up to the task."

Miss Dix straightened and clasped her hands in front of her. "My nurses are carefully selected and held to rigorous standards."

"Rigorous?" He sneered. "Rigor mortis best describes the one who just bailed on me."

She shifted her stance. "What? One of my nurses quit?"

"Yes, and good riddance. If you intend to replace her, send me a man ... even if he's missing half his limbs."

"That's not my prerogative, but Mrs. Pomroy, here, can stay and take up the slack while I arrange for a more permanent solution."

He assessed Rebecca. "The others can tell you what needs to be done. Just stay out of my way and make sure those indolent Negroes keep to the kitchen and laundry where they belong. I don't want them aggravating the patients."

A Black male orderly scurried past carrying an armful of clean bedding.

The surgeon shouted at him. "What have I told your kind about entering the wards, unattended."

Miss Dix nudged Rebecca. "Let us get you settled in. I'll have your trunk brought over this evening."

Once they were out of earshot, Rebecca said, "I can't believe how rudely the surgeon treated that poor man. Are not our men fighting to end their mistreatment?"

"For some that may be true," Miss Dix replied, "but the government's immediate purpose is to put down the rebellion so the country can be made whole again. The fate of the Black race is a secondary concern."

An orderly led Rebecca to the third floor and turned her over to the military guard who was posted at the landing. She kept pace with the guard as he quickstepped past open doors of converted guestrooms. The hollow groans of suffering soldiers assailed her ears. The reek of dried urine, moldering feces, and a stench akin to rotten eggs filled her nostrils. The plaintive sounds and acrid odors weighed on Rebecca as she trailed behind the guard. They passed more than a dozen sick who languished on narrow beds jammed into a vacated upstairs parlor. By her quick count, she would be looking after at least forty bedridden patients.

At the end of the hallway, they stopped at the doorway of a repurposed storeroom, furnished sparingly with a crude military cot and a spartan stand that held a pitcher of water.

"Will you notify the nurse in charge of the ward that I have arrived?" Rebecca asked.

"You're all there is ma'am. Ain't no other nurses up on this floor. Just you and these poor souls. Half will likely die. Others will curse the morning sun, wishing they could die." With that, he returned to his post.

Rebecca surveyed her sparse accommodations then gazed down the hall. She choked as she tried to draw a deep breath. Memories washed over her—the wafts of death she had tasted at the passing of loved ones, their clammy hands gripping hers as if they refused to let go of the last strands of life. But she had never experienced the suffocating misery of so many, all crammed together in one compact place.

She collected herself and began wandering the hall to visit her charges. She buried her emotions behind a veneer of cheer, masking fatigue and resurgent sorrows that were aggravated by three nights of little sleep and sparse nourishment since receiving Miss Dix's telegram.

The surgeon arrived at four o'clock that afternoon. "Miss Dix tells me you come to us from Massachusetts."

"Yes, sir. Chelsea—"

"I have no need to hear your life story. It is sufficient that you come from a civilized region of the country. Now, before you get any fanciful ideas, you're not a healer. Your job is to sponge-bathe those who cannot make it to the washroom. Change bed linens, empty bedpans, clean up vomit, give medications, and blister patients exactly as instructed, etc., etc. Call for a surgeon if one of the patients is bleeding to death. In the event one of them commences to have a seizure, make sure he does not swallow his tongue. Everyone you see in this place outranks you. Of course, that doesn't include the darkies who do the cooking and the laundry." He thumbed through his notes. "Mrs. Pomroy?"

"Yes, sir."

"Hmm. Husband off to war, I suppose. Sons, too? You just want the world to know you are not useless. Guess I can count on you quitting like the last one."

"No, sir. My husband is dead. My children gone with him, except my oldest. He's in the Army."

"My condolences." He handed her a stack of patient cards. "Enough chit-chat. Let's get to the business of medications you are to administer."

In the middle of his instructions, her face flushed, her body quaked, and she rocked back on her heels. The surgeon braced her as her legs gave way, and the guard rushed forward to help. Anxiety spawned by the sudden changes in her life and deprivation of sleep and nourishment over the past days had caught up with her.

Once she was steady on her feet, the doctor marched off, shaking his head. The guard assisted her to her room and poured a cup of water for her to drink.

She sat on the cot for a time, sipping the water, battling over whether she had made a colossal mistake, whether Mayor Fay's initial doubts had been too hastily discarded, whether the surgeon's instincts about female nurses were grounded in truth. The words from scripture came in a rush, almost audible, "He that putteth his hand to the plough and looketh back is not fit." Her mind churned. Unfit. She wrung her hands. Was that a fact? Was she unfit? She stood. Planted her feet. Resolved not to look back. She would look heavenward for help. She would be fit. She would persevere in all that lay before her. She echoed the determination of her nineteen-year-old self, who a quarter century earlier stood before her soon-to-be betrothed and declared, "it shall be my purpose in life to ease suffering wherever I find it."

Rebecca strode into the hallway to resume her duties. As she passed the spot where she had nearly fainted, a sickly soldier called her name from one of the old guestrooms. She stepped to the doorway and peered in.

"Mrs. Pomroy," the young man repeated. "What sent you here?"

She went to his bedside for a closer look. "I am a nurse," she said. "I have just arrived."

He grasped her hand. "I am the Stevens boy who played in your garden with Willie when my family lived in Chelsea."

"Young Eddie?" she asked.

"Yes, ma'am." He broke into a brief coughing spasm. After the coughing ended, he asked, "Has Willie joined up?"

Her heart clenched. "I'm afraid he took very ill a few years after your family removed to Boston. He passed before the war began."

Stevens winced and clutched his abdomen. "Then I shall see him soon."

Rebecca cringed, recalling her neighbor Micajah Haskell's discomfort during his futile bout with the typhoid. "I will do my best to see that you are a very old man when you see him again. My George is in the Army. Where did you enlist?"

"Boston," he replied. "1st Massachusetts."

"George joined the 13th in July. He says in his letters he has survived a couple of skirmishes in western Virginia." She placed her palm on his sweat-beaded forehead, studied his red-webbed eyes. The fever was raging, unchecked. "How did your illness come about?"

"I got through the hellfire at Bull Run without a scratch. After that, got an awful bad case of the runs. Then the fever."

"Let me find some cold towels," she said. "But first, I'll open that window."

"All the windows are fastened shut," he said. "Precautions against a rebel attack."

She shook her head as she started out to find anything to relieve his fever. Her search led her into a room where a solitary patient lay, calling for his mother. Rebecca's heart twinged at the desperation in his voice. She sat with him for a long while, holding his hand and serving generous doses of soothing words in an effort to comfort him. When he was settled, she found wet towels and returned to Eddie Stevens, who had drifted to sleep. She draped the towels over Eddie's forehead.

Again, the other patient began calling for his mother. She rushed back to him and found his agitation in high pitch. She tried to administer laudanum which had been left on a small corner desk by the surgeon or a previous nurse. The young soldier put his arms around her neck and cried out, "Oh, my dear mother!" He clung to her neck with such a death grip that she had to call for help from the guard who was posted at the door to her ward. Together, they tried to pry the patient's hands off her. Even after the man drew his final breath, his arms remained locked so firmly around her neck that the guard struggled for several more minutes before he was able to wrench her free.

Rebecca lingered in the hallway outside the dead soldier's room. Tears streaked her cheeks as the guard went to summon an orderly to take the fresh corpse away. She trembled as she murmured, "hands to the plough ... do not look back."

She lifted her chin, straightened her back, and stood stock-still like a sentinel, until the orderly arrived.

The next patient she checked on writhed in a cot at the end of the hall near her small room. He moaned, gripping a bandaged wrist. When she stopped next to his cot and greeted him, he only managed unintelligible groans through gritted teeth.

"How can I help?" she asked.

He peeked up at her, his face contorted.

"Let me take a look at your wrist," she said, and without waiting for his reply, she began snipping and peeling back his bandage.

"Yow!" he cried out.

Her stomach knotted at the sight of pus seeping from the lump of mangled flesh. She reapplied the bandage the best she could. "Try to relax. I'll be right back."

Moments later, she returned with clean strips of cloth to rewrap his mutilated wrist. "How did it happen?" she asked.

He sneered. "Took a musket ball straight through."

"How old are you?"

"Eighteen. I enlisted without Mama's permission."

"You must let me write her. She will want to be with you."

"I refuse to put her through any more pain than I already have. I am all she has."

"Why don't we both sleep on the matter for tonight and see what course the surgeon plans to take."

"You can sleep on it, if you want," he said. "But my mind is set."

The next morning, Rebecca made the rounds of all the patients, ending with the boy whose wrist had been shattered by a musket ball. He told her his widowed mother lived in Methuen, near the New Hampshire and Massachusetts border, but he still refused to let Rebecca write to her. "They are going to amputate my hand." His voice croaked. "It would kill her to know."

A pair of orderlies soon arrived with a stretcher to take him away to the surgeon. He sat up in his cot and embraced Rebecca, his good arm draped around her neck. "You are much like my mother," he said.

"I shall be waiting for you when you return."

After the orderlies carried the Methuen soldier off to surgery, Rebecca sat with the Stevens boy and read to him as he slipped in and out of consciousness. She presumed he was aware of her presence at his bedside and paused her reading only to check his fever or to answer pleas for help from other patients. Despite her best efforts and fervent prayers, his condition continued to worsen over the following days.

As she read to him one day, orders came from Miss Dix for her to report to Columbian College Hospital for permanent duty. The words "Columbian College" awakened in her a nostalgia for the old Boston north end where she had lived most of her life—particularly for the Baldwin Place Baptist Church and its pastor, Reverend Stow. Reverend Stow often broadcast his affection for the college, even after the denomination fractured over slavery and the college chose to align with the pro-slavery Southern Baptist Convention.

On her last walk through the Union Hotel Hospital ward, Rebecca bid each patient goodbye and Godspeed. The Methuen boy clasped her hand in his good one and thanked her for her motherly care. When she looked in on Eddie Stevens, an orderly was struggling to keep him from hurting himself during a violent seizure. She choked back tears. She could not deny his time was fast approaching. Any moments of consciousness in his final days would be fraught with delirium. She cherished the last coherent words he had spoken to her, "It does my soul good to see a good woman from home whom I never expected to see again."

CHAPTER EIGHTEEN

Rebecca rode in Miss Dix's ambulance to Columbian College Hospital on a clear, unseasonably warm day, shy of two weeks after arriving in the Capital. The five-story masonry building loomed above an array of white tents just beyond the edge of the city at the end of 15th Street near Florida Avenue, fifteen blocks north of the President's House. The government seized the college after most of its students went off to fight for the rebels. The largest building became a hospital for sick and wounded Union soldiers who were transported there from nearby battlefields. Ten army regiments pitched camp on the grounds to protect the seat of government and the hospital from threats of violence by secessionist sympathizers.

Dr. Thomas Crosby, the surgeon-in-charge, led Rebecca to an upstairs ward where several small rooms faced a wide corridor filled with patients lying on military cots. "You have thirty beds to look after," Crosby said, "less three that are temporarily vacant. Most of your charges are afflicted with typhoid."

Rebecca replied, "I shall give them every attention possible."

"Miss Dix speaks highly of you." He pinched his brow. "You may have heard we find it difficult to keep good nurses. Many become worn down—either their health fails or emotions get the better of them. Some leave when they find a husband. She assures me you have what it takes to endure this place."

"Whatever the Army requires, I shall do to my fullest."

"I'll send up one of the other nurses to help you settle in. In the meantime," he gestured toward a doorway at the far end of the hallway, "you'll find patient records in a nurses' room we have set up with a bed and a desk. As you'll discover, I am keen on details. The patient cards show everything you need to know about the men in your ward. The typhoid sufferers should be blistered each evening and morning. I'm afraid we are short on male nurses and attendants, so you are on your own."

"If I have questions, to whom should they be addressed?"

"Direct any critical questions to the nurse matron since we don't have a surgeon for every floor. But do not leave your ward unattended. Send an orderly. If the matron is unavailable, try nurse Stevenson. She's a Massachusetts woman like yourself and has been here from the start."

"I look forward to meeting her."

That evening, singing and loud music rose from the encampments around the hospital. The easy melodies around the campfires clashed with moans and demented outbursts from patients in Rebecca's ward. After the outside revelry abated near midnight, the cacophony of misery within the hospital ran straight through the night. Calls for mother drew Rebecca from one bedside to the next. She clasped one poor soul's hand and could not release her grip until a few minutes after he drew his final breath.

She battled fatigue until she exhausted her last measure of willpower and surrendered to the fog of sleep.

A bugler's Reveille startled her awake soon after she had closed her dry, achy eyes. She rose, refreshed herself with a wet towel, and called for an orderly to keep watch over her ward while she hastened downstairs for a breath of fresh air.

A blush of morning dew kissed her cheek as she alighted on the stoop, but serenity came to a quick end. A column of ambulances rumbled up the street and stopped at the hospital's entrance. A matron, tall and thin, jumped from the lead wagon and barked orders at nurses and orderlies. Rebecca bristled. The woman, whom everyone called Fales, reminded her of accounts she'd heard in her Chelsea days of imperious foremen abusing workmen in Boston's boot factories.

Mrs. Jane Russell, an angular middle-aged nurse and widowed schoolteacher from New York City, muttered, "That Fales woman thinks highly of herself."

Rebecca held her tongue and helped a flagging soldier into the hospital—his breath oppressive and musty.

The ambulance matron brushed past, spreading the word that many of the sick were ill from drinking spring water poisoned by retreating rebels. She was followed by a rush of orderlies carrying stretchers loaded with near-dead fever victims and maimed battlefield casualties.

Rebecca continued to guide her patient to the bathroom, where the new arrivals were stripped naked and thoroughly washed before being carried to bed. Mrs. Russell warmed towards Rebecca in an older-sisterly way, and instructed her to empty each soldier's pockets, roll up his clothing, and mark his name on the bundle—if it was possible to determine his identity. Their clothing went on a shelf in a shed along with their sword and knapsack. When the soldiers' personal effects were all put away, Rebecca counted the bundles. In total more than two hundred souls were under their care.

Mrs. Russell confessed, "In this place you will become well acquainted with death."

"I am quite familiar with death, already," Rebecca said.

"Aren't we all," Mrs. Russell replied. "Next time, be quicker about storing away the men's bundles. Sometimes hundreds come in all at once and we've no time to waste."

* * *

Rebecca immersed herself in the army way during her first week at Columbian College Hospital—nurses were shown little respect and had no privileges. They were not allowed to wander outside the hospital or to stray from Miss Dix's puritan rules of conduct or dress code. Each nurse's rations of twenty cents a day went into a pool to buy rice, bread, beef, and to pay wages to a sick soldier to cook meals. Cooks were prohibited from baking bread, cakes, or pies. If a nurse wanted extras for her patients, she must write home for folks to send boxes of fruits, jellies, baked goods, crackers, boiled hams—anything that could be eaten without having to be cooked.

Mrs. Russell gave Rebecca another tidbit of advice— once the weather turned chilly, nurses would need to plead with everyone they knew to send woolen socks for the sick and wounded to wear on cold days and nights.

Rebecca toiled for hours on end—often with little or no nourishment, sleep, or help. She applied cold, wet towels to the blistered skin of her typhoid patients as they thrashed in their beds and ripped at their clothes. Many were tormented by delirium-induced fevers. For battlefield casualties, she cleaned pus-filled lesions in cratered flesh. She gagged whenever the all-too-common sickly-sweet, rotten-egg odor emanated from festering infections, especially when accompanied by the presence of maggots. She stuffed crevices in ripped flesh with lint to stanch bleeding before applying clean dressing to her patients' wounds.

With no organized ambulance corps in operation, sick and wounded soldiers were transported in make-shift ambulances—often nothing more than a crude, two-wheeled ox cart commandeered into service. Long journeys to the hospital, lurching and bouncing over miles of potholed roads, compounded many of the men's wounds.

Each night she stood watch like a solitary shepherd, guarding her flock of fitfully slumbering charges. When all fell silent, she replayed in her mind the gruesome scenes of the previous hours. Many dark nights, she sat at the bedside of a dying patient, or sometimes several, each of whom gripped her hands until the moment of death—as if afraid to let go of their earthbound existence. When each drew his final, sour breath, the duty fell on her to close his eyes and mouth and pray for God's mercy on his soul.

One evening, Rebecca sat in the largest room in her ward, watching over two soldiers who lay dying, though oblivious to their own suffering. They had been mercifully unconscious since they arrived, often beset by seizures, and their names and the names of their kin were unknown. Hollowness consumed her as the orderlies carried off their lifeless bodies after they expired. She had no names of loved ones to telegraph with the grave news.

✳ ✳ ✳

Days later, word of the catastrophe at Ball's Bluff shocked the Capital into turmoil. Even though casualties—more than 200 wounded and another 200 dead—were considerably fewer than at Bull Run, public outrage erupted. Citizens raged over the way most soldiers died and because of one who was among their number, President Lincoln's popular and charismatic friend, Senator Edward Baker. Many of the dead drowned or were shot in the back as they scrambled into the Potomac River to avoid rebel cannonade and the hailstorm of musket balls. Rigoring carcasses floated downstream as far south as the Capital and Mount Vernon, piling up wherever the river bent, in clear view of unwary spectators.

Some of the wounded landed in Rebecca's ward, adding to her existing flock of dysentery and typhoid patients. Her typhoid patients included two Indiana brothers who gave their names and other vital information when they arrived at the hospital. Seth Worth was twenty-three, and his brother James was four years younger. The Worth brothers joined the Harris Light Cavalry the preceding August, arriving in the Capital during late September. Each contracted typhoid during October while encamped south of Arlington, Virginia, near Bailey's Crossroads.

The two Indiana brothers plucked tender chords in Rebecca's memory. She revisited scenes of her own seventeen-year-old Willie's fever-ravaged last days. James Worth was first to slip into fitful unconsciousness, which often exploded into violent seizures. He passed from his world at the height of his last convulsion. His older brother followed the same course and died five days later. They were buried several yards apart in a cemetery on the grounds of the Soldiers' Home north of the Capital.

Rebecca stirred from her sleep before dawn on the morning after the elder Worth brother passed. A dream in which George lay on a distant battlefield in a pool of blood, gasping for breath, haunted her during the night. Her grogginess lifted at once. The letter she had received from Almira Cushing Fuller several days earlier remained unanswered. After scrambling to find paper and pen she wrote—

Columbian College Hospital
November 7, 1861

Dear Almira,

You must think it a long time before your letter is answered but if you know how my time was spent you would wonder that I got any time at all to write to dear friends. The bell rings in the morning at 6, for all hands to get up that can be dressed, and before breakfast I have to go my rounds with my quart bottle of medicine for my fever patients, then I go down five flights of stairs to eat my breakfast, then I have to look after 20 beds which have to be made, the patients all washed, and then their breakfast comes up which consists of tea, coffee, bread and butter. Then the sweeping process commences, and at half past eight o'clock the bell is rung again for the physicians call, and such a scrabbing to get on their beds and sit there till the surgeons have made their call. I then take my slate, go round with the surgeons, tell them what medicines they have taken the day before, also their food. When the blistering, poulticing, cupping is set down to each one, and when they have gone through my large room into my small one, where there are only five beds, and three wounded out of them, I commence my business of giving them their medicine, also applying blisters, spreading plasters, syringing their ears, dressing toes, bandaging legs which takes up all the time till the bell rings at twelve for dinner. After dinner if I sit down on the bed where the boys are, such a teasing "nurse please read my letter" or nurse please direct three letters for me or one of my boys is bleeding at the nose, or another is in chills, or another is vomiting, and another wants help to turn in bed, and then another to read, and a louder call still from a troublesome one "nurse can I have a Bologna sausage." All these and sometimes other things which are not so agreeable are added to the list. I have to laugh in spite of it all, and shut my eyes, and turn a deaf ear as I have many who have a streak of fun in them. I am graduating from one flight of stairs to the very top of the house, (which by the way is the pleasantest room in the house) and I expect when I get all through at this place, my hair will be the silver grey, and a small portion of that. A gentleman called to see me today from Washington whose name is Dr. L. A. Johnson and gave me a strong invitation to go to his house and spend a few days when I was tired, but when informed that the nurses had no privileges of that kind, nor not even a furlough he was quite disappointed, but will turn around and come and see me. I only wish you could take a bird's eye view of this place and see how happy I am with all my boys around me, some are full of fun, while others are despondent. I do not know as any inducement whatever would tempt me to come home, as I am contented and happy and have gained what I never had before, the red on my cheeks. I have warm feet and have made a friend of the steward of the bedding department and have got nicely fixed for the winter, as I shall have steam all over the house. Some of my former boys come to see me, and when I commence to read, they are sure to come. I have merchants, lawyers, mechanics, and the little sailor boy is not forgotten. I have privates, sergeants, colonels, etc. and the whole conversation throughout the wards is on the times and this cruel war. I am a confidant of the soldier, as he entrusts me with his lady's face, also money, revolver, watch, etc. I cannot stop any longer to write, so you will give my love to Mr. Fuller, Father, Mother, and the girls, Frank & Clara, and lots of kisses to my boy. Also tell Susie Currier that I have not forgotten her but will write sometime.

Good bye from Auntie.

My love to Mrs. Hartt, Sherman, Mary Duville.

Let Maria hear from me.

Several days later, visitors from Chelsea buoyed her spirits. Among them were Mayor Fay, Dr. Mason who pastored the Baptist Church, Mr. Bagnall, and Mr. Slade—husband of the elderly Methodist woman who sparked Rebecca's epiphany at Asbury Grove. Each bore gifts for her boys. The encouragement she enjoyed from their visits fortified her for the next wave.

Rebecca had barely finished preparing the last of twenty-six new beds when a train of litter bearers began snaking through the ward. "Give them any vacant bed you can find," she called out as she scurried to get them settled.

As one of the new patients was deposited in a bed, a litter bearer remarked, "They're all from the 11th Maine. There's scores of 'em."

She opened the patient's shirt and inspected the red, flat rash. She removed one sock, and the same measly blotches covered his foot. "Are all of them this far along?"

The litter bearer answered with an affirmative nod.

Another patient with a raspy cough called to her from across the room. "What will my poor mother say when I am laid away from her?"

Rebecca went to his bedside and managed to give a reassuring smile. "We shall not talk about laying anyone away just yet. We shall set our minds on getting you better." She checked inside his mouth. Small white spots were present, though not pervasive. His forehead was hot to the touch, his eyes inflamed.

She went from bed to bed, assessing her new patients.

A surgeon arrived and interrupted her. He said, "Your ward is now on quarantine until we get this infection under control. At the present rate, it may wipe out an entire regiment."

"All of my patients quarantined?" she asked.

"Yes, and you included. You are not to leave the ward. An orderly will deliver your meals."

"Yes, sir," she said. "I understand."

The measles quarantine eclipsed the Christmas season and stretched into the new year, leaving a wake of death in its path. After wasting away for weeks and reduced to a mere skeleton, the regiment's bugle boy called for his nurse. "Mother," he said in a reedy voice. "May I have my bugle?"

She turned to an orderly and directed him to request that it be brought up to the ward. When the bugle arrived, the young bugler was too weak to hold it on his own. The orderly placed the bugle in the emaciated soldier's hands then helped him raise it to his lips and hold it in place. With what little energy the faltering bugler had, he managed to blow two or three weak strains. His eyes lit up for an instant before the bugle's wavering tones joined his final breath as echoes in the night.

A few days later, she sat with another Maine boy who was thought to be on the cusp of recovery from measles, though his fever, fatigue, and headaches persisted. As she dabbed him with a cool, wet towel, she detected pus-filled spots. They were distinct eruptions rather than the blotchy rash of measles. She fought back panic as she opened his shirt to discover his torso was infested with the same oozing lesions. She sent word of the boy's condition to the surgeon-in-charge. He responded with instructions for her to isolate the patient in an empty room and sit with him alone during the night.

The ward surgeon blanched when he checked her patient during his rounds the next day. The lesions were starting to flatten and blacken.

"Smallpox," he whispered. "It's advancing rapidly. We must send him over to the smallpox ward at Carver Barracks."

"What shall we do if the infection spreads?" she asked.

"We cannot let that happen. Go downstairs at once and be inoculated. Then gather our entire supply of vaccine and administer it to every last soul in this hospital. Start at the top of the building and work your way down."

"Will it not be faster if the other nurses helped?" she asked.

"We do not know whether the infection has taken root elsewhere, and I wish not to expose our entire staff. If there must be a sacrificial lamb, due to your exposure to this patient, fate has chosen you."

After Rebecca finished inoculating every arm at Columbian College Hospital, news reached her from the Carver Barracks smallpox ward. The young Maine soldier who had been under her care died. She fell to her knees and wept. After a while, exhaustion and grief yielded to relief. At least no other cases of the wretched disease had been found.

* * *

Rumors had been whispered through the hospital—like an infestation of termites gnawing within the walls. Since Rebecca's arrival, she had chosen to ignore what she hoped were tall tales told behind the backs of her superiors. Then shortly after the new year, a young patient from Massachusetts limped up and planted himself in her path. "We're being cheated out of our meal allowance," he said. "The Government gives a certain amount for meat each day, but we rarely get any. When we do, it's tough and tasteless as boiled boot leather."

She furrowed her brow. "I will talk with the surgeons and see what can be done."

The soldier folded his arms across his chest. "If something isn't done, I shall write to Governor Andrew in Boston and see if he can solve the matter."

She mulled the complexities of hospital politics as he hobbled off. There was frequent contentious jockeying and wrangling within the ranks of officers and staff.

Several nurses and attendants had lost their positions during the three months she had been at the hospital. Each dismissal occurred curiously after an incident of bribery or theft had been exposed—offenses committed against defenseless patients by greedy hospital officials.

Rebecca sent an orderly to bring her a copy of *Army and Navy Regulations*. After reviewing the volume, she dispatched her attendant to the hospital steward with a request for her boys to be served meat for breakfast the following morning.

The attendant returned in short order with the steward's reply, "Mrs. Pomroy cannot have it; it is not allowed. She is the most extravagant nurse we have."

A proverb came to mind—one she had learned from her long-departed sea-captain father. "Still waters run deep." She had remained passive in the face of corruption long enough. The steward's indignation was the last straw.

Rebecca left her attendant to watch over her patients while she hastened downstairs to call on Dr. Crosby, the hospital's surgeon-in-charge. She found him in the officers' messroom finishing his noon meal.

"Doctor," she said with the sternness of a schoolmarm. "Is it not true that the government gives an allowance for certain ounces of meat per day?"

Doctor Crosby averted her glower. "I believe there was a provision somewhere of the kind, but the number to feed is so large and the army expenses so great that it is impossible to furnish it."

She angled into his field of vision. "Is there not an appropriation of money to cover it?"

"If it is supplied to your ward," he sputtered, "it will have to be given to all the rest."

"Why should it not be?" she asked. "All of the boys need it as much as mine."

He lowered his head.

She continued. "There are some smart boys on my ward who think they are being defrauded by officers in this hospital. I imagine more than one has a well-connected father at home who takes his son's welfare seriously. If the matter is not righted very soon, they will surely see to it that something is done."

Dr. Crosby surrendered a timid smile. "Tell your boys it will not be necessary to disturb their families with the matter. I shall deal with it."

The next morning the aroma of fried steak surprised all the patients at Columbian College Hospital, and Rebecca became known thereafter as "the woman who got us the beef."

CHAPTER NINETEEN

News of eleven-year-old Willie Lincoln's death rocked the Capital a few months after Rebecca arrived at Columbian College Hospital. The shock came as preparations were under way to commemorate President Washington's birthday. Miss Dix was one of the first to receive word. She scurried from her Fourteenth Street office, past the Treasury Building and across the broad lawn, to the President's House.

Dr. Stone met her in the vestibule at the mansion's entrance and led her upstairs to the family parlor where the president sat raking his fingers through his hair.

Lincoln rose from the sofa. His drawn countenance and sunken, bloodshot eyes evidenced his sorrow. He greeted Miss Dix. "Thank you for coming."

"Please accept my condolences," Miss Dix replied. "Dr. Stone tells me your boy Tad and Mrs. Lincoln require attendance."

Lincoln nodded. "Tad is afflicted by the same fever that took our Willie. Mrs. Lincoln is too distraught to leave her bed. She was up briefly this morning when the Cabinet and their wives came to offer their sympathies, but soon after they left, she became hysterical. I am at my wits' end. Any help you can offer is much appreciated."

Dr. Stone added, "I put her to bed and administered laudanum. Both she and Tad require constant care, better than the old colored nurse is able to provide."

"Could you recommend someone?" Lincoln asked.

Dix already had a name in mind. "Yes, sir. There is an excellent nurse in my corps. She is intimately familiar with the typhoid and with the emotions of losing a precious child. She is my best nurse—reliable, reserved, observant, capable, gentle."

"Yes," Lincoln replied. "She sounds just right."

"I shall bring her at once."

Miss Dix rushed back to her office and sped her carriage up Sixteenth Street, one-and-a-half miles to Columbian College Hospital. On arriving, she sought out Dr. Crosby and informed him that Mrs. Pomroy's services were required immediately at the President's House.

"We have no one to replace her," he protested.

"The president's needs are paramount," she replied. "The nation and its principles are the best hope for humanity, and it cannot endure without Mr. Lincoln giving his full attention to his duties. Mrs. Pomroy is better prepared than any nurse I know for shepherding the president and his family through the valley of illness and death in which they are mired. Please summon her."

Rebecca's stomach looped into knots over being ordered to report to Dr. Crosby in the middle of her duties. On her way to his office, she stopped in Mrs. Russell's ward, hoping for a word of encouragement. "I may have ventured too far out onto the limb when I demanded meat for our boys," she said. "I'm afraid that bough is about to be sawed off by Dr. Crosby."

Mrs. Russell offered a reassuring smile. "If they thought they could afford to lose you, they would have sacked you on the spot and not given us the beef. You're one of the best nurses this place has seen."

"You've been so kind to me since I came here."

"I go out of my way for people I respect, and who show respect for me."

"Thank you." Rebecca sighed. "However, I cannot think of another reason he would call me in for an audience."

"If they sack you," Mrs. Russell replied, "you can count on me to be right out the door behind you."

"Let's hope that won't be necessary."

Rebecca entered Dr. Crosby's office and braced herself at the sight of Miss Dix standing beside him. Her reprimand and dismissal were surely imminent. But the words coming from Miss Dix jumbled and somersaulted in Rebecca's mind—something about President Lincoln.

The next thing Miss Dix said was clear. "I need you to be ready to go in ten minutes."

Rebecca replied, "I don't understand what's going on."

"I said you have ten minutes to pack some belongings. You will be attending to the president's family."

"What about my boys?"

"They will be cared for," Dr. Crosby replied.

"You don't have enough nurses as it is," Rebecca argued. "Besides, some of my boys have only a few days of life left. I must hold their hands in their final hours."

Miss Dix shook her head. "You must do what the Army requires of you. Now go upstairs and pack. You can say goodbye to your boys but be quick about it. I will be waiting in my carriage."

As Miss Dix's carriage clattered down Sixteenth Street, Rebecca replayed mental images of the last moments she shared with her boys. They had pleaded nearly in unison, "Don't leave us, Mother." She gave each of them a parting hand and for the last time she adjusted the pillows of those near death. The expressions on their faces were imprinted in her mind. She murmured, "Oh, if I could only have stayed with my boys."

Miss Dix said, "Dear child, you don't know the Divine work you have been called to. Others can look after your boys, but I have chosen you out of two hundred and fifty nurses under my supervision to minister to the head of the nation. What a privilege is yours!"

* * *

Lincoln left Tad under the care of Mary Jane Welles—wife of Secretary of the Navy Gideon Welles—while he went to check on Mrs. Lincoln. When he entered his wife's chamber, he found the curtains drawn and the room dark. Eliza Browning—the wife of his close friend, Illinois Senator Orville Browning—sat at the First Lady's bedside. Eliza said that Mrs. Lincoln demanded the curtains be closed and insisted on more medication to help her sleep.

As Lincoln opened the drapes, Miss Lizabeth, his wife's mulatto dressmaker and confidant, entered the room accompanied by Rebecca.

Lincoln took Rebecca's hand. "I am glad to see you. You will surely be a comfort to us. My wife is hysterical over our boy's death, and another son is stricken with fever."

Rebecca had already learned from Miss Lizabeth that the lady of the house had a kind heart but could be difficult even on a good day, and the present day was a day from hell for the entire household.

Rebecca replied, "Sir, I am humbled that Miss Dix thinks me worthy to serve your family. But I must confess. I worry over leaving the young soldiers in my ward at the hospital."

"You mustn't worry." Lincoln offered a weary smile. "Miss Dix is a capable administrator. She will see that they are well-tended to." He glanced at his wife lying in her bed in a laudanum-induced fog. "Come, Mrs. Pomroy. Mrs. Browning and Miss Lizabeth can watch my wife while I introduce you to Tad."

Lincoln led her across the hall, through the Prince of Wales Room, and into an adjacent bedroom where two doctors attended to his eight-year-old son. After introducing Rebecca, he left them to discuss Tad's medications while he walked down the hall to his office.

That evening at half past six, Lincoln checked on Tad and found him sleeping peacefully. Rebecca reported he had been tossing and turning earlier, whimpering several times he would never see Willie anymore.

"They were inseparable," Lincoln said. He gazed at Tad for a moment then invited her to join him in the family dining room. She thanked him for the courtesy but insisted on staying at Tad's bedside.

After supper, Lincoln and Senator Browning viewed Willie in his coffin in the downstairs Green Parlor. As Browning described the revolutionary embalming technique the doctors had used—a process proven in Europe to keep bodies preserved in nearly perfect condition for a decade or longer—Lincoln's knees buckled. After steadying himself, he rushed upstairs to his office and locked the door behind him. He sat in a chair by a window and sobbed.

When the clock on the mantle chimed ten, he emerged from a mental fog and fixed his gaze on sparse embers nestled among smoldering ash in the fireplace. His little dog Jip, a mutt he rescued the previous autumn while reviewing troops in the field, nuzzled him. He reached back in his memory to recall the moments since viewing Willie's lifeless form in the coffin, but all was a blur.

His thoughts turned to Tad. He leapt from his chair and rushed, with little Jip close on his heels, to his son's bedroom to find the boy asleep. Rebecca was still seated at his bedside.

"How is he?" Lincoln asked.

"Little changed. His fever remains the same as when I arrived." She fidgeted with the small green bottle in her hands. "I am hoping Dr. Sappington's miracle pills will keep the fever from worsening. I've been pondering whether to wake him for another dosage. Sleep is sometimes the best medicine."

"How's his rash?" Lincoln asked.

"It has neither advanced nor retreated."

Lincoln set a chair beside her and leaned to touch Tad's forehead. "The fever seems to have lessened."

"I opened a window," she said. "The cool night air gives

that impression." She glanced down at Jip. "Does he follow you everywhere?"

"His loyalty is unmatched."

They sat in silence for a while, then he asked, "What does Mr. Pomroy do while you attend to our soldiers?"

"I am widowed," she said.

"I am truly sorry. What of your family?"

"My father was a sea captain." She folded her hands in her lap. "He was rarely home and died when I was a girl. After that, life was lean. Mother raised us four girls and our younger brother on her own, sewing for an upholsterer. Daniel and I married when I was nineteen, and he was sickly even then. We were together for two dozen years. During the last twelve he grew progressively worse. His body finally gave out two years ago and he joined two of our children in the other world. Our Clara Jane died five years ago. She was eight. Willie passed on when he was seventeen, two years after Clara Jane. I have one son remaining, George. He joined the army when they first called for volunteers."

"Did you always feel that you could say, thy will be done?" Lincoln asked.

"No," she replied. "Not at the first blow, nor the second, not even the third. After burying Daniel, I drifted for the next year and a half, feeble and heartsick." She shifted in her chair. "God met me when I attended a camp-meeting. With my faith restored, I answered the call to serve our sick and wounded soldiers. My preparation was nineteen years in the school of affliction that began when I held my sister's hand as she drew her last pain-riddled breath."

"Watching our Willie waste away," he said, "and seeing him laid out in that coffin—it's as if my heart has been ripped out and carved into a thousand pieces. I don't know if I can carry on."

Rebecca recounted the many times she almost gave up. She had often been angry with God. "But something inside me," she said, "sparked a glimmer of hope."

"What made you decide to become a nurse?" he asked.

"When I was a girl," she replied, "my father took me along when he went among the forgotten families of sailors who had been lost at sea. We took them gifts to help soften the pain of their poverty. My heart was touched by what I saw, by the desperate cries of hungry children smaller than myself, by the pleas of their poor mothers. The children were like my Olivers—from the Dickens novel. I resolved to follow in Papa's footsteps and shine a light of hope on those children, but circumstances steered me far away from my youthful dreams. I offered my services to the nurses' corps as a way of returning to the path God laid before me all those years ago."

"Why? Why?" Lincoln cried out. "This trial heaped on me is more than I can stand."

"The Almighty will sustain you as he did me," she answered. "Thousands of prayers go up for you daily, and for your family."

Lincoln fell to his knees, sobbing.

She knelt beside him and intoned a hopeful psalm.

The next morning when Lincoln failed to show for breakfast, William Slade, the middle-aged, light-skinned chief butler, took a tray upstairs to the president's bedroom. "Sir, shouldn't you be getting dressed for President Washington's birthday ceremonies at the Capitol?"

"I won't be going," Lincoln replied.

"I suppose there are some Democrats who will be pleased not to see you, but your nation needs you. There's a war going on."

"I will not be going," Lincoln repeated.

"Be that as it may, you look a sight. How do you think young Master Tad will feel if he sees you in this condition, not to mention Mrs. Lincoln? Your gloom is not going to cheer them in the least. Besides, Johnson is on his way up to trim you."

Shortly after Slade left, Lincoln's barber and confidential messenger, William Johnson, a former slave in his twenties, entered the room.

As Lincoln rolled out of bed and sat in the barber's chair, William spoke softly. "I'm so sorry about young Willie. Maybe if we clean you up, your burdens might seem a bit easier to carry."

Lincoln scoffed. "Not even Merlin-the-Magician can help me this morning."

William worked the razor along the leather strop. "Now just sit back and try to put your sorrows aside."

"I don't want—"

"Hush. I didn't say to talk about your tribulations. Just relax and let me freshen you up."

Several times William tried to engage in light conversation, but Lincoln's silence made dialog impossible.

Afterwards, Lincoln went into his office and shut the door. Rain drummed the windows as evening fell, and a truth struck him—the day had passed. He missed Washington's birthday ceremony. He plodded to the water closet, doused his face, and went to check on Tad.

As he entered Tad's room, the sight of Rebecca at the boy's bedside brought him a modicum of relief. He pulled up a chair and sat beside her as he had the previous evening. "How is he?"

"Stable," she whispered. "He slept all afternoon. No signs of discomfort."

"I fret he may take the same turn as his brother. I could not go on living if I should lose them both."

"We can hope and pray," she replied.

Lincoln folded his hands in his lap, and they sat in silence for a long while. Then he said, "Tell me again how you obtained your faith in God and how He sustained you through your afflictions."

"There isn't much more than what I told you last night."

"Please, tell me again and do not leave out the slightest detail. I am trying as hard as I can to place my trust in the Divine, but I cannot seem to."

She repeated her story, adding more details—she held not only her husband's and children's hands until they drew their final breaths, but also nursed a beloved sister, sister-in-law, mother-in-law, her own mother, two of her husband's elderly aunts, and neighbors, all of whom passed from this world under her care. She told him she never had the benefit of formal schooling but had learned to read and love literature, nonetheless. She talked of rising each morning as a girl—even before the others in her household—so she could finish her share of the piecework and still have time for the urchin children and their indigent mothers on the streets of North Boston.

He recalled for her the many trials of his life and mused at the common chords that entwined their individual experiences. He added, as a boy of three years old, he had watched his angel mother weep inconsolably as they buried little Tommy, his infant brother. Although he was too young at the time to comprehend the meaning of death, her anguish passed into his own soul.

Rebecca nodded her understanding. "As a girl, I watched Papa and Mama bury two infant sons. I carried a hollowness in my heart over many years. Not until I lost my own children was I fully able to grasp their pain."

"How did you come to say, 'He doeth all things well?'" he asked.

She repeated all that she had said the previous night about falling into such darkness that she lost the will to live, but she was rescued from the depths of despair by a saintly old woman at Asbury Grove.

At last, Lincoln said, "The principles you describe are easily understood. It's the practice that is so difficult." Then he bowed his head and murmured, "Oh, why is it?"

After a long silence she replied, "God sees the whole of eternity while we see only the speck of time and merely the things which lie in front of us. Sometimes our calamities help others learn to practice mercy. It is also said that suffering teaches us humility and dependence on the Almighty. In ancient times a good shepherd would break the leg of a wayward lamb to discourage it from wandering again. While we obsess over protecting our bodies and temporal possessions, we overlook perils to our souls. Afflictions can help us focus on eternity."

"I would offer each of my limbs to be broken," Lincoln replied. "I would suffer one hundred, no one thousand lashes of the whip to appease the Almighty and win His favor. Anything, if only He would bring poor Willie back."

"That is not how the Lord works," Rebecca said. "Everything that comes to us from God is free. He extracts nothing in return. Trust God who doeth all things well."

"I shall tell you a story if I may." He drew his lips in a tight line as thin as a dagger's edge.

"Of course," she said.

"When I was out on the circuit with a cabal of lawyers in a modest little town, we spotted a finely dressed young woman in front of the hotel across the town square. She stood staring at a piano in the back of a wagon and called for our help. After we unloaded it and set it up in the parlor, she serenaded us. Her last song was *He Doeth All Things Well*. The final refrain left me weak-kneed and humbled—Oh! that cup of bitterness ... let not my heart rebel ... God gave ... He took ... He will restore ... He doeth all things well." Lincoln's voice pitched. "I have always hoped I could embrace the sentiment of the song, but circumstances have nurtured seeds of doubt in my mind."

"Your heart can heal," Rebecca said in a gentle voice. "Grieve for a while. Rail at God if you must. But do not rebel against Him. Remain faithful and he will restore you and make you stronger than before."

Lincoln patted her hand. "Thank you. I should look in on my wife, and maybe you can go check on her after a while. I do wish she could find some reprieve from her own grief."

* * *

Three days later when Willie was to be laid away, Mrs. Lincoln remained bedridden. Only in the last moments before the funeral service began did she agree to go downstairs and bid her fallen child goodbye. Miss Lizabeth and Eliza Browning helped her, still in her nightclothes, to the Green Parlor where Willie lay. When Mrs. Lincoln gazed at his waxen face, she shrieked and threw herself over the coffin, sobbing—her arms spread wide as if clutching shipwrecked debris to save herself from roiling swells. Miss Lizabeth and Eliza Browning came by her side, calmed her, and took her back to bed.

All the downstairs mirrors were covered in mourning drapery, their frames wrapped with black, and the glass concealed by white crepe. Mirrors were not needed to reflect Lincoln's grief as he viewed his son laid out in his little brown suit. No matter how many times he had buried loved ones, death's dagger pierced his soul as if for the first time. On this occasion, the dagger's thrusts came like a cannonade.

While Lincoln lingered beside Willie's lifeless form, mustering the willpower to murmur his final goodbye, an old nemesis—melancholy—cloaked him. An inaudible chorus of groans reverberated in his soul.

He wept as the household servants took their turns bidding Willie farewell. Their sobs echoed into the lobby.

When Rebecca approached, she whispered to him, "Look for strength from on high."

Lincoln replied, "I shall go to God with my sorrows."

She stepped to the coffin, kissed the tips of her fingers and pressed them to Willie's alabaster forehead. Though she never knew the boy, her heart twinged as she revisited memories of a son and daughter laid out in their coffins.

William Johnson's chin quivered when his turn came. Slade draped an arm over Johnson's shoulders and walked him back to his quarters.

Nature was unrestrained at that hour. Storm clouds, pushed by violent winds, raced through the sky. The room darkened and windows rattled as if the entire mansion quaked with sorrow. On the portico and out on the drive, torrents of rain pummeled a large crowd. Some fortunate souls avoided the storm by cramming into the lobby. None of them had any hope of joining the cadre of generals, commodores, government officials, family, and friends who followed Lincoln into the East Room where the ceremony took place.

As invited guests settled into seats, Lincoln's eldest son, Bob, sat stiff-backed at his side. His demeanor was more fitting for a general's aide de camp than a mourning brother. Lincoln slumped forward and bowed his head as tears spilled out of him.

Reverend Dr. Phineas Gurley's sermon caught in Lincoln's throat like a bitter pill. Consolations from women like Rebecca and Miss Lizabeth, who had suffered life's tribulations, were one thing. Words of comfort from a man who had never suffered personal calamity and whose business was the Almighty were a different matter. The eternal blessings Gurley recited were dim and far removed compared to the sorrows that lacerated the anguished father's heart. The preacher's words provoked questions for which Lincoln's soul demanded answers. If a tender boy's death, if the deaths of thousands of young men and boys on battlefields across the land, were examples of a Divine who doeth all things well, what hope did heaven hold? Was it not cruel for the Almighty to test virtue with affliction? How could a future ever brighten when unbearable misery hung like a perpetual storm over one's remaining days?

By the conclusion of the ceremony, rainsqualls had subsided, giving way to a monotonous drizzle.

The funeral procession slogged through muddy streets toward Oak Hill Cemetery in Georgetown. Twelve pall bearers led the way, each with a wreath of flowers on his arm and a yard of white silk tied around his hat. Then came the hearse, drawn by two white horses, their legs and underbellies collecting layers of grime as they plodded through muck and mire along the route. The president's private carriage, drawn by two mud-spattered black horses, was next in line, followed by the Cabinet and their families, a host of private carriages, and last of all, the colored help on foot.

Following a brief ceremony in the intimate cemetery chapel, workmen carried Willie's casket to a borrowed vault where he was to remain until the Lincolns returned to Illinois.

CHAPTER TWENTY

Mrs. Lincoln summoned Rebecca to her room early one morning, several days after Willie's funeral. She was keen to hear news of Tad's condition.

"Much improved," Rebecca replied.

"Are you certain he's not rallying before he ... it happened with our Willie, you know."

Rebecca adjusted Mrs. Lincoln's pillow. "I wasn't here to observe Willie in his illness, but Dr. Stone tells me Tad's course is very different. In the week I have been here, Tad's symptoms have lessened. His rash has stopped spreading, and there is no sign of splotching."

"I will not get my hopes up," Mrs. Lincoln said. "I fear God has forsaken us. He punishes us by taking away so lovely a child as our Willie and he is likely not yet done with us. We have become so wrapped up in the world, so devoted to our political advancement that we think of little else."

"I do not believe that is so," Rebecca said.

"It is such a strange thing, that you can bear to nurse the children of strangers after your own family's devastation. How is such a thing possible?"

"I choose to hold fast to the hope we will see our loved ones again in heaven." Rebecca's heart wrenched.

"My dear friend, Mary Jane, and Mr. Welles have lost five of their own and she clings to the same belief."

"You are fortunate to have Mrs. Welles and her husband as friends," Rebecca replied. "She was with Tad all through the night and just now went home to rest. Mr. Lincoln is with him now."

"In Willie's last days, Mary Jane was a Godsend," Mrs. Lincoln said. "She loved him as if he were her own. She and her husband came at once when Mr. Lincoln sent word that Willie had gone to be with the angels."

"Mrs. Welles is a strong woman, as are you."

"I suppose that is so," Mrs. Lincoln replied. "Though we are different in so many ways. I have always imagined, if I should be tried and tested as she has been, my faith would sustain me—it did so after my Eddie died years ago. But it has not in this case. Willie is our idolized one. If I could only believe he is happier now than he was when he was on earth." Mrs. Lincoln pressed her hand to her chest. "It would be so much easier to endure my grief. But I am not able yet to say, His will be done."

Miss Lizabeth appeared in the doorway.

Mrs. Lincoln acknowledged her and remarked, "Here we have another good friend."

"Young Master Tad is asking for his nurse," Miss Lizabeth said. "Seems he only wants to be attended by his papa or Mrs. Pomroy. Don't worry. I can look over Mrs. Lincoln while you go see to him."

Rebecca crossed through the Prince of Wales Room into Tad's sickroom. The boy sat up as she entered.

She balked at finding the president seated at a child-sized desk near his son's bed then proceeded to Tad's side and cupped his forehead.

Lincoln glanced up from a stack of papers. "I am not sure which of us is more pleased to see you."

"I didn't mean to disturb your work." She gestured to the papers on his makeshift desk.

"Not at all," he replied. "I bring my work here, so I'm not distracted with worry. It brings me comfort to be near him."

"Sir," Rebecca said.

"There is no need to be so formal," he replied.

"Very well. But there is a matter we seem to be ignoring."

"Go on ..."

"How are you faring?" she asked.

"I have precious little time to worry about myself."

"I worry about you."

"I appreciate your concern, but you mustn't." He returned his attention to a document on the desk.

"On the contrary, as your family's nurse and as a countryman, I must."

"In that case, when I take note of any matters concerning my health, I shall bring them to your attention."

She crossed her arms. "And I shall consider it my duty to make sure you take note of any which I observe. Not only physical, but spiritual also. After all, the two are intertwined."

"I see why your boys call you, 'Mother.'"

✳ ✳ ✳

Lincoln left Tad's room a few moments before five o'clock that afternoon and wandered downstairs to the Green Parlor. He locked the door behind himself, staggered to the place where Willie's coffin had been on display exactly one week earlier, and dropped to his knees.

"Why, oh why," he mumbled. The weight of despair dropped him to his knees. Tears flowed. In part, he envied his wife—shutting herself in her room, dulling her heartache with laudanum, shrouding misery in a mental fog. He didn't begrudge her any of that. He only wished he had some place to lock away his anguish so he could soldier on and bear the weight of the mantle that had been thrust on him. He recalled the patriarch's lament, "better is he ... which hath not yet been, who hath not seen the evil work that is done under the sun."

Later that night, Lincoln rode off to Oak Hill Cemetery accompanied by William Johnson. A bright moon illumined the short ride to Oak Hill as frigid air numbed their cheeks. An image of Willie lying in a cold granite vault flashed through his mind. His blood ran cold.

At the cemetery, a caretaker offered to lead them to the crypt. Lincoln thanked him for the courtesy but reminded him that he knew his own way. The caretaker insisted on serving as their guide and stayed outside the burial chamber with William while Lincoln went inside.

Lincoln knelt on the cold floor and caressed the rosewood trim of the child-sized coffin. He glided his palm over the cool metallic lid. His hand came to rest on a latch, his breath caught. He unfastened the lid and raised it gently. Locked it upright. Willie lay before him, calm, peaceful, as if he merely slept. He lamented, "Oh, if you were only asleep." He reached under the boy, cradled him, brushed a wisp of hair into place.

"Willie," he murmured. Salted whispers of grief traced the contours of his face and found the corners of his mouth. "I should not have allowed you to play so near that canal full of sewage and disease. I should have called you and your brother in when the weather turned foul, or at least told you to put on your coats. You cannot know how much I wish it was me locked up in this place instead of you. You had so much to offer this world. Your smile, your laughter, your wit, your inquisitive mind. You lifted me. Without you to cheer me, how can I carry the burdens that bear down on me? My load is so heavy. Your brother, Taddie. He calls for you every hour. Your Mother. Your dear Mother. Almost insane. Oh, poor Willie! Why did you have to leave us so soon?"

After hours of weeping, stroking his boy's marbled cheeks and silky locks, spilling out his grief to Heaven, Lincoln laid his son's lifeless frame back in the casket. He rose and called for William and the caretaker to help him lift Willie's coffin into the vault.

As Lincoln and William returned to their horses, a swirling wind howled through the sturdy oaks that lined their path, as if a chorus of ghosts and ghouls chided them for disturbing the sleeping dead.

The night fell silent once they passed out of the cemetery, and the air remained stone-cold quiet for their journey back to the mansion.

CHAPTER TWENTY-ONE

Rebecca packed her trunk three weeks after arriving at the President's House to care for the family. The time had come for her to return to the hospital. As she closed the lid, she gazed around the luxurious furnishings of the Prince of Wales Room. She had experienced nothing so grand in her life. Mary Jane Welles said Prince Albert Edward, heir to the British throne, had slept in the suite on his stay at the mansion in 1860. The prince was born the same year as her Willie.

The mansion lacked something in comparison to the hospital. Despite its battened-down windows, bare walls, thin mattresses, odors of disease and death, and the moans, groans, wails of suffering souls, the hospital was home. The President's House was not.

William Johnson appeared in the doorway. "If you are all packed, I'll take your trunk down to the carriage."

"Thank you," Rebecca replied. "Give me a minute to say goodbye to Mrs. Lincoln."

"Take your time. I am at your disposal."

While she'd been in residence with the Lincoln family, she had learned that William was more than the president's valet and confidential messenger. He was the keeper of everything and anyone Lincoln valued highly.

Rebecca crossed the hall into Mrs. Lincoln's chamber where the First Lady was sitting up in bed, passing the time with Mary Jane Welles and Miss Lizabeth.

"I came by to say goodbye before I return to the hospital," Rebecca said.

"You will be sorely missed," Mary Jane replied.

Miss Lizabeth added, "You have been a great help."

"I do so hate for you to leave," Mrs. Lincoln lamented. "Come here and let me give you a kiss."

Rebecca approached and leaned forward to receive Mrs. Lincoln's kiss on her cheek. Mrs. Lincoln then turned her cheek to Rebecca who returned the gesture.

"Mary Jane is exactly right," Mrs. Lincoln said as she held Rebecca's hand. "You will be sorely missed." She released Rebecca's hand and gave her an envelope. "You must come back whenever you are able. Here is a letter for Miss Dix. It is my earnest plea that she allows you to come often to stay with us."

"I will come when my duties allow," she replied. "But I cannot make any promises."

On her way out, Rebecca embraced Mary Jane and Miss Lizabeth in turn, thanking them for their friendship. When she stepped out into the hallway she almost collided with Tad. It was the bleating goat that warned her to watch her step. A few feet from his mother's bedroom door, Tad knelt in the hallway, attempting to harness his goat to a chair. Rebecca lowered her voice an octave or two. "You should not overexert yourself. You're still not fully well."

He struggled at looping a piece of rope around the goat's neck.

She thought better of her reaction and began laughing. "Well, I suppose if you cannot go outside to play on the lawn, the next best thing is to bring the outdoors inside."

Tad stared up at her and his chin began to tremor. He said, "Do you think Willie is watching me? I want to show him I can harness a goat all by myself."

Rebecca stooped and wiped his tears. He threw his arms around her and sobbed. As she held him and whispered soothing words, memories washed over her.

On those many occasions when she held the hands of dying loved ones and friends, she had no time or life, or spirit left in her to be the mother her children needed. When her Willie beamed with pride over the launching of a ship he had helped ready for voyage, she was so consumed with grief over Clara Jane's death that she refused to attend the christening ceremony. When George left to join his army unit, she shut herself up in her room.

She glanced back at Mrs. Lincoln's bedroom door. Her heart pinched. She reached with one hand for the rope. "May I help?"

"No," Tad replied. "I want to do it myself."

"I'll leave you to it, then. I'm off to see your father. But I need you to understand I must go back to the hospital to see to my other boys who have been in the war."

"Will you come back?" he asked.

"Yes. And very soon, I hope."

Rebecca kissed the top of his head and left him to the goat and harness. Then she angled through the packed reception area outside the president's office, passing callers who were anxious for a chance to lay their petitions before the nation's Chief Magistrate. The president's secretary smiled and gestured to the doorway. "Go ahead," he said.

Lincoln stood when Rebecca entered his office and held her hands in his. "My dear Mrs. Pomroy," he said. "You have been a Godsend. I speak for Tad and Mrs. Lincoln, as well as myself, when I say you are as family to us. And when you are an old woman, please tell your grandchildren how indebted the nation is to you for holding up my hands in time of trouble. I might have come completely undone these past weeks without your ministrations, and we would not have wanted the rebellion to get off the hook that easily."

"If I have been able to serve our nation's Moses, even in the smallest way, it has been my honor. However, I must return to my boys who are in desperate need, to say nothing of relieving the other nurses from the added burden they have carried while I have been gone. The army is shorthanded."

William appeared in the doorway with a bouquet of flowers. "Ready, sir?"

Lincoln took the bouquet and gave it to Rebecca. "These are for you. I understand Mrs. Lincoln instructed the gardener to collect them for you from the conservatory, so that your hands shall not be entirely unoccupied on your ride back to the hospital."

A knot rose in Rebecca's throat. "I suppose it is goodbye."

Lincoln gestured to the door. "I shall escort you to the hospital."

"That is very kind, but unnecessary," she replied.

"Nonsense. It is my privilege. And I shall make it a point to exercise that privilege whenever you come to see us, which we all hope will be often."

Rebecca blushed. "Then I suppose the matter is out of my hands."

Lincoln tugged at his cuffs. "I have wanted to tell you how much I value your friendship. I am acquainted with others whose lives have been marked by loss and grief, but none understand my heart better than you. In many ways, our lives have mirrored one another. You have emerged from affliction stronger than you might have become without such severe trials. I, on the other hand, am still searching my way through, and I trust your wise counsel. You are an inspiration to this tired soul, and I owe you a great debt for the help you have given me and my family."

She blushed. "Your family is dear to me as well."

✳ ✳ ✳

Lincoln returned from escorting Rebecca to the hospital that afternoon at almost five o'clock—twenty-one days to the hour after Willie's time on earth had passed. Images of his visits to Willie's crypt had followed him the entire day—frigid air stinging his eyes and chafing his lips along the ride to the cemetery. The hollowness of the crypt. Willie's alabaster cheeks and wispy locks.

Rather than going upstairs to his office, Lincoln closed himself in the Green Parlor, accompanied only by little Jip, and locked the door. He fell to his knees, begging to know why the Almighty saw fit to take away his perfect son—the bright star of his life.

He demanded answers. What good had come from the afflictions heaped upon him in all his time? Why must children suffer for their fathers' sins, even unto the third or fourth generation? How much punishment must he, must the nation endure before the Lord is satisfied?

He gazed up to heaven and cried out, "Oh, why did you have to take him from us so soon?" He sobbed. "Lord, can you not see that I am now the most miserable man living. If what I feel were equally distributed to all humankind, there would not be one cheerful soul on the earth. I beg of you. Release me from my misery or let me die."

✳ ✳ ✳

When Rebecca returned to her ward, she attended to a new patient who arrived during her absence, thirty-five-year-old Thomas Mack from Massachusetts. He suffered from delirium. A battle raged in his head—beat, beat, beat ... faster, faster ... rata-tat-tat ... drummer boy ... forward ... attack ... attack. He had wheezed as he sucked for air while ripping each word from his lungs. She draped cold towels over him for several days to reduce the fever, but her efforts bore little fruit.

She considered it a tiny miracle, when a couple of weeks later, still hanging to life by a thread, his fever ebbed enough that he could achieve spurts of consciousness. In some of those moments, he was lucid.

His patient record listed some of the necessary details—captured at Ball's Bluff more than four months prior, confined at Richmond under horrid conditions, exchanged only weeks ago, emaciated, pneumonia.

She asked, "Where's your home?"

"Mayo," he said.

"My home is ... was ...," she paused. "It doesn't matter. I'm from Chelsea."

"They told me I'd meet a good Massachusetts mother ... if I held on ... until you came back."

"I'm certain Mrs. Russell has given you excellent care."

"She is efficient," he replied. "But anybody's mother, she isn't."

A spasm of dry heaves returned, doubling him over— he had given up the last traces of sputum hours earlier.

He languished through the late afternoon and into the night. Profuse sweat soaked his nightclothes, and the redness around his pupils deepened. He winced each time he strained to draw a satisfying breath, and his lungs rebelled, triggering new coughing spells. No longer deep spasms but shallow sputtering.

She stroked his placid hand as he sank back into the bed and fell unconscious.

By dawn, his life reached its conclusion. As two orderlies transferred him to a stretcher and covered his body, Rebecca laid her hand on his chest and murmured, "Another cherished son returns home."

One of the orderlies replied, "No ma'am. He ain't goin' home. Just to the Soldiers' Home Cemetery up the road. We been sending a lot of the boys there lately."

The same orderly drove Rebecca to the President's House the next day, after they picked up supplies at the Sanitary Commission office. She told him he needn't wait. She would find a way back to the hospital, even if she had to take a city streetcar to the end of the line and walk the rest of the way.

An anxious mood hung over the waiting area outside the president's office as she reached the second-floor landing. She paused to eavesdrop on a conversation. The pitch in one man's voice telegraphed his alarm over rumors that the rebellion's *Merrimack*—a sunken Union frigate, later raised by the rebel navy and covered with iron plating—was running up the Potomac to bombard the city. Only a month earlier, the rebel ironclad defeated three Union warships within one-hundred-and-thirty nautical miles of the capital. The man's companion urged calm.

Lincoln's private secretary, young John Hay, emerged from his office and crossed over to greet Rebecca. "Is he expecting you?" he asked.

"No," she replied. "Don't bother him. I'm sure he has much on his mind right now. I shall just go down the hall and look in on Mrs. Lincoln."

"She will be happy to see you. Anything that pleases her makes the rest of us happy, too." He started to turn away but hesitated. "I shall let him know you are here."

"That's not necessary."

"He will be glad to know you'll be putting Mrs. Lincoln in a good mood."

Rebecca offered a polite smile and turned down the hallway toward Mrs. Lincoln's chamber. After knocking, she eased open the door and stepped inside to find the First Lady in bed with the curtains still drawn, even with the morning well under way.

"Go away," Mrs. Lincoln groaned.

"It's Rebecca. I came to see how you are doing."

Mrs. Lincoln sat up, her tone welcoming, revealing an instant change in mood. "Oh, my dear friend. Come and sit with me."

"Shall I open the drapes?" Rebecca asked.

"Yes. Seeing daylight may give my life a little spark."

Rebecca opened the curtains, letting sunlight fill the room, "Has Mary Jane come to call of late?" she asked.

"She was here all of yesterday. We had a pleasant time. She is the best of friends, though I have not made many since we arrived in this wretched city."

Rebecca adjusted a pillow to help Mrs. Lincoln sit more comfortably.

Mrs. Lincoln asked, "How are things at the hospital? When I feel better, I must accompany Mary Jane on one of her visits to look in on your poor boys."

"We have parted with a number of nurses who would not answer after failing to report for their shifts. Another dear nurse died from fatigue. She was overtaxed and would not go home to rest until she was called to heaven." Rebecca pressed her tongue to the roof of her mouth and held it there until a wave of sorrow dissolved. "I am now in charge of the fourth floor where there are eighty beds to look after, which is more than I feel able to do. There has been so much trouble about the nurses that I am doing the work of three. God helping me, I will do all that in me lies."

"How are your boys faring?" Mrs. Lincoln asked.

Rebecca sighed. "Many are plagued with measles these days, and of course, some of the wounded must die, and those who survive will go home to very hard lives."

"How I wish for this war and all its misery to end."

"I agree," Rebecca said. "But in the midst of trials and afflictions, God can do a great work in each of our lives."

Over the balance of the morning and into early afternoon, Rebecca recounted the sufferings she endured from her fourteenth year until that thunderstorm at Asbury Grove. How drawing close to God continues to sustain her in her darkest hours.

Mrs. Lincoln whimpered. "I fear I could never be so happy as you. How I wish I could."

A memory struck Rebecca—George on his way to join the 13th Massachusetts. It was as though she had been swallowed into an abyss, or more like Jonah, wallowing in the belly of a whale. "I once felt the same," she said. "But I can assure you it is possible. Only trust in God's goodness, and peace will come to you as you have never known it before."

Mrs. Lincoln wiped her tears. "You are such an angel to try and lift my spirits. I shall make an effort to do all that you have said. But I am certain I have kept you away from your boys for far too long today." She rang the bell to summon one of the household staff.

When a maid appeared, Mrs. Lincoln instructed her, "Run downstairs to the conservatory and tell the gardener I wish for him to cut a bouquet of the richest flowers for Mrs. Pomroy to take with her."

"You are so kind." Rebecca offered a weak smile. The memories she had shared and the depth of Mrs. Lincoln's grief sapped her energy.

"Just a little something to bring some cheer to your ward."

"Thank you." Rebecca leaned and kissed Mrs. Lincoln's cheek.

"Now, you better not leave without peeking in on little Tad. He will be out of sorts if you don't. He misses you terribly."

"Of course."

"And please come see us as often as you are able."

Rebecca turned and smiled as she reached the doorway. "I shall." She walked down the hall to the family parlor where she found Tad and Lincoln stretched out on a sofa.

Lincoln glanced up from reading to Tad and held his place in a copy of Dickens's *Oliver Twist*.

"I have a copy of that," she said. "Autographed by Mr. Dickens, himself."

"You don't say," Lincoln replied as he sat up. "How did you come by his signature?"

She sat across from them in a brocaded chair. "When I was a girl in Boston, I once worked for a famous preacher who served indigent families of sailors on the waterfront. Father Taylor. Maybe you have heard of him."

"I know only of his legend. I have not had the pleasure of meeting the man."

Tad left his father's side and stood next to her. She tousled his hair. "After Papa died, he became like an uncle to me." she said. "Several years after, when I no longer worked at the mission, Mr. Dickens visited Boston and was keen on hearing Father Taylor preach. I was invited to meet the author in the parson's study. That is when he signed two volumes of *Twist* that my husband's aunt gave me. Mr. Waldo Emerson, Mr. Longfellow, and Mr. Charles Sumner were there as well."

"I am impressed with the company you keep," he said. "I have met only two of those gentlemen. Senator Sumner, I see often, and Mr. Emerson visited me weeks ago."

"Both are household names in Massachusetts," she said. "May I ask the purpose of Mr. Emerson's visit?"

"He came with Senator Sumner and asked me to deny an appeal by a slave trader who was condemned to die."

"Were they successful?"

"If you mean, did I let the man hang, I did. I may have been swayed to some degree by the knowledge that both men ardently oppose capital punishment. Neither would have made an exception to their beliefs without good cause, so their opinions carried more weight than many others might. However, I found the trial judge's views to be a valuable influence on my decision to deny the man's appeal. The judge cited the enormity of the accused's sins—the cruelty and wickedness of thrusting nearly a thousand fellow beings beneath the decks of a small ship to die of disease or suffocation. Those who survived and their posterity were consigned to a fate far crueler than death. He carried off not only men to such a fate, but women and helpless children as well. Not a single one of those poor souls ever did him any harm."

"I suppose," she replied, "we have more in common than our afflictions. I, too, agree with that judge."

"Don't leave out our common appreciation for Mr. Dickens' novels. So, what do you think is the point of young Oliver Twist's story?

"Young Oliver's condition at the beginning was not of his own making, and those who were entrusted with his care did him no favors. It is not his fault he fell in with an immoral lot who led him astray."

"So, society should excuse his behavior?" Lincoln asked.

"Of course not. Nor is simply reversing their fortunes the answer, as we saw in the character named Monk. We must also plant their feet on high moral ground and nurture their growth. I was taught those things by my father."

"Your father was a very wise man."

"I like to think so," Rebecca replied. "Without the example he set for me and without my mother's hard, honest work after he died, I might have been no better off than those young thieves in Mr. Dickens' story. That said, I do not discount the many mercies of my dear sister, neighbors, and friends, especially Father Taylor and his wife. They were invaluable to me, just as the characters Rose Maylie and Mr. Brownlow were to young Oliver."

Lincoln shifted in his seat. "You've had a good visit with Mrs. Lincoln, I presume."

"Yes, and she is quite more cheerful than when I arrived. She has even instructed the gardener to cut some flowers for my boys at the hospital."

"You will be staying for a time, I hope."

"Yes, please stay," Tad chimed in.

"I'm afraid I must get back to the hospital."

Tad stuck out his lower lip and crossed his arms.

"We have lost several nurses, and my ward is now up to eighty beds. I should be seeing if Mr. Hay can arrange for a carriage to take me back."

"Nonsense," he said. "I shall make the arrangements directly and be your escort."

"But I should not bother you with such a small matter. You have more important things to attend to."

He stood. "My dear, there is no person in this family more important than you. Do not underestimate your influence on Mrs. Lincoln or on me. At times, I have worried that nothing can be done for her. Then I see her anxieties lifted when you are here. Your mere presence is a balm to her. As for me, I might well have shaken my fist at the Almighty and turned my back on Him, had it not been for your example and encouragement. Your words lift my spirits more than any preacher's or of all the esteemed men in the halls of government. It is my honor to escort you. I will have William bring the carriage."

As they crunched along Fourteenth Street toward the hospital, Rebecca asked, "How are you these days?"

"I am fine. Why do you ask?"

"It is my duty to ask my patients how they are," she replied. "And before you answer, I expect candor from my patients."

"If you insist on knowing, I am often unwell."

"I heard banter outside your office about a rebel ironclad running up the Potomac to attack the Capitol."

"There was a recent battle in the Hampton Roads waterway," he said, "where their ironclad frigate sank some of our wooden warships. We'd hoped our own ironclad could have defeated theirs. We did manage in chasing the monster back to its port in Norfolk, but our armored boat was severely damaged."

"So, there is no attack."

"We don't know what they plan. But if I were in their boots, I would strike."

William pulled the carriage up to the hospital entrance as dusk fell, and Lincoln helped Rebecca down. As she entered the hospital, she glimpsed gawkers standing at the windows, showing their surprise at the president's chivalry toward their Massachusetts nurse. Mrs. Russell grinned broadly and waved.

✳ ✳ ✳

When Rebecca rose the following morning, she gazed out the large bay window of her ward and took in the view of Washington City—its Capitol Dome waiting to be completed, the half-constructed Washington Monument, and the broad, placid Potomac River. Her focus retreated to the field that bordered the hospital drive where cows grazed, and the surgeons' horses roamed loose to feed.

Her mind reverted to memories of her years in Chelsea. She recalled the scene through which she passed there two years earlier. In the seclusion of her simple home, she sat at her husband's bedside, holding his hand, and encouraging him to trust in God when the time came, which was already at hand, when they would be separated by death. It had been beyond her comprehension at the time that someday she would offer the same encouragement to the head of the nation, shining light into his darkness.

Before she began her day, she wrote to Almira.

Columbian College Hospital
March 10, 1862

Dear Almira

Do not think I have forgotten to write to you, Oh! no, but I have sometimes think I shall be obliged to give up writing altogether as it is such a tax on my time and head. Since I returned from the President's House I have had more letters from strangers than you can imagine, but I shall not be able to do anything for them. I did not come to Washington to serve in any capacity but that of being the soldiers' friend, and that I shall stick to, if I only have health. I was three weeks at the President's House, and had a pleasant time. O! if I could only sit down on the lounge in the writing room, how much I could tell you with all my dear neighbors. But we all expect to be at home on the 4th of July, and then such a time. Well, I shall not know where to begin, for I have much to tell you all. Last Tuesday I went to Washington and called upon the Sanitary Commissioners, and obtained 200 Shirts, 50 Flannels, 125 Towels, 150 Handkerchiefs, 150 Drawers, etc. which pleased the Steward of the Hospital very much. I went down on my own responsibility and done well. From there I went to the Presidents house, and took dinner, and towards night the President ordered his span of horses to be harnessed, and I was then invited to ride, which of course I could not refuse. I was riding in great style with the President in his open carriage, with a driver mounted on his seat with white gloves, and a tall hat, when a gentleman the Rev Joseph Driver (one of Mrs. Holden's friends) saw me and the next day he told me he thought I was highly honored in riding with the President in the streets of Washington. The President rode with me up to the Hospital to the great surprise of its inmates, and the news "the President's carriage is coming" started all to the windows, and the Chelsea Nurse alighted and the Steward of the Hospital waited upon me up the steps. The flowers I brought home for my boys were magnificent, and Mrs. Lincoln says whenever I want to come if I will let them know she will send her driver for me and return me in safety. You do not know how kind of Presidents family all are to me, and if George lives and does well the President will be his friend as well as mine. I have given the President all the particulars, age, name, residence, etc. and they both say to me when the war is over come and stay with us. That looks like going to the old lady home does it not Almira? Well, so it is, and I am still trying to live by the day, pleading with God to direct me in all my doings, that wherever my lot may be cast, I may honor Him who has done so much for me. When the President left me, he said he felt that he was still in my debt, but he hoped to see me some day at his house. I am again promoted, as I have been here the longest. I am put in charge of the whole of the 4th floor, which includes 84 beds. I had a letter from George, he is well, and near Winchester, Va. I wish you could only see the tents that surround us and hear the music from the different bands. Three nurses have been discharged and one has died from fatigue.

Give my love to all, and plenty of kisses to little Georgy. good-bye From Auntie Pom

Give me some credit for good long letter. I send you an envelope with A Lincoln on it keep it, for it is wartime.

✳ ✳ ✳

Rebecca visited the President's House infrequently over the remainder of March. During that period, Mrs. Lincoln grew restless from languishing in bed and her vitality increased. But with renewed mobility, she came face to face more often with reminders of happier times. Each such encounter prompted her to redouble her defenses against thoughts of the idolized one. She refused to enter the Green Parlor where Willie's coffin had been displayed. Neither would she venture into the Prince of Wales Room where he grappled with and succumbed to that wretched fever. She could not bear the slightest glimpse of any photograph bearing the boy's image. Anything that reminded her of Willie distressed her, and that included Tad. She could barely endure the sight of him, leaving him all but motherless for a season.

Tad flew into Rebecca's arms on one of her visits and burst into tears. "What's the matter?" she asked.

"Ma is giving away everything. She says my friends can't come to play anymore. I cannot even go to see them. It isn't fair. How can I remember Willie if all the toys we played with, if pictures of us, are given away?"

"Your mother is very sad," she said.

"I am sad, too! I want to keep our toys and pictures, so I can remember the fun we had."

"Let's just give her some time. I promise she will start feeling better."

"I miss the way she used to be." He buried his face in her chest and wept.

"I will talk with your father and see what can be done."

Rebecca left the mansion that day without speaking to Lincoln. He had made himself inaccessible to everyone. It was well known within his inner circle that he had spent every Thursday afternoon during March, precisely from five o'clock until six, in the Green Parlor. He kept the door locked while he mourned in private. It was also known that the edge on his grief had begun to dull. But for the period surrounding the first month's anniversary of Willie's passing, he had secluded himself entirely in his office and declined to see visitors or interact with his aides.

Rebecca returned to check on Lincoln the next day out of concern he could be descending into melancholy. As she stood in the doorway to his office, she could tell that the days of isolation had taken a toll on him, both in spirit and in vitality. His weary, drawn countenance and dark sunken eyes told the story of a deeply troubled soul.

His face brightened when he glimpsed her standing before him.

"I must get back to the hospital right away," she said. "I am in the city to pick up some supplies, but the surgeon gave me permission to stop in to see if all is well. My driver is waiting downstairs."

"The sight of you cheers me. Give me a few minutes to finish some work while you look in on Mrs. Lincoln. She is having a hard time today."

"Yes. But we must be quick about it," she replied. "The driver—"

He beckoned one of his private secretaries. "Go downstairs and tell Mrs. Pomroy's driver to go on. I shall see Mrs. Pomroy home. Tell him we shall not be long, I promise."

Lincoln turned to Rebecca, "You should find Mrs. Lincoln in the family parlor. I will join you shortly."

As Lincoln requested, Rebecca hurried to the family parlor where a morose Mrs. Lincoln sat reading.

"How are you?" Rebecca asked.

"I should be the vision of gratitude and contentment," she replied. "But my life is so empty."

Rebecca sat next to her and took both her hands. "Believe me. I understand. I have been in your place and am able to tell you the sun will shine for you once again. In time the heart will heal and grow stronger."

"It would help me if I could somehow become assured that my Willie is happier now."

"There will come a time," Rebecca said, "when we shall be reunited with our loved ones. I am certain of that."

"That time cannot come soon enough for me," Mrs. Lincoln replied.

"I am needed back at the hospital," Rebecca said. She did not know what more she could say to console her friend. "So many of our boys are suffering. Many must die. I cannot let them die alone."

"Yes, you must," Mrs. Lincoln replied. "But first let me give you some gifts." She stood and took Rebecca's hand. "Come."

They walked hand-in-hand to Mrs. Lincoln's chamber. On a table at the First Lady's bedside rested a small rosewood box, elegantly carved. She opened it and took out photographs of Willie and Tad which she put in Rebecca's hands, careful not to so much as glance at them. "Here," she said. "Put these up so your boys can see how our family loves them and appreciates their sacrifices."

"Thank you," Rebecca replied.

"I shall order some fruit and other delicacies from the kitchen for you to take, as well. For you, I have set aside some potted plants in the conservatory. I had planned to bring them to you myself, but I have been unwell of late."

Lincoln soon appeared in the doorway. "Ah, here you are. My promise is kept. The carriage awaits."

"Be sure to collect the potted plants I have set aside for her," Mrs. Lincoln said. "And wait while I have the kitchen make up some boxes for her to take."

"Yes, Mother," Lincoln replied.

On the carriage ride to the hospital, Rebecca told Lincoln, "Yesterday, when I said goodbye to Tad, he was nearly inconsolable. He misses his brother terribly, but more than anything he needs his mother. Giving away everything that reminds her of Willie is not helpful for him. Will you speak with her?"

"I will do what I can, and if my efforts produce no fruit, I will put Mary Jane and Miss Lizabeth on the task."

CHAPTER TWENTY-TWO

A spate of measles deaths kept Columbian College Hospital under quarantine for most of April. Even late in the month, when Lincoln suffered severe headaches and called for Rebecca's aid, she was denied permission to leave. But when the quarantine was lifted on the first day of May, Lincoln wrote to Miss Dix.

> *Miss Dix's permission for Mrs. Pomroy to remain at the White House two weeks, or any shorter time, if so long is not possible, would greatly oblige Mrs. Lincoln and myself.*

After reading the president's note, Miss Dix summoned Rebecca to her office and explained, "As you are aware, my policy is to give no furloughs to any of my nurses, and if any choose to go away, they must stay away altogether."

"Until you reminded us recently of your policy," Rebecca replied, "I was wondering whether I had better get one for two or three days, for I need the rest and feel as though I am growing old fast. But I have not made any request for leave."

Miss Dix showed Rebecca the president's note. "Did you have any hand in this?"

"No Ma'am. This is as much a surprise to me as it is to you."

"News from a battle near Williamsburg is grim." Miss Dix said. "The Army estimates more than two thousand casualties among our ranks. Hundreds of wounded will be flooding into hospitals in this city, and Columbian College will have its share. You see the kind of bind this puts me in."

"Considering how it might look to the other nurses," Rebecca replied, "I would not take furlough even if it be offered."

"There shall be no furlough, but neither of us are of sufficient rank to deny a request from His Excellency. Get over to the President's House and report back to me on the family's state of health. I will arrange for Mrs. Russell to cover your ward while you are away, and I can spare you only two days."

Lincoln was in the upstairs family parlor, stretched out on a sofa with his eyes closed, when Rebecca arrived at the mansion that evening. A cool towel rested on his forehead as he recited a poem to Senator Browning who sat in a chair close by.

Senator Browning leaned toward Rebecca and whispered, "You should check on Mrs. Lincoln. She's in a severe state. My wife and Mrs. Welles are with her, as is the dressmaker. They are trying to calm her."

"Is that Mrs. Pomroy?" Lincoln asked.

"Yes. It's me," she replied.

Lincoln removed the towel and sat up. "We are so glad to have you come."

"I cannot stay long," she said. "I must get back to my boys soon."

"You must stay the night," he said. "William will see that a room is made ready."

"Yes, but in the morning I shall go back."

Chills and fever attacked Rebecca during the night as she sat with Mrs. Lincoln. Mary Jane had gone home, and Miss Lizabeth was napping. When Miss Lizabeth woke and returned to Mrs. Lincoln's chamber, she found Rebecca huddled in a chair, wrapped in a blanket, and her teeth chattering.

"Let's put you to bed," Miss Lizabeth said as she cupped Rebecca's forehead to test for fever. "My Lord, we need to get some of the lady's quinine in you."

Rebecca offered no resistance as Miss Lizabeth administered a dose of medicine then walked her down the hallway to a guest room.

The next morning when Rebecca awoke, her symptoms had receded sufficiently that she went to look in on Mrs. Lincoln. She found the drapes open and the First Lady sitting up in bed, basking in dawn's gentle blush as she bantered with her dressmaker.

Mrs. Lincoln shifted her attention to Rebecca. "My dear, what is this I hear? You have taken ill?"

"Only a fit of exhaustion. I am better this morning. I shall return to the hospital and my boys after I see to Mr. Lincoln and Tad."

"I shall not hear of it. You have taken care of us all these weeks. Now, we must return the favor. Surely, someone can cover for you while you take some rest."

"But the hospital is overrun with a large wave of wounded, and we are desperately short of nurses. All are overworked. It is not fair that they must work even harder so that I may rest. The surgeon-in-charge would be within his rights to demand that Miss Dix replace me."

Mrs. Lincoln smoothed wrinkles in the sleeve of her night dress. "My husband has already sent a note to your surgeon-in-charge instructing him to reserve your place at the hospital. You are safe here under your president's protection until you are better rested. Now, your assignment is to rest. Off to bed with you."

After Rebecca woke from a short nap, Lincoln invited her to join him for lunch in the downstairs family dining room. As he fed his dog, Jip, from his plate, he said, "Mrs. Pomroy, I want to do something for you. What shall it be? Be perfectly free to tell me what you want most, and if it is in my power, you shall have it."

She shifted in her seat, floundering to form a reply.

Then she said, "All through each day, I lean on Divine favor to carry me through this strange, new life to which I have been led. I have no wants uppermost for myself."

"Promise me you will think on it," he said. "It would do my soul good to help you in some measure."

"I promise I shall." She folded her hands on her lap. "May I ask you something?"

"Of course. To you my soul is an open book. I trust you with my life."

"Are you yet able to say, 'thy will be done?' At least in some small measure."

"Since Willie left this earth, I have struggled to do so. More so than at any point in my life."

"Have you found what holds you back?" she asked.

"I believe I have always known the answer to that question. It is the principle of forgiveness that I stumble over. How am I worthy of such compassion from one so great as the Lord?"

"No one is," she said.

"Through all my days, Providence has seen fit to punish me. Since my boyhood, the drumbeat of death has carried off those I cherished, my infant brother, my angel mother, my sister Sarah, my sweet Annie, two sons, dear friends. When will such torment end? Have you not felt the same?"

Her chin quivered. "Indeed, I have. As I have told you, it began with Papa and later my own sister Sarah. The siege of affliction continued for almost thirty years."

"So, by what formula did you find an end to your affliction?"

She hesitated. "There is not a formula outside of surrender."

Lincoln drew a deep breath. "It would be good for Jeff Davis to heed those words."

"If he did," she replied, "would you forgive?"

"I might find forgiveness harder than surrendering."

She said, "Maybe one is the key to the other."

He arched his brow. "I think you have just tied me in a knot that I know not how to undo."

After lunch, Rebecca went to the upstairs family parlor to read while Lincoln walked with Tad to Stuntz's Toy Shop in a small two-story brick row house on New York Avenue. The shop was a few short blocks from the mansion. As they approached the shop, Lincoln asked, "What are we buying?"

"A soldier," Tad replied.

Lincoln laughed. "You sound like General McClellan. He's always asking for more soldiers."

"It's for my nurse."

"Mrs. Pomroy?"

"Yes. She loves her boys so much. If we have more of them at our house, she might come to live with us."

"Someone has big ears," Lincoln said.

"I hope mine are never as big as yours," Tad replied.

When they returned to the mansion, Tad ran upstairs and burst into the guest room where Rebecca was staying. She wasn't there. He darted down the hall toward the family parlor, clutching the toy soldier to his chest. On finding her lounging on a couch, reading, he stopped in front of her and held out the soldier. "Here," he said. "This is for you. If you want to be a nurse to more, we can buy all that you need."

Rebecca reached for the toy with one hand and wrapped the other arm around Tad. "My precious boy, you are my very favorite boy." However, she was unable to stay. The next morning, she was called back to the hospital, and Tad refused to come out of his room.

A week later, however, Rebecca moved back into the mansion, and Tad was all smiles. She was to watch over Mrs. Lincoln while her husband embarked on a clandestine mission.

The excursion kept him away for nearly a week, and for the first time since Willie's death he did not mourn in the Green Parlor on a Thursday at the hour of his son's passing. Instead, on the preceding Tuesday, he boarded a battleship under the cloak of secrecy, accompanied by two Cabinet members and an Army engineer. The ship steamed from the Navy Yard to Fortress Monroe, near the mouth of the Potomac, across the Hampton Roads waterway from the rebel navy's strategic base at Norfolk, Virginia. The voyage consumed twenty-seven hours.

His primary objective was to put an end to the rebel ironclad's reign of terror on vital waterways, and to block the rebel navy's access to Washington. Without consulting General McClellan, Commander of the Army of the Potomac, Lincoln directed a joint Army and Navy assault that succeeded in capturing the rebel navy base at Norfolk and forced the rebels to blow up and sink their celebrated ironclad.

Rebecca remained in residence at the mansion for several more weeks after his return, thanks to Miss Dix's revised furlough policy. On many of the days during her stay, either President or Mrs. Lincoln, and sometimes both, escorted her to and from the hospital.

Mrs. Lincoln told her on the afternoon she arrived, "You have nothing to do but be waited upon."

"Is there nothing I can do to be of use while I am here?" she replied. "I care not to be a burden on anyone."

"You will not be a burden. We employ many dedicated servants, and they are at your disposal. Your only obligation will be to join the family for meals—breakfast at eight o'clock, lunch at one, and dinner at five."

"I hope your servants will allow for the fact that I am not accustomed to a life of such ease."

"It is not their purpose to judge you," Mrs. Lincoln said, "but to be attentive to your comfort in all ways. And speaking of comfort, please call me Molly. It is the familiar name my family uses, and you are as a sister to me."

"I ... I am overwhelmed," Rebecca replied, baffled that a lady of such status and privilege would readily take a humble stranger into her home and regard her as a sister.

Otherworldliness might have been a more apt label to hang on their entire conversation, but she feared such characterization might offend. "May I ask one small favor?" Rebecca added.

"Certainly."

"I would like to be secluded from the public eye while I am here."

Mrs. Lincoln arched her brow. "Why is that?"

"I am not embarrassed. It is only that notoriety is a burden I wish not to carry. Already my name is far too widely known. Visitors call almost daily. Some merely want to meet the Massachusetts nurse, others come to see how I work. Most, but not all, have sincere intentions. Regardless of their purpose, by being so many, they distract me from my work with my boys."

"I understand," Mrs. Lincoln said. "There are times when I would rather be anonymous, myself."

One afternoon during Rebecca's residence with the First Family, Lincoln arrived early at the hospital to pick her up and return her to the mansion. He was accompanied by his Illinois friend, Senator Orville Browning.

Rebecca had been in her little room with her nose buried in patient medical cards when she was called downstairs. As she entered the lobby and discovered Lincoln waiting for her, her embarrassment drew a chorus of laughter from the assembled surgeons, stewards, cadets, and nurses.

"I told you," he said, "name any favor and it would be granted. So, I am now here to greet your boys, just as you asked."

She took a moment to collect her wits then thanked him and began by introducing him to each staff member, giving special attention to her dear friend Mrs. Russell. When the last introduction was made, they all went up to the wards. On each floor, wounded and sick soldiers were called up and arranged in a straight line. Even the lame, faltering, and feeble insisted on straggling forward to greet the president. Lincoln took off his hat and shook hands with each one, asking his name, his home state, and the name of his regiment and company.

For the few who were unable to rise, Lincoln stopped at their bedsides to greet them in the same manner and offered his thanks for their sacrifices. Once they had visited each ward inside the hospital, they went out to the tents where additional infirm soldiers were housed and repeated the ceremony.

Before Lincoln left, Rebecca led him to the kitchen and introduced three colored staff. "This is Lucy, formerly a slave in Kentucky. She cooks the nurses' food."

Lincoln nodded. "A pleasure to meet you, Lucy."

Lucy put her hands over her mouth to contain a squeal of excitement.

Rebecca gestured to two men on her left. "This is Garner and Brown. They serve their country by cooking the low diet of bread and gruel for our sickest boys."

Lincoln shook hands with each of them. "How do you do, Garner? How do you do, Brown?"

Garner answered for them both, "Fine. Thank you, sir."

Rebecca joined Lincoln and Browning afterward and returned to the President's House to retire for the night. The next morning when she returned to the hospital, one of the surgeons wagged his finger in her face. He accused her of playing a mean, contemptible trick by introducing Black servants to the president.

She replied, "Does God think less of those poor souls because their skin is black?"

Hospital officials who had been grumbling along with the surgeon changed their tunes abruptly. They expressed their gratitude for having received the honor of meeting President Lincoln.

That evening, she arrived at the President's House to find Lincoln sunken in a chair next to a window in his office, haggard and weary. He invited her to sit with him while he read. He indicated a stack of books on a table next to him. "Which shall it be?" he asked. "The Word of God? Perhaps the Bard's tragic story of King John's reign? Maybe the philosophies of Mrs. Partington who cared not whether flour was dear or cheap, because she invariably had to pay the same money for a half-dollar's worth regardless of its weight?"

"It looks as though you need something that will help you laugh," she said. "Something to push away the cloud of weariness that seems to have settled over you. But I do enjoy hearing you read Shakespeare."

"Shakespeare it shall be," he said. "Nothing shall lift my spirits more than delighting a dear friend, and possibly you can help answer a question that plagues me." Lincoln's voice became tremulous as he read from *King John*—a part where Constance bemoans the loss of her son.

> *And, father cardinal, I have heard you say*
> *That we shall see and know our friends in heaven:*
> *If that be true, I shall see my boy again;*

Lincoln paused. "My greatest wish is to see my dead boy someday, but here's the part that wounds my soul."

> *There was not such a gracious creature born.*
> *But now will canker-sorrow eat my bud*
> *And chase the native beauty from his cheek*
> *And he will look as hollow as a ghost,*
> *As dim and meagre as an ague's fit,*
> *And so he'll die; and, rising so again,*
> *When I shall meet him in the court of heaven*
> *I shall not know him ...*

"Such a thing might be true for my poor Willie. I shall not recognize him when my time comes to join him on the other side." Lincoln laid down the book and asked, "Do you think my boy and I shall know each other when we meet again?"

She folded her hands in her lap. "It is a certainty that you will."

"Certainty?" he said. "What a notion, but how does one attain it?"

"Faith is the key."

"Faith. I understand the meaning of the word, but how to do the thing is vexing."

"Did you not say once, 'the mystic chords of memory ... will yet swell the chorus of the Union, when again touched, as surely they will be, by the better angels of our nature?' Did you not possess faith in our better angels when you spoke those words?"

Lincoln laughed. "I do believe you caught me on that one."

"Maybe you can relieve my mind on a matter that has me troubled," she said. "Did I hurt your feelings by introducing you to the colored servants at the hospital?"

"Hurt?" he replied. "It did my soul good. It will not be long before we shall have to use them as soldiers and call them into the ranks side by side with their white brothers. To make my feelings clear, it shall be my delight to extend to you any favors you request."

"There is one other thing I wish for but do not want to take advantage of our friendship."

"Name it," he said. "There is nothing you should be in want of if it is in my power to give it to you. It would be impossible for me to repay you for all you have done for my family."

"That is kind of you to say. I wish for what any mother would want for her only remaining son. Is it possible for him to be commissioned as a lieutenant in the regular army? I am so anxious for him in these perilous times."

"It is a difficult thing that you ask, but I will do my best to make it happen."

One of Lincoln's secretaries barged in. "Sir, that young sprite of yours is wreaking havoc again."

"What is it this time?" Lincoln asked with a grin.

"It's the artist who is painting your portrait. Tad locked him in a closet and ran off with the key. The servants have canvassed the entire house. The boy is nowhere to be found."

"Let me suggest that you find an alternative strategy for liberating our imprisoned artist."

"Such as?" the secretary asked.

"I have found during my years on this earth that an axe can be useful in some situations. As for young Tad, I doubt he will have run far. He shall be back with us by suppertime."

After the secretary tossed up his hands and left, Rebecca excused herself to check on Mrs. Lincoln.

When she entered Mrs. Lincoln's chamber, she asked, "Are you comfortable enough?"

"Oh, I am so tired of being a slave to this world. I would live on bread and water if I could feel as happy as you."

"Healing comes with time," Rebecca said.

"Our home is beautiful, the world smiles and pays homage, yet the charm is dispelled. Everything appears a mockery. Poor Willie, our idolized one is no longer with us."

Rebecca had heard the same lament many times. She knew patience was the best course. "Cherish the sweet memories he gave," she said. "The pain will never go away, but in time it will become bearable."

"No. I wish to remember nothing of him. I cannot bear to look at things that remind me of happier days with our dear Willie." Mrs. Lincoln whimpered.

"I was once where you are. Desperate to escape all the evil work that is done under the sun. Hoping to find release, even in my own death."

"How did you overcome your grief?" Mrs. Lincoln asked.

"I looked on high for help beyond earthly horizons. I also found that being a friend to the friendless helps take my mind off my own troubles."

"I try hard to follow your example. If only I could be that strong. Will you help me do the same?"

"I will do my best," Rebecca said.

Mrs. Lincoln took Rebecca's hand. "You will be staying with us a while longer, won't you?"

"I will remain here as long as possible, but my boys need me also. And I must be fair to the other nurses."

"Isn't it time you considered giving up the hospital. My husband has said you do as much good for the nation by being in our family as you do by caring for your boys."

Rebecca's heart ached for her, but in the height of Mrs. Lincoln's pleas for her to abandon her work in the hospital, urgent news arrived. Hundreds of casualties from a battlefield near Winchester, Virginia, were enroute to the hospital. Not a soul could be spared—not even for service in the President's House.

Before Rebecca left for the hospital, she wrote another letter to Almira.

> *White House*
> *May 1862*
>
> *Dear Almira,*
>
> *I have got a furlough for three weeks to keep Mrs. Lincoln company. My health is fast improving, as I ride out every day with the President and his wife, and they do all that they can for me to enjoy myself. I am one of the fortunate women, as not a nurse which Miss Dix has, (which is two hundred) is allowed a furlough, and this comes to me so very singular, as I was not very well, that I can see Providence in it all. If I had come home, I should be obliged to stay, for if the nurses once go away, they have to stay for good. The President wrote to Miss Dix to have me come to the White House, and she did not object, and then he wrote to the Surgeon in*

Charge who could not refuse. Nothing is the matter with Mrs. Lincoln, but deep sorrow, such as others have felt, and being a fashionable woman of the world, the blow falls hard, but it was intended to soften and make her realize her position in the eyes of the world, but more especially her obligations to that Being who has crowned her with loving mercy. To many her position is enviable but to me, I would rather be a friend, and go from door to door doing some good in the world and have a name that will live when I am dead. The house is splendidly furnished, the grounds are magnificent, the parks are full of splendid flowers, and the large Conservatory looks like July, as everything is in blossom. The trouble with me is I am living too easy, as I have nothing to do but be waited upon, as there is any quantity of servants. She has taken me, although a stranger, like a sister and does the same towards me. I have told her several times that I would like to be secluded from the public eye gaze, and she understands me, so it is only occasionally when we ride out that I have an introduction to the great men of the day. We have breakfast at eight, lunch at one, and dine at five. Mrs. Lincoln thinks I had better give up at the Hospital, and stay with her this Summer, but I would like better to look after the poor soldier who has no friends. I am thinking what is the best to do, as the President thinks I am doing as much good in his family as I am in the Hospital, so I leave my case in the Lord's hands, knowing he will direct my steps right.

Write soon and direct your letter to the C. C. Hospital.

Love to all

Auntie Pomroy

Let Maria Borin know I am better.

CHAPTER TWENTY-THREE

More than three hundred wounded arrived at Columbian College Hospital in the hours following Rebecca's return from the President's House. Many of them had lain for days on dank, flinty ground cushioned only by a smattering of hay as they waited for ambulances to carry them to a hospital. She and the other nurses scurried to rearrange their already cramped wards to accommodate the newcomers.

An additional sixty bedraggled casualties stumbled up the stairs after dark one night. Orderlies directed them to bathrooms to be washed and issued clean clothes. Once again, Rebecca blinked back tears as she weaved through the maze of cots, directing the least ill or wounded of her patients to surrender their beds. She indicated the bare wooden floor in reply to displaced patients asking where they were expected to sleep. Her throat ached—the pain her boys suffered from wounds and surgeries was already enough of an obstacle to their healing.

Some new patients arrived without money to pay for washing their clothes, for postage to write to loved ones, or for luxuries, such as beef to supplement their diets, let alone for sweets. She gave them what monies she could spare and wrote letters to friends—new ones she had met while in residence with the Lincoln family and old ones from home—pleading for gift boxes to help supply her boys' needs. She asked for shirts and drawers, cotton socks, coarse combs, small pins, handkerchiefs and old linen—things that were not supplied to the hospital.

Gifts beyond what was needed for patients often made it to families that lived in a shabby tent city behind the hospital. Anxiety ate away at the hopes of destitute women and children who waited in squalor, often for months, for husbands, sons, or brothers to heal in the hospital wards or to return from distant battlefields. The huddled masses encamped there, braved every kind of weather from suffocating heat to bone-chilling winter storms. Whenever Rebecca delivered bread and milk, or anything else she had scavenged, into the small hands of a child or the frail palms of a mother, her memory rewarded her with scenes from lower Ann Street. Perhaps one day she would return to those corners and relive those times.

Mrs. Russell met Rebecca one morning in the nurses' messroom and pulled back a blanket she had used to conceal a crate of Borden evaporated milk in ten-ounce cans. "They're for the families out back of the hospital," Mrs. Russell told her.

"Where did they come from?" Rebecca asked. Her eyes narrowed.

"Don't ask. But we should get them out of here before the hospital steward finds us out."

"I shall collect a basket of soiled shirts and pantaloons from the boys in my ward," Rebecca said. "We can hide the cans under the laundry to carry out back. The poor mothers will be delighted to do some wash in exchange for milk."

Mrs. Russell asked, "If Miss Dix moves the city's nurses to Fortress Monroe, what do you suppose will happen to these mothers and their little ones?"

"Do you think it will come to that?"

"Many in the last batch of wounded from the battles down in Virginia are pretty down in the mouth. They say it's only a matter of time before General Lee's army is at our doorstep. Washington is full of secessionists waiting to welcome the rebel hordes if they assault the city."

"I am not certain I can leave my boys," Rebecca replied. "We shouldn't leave these mothers and children, either— even if the army orders us."

"You've heard about the nurses who were killed when rebels assaulted their field hospital near Winchester, right? And another eight who fled and are still missing."

"Attacking hospitals. What will those cowardice rebels do next?" Rebecca said.

"It could happen to us." Mrs. Russell paused. "And to those families."

"Mrs. Lincoln hopes I will make my home with her."

"You should."

"I do not encourage her in the least," Rebecca replied. "I am happy here doing my duty for these brave men and would not change places with Mrs. Lincoln for all her honors. She suffers from depression of spirits, but I do think if she would only come here occasionally and see these poor soldiers it would be better for her."

"Do you never tire of this place?" Mrs. Russel asked.

"Tire from all of the work, yes. Tire of the abuse we suffer, as women, from the arrogant men who lord over us. Tire of the constant need to beg for necessities. Yes, to all of that. But tire of offering healing and hope to my boys? Never. It is not for want of offers to work elsewhere. One gentleman from far out west offered to pay me to write for his Sunday School newspaper. Another invited be to work in his orphanage for a scandalous salary. Miss Dix even encouraged me to accept an offer to become matron in a fine Connecticut hospital. I was offered a position as head of a prestigious girls' industrial school. There is no higher calling for me than to care for my boys and the president's family."

"You are certainly a better woman than I," Mrs. Russell replied with a smile.

* * *

A few nights later, Lincoln strode through the entrance to Columbian College Hospital and ascended the stairs to Rebecca's ward. He found her at an ailing soldier's bedside and said, "I see you have a full house. I won't keep you long."

"What a pleasant surprise," she replied. "By all means I am at your disposal."

He glanced around. "I wanted to bring you good news in person. I informed the War Department I will give your George a lieutenancy in the regular army as soon as one comes available."

Tears welled in her. "Thank you," she whispered.

"Think nothing of it. It is my delight. Now, as I see how busy you are, I will not detain you any longer. I mean what I have said. Anything you need, you only need ask for it."

"You are most kind," she said. "Let me see you to your carriage."

As they descended the stairs to the lobby, Lincoln said, "I shall be passing by this place often for the next few months. For the hot season, we are moving our household to a cottage at the Soldiers' Home a little north of here. Mrs. Lincoln is very anxious for you to stay with us for the summer."

"It is a generous offer, but as you can see, we nurses carry a heavy load."

"That is obvious. Promise me this, though. I fear this will be a long war with much more suffering. You are certain to need a place to rest from time to time. If you are unable to make your residence with us, at least let our home be your refuge—a place of respite when needed."

"You and Mrs. Lincoln are so generous," she said.

"I believe we are more indebted than charitable. And selfish. You are a great friend, and we cannot bear the thought of losing you. So, you see, we will do anything for your well-being."

She blushed. "Then I shall consider it my patriotic duty to remain well."

"Now, if only I could have my generals follow orders as readily as you, we might at last finish this war."

They shared a good laugh, and Lincoln took his leave.

Another visitor took her breath away a few days later as she stood in her ward in conversation with Mrs. Russell. He was among several newly arrived patients. Her knees wobbled. Mrs. Russell gripped her elbow and held her steady.

"George," Rebecca mumbled as she covered her mouth with her hands. "My George."

He faltered toward her. She spread her arms, and he fell into her embrace. "Ma," he said.

She leaned back to assess his condition. Worry lines crinkled her forehead. "Why are you here?"

"We were in heated battle for a full week. When the rebels retreated into Richmond, about a hundred of us who were too wrung out to fight were put on trains for New York to recuperate. A conductor who knew of you arranged passage for me to Washington. The surgeon who admitted me at Armory Hospital transferred me here."

"Thank goodness you are safe, and thanks for those kind souls who guided you to me." She dabbed her eyes with a kerchief.

"I was unaware my mother is so famous."

"It shocks me, as well," she said. "I make a great effort to escape notoriety."

Mrs. Russell laughed. "I suppose it is the company you keep that draws attention."

"I must go where the army sends me," Rebecca replied.

George stiffened. "I pray they don't send you for battlefield duty. Rebs don't seem to care where they aim their cannons."

Rebecca slapped her forehead. "My goodness. I apologize. I don't know where my manners have gone. George, this is Mrs. Russell. She's a nurse from New York who has become a dear friend."

"Your mother speaks of you constantly," Mrs. Russell said. "She is quite proud."

"That I am, and now that you are here, young man. You are in my care the same as the rest of these boys. And I will see to it that you are well mended when you leave."

"Yes, ma'am," he said.

"Fortunately, a spare bed has become available. Come with me and I'll get you settled in."

She pointed out George's cot just as orderlies arrived to carry a New York patient named Charlemagne to surgery. "I better follow them," she said. "Wish us luck."

When she arrived in the operating room the surgeon asked, "What do you want, nurse? Can't you see I am about to amputate a man's leg?"

"Sir, he is my patient. I promised I would stay with him during surgery."

"And who's tending to your ward?"

"Mrs. Russell," she replied.

He scowled. "If you must stay with him, at least make yourself useful. Have you ever seen a surgery up close?"

"Never an amputation," she said. "But I have dealt with the aftermath of many."

"I suppose that will have to do, seeing as how I have no assistant at the moment and there's a lineup of patients waiting to be sawed on. So don't go fainting on me or making any kind of fuss. If you do, I'll send you home on the next train." He gestured to the shelf. "Fetch that sponge and cone. A bottle of chloroform, too."

She darted to the shelf and returned as quickly.

"Dab the sponge," he said. "Not too much. An overdose can kill the poor man."

She did as she was told.

"A little more," he barked. "You don't want the patient dying from pain while I'm sawing on him."

When she had applied enough on the sponge to satisfy the surgeon—at least she hoped it wasn't too much or too little—he said, "Stop. That'll do. Now put the wide end of the cone over his nose and mouth and ready the sponge on the small end."

The skin on her arms and neck prickled as she followed his instructions and stood ready for his next order.

"Steady now," the surgeon said. "Squeeze the sponge. Not too hard. Let the chloroform drip gradually. Too fast and it will shock his system. It'll take a few minutes for the drug to take effect."

She took a deep breath and teased a few drops into the cone. The surgeon said, "That should be enough. It is only necessary that he be insensitive to pain."

After almost ten minutes, Charlemagne remained restless, as if in a fitful sleep. The surgeon instructed her to replace the cone and chloroform on the shelf.

She did as he said and when she returned to the operating table, he ordered, "Over here. I'm sure you have experience with tourniquets."

She positioned herself as directed and braced herself. Her whole body tensed.

"Attach the cord about here." He indicated a point on Charlemagne's mangled calf, just below the knee.

When the tourniquet was applied, he said, "Hand me the scalpel and hold his leg steady while I detach the soft tissue. Be ready with the sponges and ligature threads." As he cut flesh away from the bone above Charlemagne's wound, he gripped the loose flaps of tissue with a long piece of muslin and pulled them back.

Rebecca ligatured severed veins and dabbed up blood as it dribbled out. Her pulse quickened when Charlemagne twitched, and his leg jerked. Several minutes later, a clean section of bone, several inches below the tourniquet, was ready for cutting.

The surgeon took up his saw. "Grab his ankle and hold the leg steady," he said. "When I'm done, discard the severed part in the refuse bin and get back over here to help me dress and suture the stump."

After the operation, the surgeon said, "You're quite adept at this, especially for a woman and first timer. Most new male assistants get queasy, and women generally swoon by the time the saw is put to the bone. I hope to see you in surgery more often."

CHAPTER TWENTY-FOUR

Rebecca visited Lincoln in the President's House in mid-July, a little more than a year after the war began. She had been at the Sanitary Commission, collecting clothing and medical supplies for her boys at the hospital. His weathered face was pale, his eyes reddened and bleary, and his shoulders stooped more than was normal for him, as if he had borne ten thousand fallen soldiers to their graves. The sight of him pained her soul.

"You look as though you have lost your last friend," she said.

"I've hardly slept for days. With Tad and his mother gone off to New York, there is no one to distract me from the mountain of bad news coming from every front."

"What can I do?"

"You can pray for me."

"I do so constantly," she said.

"I have proffered a bargain to the Almighty. If he should give me just one victory on any field of battle, I shall give every slave under my jurisdiction their freedom."

She hung her head. "If the Lord bargained with us, I might have avoided nearly all the affliction I have suffered in my life."

"What use is there, then, in praying?" He raked his fingers through his hair.

"I shall pray that he gives you strength to do his will."

He smirked. "Strength to endure my troubles would be helpful, a general who is not too bashful to fight would be better, but if he could see fit to give me a victory, I would be eternally grateful."

"Fear shrouds every face in the city," she said. "Everyone frets that the enemy will soon make a bold move against our Capital. Are things truly as grave as the newspapers report?"

"Our generals have given up on taking Richmond. With their capital secure, the enemy is determined to make this a long and brutal war. That is unless they can take Washington. In which case, catastrophe will fall swiftly upon our necks."

Secessionist threats were not the only tinderbox distressing the city. During August, the thermometer threatened to surpass 100 degrees. In the hospital ward, temperatures ranged even higher, and the air indoors was stifling, especially with the windows fastened shut out of fear of rebel attack. The healthier patients grumbled, restless from nature's oppression, while those suffering from fever lay in their cots, lethargic and feeble.

The nightly scene of wooden legs and arms stowed under amputees' beds had also begun to play out under the sweltering daytime heat. One of the boys whittled his own wooden leg after losing one on the Fair Oaks battlefield. When not using the artificial limb, he kept his handiwork on prominent display, hanging by a strap at the end of his bed.

Mary Jane Welles called on Rebecca one tyrannically hot afternoon and said, "I have ice cream at home in the cellar. I shall send up ten quarts for your boys."

"I will keep watch by the window, the best I can," Rebecca replied. "If the steward finds us out, he will make every effort to abscond with your gift."

"If your steward tries, my husband will throw his navy at the problem—the same navy that conquered the rebel ironclad and captured its home port."

"I will do my best to keep the President's Cabinet out of the matter." Rebecca giggled. "We cannot have our navy at war with the army over a sick soldier's ice cream."

Rebecca darted from the window to her patients and back to the window for shy of an hour before she spotted Mary Jane's carriage and hurried downstairs. The moment the footman alighted and began unloading his cargo, the hospital steward rushed out to confront him.

"Boy," the steward said. "Take those items to my office."

"Excuse me, sir, but these are for Mrs. Pomroy's sickest men."

"Look here, boy. You best do as you are told, or else."

Rebecca angled into the space between the two. "Those are a gift for my boys," she sputtered at the steward.

"All gifts go through my office," he retorted.

"Once you get your hands on them, they never make it upstairs to the suffering men for whom they are intended."

"We have been through this before." The steward glowered at her.

"Yes, and each time you have been set straight. Shall I let the Secretary of the Navy know you are diverting his gifts for your own use?"

He rocked back on his heels.

She continued. "Secretary and Mrs. Welles intend for this ice cream to be enjoyed by the boys in my ward and the sickest in the other wards. If you would like for the President's Cabinet to weigh in on the matter, Mr. Welles can raise the issue at their next meeting."

The steward turned to the footman. "Take it upstairs as the woman says." Then he shook his fist at Rebecca and retreated to his office, emptyhanded.

Rebecca's patients celebrated the arrival of their ice cream, a treat that never made it to battlefield encampments.

Often in the field, even a cup of drinking water could come at a dear cost.

＊ ＊ ＊

Soldiers on both sides of the contest faced a choice between two bad outcomes at the end of August. They camped on opposite banks of Bull Run Creek in Virginia, near the Manassas railroad junction—separated by a narrow stone bridge. Men in both armies could go thirsty with temperatures still peaking at near one hundred degrees or hope they survived dysentery, or the like, long enough to reach a hospital. Unless the hospital came to them.

Reports of massive casualties on the Union side drew everyone who could procure a horse to the battlefield to render aid to the sick and wounded. Rebecca was one of the few at Columbian College Hospital who were chosen to stay behind and watch over the overcrowded wards.

Saturday night, she learned that wagons, carriages, omnibuses, all types of make-shift ambulances loaded with battlefield wounded and dying were log-jamming Washington's streets. A dispatch from the War Department advised all city hospitals to prepare for a flood of 8,000 new casualties. By the early hours of Sunday, a call went out to all orderlies, stewards, physicians, and cooks who were not already on duty to return to their posts and prepare for the new arrivals.

All previously admitted patients who were not too weak for transport were to be carted off for convalescence elsewhere. By daybreak, the first of three hundred new patients were deposited at the entrance to Columbian College Hospital. Several were so exhausted or severely wounded that they died as they were lifted out of vehicles onto litters.

Before noon, every bed in the hospital was filled, and the surge of wounded continued. Floors of the lobby, hallways, and wards became so thick with languishing, distressed souls that Rebecca watched her feet to avoid stepping on some poor sufferer. Blood leaked onto the floor from sockets where eyes had been put out or dripped from holes in arms where a ball had torn through or seeped from cratered chests and backs. More blood oozed from legs that were shot off or mangled. Men wept like children, as if waiting for a mother's care.

The cacophony of pathetic appeals might have driven her insane. "Lord, take me quickly!" "Water, please!" "I'm so faint!" "God, but I'm in so much pain!" "If my mother were here, she would not let me die so." But she braced herself, willing her senses into a state of numbness.

Rebecca, with whoever was available to assist, gave each new patient water, tea, coffee, or wine—whatever was within reach—then washed and dressed their wounds, cut and combed their hair, put them in clean clothes, and gave them a place to sleep. Each task was performed with the greatest haste and the most compassionate care, often evoking a soldier's tender memories of home and a wife or mother.

She assisted surgeons as they performed urgent surgeries deep into the night. An old gray-haired man, his matted locks saturated with blood, gritted his teeth as she stuffed gobs of lint into his wound. Her knuckles disappeared inside the shredded flesh. "Tell me when it hurts," she said.

A stout man of forty, his hip mangled beyond repair, called her God's angel. Tears streaked his grimy cheeks moments before the surgeon knifed into the hip joint to remove his leg. Still another, whose ankle was cut through by a musket ball, sank his fingers into her arm's sparse flesh. She gripped his leg and held it with all her strength as the surgeon amputated it without sedation— time was too precious to stop and give him chloroform.

By midnight on Sunday, the hospital was filled to the brim with eight hundred wounded, and Rebecca still was without help—as most of the other nurses had not yet returned from the battlefield. She did not have the luxury to think, nor could she afford to weigh what made sense against the things that did not. Judgment was no longer under the jurisdiction of her mind. It had been given over to the tips of her fingers and the balls of her feet. She acted speedily, lest she lose her mind.

It was almost dawn on Monday when she sneaked into her room to be alone. She had ninety-one men in her ward. Many scenes from the previous days' most gruesome moments had carved themselves into her consciousness. She could not cleanse her mind of them. She pounded her head with her fists, battling to drive the memories into the past where they belonged.

Her break from chaos came to an abrupt end when an orderly rapped on her door post and said, "Surgeon called for you in the operating room. Said to bring your basket of bandages and lint. He hopes you have scissors, too."

She collected her supplies and hurried past moaning and groaning soldiers to attend the surgeon. He pointed to a table, empty of everything except a puddle of blood. "Get that cleaned up and stocked with sponges, basins, an oil cloth, and a tub. We have over a dozen waiting to be cut into or more men will die on us. We're almost out of time and the stock of chloroform is nearly gone."

Before noon, Rebecca assisted the surgeon in amputating fifteen legs, and over the next week the influx of casualties from the battle at Bull Run continued. A fifteen-year-old boy from Ohio, John Schlotterback, was among them. He fought through six battles before a rebel minié ball tore through his left leg. For four days he lay bleeding on the field without anything to eat or drink. He lay in a field hospital four days longer before being transported to Columbian College where Rebecca assisted the surgeon in amputating his mangled leg.

Timothy Scannal, a young cavalry man from Maine, was another of those Rebecca attended to in surgery. About a week later he complained of a crawling and biting sensation in the stub of his amputated leg that was sheathed in a wooden box. When she reported Scannal's complaint, the young surgeon shook his head and replied there was nothing that could be done about his patient's discomfort.

Later that evening, when the surgeon was off to the city, she took matters into her own hands. When she unstrapped the box, she jerked back at the sight of dozens of worms gnawing at the festering wound. She picked away at the larvae until the last was removed, then cleaned and dressed the wound before putting the box back into place just as she had seen the surgeon do when it was first installed. That night her patient enjoyed his first peaceful sleep since arriving at the hospital.

A virulent state of agitation permeated the hospital wards once the tidal wave of casualties ebbed to a ripple. After the Union Army's collapse at Bull Run Creek, patients, surgeons, nurses, cooks, and the rest grew increasingly despondent over waning prospects for near-term victory. Many were ready for peace at any price.

Soldiers, once eager to return to their regiments in good health, angled for lengthy convalescence furloughs or full discharges based on invented disabilities. Wealthy parents visiting their sons sometimes lobbied surgeons to embellish medical records, some even offering bribes.

* * *

Rebecca fretted her dear friend, the president, would be struggling over the Union Army's demoralizing defeat in Virginia. The last time they spoke, he was desperate for a victory on the battlefield. She imagined his melancholy might be so thick it would blot out the sun. Even so, Mary Jane Welles's news that Lincoln claimed he was almost ready to hang himself stunned her.

"When did this happen?" Rebecca asked.

"During a recent meeting of the Cabinet," Mary Jane replied. "My husband was present when it was said. I saw Mr. Lincoln this morning while visiting at the mansion. He seemed fine."

"The poor man. I must go see how he is. And what of Mrs. Lincoln? How is she?"

"She talks of returning soon to New York to visit friends. My husband said Mr. Lincoln passed off his remark as a speck of hyperbole in a dustbin of disasters. He is besieged by a swell of angry politicians and journalists, outcries of public distress over General McClellan's procrastinations, and reports of General Lee crossing the Potomac into Maryland."

"Will you be returning to the President's House this afternoon?" Rebecca asked.

"I can if you need me to."

Rebecca scribbled a note. "Please give this to the president. I need a night of respite, away from my boys, and would like to join the family at the cottage if it is not too much of an imposition. Hopefully he can stop here and collect me on his way home."

Lincoln directed his driver later that afternoon to stop at Columbian College Hospital. He had spent most of the day agonizing over the dearth of news from a region of karst geography along the banks of Antietam Creek in Maryland, where limestone bedrock had been eaten away, leaving behind hollows and outcrops. One hundred and fifty thousand Union and rebel soldiers were poised on the Union side of the Potomac River to decide the fate of the nation.

As Rebecca seated herself opposite Lincoln in the carriage, she asked, "How long has it been since you had even half a night's sleep?"

"I could ask you the same question," he replied.

She tilted her head, angling into his field of vision. "You can't save the country if you're dead."

"I see why your boys call you Mother, but why do you call them your boys? You have a son of your own."

"In my heart, I think of them as my Olivers, but it would not do to call all of them by the same name. They would not understand. Besides, if I am their mother, does that not make them my sons?"

"When you put it that way, I reckon it makes perfect sense."

"Speaking of my Olivers," she said. "I worry about you."

"Then pray for me." He glanced away. "Maybe it is the will of Providence that I should die."

"You shouldn't say things like that. Especially in front of your Cabinet ministers."

"Oh, that again. Are you saying I cannot blow off a little steam?"

"Of course, you can." She folded her hands in her lap. "If done discretely."

"When I consider the state of things, how can I not wonder whether it is God's will to strike me down?" He slumped forward in his seat, wringing his hands. "Our attempt to take Richmond thwarted with thousands lost. Harper's Ferry surrendered to the rebels with twelve-thousand men and their armaments captured. Lee's army crossed the Potomac into Maryland and is amassing on Union soil. A great victory for the rebellion would bolster their chances of drawing European nations into the conflict against us."

Rebecca sat back in her seat. "A rebel victory surely is not what God wants."

"How can you be certain?" he asked. "Each party claims to act in accordance with the will of God. Both cannot be right, and at least one must be wrong. God cannot be for and against the same thing at the same time."

"But you are in the right. Slavery is a blight on humanity and an affront to God."

"I have weighed that question for weeks now. Is this proclamation for the emancipation of slaves the will of Providence? If so, why is now the time to end the scourge of human bondage? The Almighty has had centuries to do so, with or without human instrumentalities."

"I cannot answer why. But he has given you the position, the opportunity, and the inspiration to carry it out. So now must be the time."

"Maybe there is a different purpose," he replied. "Maybe the purpose is the struggle. The struggle to save the Union or to divide it. The struggle over keeping slavery or ending it. The struggle over whether to end it at once or over time. The struggle over whether we end it because it is right or out of expediency."

Lincoln unfolded a document. "Speaking of discretion, you are the only one to see this, and I do not know whether anyone else should know of it. I wrestle with these ideas and have jotted them down that I might not lose track of what I believe to be true."

He studied her expressions while she read.

> *In the present civil war, it is quite possible that God's purpose is something different from the purpose of either party—and yet the human instrumentalities, working just as they do, are of the best adaptation to effect His purpose. I am almost ready to say that this is probably true—that God wills this contest, and wills that it shall not end yet. By his mere great power, on the minds of the now contestants, He could have either saved or destroyed the Union without a human contest. Yet the contest began. And, having begun He could give the final victory to either side any day. Yet the contest proceeds.*

After she read it, she handed it back to him, her face somber.

"It is my earnest desire," he said, "to know the will of God in this matter. And if I can learn what it is I will do it."

"I shall pray that God gives you the wisdom to do His will."

When they arrived at the cottage, Rebecca joined the family for supper. Afterwards Lincoln went to his office where he worked through the night.

Early the next morning, as he drove Rebecca back to the hospital, his smile prompted her to ask, "Did you get some rest?"

"No," he said. "But I am more cheerful today. I finished the preliminary proclamation. Now I shall let it simmer for a time, after which, I will present it to the Cabinet, providing we soon achieve success up in Maryland or elsewhere.

Three days later, after the Union's mid-September victory at Antietam Creek, Lincoln was clear on two things. First, the rebel army had been chased out of Maryland back into Virginia—spoiling Lee's plan to gain Europe's favor. Second, although the Union Army's success came at a great cost of lives on both sides, the outcome provided an opening for him to publish the preliminary proclamation.

CHAPTER TWENTY-FIVE

Rebecca and Mrs. Russell drove to the Soldiers' Home, on the last day of September, even as the sea swell of Antietam casualties further strained Washington's overtaxed hospitals. They accompanied the body of a Pennsylvania boy, Adam Burge—dead from wounds suffered at Antietam. Three days earlier, Rebecca had gone alone to attend the interment of Emanuel Slaughter, a Union soldier from Virginia who was struck above the right knee by a minié ball shot from the enemy's cannon at Bull Run. He was removed from the battlefield and taken to Columbian College Hospital where he lay for almost a month before surgeons amputated his leg. He died the same day.

As the two nurses parked in front of the president's summer cottage, Rebecca said, "That's where the family stays. They aren't home today."

Mrs. Russell teased, "You keep their schedules?"

"No. Mrs. Welles called on me yesterday and said the president is at the mansion, preparing to take a train to the Antietam battlefield tomorrow. Mrs. Lincoln is in the city to see him off but wishes me to stay with her here while he is away."

"You should."

"My boys need me."

"They need you to be well. We all worry that you are working yourself into an early grave."

Rebecca replied. "I will think on it."

When an ambulance arrived with Private Burge's remains, the nurses followed behind a cart bearing the coffin with a chaplain walking beside it. Rebecca's voice was flat. "No drum and fife. Only a chaplain to say prayers for those left behind."

"Such is wartime," Mrs. Russell replied. "And the end is not yet."

After a short prayer by the chaplain, the body was lowered into the grave. Rebecca whispered to her companion, "Walk with me."

They wandered on the paths between rows of wooden markers, looking for familiar names. Rebecca said, "Two dozen of mine are laid here. How different a place this is from our beautiful Woodlawn back home, with its clinging vines, ornamental shrubbery, and costly monuments. Here, there is hardly a flower or tree in sight."

∗ ∗ ∗

Lincoln maundered through a field hospital, formerly the Grove family farmhouse near Antietam Creek in Maryland. Two weeks after the mammoth battle, maimed and dying rebel soldiers lingered on cots under the care of Union surgeons. A large, toothy saw—purple stains on its wooden handle—hung on a wall in what had been a dining room. Its ornate table bore puce markings of its converted purpose. Parked nearby was a wheelbarrow coated with gelatinous dregs from countless loads of discarded body parts. The rum scent of chloroform hung in the air, mingling with pungent odors from festering wounds.

When Lincoln paused at one of the cots, a surgeon whispered, "A Georgia boy, near his end."

The Georgian's face was drained of color. His chin quivered as his vision flitted around the ward at suffering comrades and their Yankee wardens.

"Are you in great pain?" Lincoln asked.

The rebel peered up at Lincoln, as if searching for an anchor to bind himself to another living soul. "My leg is gone. I am sinking from exhaustion."

"Would you shake my hand if I were to tell you who I am?"

"There should be no enemies in this place," the rebel replied.

"I am Abraham Lincoln, president of the United States."

The soldier made a great effort to smile and extended his hand.

Lincoln clasped the young man's hand and held it in both of his own for some time. He raised his voice so everyone in the room could hear. "The solemn obligations which we owe to our country and posterity compel the prosecution of this war. It has followed that many have become enemies through uncontrollable circumstances. Nevertheless, we bear no individual malice and are able to take each other by the hand with sympathy and good feeling."

Those who were able rose from their cots and went forward to shake Lincoln's hand. When he had greeted each of them, he passed by those who were too wounded to leave their beds, offering them sympathy and kind words, promising that despite their enmity on the battlefield, every possible care would be taken to nurse them to good health.

✳ ✳ ✳

Lincoln stared out the window of his mansion office in early December, his hands clasped behind his back. The year began with Willie's death in the midst of hearings in Congress over his wife's suspected treason. At last, the new year was days away and he would take up a pen and sign the Emancipation Proclamation. In the meantime, hundreds of documents lay scattered on the long table when Rebecca tapped on the doorframe.

"Am I disturbing you?" she asked.

He turned. His melancholy mood ceded to a weak smile, though his complexion remained sallow. "How was your furlough in Massachusetts?"

"A much-needed rest among dear friends and family. It was a relief to see my sisters, nieces and nephews are all well. Little Georgy Fuller is a beautiful two-year-old boy—full of imp and perverse. Some of the old ladies say he seems Black, but I don't see it in him. His mother, Almira, does her best to keep up with him. Mr. Fuller is not so lenient a father as you are."

"Maybe I should be firmer with Tad," Lincoln said.

"You look unwell," she said. "Is there something in particular that weighs on you?"

He gestured to the table. "Our people in Minnesota want to hang some three hundred Indians—three-hundred-and-three to be exact."

"For what offense?"

"They appear to have been defending their families against corrupt government agents."

"It seems unfair to execute men who did what is right."

"The corruption was perpetrated by men I appointed as stewards. I put them under the supervision of a long-time trusted friend. They have betrayed innocents, robbing them of food and medicine, blankets and warm clothing, necessities of life. Not only the Indian, they betrayed this government and me."

"What do you plan to do about it?" she asked.

"Whatever I do, I will be someone's goat."

"Then do what is just."

"Our people have made up their minds that these Indians are murderers and that hanging them is justice," he said. "They are accused of slaughtering innocents as well as those who stole from them."

"Do not condemn the ones who rebelled against corruption for the sake of their families but mete out justice to those who intended only to murder."

"If only it were that easy," he said.

"Right rarely is," she replied.

"It appears there was wrongdoing on both sides," Lincoln lamented. "So, it falls on my shoulders to decide who shall forgive whom. The Almighty ordains that all should forgive, yet no one does. Everyone accuses their victim to escape blame." He rubbed his brow. "I doubt my decision will fix anything."

"Corruption appears to be everywhere," Rebecca replied. "In my ward I try to bring a measure of joy to my boys' dreary lives. Twice our dishonest steward attempted to divert gifts sent by Mr. and Mrs. Welles. Once he almost absconded with several gallons of ice cream when the weather was brutally hot. I caught him in the act and told him it wouldn't do to have Mr. Welles's navy fighting the army. He relented and allowed the ice cream to go to the wards. Another time he refused to allow the kitchen to give us hot water so the boys could have good northern tea. Afterward, Mr. Welles delivered an oil stove to my ward so I could boil my own water. When the steward discovered tea brewing in the ward, he threatened to take the stove for his own use. Again, the specter of facing Mr. Welles's wrath and my threat to put the issue before your Cabinet forced him to back off. Now, do not let me go on about Carver Barracks."

"What about Carver Barracks?"

"One of the nurses from my hospital, Mrs. Russell, accompanied me a few days ago on rounds through the derelict Carver wards where they have no female nurses to be mothers to our sick and wounded. In each barrack we faced a chorus of cries for slings, clean shirts, and socks. A mother with a toddler in hand ran towards us, desperate to know where she could find her son, a Michigan volunteer who had been wounded and carried there from the field. After a lengthy search, he was found—dirty, hungry, and weak from pain. Mrs. Russell hurried back to our wards to find supplies we could afford to share. She returned with a comb, jelly, clean clothes, sheets and lint to bind up his wounds. The mother radiated gratitude for our kindness, and she wept when I offered her a small handful of copper coins. Whenever I visit those barracks or the families camped in tents nearby, I am reminded of lower Ann Street."

"You mean," Lincoln said, "the officers who run those barracks do not have the means to run an adequate hospital?"

"I have no direct proof," she said. "But I think that something untoward happens to the government's money when it reaches those officers' hands. I cannot bring myself to forgive those who are responsible for such offenses. Maybe such forgiveness requires more humility than I possess."

"The condemned Sioux warriors, whose files are on my table, tired of taking the path of patience and humility," Lincoln said. "When their patience was exhausted, they took a firm stance for what they believed to be right—too firm in some folk's view. To stand firmly for the right and also humble ourselves sufficiently to forgive is a contortion not easily performed."

Over the next several days, Lincoln sorted transcripts from the trials in Minnesota—one stack for those to be spared and another for those he would allow to be hanged. He commuted the sentences of two-hundred-and-sixty-four. He found that the other thirty-nine had participated in atrocities against innocents off the field of battle—two of whom had committed violence against females. The thirty-nine condemned were hanged on the day after Christmas. Six days later, he signed *The Emancipation Proclamation.*

CHAPTER TWENTY-SIX

Winter snows and hammering rains paralyzed troop movements throughout the east in early January. In a letter from George, Rebecca learned his company was ordered to cross a swollen river and they were raided by rebel cavalry after making it over. Most in his company escaped the skirmish alive, but their ammunition, blankets, and clothing were gone. All George had left besides his musket were his soaked leather pouch of paper cartridges and the drenched outfit he had worn while battling to keep his head above water in the river's currents. He almost froze as temperatures dropped during the night—his shaky handwriting bore witness to the shivers that rolled through his body.

At the hospital, half-frozen crystals splattered windows then torrential rain turned streets into creeks. Absent the chaos of battlefield casualties swamping the hospital—as had been the case in recent months—boredom and disease emerged as the convalescing soldiers' leading enemies. Checkers and dominoes kept a good many minds occupied when the boys weren't stringing red, white, and blue beads to make collars that were popular fund raisers at soldiers' fairs. Some patients indulged in carving pieces of dead rebels' bones into rings—a means of exorcising demons that inhabited their memories.

Rebecca's sewing circle—often attended by a dozen or more soldiers surrounded by balls of yarn—met regularly at three o'clock to mend socks. Each day, everyone huddled around as she read to them for an hour. Her sickest boys latched onto *Cora's Picture Books*, filled with rhyming stories and illustrations. One patient, whose mind was nearly gone, clung to the picture of *Cock Robin*, and cried inconsolably when she pried it from his grasp.

An album quilt, sent by northern ladies, raised spirits whenever Rebecca brought it out. In the white center of each multi-colored square the women stitched inspirational or witty inscriptions, such as, "Fear not Abraham, for I am thy shield and thy exceeding great reward." The boys passed the quilt around. Occasionally, a distressed patient might cling to it for over an hour, tracing its inscriptions with his finger or entranced by the variations in its colors. A young man whose mind was failing him in his dying hours could only be consoled by having it held up at his bedside for him to gaze at.

DeWitt Ray, a Vermont boy of sixteen, had become one of her favorites. He arrived at the hospital in late December, days before the winter lull in fighting began. His physical wound was not life-threatening, but he carried the cumbersome burden of having been orphaned in early childhood. He ran away at the age of fifteen to get out from under the thumb of strict grandparents and joined the army. It did not take Rebecca long to discover he could not read a single word or write more than a jot.

Rebecca took advantage of quiet days in the ward to teach him to read. On one occasion, she gave him a piece of pie as a reward for his progress.

DeWitt told her, "You are the only mother I have ever known. Can I call you mother? If only you knew how that word sounds in my ears, you would not deny me the pleasure to use it. I never knew the worth of a mother until I received your kindness—until your soothing words cheered me through sadness and dark moods."

How can I not honor his request, she thought. She smiled. "You may call me Mother."

* * *

Rebecca's concerns over Lincoln's state of mind had grown after the December debacle at Fredericksburg, Maryland. Word reached her through Mary Jane Welles that the president confessed to being heart-broken over criticism by Republican allies in the senate, calling him, "a weak man." Newspapers began to describe his condition as "nervous excitement bordering on insanity." Lincoln had made an alarming confession to Secretary Welles, "If there is a worse place than hell, I am in it."

The surgeon-in-charge acknowledged that the lull in fighting opened a door of opportunity for Rebecca to be away from her boys and granted her a few days leave to spend with the Lincoln family in late January at the mansion.

She shivered under a musty, wet woolen blanket as William Johnson drove her to the President's House. A chilly rain had turned the roads to slop.

When she reached the upstairs landing, drenched, Lincoln's voice blared through his office doorway, "Stanton's so-called certified practical meteorologist knows nothing about the weather in advance. He assured me it would not rain until Friday, but lo, it's only Tuesday and here we are, deluged for the entire day."

William appeared at the top of the stairs, moments later, carrying Rebecca's trunk. "Let's get you settled in the Prince of Wales Room," he said, "so you can get into some dry clothes."

Rebecca sniffled as she followed William to the opposite end of the hall. She began a sneezing fit after he deposited her luggage, and she sneezed more as she unpacked. When she had changed clothes, finished closeting her dresses, and tucked the rest into drawers, William returned with an armload of wood and started a fire. She stood shivering as she watched him and imagined the relief heat would bring. Mrs. Lincoln knocked on her door a short time later and welcomed her "home."

Rebecca passed the rest of the afternoon sitting next to a window, listening to the patter of rain and reading. Though the blazing fire had given way to the rusty glow of coals, she was no longer merely warm, but overheated to the point of agitation. By suppertime, her energy was nearly depleted, and her appetite was as meager as a miser's alms. Nevertheless, she joined the Lincoln family downstairs in the dining room.

She picked at her meal and struggled to join in on conversations. Young Tad's rambunctious behavior seldom bothered her, but at that moment it put her on edge. After half an hour, she excused herself to retire for the night.

Mrs. Lincoln asked. "Are you unwell?"

"No," she replied. Her smile was tenuous, and she flashed hot and cold. "I suppose I am more exhausted than I realized."

As Rebecca ascended the stairs on her way to the guestroom, her knees quavered, and she ached all over. When she crawled into bed, she began coughing in spasms that waxed and waned, blocking her from sleep for a time and wasting away the little strength there was to give up. She curled into a tight, clammy knot.

While she slept, Tad, clad in his child-sized Union uniform, sneaked into the Prince of Wales room carrying one of his toy soldiers. He placed it as a sentry on a bedside table and instructed it in hushed tones to stand guard over his favorite nurse.

He stood at attention as he warned the soldier, "If she dies on your watch, you shall hang." He saluted, turned, and marched back to his room.

When President and Mrs. Lincoln checked in on her just past ten o'clock, Rebecca's night gown was damp with sweat and her forehead was tacky.

"I will send William for the doctor," Lincoln said.

"No," Rebecca murmured. "I must go back to my bed at the hospital."

"Let's get you into some dry things," Mrs. Lincoln said.

"I wish to be back in the hospital," she replied. "I shall be well cared for there."

"We can care for you just as well here," Lincoln rebutted.

"Please," Rebecca pleaded. "I shall feel more comfortable there."

Mrs. Lincoln replied, "If that is your wish. We want whatever is best for your health."

As soon as Lincoln returned her to the hospital, the surgeon-in-charge took control of her care, assisted by two ward surgeons. They began administering chloroform at midnight to dull her pain.

By noon the next day, they started injecting opiates into her arm, and later that evening, her symptoms subsided, though she remained weak. After the doctor gave her brandy to stimulate her mind, she told them in halting speech, "Woodlawn is the place where I laid my family to rest. It seems now the time has come for that beautiful place to open its bosom and receive this poor, feeble clay as well. If I do not recover, I wish to have my body embalmed, as you often do for the soldiers." She asked Mrs. Russell to write down what she had said, so she could sign it and make the document official. A copy was sent to the cemetery in Chelsea.

During the entire time of her illness, sick soldiers from every ward and some from Carver Barracks paced outside her little room, refusing to go to bed until she was better. The president and Mrs. Lincoln called on her several times and instructed the doctors to return her to their home when she was able to travel. Mrs. Lincoln assured hospital officials that Rebecca would get the rest and care she needed.

The surgeon-in-charge closely monitored Rebecca's condition, worrying that the opiate treatment might do more harm than good, but he was desperate as well for her recovery. He continued the aggressive treatment, and after nearly a week, the sight of her sitting up in bed cleared the wrinkles from his brow.

"How are you feeling?" he asked.

"Stronger," she replied.

"Strong enough to stand and possibly to walk some?"

She pushed off her blankets and pivoted, swinging her legs over the edge of the mattress. She stretched her feet to the bare wooden floor.

The surgeon offered her his hand and braced her.

"I am anxious to see my boys." She smiled as she steadied herself, clinging to his arm as they took the first tentative steps through the doorway into her ward. She gawked at the room full of beds, arrayed in rows with only inches of separation between them. "Oh my."

"They keep coming from field hospitals," the surgeon said. "A hundred more have arrived since you fell sick."

While they moved about the ward, she flinched at the sight of wounds as severe as any she had encountered. Many of the new patients lay senseless, others managed only whimpers.

"You must let me help," she murmured.

"The president and his wife expect you to spend a few days in their home to regain your strength."

"That would be unfair to these boys and to Mrs. Russell. She must be fatigued from watching my ward as well as her own."

He pinched his brow. "If Miss Dix has her way, Mrs. Russell will have to bear the burden even longer once you are able to work. She has asked me to send you to Fortress Monroe where there are as many men in dire straits, but with no female nurses able to dress wounds."

"Certainly, she can find—"

He held up his hand to interrupt. "I have told her you cannot be spared. Already, there are seven lying here who will not survive without your care."

"Give me one more night of rest. I shall be back to my duties tomorrow after breakfast."

"We will keep a close watch to make sure you do not overtax yourself." He drew his lips in a thin line.

Before Rebecca fell asleep that night, she wrote letters to Chelsea friends. One of her first letters was to Almira.

Columbian College Hospital
Feb. 10th

Dear Almira,

I received your letter today and was glad to hear that little Georgy was better, also that you were all well. I have just had a friend call from Boston who has seen George and says he is looking finely. For a week past, I have been confined to my room sick, but the Surgeon General who comes daily in to see me, with three of the other Physicians, tells me today it is only debility and by resting I shall soon get up again. I never was so completely frustrated as for four days I kept my bed, and if I moved much, I commenced vomiting, which weakened me very much. I am sitting up a little while today to let you know how I am. My cough is better. I have had some of the worst cases that ever came to the hospital. Two poor soldiers came from the Camp Hospital in such a neglected condition, that the smell was insufferable, they were the greatest curiosity that we had in the Hospital, as they were living skeletons and the Physicians when they made inquiries about them, always asked how my living skeletons got along. One had three large bed sores, and his leg had a very large sore, that had been so neglected that when my attendants with my help dressed the sores, we had to open all the windows and doors, and even change our own clothes, he was so offensive. I think that I inhaled too much of the foul air, and perhaps over done, but I could not help it, there is so much that a woman can do, that a man never thinks of. The walking is so bad that a man can hardly get along, unless on horseback, as the mud from the Hospital down to Washington is so deep, so of course I have not been able to breathe much fresh air! I long to ride somewhere, and have a change, but if I ever live to get home again, I shall enjoy all the more. My great desire is still, to have health and be able to do more for the poor dying soldier, for if you was here you would see much that would set you all thinking. Yes, much that makes the heart ache, and calls forth all our sympathies. Three of the nurses are down sick, which makes the Surgeon General swear enough to take the roof off, but we try our best to keep cool, hoping the war will soon be over. Every few days we hear the nurses are to be sent to another Hospital, so we live only by the day, sometimes looked upon as only slaves. But I have tried to do as near right as I can, and have the good will of all the Physicians, and a few of the nurses begin to love me. They can all boast of fine education, moving in high circles, attending medical lectures, understand Medicine, Anatomy, Phisiology, Phrenology, Psychology, etc. so poor old Chelsea nurse stands all alone. Yet not alone, for my dear boys think very much of me, and as long as I have my dear Savior as my friend I am safe. I can truly say "Thus far the Lord hath led me on" and in Him is all my trust. No arm like His in this my time of trial and affliction, and at night although far from you all, I feel to say I will lay me down to rest, for the Lord will keep me. I shall write to some of the Chelsea friends soon again, as I have made my Physician promise me that there shall be no post mortem examination ever made upon me, should I die suddenly in this place, as it is the rule that every one that dies here, has to have the examination made. I am not very sick, but just as soon as I feel I can be of no use, I shall get a furlough for home.

So good bye to you.

Read this to Mrs. Holden and Maria but do not I beg of you tell any body that I am sick, for you know what Chelsey people are. I should like to lay in my little room in Chelsea a week.

A kiss to Georgy RRP.

Lincoln called on Rebecca at the hospital after hearing from Mary Jane Welles that her health had improved and she had resumed her duties. "We are so relieved you are on the mend," he said.

"Each day, I feel a margin better," she replied. "If I do not try to do too much, too soon, I shall be back to full health in no time. I hope my condition did not cause you and Mrs. Lincoln any great anxiety."

"If it did, it was our own choice. You are like family to us, so your welfare is always on our minds. If fact, only today when I was visited by a so-called one-legged brigade of two dozen amputees, you must have been in my thoughts as I called them 'my boys.'"

* * *

Rebecca had barely returned to her duties in mid-February when nurses were rousted from their beds in the early morning hours to receive an ambulance train of ill soldiers. The incoming sick had been languishing, beyond help at a regimental field hospital. Several were barely able to crawl up the stairs to Rebecca's ward. One told her he had not slept on a bed for two years and doubted his body could rest on one.

Rebecca blanched while putting one of the new arrivals to bed. Her knees buckled. She crumpled into a heap in the middle of the ward, like a rag doll tossed aside by a petulant child. DeWitt Ray rushed to her aid. Still conscious, she leaned into DeWitt as he helped her stand.

"Mother, are you all right?" DeWitt asked.

The ward surgeon crossed over from the far side of the room and asked, "What's wrong?"

"I am fine," she said.

In the bed next to where Rebecca had collapsed, a frail old soldier lay wheezing and coughing. At the sight of his feet and ankles—swollen with the rising waters of dropsy—a memory of Daniel's final days slipped out of the past and put a mask over the old soldier's face. It carried her back to a time and place she had tried to block from her consciousness by immersing herself in the rush and din of work—as she held the stubs of amputated legs, as she ligatured veins oozing blood, as she stuffed lint into cratered chests, as she closed dying eyes without shedding tears. She had grown proud of her composure in the presence of suffering. As she stared at that helpless, hopeless soldier—with wisps of his hair whipping about with each convulsion of his lungs—her weakness prevailed, and she melted.

The ward surgeon presumed exhaustion had gotten the better of her and directed DeWitt to help her to her room and put her to bed.

She was too vexed to argue.

Once the surgeon-in-charge learned of Rebecca's fainting incident, he insisted she take a few weeks' furlough during the first week of March. With renewed fighting on the horizon, he expected a surge of battlefield casualties and needed her to be rested and in the best of health. She agreed there would likely not be a better time to be absent from her boys for a short stay at the President's House. She could use the time to distance herself from the past and get a firm grip on the present, just as she had learned to do with the memories that haunted her for nearly thirty years after Papa's death.

⁂

Mrs. Lincoln called for the president's carriage on Rebecca's first Sunday of furlough at the mansion and directed the driver to take her guest to the Capitol. Miss Eliza Rumsey, one of Rebecca's friends and a niece of Chelsea's Mayor Fay, was to be married in the House of Representatives chamber that afternoon. Mrs. Lincoln gave Rebecca a bouquet from the conservatory to give to the bride. After the ceremony, the carriage returned to take her to the mansion where she dined with the Lincoln family.

During dinner Mrs. Lincoln made it clear that Rebecca was to attend the last formal reception of the season the following day—planned to be the grandest in history. Rebecca responded by asking and obtaining permission to invite Mrs. Russell and others from the hospital. Mrs. Lincoln's only instruction was for the men to wear white gloves and she offered to loan Rebecca one of her gowns.

On the day of the reception, Rebecca dressed in the Prince of Wales Room. She mused at the notion that royalty, and likely other great people, had preceded her as guests in the very room where she slept and lounged.

A floral display perfumed the President's House lobby as Rebecca descended the stairs wearing one of her own plain dresses, having declined the First Lady's offer to loan her a gown of her own. The head dressing of white flowers she wore had been the inspiration of Mrs. Lincoln, who picked the flowers herself from the conservatory.

Although the eight-and-one-half o'clock reception would not start for two more hours, a throng of hundreds, members of the public who hoped to be admitted, had already gathered on the portico and spilled out onto the drive. Ambulatory patients from the hospital, clad in dress uniforms, served as guards at the mansion doors.

Soon after eight o'clock, Rebecca and her guests—doctors and nurses from the hospital—fell in line behind a host of dignitaries in the Great Hall. Each shook hands with President and Mrs. Lincoln before passing into the large East Room for the promenade. The night of reverie finally took its toll on Rebecca by midnight when she bid her friends goodnight and retired to her room. As she passed the soldiers guarding the mansion doors, she said to them, "I am happy you boys could come."

Each thanked her, with several saying they would never forget the night they shook Mr. Lincoln's hand.

"Indeed," she said. "And I fervently pray that each of you shall be spared from harm, so that you can tell your children's children of this night."

Boredom overtook Rebecca during her first week in residence at the President's House, and she could not restrain herself from returning to her ward for short visits. Sometimes those visits kept her there for most of the day and for overnight. On one such night, she took a piece of mansion stationery and penned a letter to Almira.

Col Col Hosp.
March 7ᵗʰ, 1863

Dear Almira,

It is Saturday and I have just seated myself to rest, and find myself very much indebted to friends, as a huge pile of letters are before me to answer. I have so little time to write, and then again I think I ought not to tax my brain so much as I have, and at my age I ought to be careful, so in order to keep my health good, I have so much other work of importance that must be done in the Hosp. that friends must excuse me if I do not write often to them. My health is good, although care and anxiety for my patients often change my looks as well as feelings and I am obligated to rest. I have been to the White House five days and was at two grand receptions. The one in the evening was the most brilliant of anything I ever saw. Every room was lighted and splendid flowers in all the rooms below, and Mrs. Lincolns dress was magnificent. Mrs. Lincoln was anxious that I should wear white flowers for my head and she offered to lend me anything to wear that I wanted, but you know my way is not to borrow when I can do as well without. I thought I would see all I could while there, for I had every advantage of riding or seeing all I liked. Mrs. Lincoln ordered the carriage on Sunday morning for me to ride up to the Capitol, and see the marriage of my friend Miss Rumsey, and she gave me a splendid bridal bouquet to give the bride. The carriage came for me to go home, and then I dined with the whole family and some gentleman from the West.

The nurses here at the hospital are engaged in cleaning up the messroom, where four hundred boys eat their meals, and it is so dirty that it looks like a pig pen. They have only boys who are sick or lame to do the work, and they do the best they can. We try to encourage them by helping them clean and showing them how to work.

How are all the friends in Chelsea? I do not hear from them often. It affords me much comfort when tired, to sit down and read letters from home, and often the tears flow when I think I am so far from all of you, and often have so much that I would like to say to you, but I have only one attendant and I have more care than I ever had before. I love to look at the Father and Georgy and Eliza, and wonder when I shall have the rest of the family, as every boy sees my friends, and all the Surgeons think Georgy Fuller is a beautiful boy, just as Auntie Pomroy always said he would be, but one of the nurses thinks I do not know what beauty is if I could see any in him. Well Almira, as it is late I must say good night, and will you say to all the friends that I would like to hear from any of them. Tomorrow I shall return to the Lincoln family.

Love to all

Auntie Pomroy

Tell Frank and Clara I have not heard from them yet!

✳ ✳ ✳

Six weeks after Rebecca returned from her month-long furlough at the President's House, her pale complexion was a hue duller than usual. Lincoln and his wife were quick to notice her appearance when they stopped at the hospital, while on an afternoon carriage ride.

"Your sweet voice has grown a bit thin and raspy," Mrs. Lincoln said. "Are you taking care of yourself?"

Lincoln added, "When you were with us earlier, I worried we overtaxed you. You must come again soon, and this time we shall see that you get plenty of rest. I want you to live to a good old age."

Mrs. Lincoln took Rebecca's hand. "Poor thing. You're working yourself to the bone, and likely starving yourself too."

Rebecca put her hand to her forehead and sighed. "I suppose you may be right. If another hundred sick or wounded should show up tonight, I don't know if I have the energy to be of any use."

"Then, it's settled," Lincoln said.

"I agree I must get on top of whatever is ailing me, before the next big battle. Please send the carriage for me on Tuesday. I would like to put a few things in order before I spend more time away."

Shortly after the Lincolns left the hospital, Rebecca entertained another caller, Senator John Parker Hale from New Hampshire.

"What can I do for you?" she asked.

"I should turn the question around," he replied. "What can I do for you? The president has told me you are the best friend he has known in this city. He said I should meet this good Massachusetts woman who works in one of our hospitals."

Rebecca smiled. "We could use more of most everything we have and there are things we don't have."

"I understand you often receive boxes for our sick and wounded, sent by friends and good New England people."

"Without those I fear we would be in desperate straits," she said.

"I know many good New Englanders. Do they ever let you out of this place to go visit friends or family in Massachusetts?"

"They have, and hopefully they will again."

"Do I understand your home is Boston?"

Rebecca gestured around the ward. "These days, this is my home. But I came here from Chelsea and have a good many friends and family there, still."

"When you are next in Chelsea, I wish for you to go and meet my family in Salem. The Hales have deep roots in that place and I can introduce you to many of the town's citizens who would consider it a privilege to assist your efforts here."

"It would be my honor to meet your family," she replied. "I will write to you if the army gives me another furlough long enough to travel back home. Of course, it will be a blessing if this war is over soon, and such a journey becomes unnecessary."

"Even if peace comes soon, which we all hope," he said. "The invitation stands."

CHAPTER TWENTY-SEVEN

A soldier barreled through the doors of the War Department in July, on the second day of the behemoth battle at the town of Gettysburg. He blurted, "I have an urgent message for the president."

"What's your message?" a guard asked.

"Mrs. Lincoln has been in an accident."

The guard pointed. "In the telegraph room."

When the soldier delivered news of the carriage mishap, Lincoln demanded, "Where? How is she?"

"She was coming into the city from the Soldiers' Home. The horses took fright and bolted. She either jumped or was thrown from the carriage."

"Is she hurt?" Lincoln tossed aside dispatches he had been reading, updates from a massive battle—a match to the death that pitted almost two hundred thousand American countrymen against each other.

"Only stunned, according to the doctor," the soldier replied. "Maybe some bruises, but nothing broken."

"I need to get to her at once," Lincoln insisted.

"The surgeons at Mount Pleasant are attending her," the soldier explained. "I was told she will be brought straight here when they finish examining her."

Lincoln turned to Secretary Welles who was standing close by. "Go over to the Treasury and find William

Johnson. He should be there running errands. Tell him to bring Nurse Pomroy to the mansion, at once. As soon as I saddle my horse, I'll be off to the hospital."

"With your cavalry guard, I hope," Welles said.

"There's not time for that," Lincoln replied.

He retrieved the last telegram he had read before the soldier burst through the door—General Meade's dispatch reporting the death of Major General John Reynolds. He crumpled it and threw it as hard as he could in no particular direction. "Why is there no grace when I err?" he muttered.

When Lincoln arrived at Mount Pleasant Hospital, about two miles north of the President's House, doctors said they had sewn up a nasty gash on her head—likely caused by a sharp rock she may have struck when thrown from the carriage. Otherwise, she sustained no significant injuries.

He took his wife's hand as the surgeon went to arrange for an ambulance to transport her to the mansion. "I should have insisted," he said. "A detail of cavalry guards should have accompanied you into the city. Surely, they would have been able to help in some way to get the carriage and horses under control."

"There was no way to know they would be needed." She winced. "Besides, if there had been a secessionist attack, it would have been against you. If such a thing happened, you may have needed every last one of them to defend you."

"Still, I feel responsible."

"You mustn't," she said. "You might be interested to know the good doctor came down from Pennsylvania last night with a train of ambulances full of wounded."

"I've been studying dispatches all morning. Lee seems to have sneaked his whole army into Pennsylvania. Hopefully, General Meade is throwing everything he has at them."

"Then you should get back. I can take care of myself."

"I will see you home and there is no sense arguing about it. Mrs. Pomroy will be there to take care of you until you are fully healed."

"Good. I shall not be a great burden on her. It will be a good chance for her to get some badly needed rest."

Lincoln stood at the long table in his office the next day. The rebel invasion of the north was turned back at Gettysburg, and General Grant—Commander of the Union Army of Tennessee—reported rebel forces would surrender the Mississippi River city of Vicksburg in a matter of hours. He brushed Grant's message aside. He could not drag himself into a celebratory mood. The burden of 60,000 men lost between both sides at Gettysburg and Vicksburg combined would have been heavy enough. Add to it the weight of guilt he already shouldered because of General Reynolds' death and his wife's injury, it was as if the earth had escaped its orbit and was careening toward the sun.

His distress deepened when he opened a note from Rebecca, passed to him by his private secretary. He should come to Mrs. Lincoln's chamber as soon as he could. She went to bed in the middle of the afternoon, suffering from fatigue, headaches, and a slight fever.

He stepped into the hall and was waylaid by a messenger from the War Department. "Mr. President, I have news regarding your carriage."

"What is it?"

"It appears the screws that held the driver's seat in place, had been removed by unknown hands. When the carriage started down a steep grade, the seat gave way, throwing the driver to the ground."

Lincoln pinched his brow. Oh! What a deadly web I weave, he thought. His chin quivered. "She could have been killed in what was intended to be an attack on me."

He continued down the hall to check on Mrs. Lincoln and found her asleep with Rebecca seated in a chair beside the bed, reading a book.

"How is she?" he asked in whispered tones.

"There has been no improvement," she replied. "The doctors think she should continue her convalescence at the quieter environment at the Soldiers' Home."

"Then it shall be done," he replied. "Let her have a good night's sleep and we shall carry her there in the morning."

"You should send a letter to the surgeon-in-charge. Tell him I will be a good bit longer and he should send messages to the Soldiers' Home if I'm needed urgently."

∗ ∗ ∗

Rebecca unwound the bandage on Mrs. Lincoln's head a few days after they moved to the summer cottage and discovered an abscess filled with pus. She retrieved a lancet from her nurse's basket, a tool that came in handy when she treated her boys' wounds.

"You will likely feel a slight pain," she said.

Mrs. Lincoln replied. "My head hurts too much to feel any discomfort you might inflict."

Rebecca incised the abscess enough to drain the fluid. When she had cleaned the gash, she said, "I shall leave the bandage off for a while. The fresh air will dry things out, and a little sunlight should help you heal faster."

"Having you near is healing power enough. When I can travel, you must go north with me for a little holiday."

"Shall I read to you?" Rebecca asked.

"It is always a delight to hear you read. But are you not going to give me an answer?"

"We best focus on getting you better." Rebecca opened a book and read until Mrs. Lincoln nodded off to sleep.

Lincoln paced the anteroom outside his cottage office while his wife slept, pausing occasionally to stare out the window toward the cemetery. He replayed in his mind something Emerson said to him months earlier, "Fires, plagues, revolutions, and calamities of all sorts serve to break up entrenched routines, clear the arena of corrupt contests, and open a fair field to all men."

When Rebecca appeared in the doorway later that evening to report on his wife's progress, Lincoln stood gazing out the window. He sniffled as he muttered, "Lord, if you cannot show mercy for my failures, at least shower those poor souls with your grace."

"He will," she whispered.

"Am I cursed of God?" he asked, "So many loved ones taken too soon ... so much pain suffered by innocents on account of my misdeeds ... such a high price the nation must pay for allowing the scourge of slavery to persist." His eyes glazed with a sheen of tears.

"No. God does not curse us," she replied. "I still mourn each of the loved ones I have lost over the years. Torment filled their eyes through the pain of disease, but once they drew their final breaths, a peace settled over them. I agonized through a long season of grief before I understood—they who leave this life early are more blessed than we who remain behind. Then I asked, why does God not take me out of this life and grant me eternal peace. Often, I sit in my hospital ward late at night, when all is quiet except for the sound of weeping from those who cannot sleep. I know that I tarry on this earth to be a blessing to my boys and to your family. How do I endure the evil of this world? I remind myself I am his instrumentality to salve the wounds evil men inflict on one another. And that is cause enough for celebration."

Lincoln arched his brow. "You threw yourself into a cause greater than yourself. A doctor once told me that doing so would help me whip the melancholies."

"Let nothing overshadow the purpose which God has laid on your heart."

"I was responsible for General Reynolds' death at Gettysburg." Lincoln hung his head. "When I offered to make him commander of the Army of the Potomac, he said he would accept on the condition that he would be free from political influences. I told him I could not do that. The truth is that it would have been in my power to do so, but I did not want to shoulder the burden that would accompany that promise. Had I agreed, he would not have been in the field and in harm's way. Does not the Almighty judge us for our evil acts?"

"He judges," she replied. "Yet he forgives."

"Even if it is true that the Almighty forgives, is it possible for a man to forgive himself?"

"Life is sometimes cruel," she said. "And war is the cruelest part of it. Your act was not evil. But men killing and maiming to defend their supposed right to inflict unspeakable cruelty on others—that is evil."

"I must believe this is a righteous war," he insisted. "And God will protect the right, though with many lives sacrificed."

"And those sacrifices shall be rewarded in Heaven," she replied.

"I have done the best I could, trusting in God," he said. "Even now, our troops are engaged with the rebels at Port Hudson on the Mississippi. If the rebels prevail there, we are all but lost. But if we could only take it from them, I think we shall have full control of the entire Mississippi River and the rebellion cut in half—a great deal to thank God for."

"Prayer will do what nothing else can. Will you not pray?"

"Yes, I will." He pressed his forehead against the window. "And you should pray for me."

"I do so constantly, as does Mrs. Lincoln."

"How is she doing this evening?" he asked. "Has she improved since you lanced her wound?"

"She has been sleeping. I was on my way to check the dressings when I came in here to say goodnight. If there is any great change, I will let you know."

"Thank you. You are truly a Godsend. I don't know how we would manage without you."

One of the cottage guards delivered a telegram to Lincoln around midnight. After reading it, he ran down the hall and burst into the room where Rebecca sat with his wife who had been woken by the thunder of her husband's footfalls.

"Good news!" he shouted. "Good news! Port Hudson is ours! The victory is ours! God is good. The rebellion is split in two, and the Father of Waters again flows unvexed to the sea."

His wife smiled for the first time since the carriage mishap. "Yes, God be praised. It is wonderful at long last to see such relief on my husband's face."

✳ ✳ ✳

Mrs. Lincoln clung to Rebecca's arm, nearly three weeks after the accident, as they meandered the broad field behind the cottage. "These walks do me so much good," she said.

Rebecca replied, "I wish I could bring all my boys to a place like this. I imagine I would see a good deal more healing than we accomplish in our hospital wards."

Mrs. Lincoln drew in a deep breath and with it, the fragrance of honeysuckle. "I often find myself ruing the day we left our sweet Springfield for this harsh city. And this war. The nation has become by husband's mistress, but it is a sacrifice I must make for the good of all."

"When this war is over, you shall have your husband back," Rebecca replied.

"You should go back to your boys, soon. It is selfish of me to keep you away from them."

A few days later, when Lincoln escorted Rebecca back to the hospital, Mrs. Lincoln heaped bouquets of flowers onto their laps and into every available space in the carriage. She had cut them from the beds and gardens around the cottage and grounds of the Soldiers' Home—some because of their brilliant colors, others for their sweet perfumes.

As the carriage creaked down the drive, Lincoln selected a long-stemmed rose from one of the bouquets.

"This is for you alone—to say thank you for saving my wife's life. The rest, I presume, are for the boys."

Rebecca smiled, hoping to hide her fatigue and achy joints. "I worry that no one looks after you. I pray the Lord will preserve you and comfort you in these tumultuous times."

DeWitt Ray was one of the first to greet Rebecca when she returned from nursing Mrs. Lincoln. He stood in the doorway to her room, his shoulders slumped, his eyes downcast.

"What is the matter?" she asked.

His lips trembled. "They have ordered me back to my regiment."

Rebecca's throat tightened.

"Mother," he said. "If I die on the battlefield, I have found two good friends—a Christian mother and a loving Savior."

Rebecca's eyes watered as he flung himself into her arms. Her soul ached. How lonely she would be without him. The only worse news she could imagine would be that her George had fallen in battle.

CHAPTER TWENTY-EIGHT

Rebecca fell ill in mid-September and lay in bed, suffering, for several days. The doctor called her condition a nervous affection of the heart and convinced Miss Dix to grant a month-long furlough.

She choked on tobacco smoke and exhaust from the coal-fired steam engine a week later, as she rode the six-and-a-half o'clock night train to New York City. The leather satchel that Secretary and Mary Jane Welles gave her for her journey home remained snug against her hip, its strap pulled tight across her chest. The Welleses warned her to guard it closely and to suspect every passenger jostling aboard the overnight train—except for soldiers and mature women. She didn't need their caution to be wary of the crude, beady-eyed man, who crowded too close to her on the wooden bench seat.

As soon as she deboarded in New York, she hurried to catch the eight o'clock morning train to Boston. Though the coach soon filled with caustic vapors, at least the passing landscape was visible through windows, and the seats were less crammed and more comfortable than on the night train from Washington.

Once away from the chaotic New York metropolis, the train's clanging settled into a monotonous rhythm, and she was lost in thought. She reflected on the duties she had left undone before hurriedly leaving Chelsea for Washington two years prior. The first thing she resolved to do on her return was to go directly to Woodlawn Cemetery.

She stood at her family plot the day after her arrival home, weak-kneed and clutching bouquets she cut from a friend's garden. She spoke to Daniel. Her tone was no different than if he had just returned from a long day at the upholstery shop. "We have gained a second Almira in our lives—our new daughter. She and George were wed a month ago. I have not met her yet but will in a few days. I don't mean that she replaces our sweet Clara Jane."

She fidgeted with a button on her dress. "I know I should have tended to certain affairs sooner. You will forgive me for not being more diligent about the business of having a slab to mark your place here, won't you? I have taken care of it today. I shall sell the last of our furniture in a day or two. The president has promised to make George a lieutenant in the army. Mr. Lincoln and his wife call me their friend. Yes, Mr. Lincoln is now our president. When I am in their family at the mansion, I stay in a grand suite with its own water closet. Can you imagine? They see that all of my needs are met. I have made a dear friend at the hospital. She is also a widow."

Rebecca knelt, weeping, murmuring. "Seeing so much death and suffering, one would think that I should not be so overcome by such sorrows. But I miss you. Each of you. I miss you more than I can bear at times. See, I brought flowers and I pray you are at peace. Maybe soon, the Lord will finish the work he has for me and let me join you." After laying bouquets at the graves of Daniel, Clara Jane, and Willie, she said good-bye and carried on.

Rebecca called on old friends in Chelsea, Boston, Somerville, and Newton Centre before she made the trip to Winthrop to meet her new Almira. She carried with her a bridal box and a silver spoon that Daniel's Aunt Prudence had given George when he was first born. Her new daughter-in-law received her with warm affection. They formed a bond that was both quick and deep, and when Rebecca left for Chelsea, she gave Almira a mother's kiss and a loving embrace.

Her first Almira—Almira Cushing before she married Solomon Fuller—brought her three-year-old son, Georgy, when she visited Rebecca a few days later at the Derbys' farm. Rebecca reached out for Georgy, a broad smile on her face. "Come to Auntie," she coaxed.

"It's okay, Georgy," Almira said. "You remember Auntie Pomroy."

Georgy flew into Rebecca's arms, and she gave him a big kiss on his cheek. "I can't wait to have a grandchild of my own. My George is married now. To a girl named Almira, no less."

"I told you he would marry a wonderful young woman someday—how could she not be so with the name Almira?"

"Tell me about everyone ... Father, Mother, Frank and Clara, the girls ... Mr. Fuller."

"All are well. Frank and Clara moved to Pearl Street after Father sold your house."

"It was kind of your father to take care of that business for me. With both George and me off in the war, it would not have been possible to sell without his help. Now, tell me about you and Mr. Fuller. Is everything going well?"

"All is well," Amira replied. "He didn't see much fighting in the war. His unit was used mostly as reinforcements, and his enlistment was over in August. It has been good to have him home. He would have come with us today, but he's in Boston on business."

"I would have liked to see him. I'm afraid we weren't on good terms when I left."

"You were a bit hard on him."

"I have always thought of you as the young woman I had hoped my Clara Jane could have grown into had she lived," Rebecca said. "When you came to me and said you were to be married, then you were in the family way so soon after, I grew concerned you were making a grave mistake. After all, his reputation wasn't sterling."

"And your motherly instinct was to protect me. Both Solomon and I understand that. You can rest assured that all is forgiven. He does not hold that against you."

The knots in Rebecca's shoulders unwound. "That is a great relief. Maybe I will be able to see him before I return to Washington … to set things straight."

"We shall do that," Almira said. "Now, tell me. Is there some secret from the President's House that you can share? A piece of gossip the public would not know."

"I am not a gossip, so I will not give you anything scandalous … not that there is anything of that sort. It is little known that Mrs. Lincoln is a highly intelligent woman. She speaks French fluently and has taught her eldest son to speak it as well. They often converse in the foreign tongue behind the president's back so that he cannot understand what they are saying. Knowing of Mrs. Lincoln's refinement and Mr. Lincoln's humble youth, I can only imagine that what they say is unflattering."

"That is the best you have?" Almira asked.

"That, young lady, is all you are getting."

✳ ✳ ✳

The following Saturday morning Rebecca set out for Salem and the home of Henry Hale, the proprietor of a hardware store and one of Senator Hale's several cousins. Henry Hale and his wife, Lydia, had invited her to join their family for midday dinner. Their son, Henry Augustus, the same age as George, was away in the Army and would not be able to join them.

The three-story wood house on Northey Street had a narrow front which created the illusion of a small cottage. Its long hallway that led to the spacious dining room and a large kitchen dispelled Rebecca's first impression. She delighted in meeting the Hales' teenage daughters, Lydia and Charlotte. Senator Hale's sister, Eliza, whom Rebecca had met a few days earlier for tea at her home in Malden, was another dinner guest. So was the Hales' next-door neighbor, Reverend Charles Palmer of the Tabernacle Church.

The doorbell rang incessantly as they dined, though no one rose and went to greet the callers. It was not until after they finished eating and everyone retired to the main parlor that she suspected there was more in store for her than a pleasant family repast. Many neighbors and guests mingled about in the parlor, waiting to meet her.

Henry Hale raised his voice over the conversations of those gathered, most of whom were ladies. "Ladies, gentlemen, it is my honor to present to you, on recommendation of my distinguished cousin Senator John Hale, a dear woman who is called by our president, 'the best friend I have known.' Mrs. Rebecca Pomroy is not only a nurse to our sick and wounded soldiers, but to the president's family during their recent times of trouble. Mind you, I have not pre-warned her that she would have such a large audience to address, but I hope she won't mind enlightening us on her intimate experiences within the halls of the President's House and among our brave men in arms."

Myriad stories, thoughts, and emotions swept through Rebecca's mind as she considered how to begin, until her sight landed on Lydia, the Hales' thirteen-year-old daughter. She nodded in her direction. "When I was only a couple of years older than your daughter, I called on the merchants of Boston's Faneuil Hall in search of donations for a worthy cause—a mission for seamen's families. A part of me wants to make a similar plea to all of you. That plea is on behalf of young men like my son, George, and like the Hale's young Henry. So far, our boys have been spared from injury or death. I imagine some of you here are not so fortunate. But all of us know at least one family which has suffered the cruelty of war. I sometimes wonder how I can withstand all the misery I see every day and every night and soldier on. Our poor boys need your help. Our hospitals run short on necessities such as blankets, warm socks, decent clothing, supplies of medicines. There are times when we are required to ration chloroform for those whose limbs we must amputate. We certainly lack luxuries like sweets, cake and bread, fruit, other delicacies. Anything you send us will be put to good use."

After she finished her appeal, she entertained questions from trivial to profound about her experiences in the President's House and in the hospital, until her voice grew pitched from exhaustion.

Henry Hale intervened. "We are grateful for all you do and for sharing your experiences in this war from which we are heretofore far removed. But before you go upstairs to rest in preparation for your return to Chelsea, let me assure you that my good neighbor Reverend Palmer is prepared to organize the members of his church to answer your pleas."

✳ ✳ ✳

Rebecca returned to Washington ten days after meeting the Hale family in Salem. She reported herself first to Miss Dix who asked if she knew Massachusetts ladies who would volunteer to become nurses. She replied, "There were several who would like to come, but they could not because of your ideas about nurses."

"I do not understand. My ideas are plain and easy."

"Plain, yes. But not necessarily easy for many. You demand that nurses must know how to cook all kinds of low diet. They must wear brown, black, or drab dresses, very small hoops, no curls, no jewelry, nor flowers on their bonnets. They must not write for books or newspapers. They must be in their own rooms at taps, or nine o'clock, unless obliged to be with the sick, must not go to any place of amusement in the evening, must not walk out with any private or officer, must not allow a private or officer in their own room except on business, must be willing to take the forty cents per day that is allowed by government to assist them in supplying what rations will not furnish in food, must pay for their own washing, shoes and clothing. If there is any surplus, it is expected that it will be spent upon the soldiers, for no nurse must come into the service with the idea of laying up one cent. Your nurses are to be quiet, careful not to offend, willing to suffer wrong rather than doing wrong in return."

"As I said, plain and easy," Miss Dix replied.

"You think it is reasonable that all your nurses should be like yourself—self-denying, self-sacrificing, with a large heart and open hands, doing all they can for the soldier. You are without doubt a worthy example—on the battlefields you do not stand back and observe but you take upon yourself the work of binding up wounds, stanching hemorrhaging, and administering stimulants until a surgeon can come. You also give your own food to fallen soldiers who are near starvation. You expect those who apply to be educated, intelligent, with a large share of patience, forbearance, and sobriety. But few women can match your standard."

"Thank you, Mrs. Pomroy, for your enlightening views." Miss Dix took up a stack of patient records to review. "There is an ambulance waiting to take you to the hospital where your presence has been missed."

The "Welcome Home" banner hanging above the hospital entrance drew a smile from Rebecca. The five-story stone building with all its blemishes was more of a home to her than any other place she could imagine.

Familiar voices rang out when she entered her fourth-floor ward.

One soldier who had been convalescing for several months shouted, "Mother has come!"

As all the patients who could walk flocked around her, shaking her hand or giving her a welcoming hug, her eyes glistened from a salty dew that welled up in her. Her heart pinched as some told stories of their suffering while she was gone. Others showed her calendars they had drawn to mark off the days until she returned.

All were doing well, except for one who took a musket ball in his back five months earlier and had lain, suffering in pain, for all that time. A surgeon finally operated on him the day before her return from furlough but was unable to find the ball.

The next morning, the muffled drum and fife from the Soldiers' Home two miles away woke Rebecca. It was a sign that another brave soldier was to be laid away in that graveyard. More than four thousand had preceded him there. The hand of death squeezed her heart whenever she visited the cemetery that lay only yards from the president's summer cottage. Her dear friend Abraham sometimes accompanied her on those visits.

Whenever she passed one of the walnut slabs that bore the inscription, Unknown, she couldn't help shedding tears for those left at home who would never know where father, son, husband, uncle, or brother was laid. The one being buried that day had a name. Sergeant Apollis Moore from the 13th New York Cavalry died of disease at the age of forty-two. During the past two years at Columbian College Hospital, she had cared for five hundred and seven brave soldiers. Thirty-one had died on her watch—two from wounds, the rest from disease.

She was cleaning closets on her second day back from furlough when visitors from Salem called on her. Mr. John Parker had come to town on railroad business and was accompanied by his wife and ten-year-old son, Eddie. Rebecca's presentation motivated them to come to see the hospital for themselves.

The Parkers' visit was followed the next day by drama surrounding barrels and boxes that Mrs. Parker told her to expect from Salem's Tabernacle Church. Rebecca's attendant was rummaging through the woodshed for kindling when he found the remnants of a demolished box with Rebecca's name stamped on it. She wasted no time and proceeded to the surgeon-in-charge to lay out her suspicions.

Rebecca reminded the surgeon that the steward had often interfered with her efforts to ease hospital life for the soldiers. She had caught him red-handed in the instances of the beef, the tea, and Mary Jane Welles's ice cream. On another occasion, the steward found out she had arranged for the nurses' cook to make up a pudding for her boys. Rebecca provided the cook with eggs, milk, and butter she had bought with her own money at exorbitant prices, along with stale bread from the messroom, which her boys had refused to eat. The steward put an immediate stop to what he called, "the extravagance of that Massachusetts nurse."

The surgeon inspected the steward's closet where he found jars of jellies, boxes of tea and coffee, and bottles of wine and sling, all marked, "For the Personal Use of Mrs. Pomroy." He ordered the steward to deliver all the items to Rebecca's ward and not to repeat his thievery.

When she thanked the surgeon, he told her, "We must keep you happy. All the worst cases in the hospital are put in your ward because you are a careful, hardworking nurse." He reached into his desk drawer and pulled out a small pouch of instruments. "I know I can trust you with these to probe for and dig out small pieces of bone and to plug the wounds when necessary."

After the steward returned the stolen items, she spoiled her soldiers, with samplings of the delicacies from Salem. She also served some to the six contrabands—runaway slaves in their twenties—whom she was teaching to read for the first time in their lives.

✳ ✳ ✳

Nurses were rousted from their sleep an hour after midnight early in November. Thirty new wounded were brought upstairs to the wards. There would have been more, but several died enroute from the battlefield at Rappahannock Station. One of the survivors had three horses shot out from under him. As he struggled on the ground, another horse trampled him almost to death, leaving him severely bruised. A second young soldier had taken a musket ball in the hip. When Rebecca removed his sock, the flattened projectile fell out. It had passed down from the hip and out his heel.

She occupied herself every waking hour of the next week dressing wounds, writing letters, and reading to a full ward of patients. As she read one day, a young soldier interrupted and pulled his Bible from his pocket.

"This is my best friend," he said. "For when I was shot through the lungs, it became covered with my own blood which I shed for my country." During those seven days, the only distraction she allowed herself was a visit from some of her earlier patients who called to thank her for being a mother to them in their time of suffering.

The chaos that swept through the ward with the arrival of wounded from Rappahannock Station had subsided by the eighth day, when Aunt Mary, the Lincoln family's African cook, stole Rebecca away to the President's House. On her arrival there, she found the president haggard and in distress. Tad had come down with fever the night before and was too ill to eat breakfast. Lincoln was determined to deliver his speech at the national cemetery dedication in Gettysburg, Pennsylvania, but Mrs. Lincoln had plunged into hysteria. Although she was to accompany her husband, she refused to leave Tad, and the special train was scheduled to depart at noon.

Rebecca carried with her a bottle of Dr. Sappington's fever pills based on Aunt Mary's description of Tad's symptoms. She also had laudanum with her, as was her usual practice when called to the President's House.

As Rebecca administered the fever pills, Lincoln paced Tad's room. "How long?" he asked.

"His fever is not high enough to be of much concern, but we likely won't see improvement before morning."

"So, what do we do in the meantime?"

"We should give him peace and quiet so he can sleep. Rest is often the best medicine."

"And how is my wife?"

"By now the laudanum should have taken effect and she will be asleep. Go to Gettysburg and give your speech. There is nothing you can do here," she said. "I will telegraph you in the morning to let you know how they are doing."

"It's no great speech. Folks won't miss me if I don't go. Mr. Everett will keep everyone spellbound for a couple of hours, and they will be happy to be out of the heat."

She shook her head. "Everybody will miss the president if he fails to show up and pay tribute to our fallen heroes. If you're not at your post, newspapers across the country will call for your head."

Later in the afternoon, Rebecca stood at an upstairs window and witnessed the spectacle of nine thousand members of the Invalid Corps, a legion of wounded heroes, march up the drive to serenade the president. They were unaware that Lincoln had already boarded the special train to Gettysburg.

Among the marchers were many who were minus one arm or both, others missing hands or feet or a leg. Some hobbled along with a halting limp, or on crutches. Many carried an arm in a sling, while several displayed empty uniform sleeves with the cuff pinned to their coats. Officers with artificial legs rode horseback. As the Marine Band played patriotic music, tears welled in her.

The next morning Tad's fever broke, and Mrs. Lincoln received the news with great relief when she awoke. A calm settled over the President's House and Rebecca returned to the hospital after telegraphing Lincoln.

CHAPTER TWENTY-NINE

Mary Jane Welles visited Rebecca in her ward the day after Lincoln returned from dedicating the cemetery in Gettysburg. She bore gifts of baked apples and pickled onions for the boys. She also brought a mixed bag of news from the President's House. Tad's health was much improved, but William Johnson had carried the president to his bed when they arrived home late in the evening. Lincoln was under a doctor's care and William was seeing to his comfort. Mary Jane assured Rebecca she would be called if he did not recover soon.

No call for her help came over the next two days, despite newspaper reports that the president suffered from a mild case of smallpox. She busied herself by reading to her boys and mending socks, distracting herself from fretting over her dear friend Abraham.

She slept fitfully that night, until the hospital matron rousted her at two o'clock in the morning. Her immediate concerns were for Lincoln.

"Prepare your ward," the matron said. "We have two hundred walking wounded and seventy-five on stretchers downstairs. The worst ones are coming to your ward."

She sat up and blinked. "Where am I to put them?"

"If any of them must have a bed, put your fittest boys to the floor to make room."

The next two-and-a-half days found her consumed by the needs of her new charges, but the dearth of news about Lincoln's health ate away at her—what was the citizenry not being told?

A welcome diversion arrived the day before Thanksgiving. Two boxes from the ladies of Salem's Tabernacle Church were delivered, containing fixings for Thanksgiving dinner—two roasted turkeys, plum pudding, apple and mince pies, cookies, crackers, butter, cheese, ham, raisins, apples, cranberries, currant jelly, wines, sugared gingerbread, cakes, nuts, and pickles.

She stored it all away in the nurses' messroom to add to the next day's feast, then she went to Mrs. Russell's ward to see to a soldier who was happy at the prospect of dying. He asked her to sing *I Am a Soldier of the Cross* and *Happy Day* while he tried to beat time with his hand. She wept for the poor soldier, far from home and friends, straining to breathe out the words in feeble tones.

Mary Jane returned with her husband later that evening and found Rebecca in her room. In the course of their visit, they remarked that the president's health had not changed a great deal, except for the onset of a mild headache. Rebecca cringed. She had witnessed enough of the disease's progression to grasp that headaches were not a good sign.

She tired of waiting for further word on Lincoln's health and called at the mansion the day after Thanksgiving. She had been on an errand to purchase supplies for her ward and instructed the ambulance driver to return to the hospital without her. When she arrived upstairs, she found the waiting area empty, except for one of the president's secretaries who told her, "He's in his bedroom, but you can't go in."

"I must," she said.

"He is under quarantine by the doctors. Not even his Cabinet can go in. Only William is allowed."

"How are the others?" she asked.

"Tad is as mischievous as ever. His mother is distressed. She didn't handle it well when the doctors insisted she leave her husband's sickroom this morning, so they gave her laudanum."

"Have the doctors given any details about his condition?"

"They do not believe he is in any danger, if that is what you're wondering. It is apparently the variola minor infection. So other than the chance of him infecting other people, there is nothing to worry about."

"Thank you. Tell him I called and wish him a speedy convalescence."

"Shall I tell Mrs. Lincoln—"

"Please tell her I was here but didn't want to bother her while she's resting. Anyway, after I look in on Tad, I had best be getting back to the hospital."

She found Tad after a long search—hunched at the base of the stone balustrade of the mansion's flat copper roof. She squatted next to him.

"What are you doing?" she asked.

He didn't answer.

She eyed a crude wooden structure, resembling a lean-to. "Did your father build this?"

He shrugged.

"Did you help him?"

"Willie and me. We built it. We call it the Ship of State." He pulled a toy spyglass from his pocket.

"What is that for?" she asked.

"We watched for strange boats on the river. If we saw anything that shouldn't be on the river or on our side, we reported it to the Commodore."

"You mean Secretary Welles?"

"No, dummy. Pa." He turned away from her.

"Do you come here often?" she asked.

"Not since Willie. This is the first time by myself."

"You miss him, don't you?"

He squeezed his eyes tight.

She sat next to him and pulled him close.

"Pa used to tell us stories about ghosts. I came up here to watch out for ghosts who might try to carry Pa off. I don't want him to die."

His ten-year-old shoulders shuddered as he sobbed.

"He's not going to die," she said. "But it may take some time for him to feel better. We just have to be patient and pray."

Tad cried in her arms for several minutes, his body tense, then he cocooned into her bosom. As he relaxed in her embrace, she recalled tender moments, long past, when she had comforted her own children in her arms. After a while Tad sat up straight and asked, "Do you want to see my soldiers?"

She followed him down to his room and watched him simulate a battle between the brave Yankees and the Johnny Rebs.

Later, when Rebecca stepped out to the portico to return to the hospital, the doorman signaled for a stable boy to bring the president's carriage around. Her downcast countenance prompted the doorkeeper to ask, "Something the matter, Mrs. Pomroy?"

She asked, "When will this cruel war end and all our hospitals be closed so we can return to our loved ones and pleasant homes?"

"I do not know the answer to that," he said as he helped her into the carriage. "I don't think Mr. Lincoln does, either."

Rebecca returned to the hospital to find her new attendant curled up on a bed under several blankets, trembling and his teeth chattering. One of her patients said the young man had been burning with fever only moments before.

When she pulled back the covers to examine her attendant, a bitter stench stung her nostrils. She covered her mouth with the sleeve of her dress as she pulled back the blankets further. The source of the odor became immediately apparent. He had been lying in a stew of his own excrement and urine.

She sent for a surgeon and called over one of her healthier boys to help her lift the suffering attendant out of bed and carry him to the bathroom. They washed and dried him thoroughly then dressed him in clean clothes, wrapped him in a blanket, and seated him in a chair.

The surgeon arrived soon after with an orderly at his side and directed her to put the patient to bed.

Rebecca gestured around the ward and asked, "Where do you propose I do that?"

He surveyed the room and replied, "I suppose we'll have to find room in another ward."

The orderly draped the trembling patient's arm over his neck and followed the surgeon out of the ward.

She stood with her arms folded as she stared at the mattress. For the first time in her three years in the nurses' corps, she had reached the end of her rope. Now, she was saddled with her heaviest load of patients, at the ebbtide of her strength, and without an attendant.

Three days passed before a new attendant arrived. He was a poor, lame invalid with the use of only one of his hands. In an earlier day, she might have rallied and taken up the challenge of becoming a mother to her needy charge. But when the surgeon made his rounds that evening, he found her listless, her complexion sallow. Her forehead was hot to the touch.

"You are too sick to be around," he said. "You are to put yourself to bed at once and not leave your room until you are well. I will see that your patients are under someone else's care, and I will check on you daily."

"How long do you expect me to be away from my boys?" she asked.

"At least a week," he replied, and he clenched his jaw, unwilling to change his answer.

That night in bed she considered whether the day had come when she should lay her burden down. Later, as she drifted off to sleep, she pondered, how could I possibly leave my work behind when this cruel war is not yet over?

She languished, flat on her back, for another couple of days with the walls closing in and longed for friends from home to gather around.

While she lay there, the hospital steward alleged that portions of turkey and other delicacies from boxes that were meant for the boys' holiday dinner had been stolen by nurses for their own use. Even though Rebecca rose from her bed to produce a letter from the Salem women stating the gifts were for the nurses as well as the boys, the charges stood. The affront by hospital officers was a bitter pill.

Her health was much improved several days later when she left her room to spend time reading to her boys. Each day after, she grew stronger and was energized by a report that the president had been well enough to attend theater with his family. On the heels of that news, she wept a mother's tears of joy on receiving a letter from George reporting he had received his promotion to 1st Lieutenant.

She was not yet at full strength when some of her boys whose healing was threatened by a diet of only coarse food wanted hardier meals. One wanted chicken broth, and another asked for tomatoes. She sent her new attendant down to the steward to deliver their request. The steward refused and repeated his complaint that she made too much fuss over her boys, and that she was an extravagant nurse.

A general's wife visited her that day, and asked if she was getting everything she needed. When Rebecca recounted the incident with the steward, the woman said, "Wait a few hours and I will send you the tomatoes and broth for your use."

When the woman's carriage returned, her footman entered the hospital with a pail of broth in one hand and a basket of tomatoes in the other. The surgeon-in-charge met him and asked, "What are you going to do with these things?"

"I am taking them up to Mrs. Pomroy's room for her sick boys," he replied.

"No," the surgeon said. "There is enough in the hospital to provide everything the patients need. Put those things back in the carriage."

The next day an article appeared in the *Washington Morning Chronicle* describing the incident and alleging a disturbing state of affairs at the hospital. When news of the scandal reached Miss Dix, she summoned Rebecca and asked her to explain the newspaper report.

Rebecca stated the unvarnished truth.

Miss Dix replied, "There will be an investigation, and you and other nurses will have to give evidence before military officers. But you are in the right, and you will prevail. Although, if you do not and you have to leave your posts, I can find other places for you."

On the morning of the examination, Rebecca packed her trunk and made arrangements for it to be sent to the President's House. She was fully prepared to be sacked. The nurses were called downstairs one by one to give their accounts, and she was last. The inquiry board consisted of a number of military and hospital officers, including a medical inspector and medical director. She was unprepared for their politeness, having readied herself to stand against any bullying they might level against her.

They asked, "Have you been obliged to send home for anything?"

"Oh yes, many times."

"And for what?"

"Sugar, rice, tea, coffee, wine, etc."

"How much have you been sent?"

"A great many barrels and boxes full. My friends have been glad to supply me, and I have always shared with the other nurses. I have sent surpluses outside the hospital, especially to Carver Barracks and the family encampments there where they were needed."

"Have you ever sent for crackers?"

"Yes. My boys often would have only two crackers apiece, and some weak tea, and I felt they needed more to make them strong again. When I had barrels come, I sent them round to all the soldiers."

After finishing their investigation, the officers dismissed her with respect.

As a result, the steward was removed from the hospital and Rebecca received the congratulations of friends who were overjoyed at the sudden turn of events.

*** * ***

A New York woman arrived at Columbian College Hospital days before Christmas, to begin employment as a cook for the nurses. She brought Catie, her three-year-old daughter. The woman's husband was a patient at a nearby hospital for invalid soldiers, his frail body eroding under a siege of consumption. He was on his way to becoming little more than skin draped loosely over a skeleton. The soldier had pleaded with Rebecca to find a way to bring his wife to him.

On the first sight of the little girl, Rebecca's imagination carried her back to an alley along lower Ann Street. She was a girl of twelve, huddled in with a flock of destitute children, reading to them and their mothers. A little tyke named Ryan had been her favorite. From an alley near North Square, they would marvel at the spire of the church where Paul Revere broadcast his signal that the redcoats were coming— "One if by land, two if by sea." Three years later, the sight of that same tower sent chills running up young Rebecca's spine. The scars from Papa's death shrouded her in foreboding for nearly another thirty years. Now her eyes turn constantly toward heaven, from whence cometh her help in times of trial.

Catie and her mother were given quarters in a small room downstairs near the nurses' messroom, but the nurses feared the surgeon-in-charge might see the girl and send her and her mother home. So, Catie was confined to their room at all times. She soon became bored with her confinement and flitted outside to gaze at the hospital on the hill where her father was being cared for. As time went on, she exchanged greetings with convalescing soldiers who walked the grounds to gain strength and speed their healing.

Catie found the courage one morning to ask Rebecca to take her upstairs to see some of the sick soldiers. Rebecca took her by the hand and led her up to her ward, past the rows of beds and gawking patients, and into her private quarters. "You may sit here and watch through my open door," Rebecca said. "But don't go into the ward and bother the sick men."

The girl's patience gave way to temptation, and she tiptoed into the ward, endearing herself to a few who had daughters and sons of their own at home. Her circle expanded until she became the pet of the whole ward. Her conquest did not stop there. Rebecca's friends in the city sewed a bright crimson dress and aprons for her to wear on New Year's Day, an occasion when the soldiers planned to present her with handmade trinkets. Catie was too ill to get out of bed and did not go to the ward at the anticipated time. The patients asked every day when they would see Catie again. Each day's news grew more dire, until word came that she was very sick with a sore throat, swollen glands, a barking cough, and difficulty breathing. Rebecca's bloodshot eyes misted as she choked on the dreaded word, diphtheria.

Rebecca returned to Catie's bedside and did all she could to make the child's final hours as comfortable as possible—giving her fluids and administering laudanum as a desperate measure to dull her pain and calm her. All the while, Mrs. Russell watched over the grieving mother.

At ten o'clock that evening, Rebecca cradled Catie in her lap as the girl wheezed her final breath. It was at that moment that Rebecca saw clearly for the first time. She had never before held someone so young as the breath of life departed through their lips. Her own Clara Jane was nearly nine years old when she passed. She had mourned the child of a friend, a neighbor, an acquaintance, though she had not been in the same room when their souls departed. Children had died on lower Ann Street but never in her presence. At twelve or sixteen or twenty, she would not have been prepared to take such a blow. Providence had been kind to her. Trials had steeled her for her present calling—for her new Olivers.

Mrs. Russell helped Rebecca wash Catie's placid body and lay her out in the crimson dress. During the next day, soldiers filed past to say goodbye to the bright star that had brought them so much joy in so brief a time. The sick and disabled, one by one, young and old, all who could hobble in on canes and crutches, came and shed tears and kissed her as though she belonged to them. Even the surgeons, who were jaded to suffering, wept. A service was held in the hospital steward's room at six o'clock. At seven, Rebecca and Mrs. Russell accompanied Catie's parents to the Baltimore train depot to carry their daughter home to her final resting place.

CHAPTER THIRTY

Lincoln sat in the smallpox ward of a Negro hospital, shortly after the beginning of the new year. He gazed at William Johnson's sweat-beaded ebony brow. His valet's mouth hung open, lips swollen, tongue covered with black ridges. More shallow dark folds formed over his face and arms as if an infestation of leeches had burrowed under his skin and died there.

The surgeon who had escorted Lincoln to William's bedside said, "Take as long as you need. This one does not have much time left."

Lincoln pleaded, "Is there nothing you can do?"

The surgeon shook his head. "All we can do is keep him as comfortable as possible." He started to walk away but turned back. "In this place, any amount of comfort is a luxury."

Lincoln's heart twinged. "There is so much need, but so little ability to act."

Two days later, Lincoln sat in his upstairs office in the President's House, mulling promises he had made and not yet kept. Especially unkept promises he had made to the young man in whom he had entrusted his life and his confidences. He held a message he had just received.

> *Mr. President, it is my sad duty to inform you*
> *of the passing this morning of your man,*
> *William Johnson.*

Lincoln's throat ached. He murmured, "He was not anyone's man but his own."

Several days after laying William's body to rest, Lincoln crossed the street to the bank. No sooner than he stepped through the door the cashier approached. "Mr. President, I hear the barber who used to groom you is dead."

Lincoln's voice trembled. "I bought a coffin for the poor fellow and gave him a proper burial."

"I do not want to seem indelicate," the cashier replied. "But I've been thinking about the loans we made to William."

"No apology is required," Lincoln said. "I was intending to take care of them."

"There is no need. The bank is prepared to forgive his loans."

"No, you don't," Lincoln argued. "I endorsed the notes and am bound to pay them. It is your duty to see that I do."

"Yes sir, but it has been our custom to devote a portion of the bank's profits to charitable objects, and this seems to be a most deserving one."

"I appreciate the sentiment, but I must fulfill my obligation. It's the least I owe William."

"I will tell you how we can arrange this," the cashier said. "The loans to William were joint ones between you and the bank. You stand half of the loss, and I will cancel the other."

"That sounds fair, but it's insidious. You are going to get ahead of me. You are going to give me the smallest note to pay. There must be a fair divide over poor William. Reckon up the interest on both notes, and chop the whole straight through the middle, so that my half shall be as big as yours. That's the way we will fix it."

"After this, Mr. President," the cashier said, "you can never deny that you endorse the Negro."

"That's a fact that I do not intend to deny." Lincoln clenched his fists to stanch his sorrow.

✳ ✳ ✳

Nearly a week after settling William's debts, Lincoln stood at his office window, his chest hollowed by grief as he stared into the night. A flash of light drew his attention to the mansion's stables. Then came a puff of smoke and a blaze of fire.

He wheeled around and bolted into the hallway, calling to his secretaries as he bounded down the stairs. "A fire! The stables. Get the horses out."

A six-foot-four hulk of a man, one of the mansion guards, blocked his path. "No," the man said. "The fire department has been called. I'll die before I let you rush into a burning building."

"But the horses. Willie's pony," Lincoln blurted.

"I'm sure both coachmen are doing what they can. Come, we can watch from the East Room."

As Lincoln watched from the East Room windows, Mrs. Lincoln, Tad, the president's secretaries, and others from the household staff crowded around him. Tad clutched his father's hand.

By the time the firemen arrived, the stables were fully engulfed. A short time later, the Lincoln family's private coachman joined them. He pressed his palms to his head. "My God, what happened?"

"Where have you been?" Lincoln demanded.

"At dinner," he replied. "I have only just arrived back."

"Where is McGee?" Lincoln asked.

"He was to remain at the stables while I was out."

Lincoln shook his head and turned back to the window to watch the fire rage.

The chief fireman entered the East Room several hours later. "I am sorry, it is a total loss."

"What of the horses?" Lincoln asked.

"I am afraid all six are lost."

Lincoln turned back to the window and sobbed.

Mrs. Lincoln tried to console her husband. "There is no need for weeping. We can get more horses."

Tad replied, "One of them was Willie's pony. That is why he cries."

"Maybe it is time we all returned to our beds," Mrs. Lincoln said as she took Tad's hand.

"Yes, go," Lincoln said. "But I shall stay here for a bit longer."

Shortly after everyone had retired, Rebecca stood at the threshold of the East Room. Rather than go in, she remained and watched Lincoln, his shoulders shaking. His head bowed and straightened, bowed and straightened again, and again, and again. Occasionally, he put a hand to his face. After a mournful sigh, he turned and started to leave. He looked up as he neared the doorway and stopped. "Oh, hello. What brings you out at this hour?"

"I came into the city for the day with of couple other nurses, and we supped in the home of friends. When we received word of excitement at the President's House, I insisted we come to see if we could be of help."

"I am afraid we have had a disaster. We lost all ..." He choked on his words and could not squeeze out the rest.

"I could see from the drive. How are Tad and Mrs. Lincoln?"

"They have gone up to bed."

"And you, my dear Abraham. How are you?"

"A few days ago," he said. "I told an old ally, who is himself on the throes of death, this war is eating my life out. For some time now, I have had a strong impression that I shall not live to see the end. And now this."

"You should rest. Get some sleep."

"I can say the same to you," Lincoln replied. "Neither of us has time to rest. The difference between us is I spend all my hours sending men and boys to be killed or maimed, and you spend yours binding their wounds and closing their eyes. When will this nightmare be over?"

"I have been asking that question more and more," she said.

"And have you come up with any answers?"

"Only the one I gave you on the night we first met."

"He doeth all things well?" he asked.

"We must trust in that," she said. "Else we lose our minds and maybe our souls."

Lincoln shook his head. "When I was a young man, a freshly minted lawyer, I had suffered several seasons of deep melancholy. I reached the point of physical and mental exhaustion and thought I had come to the end of my rope. A good doctor asked if I could think of any thread that connected those dark episodes. Having pondered the same questions on many occasions, I had a ready answer. I listed a few for him. I recalled being affected by thoughts of death, storms, and idleness. He advised me to lose myself so completely in some cause greater than myself, so that all other concerns would become trivial by comparison."

"Was the emancipation of enslaved Africans your new cause?" Rebecca asked.

"It began simply as a campaign against extremists on all sides, whether abolitionism or the extension of slavery. But melancholy continued to stalk me. When I came to live in this house, I discovered our Union, which I have loved from my boyhood, was on the cusp of destruction. I had stood by helplessly over the course of my life and watched too many cherished unions with those I loved wither or die. I dug in my heels and vowed to preserve this nation, regardless of the cost."

"That only brought more death," Rebecca said.

"As I watched the panorama of calamity unroll before my eyes, my hands became sticky with guilt from all the bloodshed—not only the blood of dear friends but of tens of thousands whose faces I had never seen, who put their trust in me. I looked for a cause greater than any I had ever pursued. I have now adopted the utter destruction of the slave power as my new purpose." He shrugged. "Then came my Willie, William, and tonight—Willie's pony. Death still stalks me, and I continue to push against the despair that wants to drown me."

Rebecca's eyes watered. "I, too, once found myself in such a place."

"What did you do?"

"I turned to a cause which is greater than all earthly endeavors. I gave over my will to God."

"Yet the contest proceeds, and the will of God prevails," he replied.

CHAPTER THIRTY-ONE

Rebecca, Mrs. Russell, and another nurse from Columbian College Hospital, boarded a ten o'clock train to Baltimore in mid-April. They were the most skilled nurses in Miss Dix's corps, and nowhere were they more needed. Miss Dix dispatched them there to help render aid to hundreds of prisoners released from the rebels' notorious Libby Prison.

The three nurses were administered the oath of allegiance before entering, and again, once inside Baltimore's West Hospital—an old warehouse on the wharf, formerly used for grain storage. Before proceeding to the patients' wards, they received strict instructions not to speak to or even look at rebel prisoners, through whose quarters they must pass on their way to the second flight where the Union men lay. While incarcerated in Richmond, the Union men had been fed only low-quality cornbread and packed like human sardines in large bays with open windows, leaving them exposed to weather and temperature extremes.

The scene that greeted the three nurses as they entered the makeshift hospital ward stopped them in their tracks. The place was dark, filled with languishing souls spread corner-to-corner across its floor. Desperation was so tangible they could have shoveled it into piles like dung.

More than two hundred hollow, vacant eyes stared back at them. Many of the eyes belonged to half-clad, leathery, bluish-hued bodies that were little more than skeletons wrapped in human flesh. The dense air reeked of odors like rotten eggs, fermented feces, dried urine, a stew of weeks-old garbage simmering under a hot summer sun. Pleas for mother, wife, or sister rose on the wings of curses from the insane among them, and the dearth of nurses was no match for the groundswell of need. Imprisonment had robbed them of human dignity.

Rebecca flashed hot and cold. Bile rose in her throat. She took a moment to recover then went to work.

Her first patient was a twentyish lad with frostbitten feet, all his toes rotted off. She cut away the dead tissue and remnants of bone. Her face was an inch from the wound. She washed him where he lay, and bandaged what was left of his feet. Her next patient said he had not changed the rags he called clothes for seven months. The odor gagged her—an invasion of festering bed sores covering his filth caked body. After him were several with matted, vermin-infested hair. She shaved their heads and rubbed salve into their scalps. They, too, were covered head to toe in smut, as if they toiled for days and nights for years on end as chimney sweeps.

Two of the brave boys she nursed that first day died under her care, and others expired before she could attend to them. Many passed from this world while being carried on litters from boats that had brought them from Richmond up to Baltimore Harbor. Some came into the hospital through the main door, others were put through windows on the waterside and lifted by elevator directly into the ward.

Rebecca's strength gave way near midnight. She had not eaten since seven o'clock that morning, and nothing in the way of food was available in the hospital. She asked a soldier if he could tell her where she might find a bed.

"There is no accommodation for sleeping here," he said. "But there is an empty bed in the attic that has been vacated by a patient. I will show you the way."

He took a half-burned candle and led her up to the next landing. The steps were odds-and-ends of unfastened wooden planks, with no railing. As she followed, in near darkness, she stumbled over something and almost fell.

"What is that?" she asked.

Her guide lowered the candle, inches away from a corpse—its open eyes frozen by death. "That's one who didn't make it. Spotted fever. A detail will take him out for burial in the morning."

She followed him up several flights and into a pitch-dark, musty room that was partitioned for stowing grain. Under the illumination of the flickering candle, he indicated a stall, set up with a crude bed and dirty quilt but no pillow.

"This is all there is," he said. "But don't undress. We have wharf rats, and they will eat up or carry off everything left about the room."

"Is there some way I can fasten the door?" She looked around as best she could.

"No," he replied. "Don't worry. Nothing will hurt you if you leave your candle burning till it goes out."

After he left, she tried to close the door and its rusty hinges creaked under the strain of its weight. An agitated voice rang out, "Who's there?"

Rebecca cringed. "Who are you?" she asked. "And why are you here?"

A woman replied, "Don't come near me. I am dying of smallpox."

"Don't worry I shall not come near," Rebecca said. "I am exhausted from caring for the sick." She sat on the bed the soldier had shown her and buried her head in her hands. Her mind filled with distressing thoughts—what if I should be taken with fever and die in this vile, unknown spot, with no one to take me to Woodlawn and lay me beside my husband and children. What would my dear friends at home say, if they knew where I am tonight? She prayed until sleep overtook her.

At dawn sunlight filtered through the cobwebs on the windows and outlined the huge rafters overhead. When she arose, she learned that the smallpox patient, also a nurse, was still living, and a colored man, who had survived the same curse of disease, was in the habit of bringing up her meals and medicines.

Rebecca left the room in haste and went down flights of stairs, past the bay full of rebels, and finally outside to a pump where she washed her face and hands. She asked for directions to the nearest restaurant and bought a breakfast of steak and coffee, nourishment to carry her through another day. Her second day was much like the first, full of cleaning bodies too weak to do other than lie in despair and await death. Three in her care passed on. When she returned to her hard bed in the attic that night, she learned the nurse with smallpox had been taken to another hospital.

News of the smallpox woman's death, on Rebecca's third day at West Hospital, incited both the better and lesser angels of her nature—the angel who forgave and the angel who avenged. As their battle raged over the course of long, grueling days, not even fatigue could inoculate her against the plague of sleepless nights.

✳ ✳ ✳

In early May, when Rebecca received orders to return to Columbian College Hospital, she had been at West Hospital for three weeks. In that time, she lost almost as many patients as she had in her two-and-a-half preceding years. The warring angels in her mind clashed again when she encountered a former Chelsea neighbor in a rebel officer's uniform. He was among the prisoners being exchanged. She shook her fist at him and shouted, "How dare you!" A guard whisked him away before she could dish out all the abuse she was tempted to unleash.

She returned to her ward, weary and with back pain, hoping to find her boys in better condition than when she left them. Instead, many had been moved to hospitals in the north to finish their healing. Her attendant was among them.

The loss of her assistant wasn't her only source of discouragement. Nurses were being sent south to help in field hospitals, even as the city hospitals were preparing for thousands of wounded and sick from the Wilderness battlefield in Virginia. Four from her hospital were among the nurses who had been deployed. Rebecca and those who remained in the city would be saddled with twice as much work.

The first six hundred new patients arrived two days after her return from Baltimore. Half of them were only slightly injured. The only care they required consisted of a good bath, a change of clothes, and wounds dressed. Afterwards, they were sent to hospitals closer to their hometowns. The next wave was like a sea wall churned up by gale force winds. For ten days, hundreds of ambulances and wagons filled Washington's streets.

A thousand new patients, most badly wounded, overwhelmed the hospital staff. Two brave men whom she attended had been shot through the face. In each case, a ball passed through their jaw, knocked out teeth, and ripped off a piece of their tongue. They could only communicate by using hand gestures. One of them carried his teeth and a part of his jawbone in his pocket as trophies. Another boy was shot through his heel, pushing the nails of his boot into his foot. One of her boys had his left arm operated on, the shoulder dislocated, and a section of bone six inches long removed. The bullet was found under his shoulder blade, and he remained very ill.

Apart from the newcomers, a young patient—who had been ill and for several months under her care with no prospect of healing—longed for home. He begged for a furlough so he could see his mother. The surgeon refused his request, but he kept begging day after day. Rebecca commiserated with the poor boy, and she told the doctor that his homesickness was impeding his recovery. The doctor relented and granted the furlough. After waiting and expecting every day for weeks to receive the furlough orders, the patient fell into deep depression and his condition deteriorated. When the orders finally arrived, he was too feeble to take them in his hands and read them.

Rebecca explained, "Now you can go home. I will get you ready tonight."

His eyes glazed over, then he broke into an insane frenzy. He was taken the next day to an asylum. When news of his death came soon thereafter, Rebecca trudged about for the balance of the morning and afternoon, her chest hollow and her mind numb.

Others died as well, and the muffled drumbeats from the Soldiers' Home cemetery thrummed and faded, thrummed and faded all day long, for days. Each volley of somber rhythms sparked bittersweet memories for Rebecca. She had read to and shown family pictures to those on the cusp of death and watched their expressions, some blissful and others wistful.

Mary Jane Welles stopped in the ward one day as Rebecca washed a dead boy's body. Mary Jane helped her prepare him to be carried off to the Soldiers' Home—dressing him in a freshly laundered, pleated shirt and tying a black ribbon on his arm. Once he was taken away, they wrote messages to his wife and five children.

The next day, Mary Jane returned to the ward loaded down with a bushel of oranges and lemons, jars of pickles, and a box of paper and books. During the following week, she visited the ward almost daily. More visitors followed—friends of the Welleses, governors, senators, representatives of Congress, as well as friends from Boston and strangers from the region around Washington.

CHAPTER THIRTY-TWO

Mrs. Lincoln had suffered from recurring headaches after the carriage accident, but none had been so debilitating as one that struck the following summer. The first thing she said when Rebecca walked into the sick room at the summer cottage was, "Did you bring laudanum? I think it will give me much relief."

"Of course," she said. Rebecca reached into her bag of instruments and medicinal supplies and pulled out a bottle. After she administered a dose, she sat with Mrs. Lincoln until the drug took effect. Then, she called on Lincoln in his office.

He set aside dispatches he had been perusing at the long table. "Mary Jane tells me you had a bad case of the gallstones."

"We had just begun receiving the wounded from Cold Harbor," Rebecca said. "Nine hundred new patients, my ward was full again, and overflowing."

"How did you manage?"

"The other nurses took turns covering for me. So, my boys were cared for. As for my gallstones, the initial attack was so painful the doctor administered chloroform for four hours."

"You now know better what your boys go through."

"I suppose so," she said. "Though, during my time at West Hospital, I witnessed the depths of rebel cruelty inflicted on our men, and no suffering I have known compares. How can anyone forgive such barbarism? The work among those poor souls in Baltimore taxed Mrs. Russell so thoroughly that she left the nurses corps soon after we returned to Washington."

"It confounds me," he said, raking his fingers through his hair. "How do their leaders whip them up into such fervor that they treat brothers with unimaginable malice? Or else they throw themselves into the mouths of cannons and impale themselves on bayonets, without any gain in it for themselves."

"But what about you?" she asked. "How then do you manage to send hundreds of thousands into the field, knowing many will perish, and those who don't will be marred forever? If not their bodies mangled, their souls tortured by what they do or witness."

"Do you not know that those rebel bayonets and minié balls pierce me, also?" Images of gravestones at Gettysburg and the Soldiers' Home weighed on his conscience. "Each time I read the record of a brave soldier struck down in a faraway field, I find myself on the plain of battle where he fell, writhing in pain with him. Distance does not buffer me from their sacrifice."

"It is an unfathomable burden you carry," she said. "I pray constantly that the Lord will sustain my dear friend, Abraham. May I tell you a story of how God extends his mercy in the midst of trials?"

"Sit," he said. "Let me hear your story."

"A poor fellow from New York was brought from the field badly wounded and was to have his leg amputated. He was very sensitive about the loss of his limb and would not let me write about it in letters I wrote on his behalf to his family. Nevertheless, he would often say as he tossed in pain on his bed, 'If I could only see Sarah.'

"Sarah was his wife, the mother of his little family of children with whom he had sung many years in the choir of a small Methodist church. I saw he was failing fast, and that he never would be able to go home to her. So, I sent word that her husband wished to see her. On the next Saturday night she arrived, weary and faint, and I gave her my own bed and rations.

"On the following morning, after the doctor had made his usual rounds, and the husband was neatly dressed for the day, I told her she could go in and see him but instructed her to not let any outburst of feeling overpower her in his presence. She entered the room and went to her husband's bedside where the absence of his leg was plainly visible from under the thin sheet. Her agitation could not be concealed at first, but she grew calmer and sat down beside him, while I sat at the other side of the bed. They talked of the children for a while, and then he said, 'Sarah, will you strike up one of the tunes we used to sing at home?' With a faltering accent, she began, *Welcome Sweet Day of Rest*. Her husband joined in, and the familiar strains were picked up throughout the ward.

"The poor woman ate her dinner in my room with tears streaming down her face. She asked, 'Don't you think he will get well?'

"I told her as gently as possible, that she must prepare to lose him and advised her to tell her husband so and to talk it all over with him. She went in and sat down beside him, and when she could quiet her emotion, she told him that she was afraid he could never recover.

"When I joined them, he looked up at me and said, 'What do you think, mother?'

"I told him he had but a little while longer to stay. He received the news calmly and said he was willing and ready to go, and they talked of the future both for him and for her. Then he asked her to sing once more. Their voices harmonized as they joined in the dear old hymns they had so often sung together, till his tenor notes grew fainter and fainter then ceased altogether. She was almost inconsolable when she became cognizant that he had left her.

"He was carried out to be prepared for the simple pine coffin that awaited him, but his wife was too poor to pay the expenses of his transfer home. Some of my kind friends who often visit the hospital—friends whom I have met because of you—took care of the expense. She left in possession of his body, which was buried near the little Methodist church where he was so well known and loved."

Lincoln leaned forward in his chair. "It relieves my heart, at least in some small measure, to hear accounts of our brave men who are at peace as they cross over into death and to know of the kindness shown by our friends. I only wish I had not allowed this war to be prolonged."

"You cannot blame yourself," she said, "for how fiercely and ruthlessly the enemy has fought."

"I could have listened to the right voices from the start and not clung to naïve notions. Appeasement was wrong, so was abiding the generals who rested their armies when the enemy was before them to be crushed. An abolitionist lion whom I ignored much too long had the right idea, 'A lenient war is a lengthy war, and therefore the worst kind of war.'"

"It is to your credit," she said, "that you allowed yourself to be bent to the truth—right makes might. Slavery must end and permitting the colored man to fight for his own freedom was the right way to achieve that end."

CHAPTER THIRTY-THREE

Rebecca returned from a second month-long furlough shortly before November's presidential election and discovered the surgeon-in-charge had fallen severely ill. As she sat at his sickbed watching over him one evening, Aunt Mary Dines, the Lincoln family's African cook, burst into the room with a plea from Mrs. Lincoln.

"The lady," she said, "asks that you come to the cottage to stay with the family for a few days."

"What has happened?" Rebecca asked.

"Mr. Lincoln has received several threatening letters. The house is guarded, inside and out, both night and day."

"Is someone ill? Or hurt?"

"No ma'am. But the lady is distraught."

Rebecca glanced at the ailing doctor. He slept soundly and his fever had plateaued. "Tell Mrs. Lincoln I must keep watch over our sick doctor through the night. If his fever breaks by morning, I can come in the afternoon and remain only for a few days."

The doctor's fever left him the next morning, and when he awoke Rebecca told him of Mrs. Lincoln's request. He gave his consent with a stipulation—that she petition the president on his behalf. The doctor's brother, a professor at the Normal School in Salem, had a son who was convicted of a theft committed in a post office and was sentenced to prison. Many months had passed, and the young man was in deep distress and withering from the effects of confinement. He was young, was led into the crime by a delinquent companion. It was his first offense. He had always been a good and dutiful son, and his mother had not left her bed since the sentence was handed down.

Lincoln greeted Rebecca with a hearty handshake the next evening when he returned to the cottage, guarded by a detail of two dozen cavalrymen. "It is so good to see my good friend," he said. "How was your time in the north. We missed you."

"I am well and rested," she said. "Happy to be back among my boys and my friends. And I have learned that Mrs. Russell recently returned to the nurses corps. She is now serving at West Hospital, the place that crushed her spirit only months ago."

"Are Tad and Mrs. Lincoln well?" he asked.

"They are. Mrs. Lincoln sent Aunt Mary for me. It seems we are all anxious over threats to your safety."

He scowled. "I cannot go anywhere these days without an army of guards. I reckon now I know what it is like to be a prisoner."

"If it cheers you, I have canvassed my boys, and all are eager to take their furloughs to go home and vote for Lincoln. I also made a proselyte while I was home. I have no doubt you will be re-elected."

"Your votes were never in doubt. It is the rest of the country that concerns me. But for now, I hope Aunt Mary has dinner ready for us."

Rebecca presented the doctor's petition to Lincoln after dinner and apologized for adding to the burdens he already carried.

He replied, "I am dogged by people with appeals like the good doctor's and I cannot always say yes. Tell me what you would think it right to do if it were your own son."

Rebecca hesitated then she said, "It is right for justice to be done, as I should want it in case of my own son. However, does this not call for mercy too? He is young. A pardon may save his own life and restore the health of his grieving mother."

Lincoln took a long pause. He entertained a memory from his lawyering days. In particular, the case of a young man accused of murder, whose parents were his dear friends. His appeal to the jury included a similar argument—mercy for the boy because of his youth and for the benefit of a grief-stricken mother. The jurors acquitted the young man. Mercy, humility, and forgiveness seemed to be tied together—a knot he had wrestled with his entire life. He had known how to forgive all along. Now he simply needed to practice. "It shall be as you desire," he said as he endorsed her petition.

* * *

While on a short furlough home to cast her vote in the presidential election, Rebecca opened a package which had been sent to the post office there. Inside she found some personal items which she recognized, including a picture of herself and a Bible. There was also a letter from Union Army Captain Orange Sampson.

Her throat tremored as she read the first lines. They explained that the contents had belonged to Private DeWitt Ray, a member of Sampson's regiment. Her fingers quivered as she turned over the picture and read an inscription on the back, "My own dear mother, Mrs. R. R. Pomroy, Chelsea, Mass."

The picture had been in his vest pocket, next to his heart, when his lifeless body was found. He died instantly when he was shot through the head at his post on July 20, while guarding a rifle pit near Petersburg, Virginia. Later, his open Bible was found on his bed where he left it before going on guard duty. He was buried at City Point National Cemetery, Hopewell, Virginia, marker 1799. The captain's letter went on to describe DeWitt's excellent character and example. Rebecca's heart grew heavy in her chest. Resentment coursed through her veins.

After a sleepless night of accusing the Almighty, the vile rebels, and DeWitt's hard-hearted grandparents, she set out to the mountain home in Vermont to which she had posted letters on her former attendant's behalf. As the cars lurched along the rails, she found herself tilling barren ground that had proven fruitless in years past. How could she forgive the stone-hearted grandparents who caused DeWitt to feel so unloved he fled into the barbed arms of war? She could never forgive the rebels.

On her late afternoon arrival, the brink of winter shrouded the tiny town. Her heart's temperature dipped as she ascended the pathway to a red house atop a nearby hill.

The old woman who answered the door clapped her hands, and her face brightened when Rebecca introduced herself as a friend of their grandson. "Come in and sit down," the woman said. Then she shouted over her shoulder to her husband inside. "We have a visitor from the hospital where DeWitt recovered from his wounds."

Even before they sat by the large, old-fashioned fireplace, the woman began singing her grandson's praises. "While he was in that hospital, he learned to read and write, and he writes us beautiful letters about a dear mother who has taught him everything. And strangest of all, he has got religion." She took out the worn package of letters from a basket near the hearth.

Rebecca's speech faltered. Was this the same strict, resentful, unloving grandmother who provoked dear DeWitt to run away? Her coolness toward the woman melted away. She awakened to the truth that her pity for young DeWitt had led her to condemn too hastily. She scolded herself—It is me who needs forgiveness, not these dear people who gave their golden years to a lost, orphaned boy. Rebecca replied, "I am that dear mother."

The old couple brimmed with anticipation over the stories their visitor might share about DeWitt.

"But I fear I have bitter news," Rebecca said. "Our dear DeWitt has passed from this world. He was killed in battle by the enemy." She went on to recount the details in Captain Sampson's letter. As the old couple clung to each other with tears spilling down their weathered cheeks, she added stories of her days with DeWitt.

When Rebecca finished, the old woman said to her husband, "Asa, harness up the horse and go round and get the neighbors. I want them to hear about our brave soldier—of his life, his service to our country, and of his death."

By dusk, the room was packed, even though the nearest neighbor lived a half-mile away. Rebecca stood in the dim light of assorted candles and coals smoldering in the fireplace as she told them of the hardships and miseries of her hospital life, of the change that had come over the wild, wayward boy they used to know. A chorus of sobs filled the tiny home. Many of the guests begged her to stay among them for a week, so they could hear more, but she felt obliged to be on her way.

The next morning, Asa harnessed the horse and took her to the nearest country store, where he purchased for her a simple gold ring—a reminder of the motherless DeWitt whom she had befriended.

Rebecca caressed the ring as the train weaved its way down from Vermont's mountains and leveled onto the lower regions through western Massachusetts. She had forgiven the Almighty whose purposes were beyond human understanding, but she could not forgive the rebels.

※ ※ ※

Soon after Rebecca returned from the short trip home to cast her ballot in the national election, the surgeon-in-charge called her to his office. When she appeared before him, she found him in conversation with Miss Dix. After brief cordialities, the surgeon said, "Miss Dix and I have agreed that you should assume the matronship of our hospital." He puffed out his chest and smiled.

A long, silent pause followed his announcement.

When Rebecca had mulled his offer for a good stretch of time she answered, "I am much honored by your confidence."

Another, shorter pause followed.

"But?" Miss Dix said.

"I think I should not give up my boys for such a thankless position. It is worse than running a boarding house. There are twenty female nurses on staff, plus the ones which are sent here for training until a position can be found for them in another hospital. Worst of all are the nosy reporters or their surrogates who come to find gossip to write about so they can stir up trouble. Besides, my boys will not hear a word of my leaving, at least not without a revolt."

Miss Dix pinched the bridge of her nose. "I suspected your answer would be something in that order, but I agreed to give it a try anyway. Your boys are privileged to have you as their nurse." She smiled. "I suppose we should not keep you from them any longer."

Soon after she returned to her ward, a young soldier from Massachusetts named Henry was brought in on a litter. One arm dangled at his side and his face was drawn in pain. When Rebecca put him to bed, she discovered his fever hovered around 100 degrees and his bedclothes were soiled from diarrhea. As she bathed him, his bowels erupted again, splattering her with a stew of excrement.

As the gray days of November inched toward Thanksgiving, Henry rallied for a while. First, he sat up. A few days later, he rose from his bed and walked a few steps in the ward. After that he plateaued and his hope for speedy recovery eroded.

His widowed mother replied to letters from Rebecca with pleas for the doctors and nurses to restore her only son's health. A letter from his sister promised she had been fattening a chicken and would send him a Thanksgiving box. He beamed and asked if he might eat some of it when it arrived. Rebecca assured him he could eat all that he was able. Then orders came to move all but the most critically ill to convalescent hospitals, as beds were needed for new arrivals of battlefield casualties. Rebecca appealed to the surgeon-in-charge, telling him that Henry was too ill and frail to walk any distance to a new hospital under the load of his knapsack.

The surgeon bellowed, "He shall go now and work. He has been petted too long here."

She helped Henry on with his blue overcoat and gave him a farewell kiss before he marched away with the other convalescents. Not quite an hour later, Henry was brought back and put to bed in the corner of the ward, weak and feverish.

The afternoon before Thanksgiving, he became restless and asked whether Rebecca would object if he laid his head on her shoulder.

"If it will help you rest," she said, "you certainly may."

"When I am gone," he said, "will you tell my other mother I have made peace with God? Tell her also that I was a good boy and minded all you said to me, and I should like to see her once more, but all is right."

Moments later, he breathed his last.

Rebecca cut off a lock of his hair and sent it with other mementos to his sister. She also placed flowers on his coffin before it was taken to the dead house.

As the orderlies carried his body downstairs, they encountered a messenger on his way up to the ward with a box. The messenger stood aside and allowed the stretcher bearers to pass before he continued on. When

Rebecca discovered the box was Henry's Thanksgiving meal, she divided it among other patients but did not tell them for whom it had been intended.

* * *

The sting of Henry's death still festered at the core of Rebecca's soul when a rebel soldier came under her care a few days before Christmas. She wasted no time telling him, "I cannot feel right towards you after seeing the abused condition of our boys who were released from your prison in Richmond."

"I do not blame you," he said. "But I suppose I am at your mercy."

"Why did you join up to fight for the rebel cause?"

"I did not want to," he said. "My father threatened to disinherit me if I did not. I never wanted to kill anyone, and never have. I joined the ambulance corps, and while I was taking wounded soldiers off the field, a ball went through my leg, and I fell."

He asked a few days later if he might call her mother, like the other boys.

"No," she said. "Not while your heart is set against our government."

"What if I take the oath of allegiance?" he asked.

"If your oath is heartfelt, it may be possible."

Over the ensuing days, the rebel went out of his way to prove his usefulness. He showed kindness to the sickest ones in her ward. Despite his effort, she told him she was sorry, but she could not call him one of her boys.

He laughed and called her mother, nonetheless.

Rebecca scolded him and said, "It does my soul good to imagine how much you must suffer when you hear our boys sing patriotic songs."

He raised his voice so all could hear, "You are a better mother than the one I have back home. You have helped me understand that I was not only fighting against the government, but against God, as well. Because of you I have resolved to take the oath of allegiance."

Mary Jane Welles was in the ward and overheard their exchange. She took Rebecca aside and said, "How much repentance is required in your book before someone is eligible to receive mercy and forgiveness?"

Rebecca winced. Mary Jane's question pricked her conscience. She asked herself, have I not pressed my dear friend Abraham with a similar question? If war bleeds color and goodness from everything, leaving nothing but a stark, iron-gray landscape, would that not mean that everyone has lost?

She turned away and pinned her eyes on one of her sickest patients.

Mary Jane caught her arm. "Don't let pride keep you from letting that poor boy call you Mother."

Mary Jane's words stalked Rebecca during the night while sharp pains spiked from one temple to the other and kept her on the cusp of sleep. When she dragged herself out of bed shortly before daybreak, she brewed a strong cup of tea and opened the previous day's *Daily Chronicle*. The newspaper reported that Lincoln ordered the release of two rebel officers from the Union's Johnson Island prison after their wives pleaded for mercy.

She reflected on the president's clemency and regarded the rebel soldier under her care. A prickle in her throat triggered a cough. She had missed something all along. Olivers were indeed everywhere. If the Lincolns, her boys, even the rebel could be her Olivers, why not those whom she nursed into the other world—her husband, children, mothers, aunts, sister, sister-in-law, neighbors. A new truth flashed through her mind—I have never wandered from the path I set my feet on as a girl of twelve. I was simply blind to where and to whom that path was leading.

The headache stalked Rebecca for days, like a predator lurking in the shadows. It was there, then it wasn't. It wasn't, then it was, or was it? Whether it was or not, it sapped her strength. A few days after Christmas the pain nearly blinded her, and it didn't stop with the stabbing behind her eyes. Every muscle in her body ached.

Her forehead wasn't hot, but she would have liked to open a window. The surgeon-in-charge forbade it. They continued to be nailed shut as a precaution against potential violence from rebel guerillas.

She shuffled her feet as she moved through the ward to check on her boys, sometimes stumbling over articles left on the floor at patients' bedsides. She tripped on an artificial leg that wasn't tucked far enough under a bed and gave the owner a piece of her mind.

A hush fell over the room.

By the end of the afternoon, her vision became blurry, and her face burned. She padded to her room, closed the door, and fell into bed.

She awoke the next morning, clammy and unrested. A stinging pain clawed the back of her throat. Tepid bath water yielded a touch of relief, as did a fresh change of clothes. But as the day wore on and she tended to her duties—changing bed pans for the bedridden, re-dressing old wounds, sewing socks, reading to the boys, and the like—her headaches, back pain, and fever gradually increased, though they receded somewhat during the night. The pattern repeated each day for the next week, with her symptoms spiking to higher levels by each day's end. The only thing that steadily regressed was her energy.

The week ended with Rebecca waking in the middle of the night, writhing from cramps and soaked in sweat. The nightmare she wrestled with in her sleep continued as she lay in bed, swatting at imaginary horned invaders clad in rebel uniforms. Her screams panicked the entire ward, and the surgeon-in-charge was rousted out of bed.

He assessed her fever at well over one-hundred degrees. A second surgeon was summoned. The two doctors, aided by a burly orderly, forced quinine into

Rebecca and administered chloroform to quiet her. A nurse was called to watch over her and to attend to her patients. After new symptoms manifested and she slipped into unconsciousness, the doctors became convinced she suffered from typhoid. News of their diagnosis, coming on the heels of Private Henry's death from fever on Thanksgiving, cast a pall over the hospital.

Mary Jane Welles and her husband were the first from outside the hospital to visit Rebecca in her unresponsive state, followed by Senator Hale and his daughter. Lincoln and his wife visited her a short time after the Senator. They brought a carriage full of bouquets and plants.

Neither Mrs. Lincoln nor the president could contain their foreboding as they viewed the too familiar rash on her neck. Memories of Willie battling the dreaded disease brought tears to their eyes and prayers to their lips.

Lincoln murmured, "She has saved both of our lives more than once, and Tad's, too."

His wife sniffled. "I don't know if I can withstand another such blow."

The surgeon-in-charge entered Rebecca's sickroom as the Lincolns were leaving. Mrs. Lincoln thanked him for the good care their dear friend was receiving then added, "Would it help her recovery if we took her home with us? Our doctor would look in on her from time to time."

"As a hospital," he replied, "we are much better able to provide the necessary care should complications arise. We can administer chloroform, if needed to help her sleep and give her morphine to numb the pain."

"Very well," she said. "Maybe when she is out of danger, she could convalesce with us."

"I will keep an open mind to that possibility."

Rebecca's dry coughing, diarrhea, and malaise receded with the arrival of the new year, allowing her to sit up in bed to mend socks. Soon she was able to make short forays into the ward to chat with her boys, and doctors grew optimistic that the worst was over.

CHAPTER THIRTY-FOUR

On a Saturday morning in early February, George arrived unannounced with news that his wife had begun the pangs of labor. Even though Rebecca had not fully regained her strength, the stone walls of the hospital could not contain her. It was time for her to become a grandmother.

Rebecca's daughter-in-law, Almira, lay in a nearby barracks where George was stationed. Cramps bore down on her like rolls of waves pushed by a rapidly advancing tide. The building had been slapped together in haste, as was the wartime way, with thin boards loosely tacked to its frame as the only barrier against outside weather. Inside, an icy draft chilled the room. An old regimental flag, draped over a military cot, provided a modicum of privacy.

At half past three o'clock in the afternoon, a little black-eyed girl made her appearance. She reminded Rebecca of her Clara Jane.

The attending doctor asked if she wanted to hold her new granddaughter, but Rebecca declined. She had no energy left after being away from her hospital bed for so many hours. Nevertheless, she stayed for several days in the barracks with George, Almira, and little Flora—her first extended time with George since the war began.

When Rebecca returned to her hospital ward a few days later she wrote to her friend, Almira Fuller.

Columbian College Hosp
Feb 13

Dear Almira,

I am well and was anxious to let you know that I have been Grandmother one week. The little girl looks like Clara and was born in Barracks not where you see them, but in another direction. It was freezing cold weather, and the Barracks was boards with not much over them, and the Colonel of the Regiment told George he could have the old regimental flag to put up over his bed, as it would keep the cold out. You would be surprised to see how nicely George fixed it all over the top and the foot of the bed, and truly the little stranger made her appearance under the Stars and Stripes.

Give my love to all inquiring friends.

Yours affectionately Auntie Pomroy

The flag was forty six feet long, and I never prized the flag so much before.

✳ ✳ ✳

Rebecca's symptoms took a sharp turn a month after Flora was born. Coughing became more severe, rising from deep in her lungs to yield greenish-yellow sputum. Her fever spiked once more to above one hundred and the locus of her pain shifted from her back to her chest. Again, she lay in bed soaked in sweat, clammy, lethargic.

She complained of heaviness in her chest as she wheezed through coughing spasms and strained for each shallow breath. Her fingers took on a purplish hue. The surgeon pronounced her condition inflammation of the lungs with pleura and began the liberal use of mercury pills and other cathartics to purge her bowels. He forced her to swallow doses of antimony to induce vomiting then blistered her skin with caustic chemicals to draw fluids out of her lungs to the surface. She lay in bed for weeks, feeble and struggling for survival. As her lungs healed, waves of typhoid symptoms came and receded, came and receded, each surge weaker than the last.

In early April, Rebecca told Mary Jane Welles, "Every severe attack helps to loosen the cords that bind me here. Whether the last cord will be snapped here, God knows best and only he knows. I have committed all into his hands, knowing that he will do all things well."

Mary Jane replied, "Gideon and I pray for you each day."

"I cherish your prayers. My heart and soul are with the Lincoln family. Sometimes, I think God has put this burden upon me for some wise purpose best known to himself. I cry out to God in behalf of Mrs. Lincoln and our dear president. I feel that I can pray for him hourly."

"What about the rebel boy?" Mary Jane asked. "Have you found room in your prayers for him?"

"I am inspired by the example of our good and kindly president. He has said of rebels who have recently surrendered, 'Let them all go, officers and all, let them have their horses to plow ... their guns to shoot crows with. Give them the most liberal and honorable terms.' Who am I to treat a rebel under my care with any less charity."

✳ ✳ ✳

Lincoln mounted his horse early the day after General Lee's surrender. He rode alone toward the Soldiers' Home, stopping along the way to call on Rebecca, where he found her asleep in her hospital room with a nurse at her bedside.

"How is she?" he asked.

"We thought she was making progress, but the fever and chills are back. She was cramping last evening, and during the night she soiled herself."

Lincoln assessed her slow, rhythmic breaths. "She seems peaceful."

The doctor shook his head. "We'll have to see how the next couple of days go."

Lincoln chafed at the unfairness—she has given so much of herself, but now that the war was ending, she might not endure to celebrate the fruits of her labors.

* * *

The next morning, Lincoln joined his family for breakfast in their private dining room at the President's House. Bob was close on his heels, having arrived less than an hour earlier from General Grant's headquarters in Virginia. He had been commissioned as a captain two months earlier and served as an assistant adjutant on Grant's staff.

Bob's blue uniform triggered his father to recall a dream that had been haunting him for several days. In it he was awakened by a loud commotion downstairs and went to investigate. On reaching the reception room just across the hall from the dining room where he was presently sitting with his family, he encountered a young sentry, about Bob's age. Inside the reception room, a crowd of mourners—women wailing and men wringing their hands—gathered around the corpse whose face he could not see. When he asked the guard who was deceased, the young man answered in hushed tones, "The president is dead. He was shot."

The memory sent chills down Lincoln's spine.

"Father," Mrs. Lincoln said. "Are you not going to greet your son?"

Lincoln blinked. His sullen demeanor brightened. He extended his hand to Bob. "Of course. Of course. Welcome home, son. We are much relieved you have returned safe."

"Father," Bob replied. "I brought a gift for you. A trophy from Appomattox." He handed his father a portrait of General Lee. "It hung in the home where the surrender was signed."

Lincoln studied the portrait in silence.

"I thought it would please you," Bob said.

"It does. Thank you." Lincoln motioned to the chair next to him at the table. "Sit here and give me all the details of the Appomattox meeting."

"Won't General Grant brief you presently?"

"At this moment, I wish to view the occasion as you saw it."

For nearly an hour Bob described the events of April 12 with great enthusiasm. Mrs. Lincoln attended his accounting with politeness, though her principal thoughts were of her relief that he had returned safely. Tad absorbed his remaining brother's every word.

Lincoln trained his attention on Bob, but his mind wandered to fatherly concerns. He recalled undeserved lacerations inflicted by his own father's hand, his father's indolence and neglect, and hard-earned wages from his own labors used to repay crippling debts spawned by his father's poor judgment. Those injustices prompted him to be a gentle, even indulgent father to his own sons.

When Bob finished Lincoln said to him, "Now that the war is behind us, it is time to put aside the uniform and resume your studies. You should read the law to decide whether it's in you to become a lawyer."

Bob rose from his seat without a word and walked over to his mother to give her a kiss, before excusing himself to rest from his journey home.

After breakfast Lincoln met with Schuyler Colfax, Speaker of the House of Representatives. "Hello Colfax," he said, "Is there something I can do for you?"

Colfax fingered the rim of his hat, holding it close to his waistband. "I came to inquire whether you have plans for calling an extra session of Congress."

"This delicate business of knitting together the strands of union is not a thing to be put in the hands of zealots and opportunists. I think I shall not be calling Congress into session but will act as much as is allowed under my own authority."

"Then I shall proceed with my plans to take an extended trip to California and the mining fields in the West," Colfax said.

Lincoln smiled. "I hope Mrs. Lincoln and I can do the same someday. But while you are out there, I want you to take a message from me to the miners you visit. I have very large ideas for the mineral wealth of our nation now that the war is over. When we were borrowing a couple million dollars a day and struggling to hold our country together, increased production in our mines was not a great concern. But now that the rebellion is overthrown and we know pretty nearly the amount of our national debt, we can ease the burden of repaying it by extracting as much gold and silver as possible."

"Yes sir," Colfax replied.

"We shall soon have hundreds of thousands of disbanded soldiers," Lincoln continued. "Many have feared that their return home in great numbers might paralyze industry by furnishing a greater supply of labor than there will be demand for. I am going to encourage our returning heroes to pursue the vast opportunities hidden in our mountain ranges."

"I agree," Colfax said.

"In addition to that, immigration, which even the war has not stopped, will land upon our shores hundreds of thousands more each year from overcrowded Europe. I intend to point them, as well, to the gold and silver awaiting them in the West."

"I'm with you all the way, Mr. President."

"Fine," Lincoln said. "Tell the miners for me, that I shall promote their interests to the utmost of my ability because their prosperity is the prosperity of the nation.

And we shall prove in a very few years, that we are indeed the treasury of the world."

Shortly after Speaker Colfax departed, General Cresswell of Maryland found Lincoln in the downstairs reception hall. "Hello, Cresswell," Lincoln said. "What are you after? You fellows don't come to see me unless you want something. It must be something big, or you wouldn't be here so early in the day."

Cresswell fingered the edges of a paper he held in his hand. "Sir, now that the war is drawing to an end, I'd like you to pardon a rebel soldier who was a college classmate of mine."

"That's not so hard," Lincoln replied. "You did right to put it in writing. I don't care to read the statement, since I know you know how to make an affidavit. But it makes me think of an Illinois story, and I'm going to tell it to you."

"I'm at your pleasure, Mr. President."

"Years ago, a lot of young folks, boys and girls out in Illinois, got up what in that region was known as a Mayin' party. They went down to the Sangamon River and took an old scow across to the opposite shore for a picnic. But when it was time to go back, the scow had gotten untied and floated downstream. At first, they thought the matter was hilarious, but after a while the thing began to look serious. There was no other boat around, and they couldn't put out a pontoon to cross the river.

"One bright young man proposed that each fellow take off his shoes and stockings and carry the girl he liked best over to the other shore. It was a great scheme, and it worked all right until all had gotten across except a little short man and a very tall, dignified old maid. That young man was in dead earnest to get her across, but she would have nothing to do with it. To say the least, he was in a great deal of trouble.

"You fellows will get one man after another out of this terrible business of mopping up after the war, until Jeff

Davis and I are the only ones left on the island. It is my expectation that he will refuse to let me carry him over, so I will be in the same spot as the young man in my story. But if Davis consents, there are people who will make trouble about my rescuing him. Do you understand my point?"

Cresswell chuckled, politely.

Lincoln scolded him. "It's no laughing matter. It's more than likely to happen. There are worse men than Jefferson Davis, and I wish I could see some way by which he and our people would let me get him over to be with us. However, I reckon when it comes Jeff Davis's turn, I'll just have to do my best to demonstrate that forgiveness is possible. We must decide to lock up the past and throw away the key." He took Cresswell's affidavit and endorsed it. "Now take this over to the War Department to be carried out."

In the early afternoon, Lincoln sifted through a stack of papers in his office, searching for a petition to release a captured rebel prisoner. When he found it, he added a condition that the prisoner take an oath of allegiance and signed his name. Before he put his pen away, a senator from Missouri appeared with a request to pardon another rebel soldier who was under sentence to be hanged. Twice before, the prisoner had been convicted of spying, and on both occasions, Lincoln sent his case back for retrial. He signed the pardon and told the senator, "Return to me if Stanton balks at freeing the man, and we will repeat the dance for an entire week if that's what it takes."

Moments later, one of Lincoln's secretaries handed him a request to pardon a Union soldier who had been sentenced to death for desertion.

Lincoln asked, "What would you do if you were sitting in my place?"

"He should not have deserted," the secretary replied.

Lincoln shook his head. "I think this fellow will do us greater good above the ground than under it." He signed the pardon and added, "Here's a lesson I have learned—we don't need to know which is the heavier load, bitterness or regret. Forgiveness saves us from either burden. If I'd been wiser two-and-a-half years ago, I might have found a different way to deal with the thirty-nine Dakotas that we hanged that winter."

After dinner that evening, Lincoln was washing his hands in a water closet in his office—preparing to dress for the theater—when he recognized a voice in the hallway. "Halloo, Dana," he called out. "Come on in. What is it? What's up?"

Dana was an intelligence officer in the War Department. "Sir," he said. "We've received a telegram from Portland, Maine. The provost marshal reports that Jacob Thompson will be traveling through Portland tonight."

"Old Thompson of Mississippi," Lincoln said. "He was Secretary of Interior in Mr. Buchanan's administration. A conspicuous secessionist when this whole mess started. What's our concern with him?"

"Of late I understand he's been employed in Canada as an agent of Jeff Davis's government. He's been organizing all sorts of trouble and getting up raids, like the attack on St. Albans in Vermont."

"And what sort of action are we intending to take?"

"When I received the provost marshal's telegram, I took it to Mr. Stanton."

"And what did he have to say?"

"'Arrest him!' But as I was going out the door, he called me back and said, 'no, wait, better go over and see the president.'"

Lincoln dried his hands. "I rather think we shouldn't arrest him. When you have an elephant by the hind leg and he's trying to run away, it's best to let him go."

Lincoln's secretary appeared at the doorway. "Mrs. Lincoln wants to remind you she doesn't like being late to the theater."

"Tell her I will be ready after I make a quick trip to the War Department. General Sherman is in pursuit of a remnant of rebel troops, and I am eager to hear news of their surrender. Colonel Crook is downstairs waiting to escort me."

"You'd best take your shawl," the secretary said. "It's a cool, damp night."

Lincoln and his escort crossed the lawn between the mansion and the War Department in darkness. Storm clouds had begun gathering in the sky, and the nippy air was laden with mist.

"Is everything all right, sir?" Crook said.

"Yes. Why do you ask?"

"Seems you're carrying a heavy load tonight."

"Reckon little Willie has been on my mind this afternoon. He would have had great fun with the city decked out and the streets overrun with revelers."

"Sorry I never got to know the lad."

"He was a good boy. Soldiers parading on the lawn always gave him a thrill."

After walking a few yards, Lincoln halted. "As my boy drew his last breath, I imagined myself flailing in a whirlpool of dark, churning waters, gasping to catch a breath. I cannot help thinking I'm the reason he died."

"How do you mean, sir?"

"When I was a boy, my father dragged our little family in the dead of winter into a wilderness where we made a new home, such that it was. It was in that place, too hostile for beauty to flourish, that my mother and sister wasted away and died. I brought Willie and my family to this city which has hosted far too much pestilence and death. All because I would not yield to the rising tide of slavery sweeping across our land."

"Sir, you are not to blame for this war."

"Maybe so, Crook. But I am to blame for bringing my family here and putting them through such agony." Lincoln choked on his words. "I held the little fellow in my arms nearly the whole time he was burning with fever, even during his fits of delirium. For almost a day after his spirit left, I wouldn't let go of him. I sobbed like a little child and ordered the staff to keep the drapes shut for days while I wallowed in sorrow."

They continued walking in silence for a short while, then Lincoln said, "There's not a moment that goes by that I do not mourn our little Willie. His death makes this city a dreadful place."

Near the edge of the lawn, they encountered a crowd of drunken men.

"Crook," he said. "I believe there are men who want to take my life, and it is possible they will do it."

"Why do you think that?"

"Death surrounds this place," Lincoln replied.

"I hope you're mistaken, sir."

"I have perfect confidence in those around me, in every one of you men. I know no one could do me harm and escape alive. But if harm is meant to come to me, it is impossible to prevent it."

At the War Department, Lincoln asked, "Have we any telegrams yet from Sherman?"

"None."

"So, the war is won, but the battle rages on. I reckon, then, I should be off to the theatre."

Lincoln and Colonel Crook walked back to the mansion without a word between them until they reached the portico.

"Goodnight, sir," Crook said.

Lincoln paused and drew in a lung full of humid night air. "Good-bye, Crook."

Crook furrowed his brow. "Good-bye? You always say good night."

"Oh, is that so?" Lincoln ran his fingers through his hair. "Of course. Good-night, Crook."

At about half past eight o'clock, Lincoln and his party arrived at Ford's Theatre with the play already in progress. When they entered the state box, the performance stopped, and the audience stood for the playing of *Hail to the Chief*. At the end of the music, people applauded politely, and the Lincoln's took their seats.

Mrs. Lincoln leaned into her husband and whispered, "The rocker you're seated in was brought over from Mr. Ford's personal quarters."

He smiled. "It fits. I should find one just like it."

Late in the play, a cool wisp of air sent a shudder down Lincoln's neck. He whispered to his wife, "Are you a little chilled?"

"No," she said. "Shall we get your shawl?"

"Not to bother," he said. "I shall just stand and put on my coat."

When he sat back down, Mrs. Lincoln leaned close and held his hand. In a hushed voice, she asked, "What will folks think of my hanging on to you so?"

"They won't say anything about it." He squeezed her hand.

A door opened behind them. Footfalls.

The actor, Harry Hawk, strode across the stage below and began delivering one of Lincoln's favorite lines. Lincoln ignored the distraction and whispered the line along with the actor.

> *Don't know the good manners of society, eh?*
> *Well, I guess I know enough to turn you inside*
> *out, old gal—you sockdologizing old mantrap!*

Lincoln slapped his knee. A sharp crack. A piercing—

CHAPTER THIRTY-FIVE

Rebecca woke a few minutes before eight o'clock on the cool, drizzly morning of April 15—still frail from waves of typhoid, aggravated by inflammation in her lungs. A chorus of wails, sobs, and moans resounded through the ward. As she struggled to rise from her bed, the surgeon-in-charge appeared in her doorway. Mrs. Russell, her friend who had been serving at Baltimore's West Hospital in recent months, was at his side. Their faces were drawn as they approached.

The doctor's voice rasped as if he had a sore throat. "We have catastrophic news."

"What?" she demanded. "George?"

"No," Mrs. Russell replied. "Not George."

The doctor's lips trembled. "The president. He has been shot. He died within the last hour."

Rebecca shrieked. She covered her face with her hands. "God! No, God." She wailed. Her body convulsed. She prostrated herself on the mattress and pummeled it with her fists. Grief overwhelmed her and she curled into a ball, as an infant in her mother's womb. Her body shook as she wept.

Mrs. Russell sat on the bed and stroked her friend's hair then patted her back. Tears welled in her as she said, "I came as soon as I heard the horrible news. You don't need to be brave for now. God knows the depths of your bereavement and will sustain you."

The surgeon-in-charge excused himself. He was unwilling to burden Rebecca with more distressing news—a threat against the hospital had been uncovered. It was feared that disgruntled insurgents intended to burn down the College. But the threat could easily have come from angry Unionists intent on taking vengeance against the school because of its southern roots.

Word of the impending danger worked its way from floor to floor of the hospital over the next several hours. When it reached Rebecca, she screamed and beat her forehead with the heels of her hands. Mrs. Russell, who had not left her bedside, threw her arms around her and held her close. "We are safe," she whispered. "A whole regiment of soldiers is keeping guard over the hospital."

Rebecca's sobs ebbed, and the tension in her back melted away as she settled in Mrs. Russell's embrace.

The crack of musket fire from the grounds below jolted the two women. A quick volley of rounds ensued, driving Rebecca closer into her friend's bosom.

Then all fell silent.

A new patient arrived in the ward later that evening—a sentry who had been shot in the exchange of fire earlier in the day. It was decided that the culprits were rebel sympathizers acting out their thirst for revenge. Mrs. Russell gave Rebecca a dose of laudanum to help her sleep and went to dress the sentry's wound.

✳ ✳ ✳

A couple of days after Lincoln's death, Rebecca's frayed nerves settled. Her aches and fever moderated as well. When an announcement was made on the evening of the seventeenth that the President's House doors would be open the next day for public viewing of the martyred president's body, she resolved to see his face one more time.

The surgeon-in-charge discouraged her at first. Although she showed signs of improvement, she was at high risk of relapse—especially considering the large throng she'd have to jostle through and the lengthy wait she'd have to endure to see her fallen friend. But her earnestness outmatched the surgeon's misgivings. He consented to her being carried to the mansion in the afternoon for a special viewing for inmates of the city's military hospitals.

A train of ambulances loaded with Columbian College Hospital's convalescing soldiers parked near the President's House near noon. A long line of the wounded from other hospitals with heads bandaged, arms in slings, and legs splinted, had already formed. When the men bearing Rebecca's litter approached, someone in line asked, "Is this woman one of your nurses?"

"Yes," one of her litter bearers replied. "She is Mrs. Pomroy from Columbian College."

"She is, indeed," another man in line said. He turned to the formation and announced, "This is Nurse Pomroy. She is the mother who saved my life and the lives of many others. For those who did not survive, she guided them with love to the other side. Now she is so ill she must be carried inside on a stretcher. Make way for these men to carry her to the front." Not a single man objected as the word was sent up the line, and each stood at attention and saluted as her litter passed by.

Once she reached the portico with its huge columns draped in black cloth, the President's House doorkeeper stepped forward and instantly recognized her. "Mrs. Pomroy," he said. "The whole house has been in distress over your illness. I hope you are on the mend, despite this great calamity."

"Thank you," she said. "However, I am more determined than healed at this moment. I cannot bear the thought of not seeing our dear president one last time. How are Mrs. Lincoln and Tad?"

"The lady refuses to see anyone, and at the present time she is kept under laudanum, so there would be no point in visiting her. Mrs. Welles has taken Master Tad into her home for now."

"Please let her know I pray for them both."

"I will see that she gets your message." The doorkeeper gestured to the closed entry door. "This way, boys. There is no exception that cannot be made for this good woman." He whispered to a guard who opened the door and let them pass before closing it behind them.

In the East Room, her vision locked onto a catafalque, draped in black cloth. Her attention was so absorbed by the sight of his coffin that she failed to observe the chandelier had been removed to accommodate the height of the canopy. Neither did she take account of the cornices and mirrors covered in white chiffon with black alpaca dressing their frames, nor the black crape curtains covering each of the windows.

A ramp enabled them to approach the open coffin for viewing, but to look on the president, she had to be helped off her litter so she could stand. She had seen his relaxed expression many times. It was his stillness that stabbed her. Nothing else about the scene drew her notice—not his black, broadcloth suit, nor the quilted white satin that pillowed his head, or the walnut, silver edged casket on which she braced herself, not even the fragrant evergreens and flowers carefully arranged around him.

As she leaned over the edge of the coffin, inaudible groans welled up from the hollows of her soul. She whispered, "My dear, kind friend Abraham, perhaps we shall be seeing each other soon, as this poor, frail vessel of mine appears to be wearing out."

CHAPTER THIRTY-SIX

Miss Dix stood in Rebecca's room on the twentieth of April. She held documents in her hands that she had been loath to sign. "I am here to implore you one more time. Please do not leave me, just yet. At least remain long enough to attend to Secretary Seward and his family while they heal from the brutal attack on their lives."

"It is time for me to return home," Rebecca replied. "In these past three years and seven months, I have cared for over seven hundred patients and closed the dying eyes of nearly eighty. The hour has come for my own healing, and to rest till Providence opens another place."

Miss Dix pleaded, "You need to do nothing for the next few weeks but dress that poor family's wounds and rest."

"I am sorry. The surgeon says I will do myself great harm if I stay any longer. He will not even let me go to Tad or to Mrs. Lincoln."

"Yes," Miss Dix said. "I suppose you are right. But I had to try. Thank you for all that you have done for your nation. There are many who owe you a great debt, but unfortunately, they will likely never know of it. God speed." She gave Rebecca the discharge papers.

"Will you do one favor for me?" Rebecca asked. "I leave this afternoon with Mrs. Russell for her new home in Newburgh, New York. It is a small hamlet where she has been hired as a teacher. Please inform Mrs. Lincoln of the arrangements for my convalescence and ask her to let me know how I may correspond with her once she is ready to face the world again. Let her know how I care for her deeply, and for Tad."

"Certainly," Miss Dix replied before taking her leave.

Mrs. Russell arrived in Rebecca's room later that afternoon and asked, "Are you ready?"

"I hope I am not putting you out," Rebecca replied.

"Nonsense. Newburgh is small and quiet. Just what you need for now. When you are stronger, we will get you back home to your family."

"Thank you. I agree. It is exactly what I need. I fear there will be too much chaos in Chelsea. All of the attention will wear me down as much as this war already has."

"Do you still believe, He doeth all things well?" Mrs. Russell asked.

"More so than ever. With each new challenge has come a greater understanding that I must walk humbly with my God, not fearing nor begrudging those who are able to kill the body but cannot destroy the soul."

"Very well," Mrs. Russell said. "Now, we must move along. We have a train to catch,"

Four of Rebecca's able-bodied patients appeared in the doorway. Among them was the young rebel. The rebel and another man stepped forward to gathered her in their arms to carry her downstairs. Rebecca turned to the rebel and put her hand on his chest. He stopped short. She smiled at him. Her eyes misted over. She cupped his cheeks. "My boy," she said.

He smiled back, folded his arms around her, and whispered, "Mother."

CHAPTER THIRTY-SEVEN

On the day of President Lincoln's funeral, Mrs. Jane Russell took Rebecca directly from her sickbed to Newburgh, New York. As Rebecca's health improved, she wrote to a Chelsea friend.

May 2, 1865.

My Dear Mrs. F,

Some weeks have elapsed since I last wrote you, and I felt for a few days that my hand might never hold the pen again; but God, who is wise and good, has once more given me health, and this morning I am feeling well. I am in a very pleasant home, where everything is being done for me, and since I have left the hospital, I have gained rapidly.

I will not attempt to describe all I passed through in my sickness while there, but the sudden death of my dear friend, the President, then the threatened burning of Columbia College and the shooting of our pickets, one of whom was brought into the hospital—these, with other things which I will describe when I see you, all helped to keep my nerves in a constant state of excitement. But, thanks to my Heavenly Father, I can still feel "He doeth all things well."

On the twentieth of April I took my honorable discharge from the hospital, where I had cared for over seven hundred patients, and closed the dying eyes of nearly eighty. Miss Dix said she had not words to express her grief at my leaving the service, feeling, as she said, as though she was to be left alone with so much on her mind, and wishing I was only able to go to Secretary Seward's and dress the wounds of the whole family. She urged me to stay in the service and do nothing but rest for a few weeks, but the surgeon on my ward told me that I was doing a great injury to myself to remain any longer, so I think I will rest till Providence opens another place.

My heart ached as I saw the tears from my poor sick boys fall, but I had served three years and seven months and felt that I must go. Two of my boys carried me downstairs in their arms.

I have passed through trying scenes, but this morning the sun shines just as bright as ever, God is still good to us, and may it never be in my heart to complain or murmur. Today I expect to go to Catskill, and in June, I hope to be at home if I am perfectly well but shall not come home sick.

Rebecca found new Olivers after two additional years of convalescence from the aftereffects of typhoid and pneumonia. She accepted employment as matron of The Newton Centre Home for Girls in Newton, Massachusetts. The Boston Children's Aid Society operated the home in addition to a farm for boys in nearby West Newton. Boys were sent to the farm from Boston's jails while girls were under court supervision for any of various reasons, including petty crimes or homelessness. All children remained wards of the court, and The Boston Children's Aid Society did not control which ones came to them, or when they left and where they went next.

In Rebecca's view, it was as if she had returned to North Boston's lower Ann Street, where nearly forty years earlier she devoted herself to offering hope where destitution was thought to reign. She extended her love, acceptance, and sympathy to all without judgment.

She remained at the Newton Centre home until it was disbanded five years later. The home only had four girls in residence and the trustees decided operating the home was no longer viable. Having put her hand to the plough, Rebecca would not turn back. The home's four remaining wards would be homeless without her aid, and she was no more willing to abandon them than she had been to leave her sick and wounded boys during the war.

Mrs. Maria Furber and Miss Mary Clark Shannon helped Rebecca establish The Newton Home for Orphan and Destitute Girls. Rebecca served as the new home's superintendent when its doors opened to accept Newton residents, regardless of race or creed. The girls lived there in a family atmosphere as wards of the home until they reached the age of twenty-one, when they were no longer under supervision.

The girls attended public schools while residents of the home. They did all the housework, so no paid domestic staff was required. They sewed, altered clothing, and made quilts to raise monies for the home. Between ages fourteen and sixteen they apprenticed as domestics in the home, preparing for placement as maids in private homes. Some girls went into clerical or nursing work, but jobs in factories were discouraged.

Food, supplies, and services were donated by local merchants, professional people, and churches. Many of the new home's benefactors took a deep personal interest in the girls' welfare. Mr. Smith P. Burton, who owned a local dairy, provided a daily quart of milk for each girl. He also offered his New Hampshire estate on the shore of Lake Winnepesaukee for use as a summer camp several weeks each year. Others in the community employed older girls from the Home as domestic servants.

The orphanage was described as "one of the more interesting examples of those 19th century protestant charities that were created and dominated by a strong female personality, and its success was largely the result of Rebecca Pomroy's religious zeal, administrative skills, and genius for managing on a limited budget."

Rebecca served as superintendent of the Newton Home for Orphan Girls until her death in 1884, after which the home was renamed The Rebecca Pomroy Newton Home for Orphan Girls.

Secretary Welles wrote to Rebecca ten years before her death, saying,

> *The many trials of the president were better known to you than his countrymen.*

Rebecca was buried at Woodlawn Cemetery, Revere, Massachusetts, in the family plot with Daniel, Willie, and Clara Jane.

EPILOGUE

Rebecca never crossed paths with Mary Lincoln after the president's death.

Mrs. Lincoln remained bedridden in the President's House, refusing to take visitors, until she left Washington on May 22, 1865, five weeks after Andrew Johnson was sworn in as president. She did not attend her husband's funeral, nor did she accompany his coffin for the funeral train's week-and-a-half long journey to Springfield, Illinois. Having endured shame from her family and public controversies over her finances, she exiled herself to Europe in 1868. She returned to Chicago in 1871, when her son, Tad, died at the age of 17. She was committed to an insane asylum by her son, Robert, in 1875, although she won her release a year later. On July 16, 1882, Mary Todd Lincoln died at the home of her sister in Springfield, Illinois.

* * *

The record is unclear as to when Rebecca returned to Massachusetts and where she resided once she arrived there. She likely lived with George, Almira, and Florence in Revere, not far from Chelsea, or with her widowed sister Dorcas at the Derbys' farm.

George resigned his commission as 2nd Lieutenant on March 21, 1865, and lived with his wife and daughter briefly in Revere. Several years later, they lived in Somerville, Massachusetts, during which time he worked as a suit salesman at Keating & Lane Men's and Boy's Clothing in Boston. By 1876 George moved his family to Almira's hometown of Winthrop, Massachusetts, where, two years after Rebecca's death, they purchased a home at 10 Madison Avenue, a short distance from Almira's parents' farm. After settling in Winthrop, George became active in the local Democratic Caucus and was a constable and sheriff's keeper at Pemberton Square Courthouse in Boston. Upon his death in 1901, George was buried in the Pomroy family plot at Woodlawn Cemetery. His wife, Almira, was also interred there.

✳ ✳ ✳

Almira Cushing Fuller, her husband, Solomon, and their son Georgy continued living in Chelsea for many years following the war. She died in Chelsea, March 16, 1889, of breast cancer and was buried at Woodlawn Cemetery, not far from the Pomroy family plot. Her husband was buried beside her after he died in 1906 from severe injuries sustained when he was run over by a train.

✳ ✳ ✳

Some of the Girls Rebecca Cared for in Newton

The Newton Centre Home for Girls
1870 Federal Census

Ella Thomas	Catherine Hagerty
Anne Tucker	Sarah Wohlers
Elizabeth Welch	Eliza H Smith
Anne Hawkins	Anne Armour
Charity Rackliff	Ellen Dempey
Catherine Gorman	Mary A Doane
Emma E Kessler	Betsey J Bowker

Mary F Chapman
Margarey McInnis
Lilla A Pinkham
Elizabeth McCuckker
Alice Hagerty
Hannah Leicester

Eliza McMinnis
Olive J Kennedy
Edith Cavenagh
Emma Cavenagh
Mary Hill
Emily Hawkins

The Rebecca Pomroy Newton Home for Orphan and Destitute Girls
1880 Federal Census

Susan Currier
Lizzie J. Robin
Annie Brunt
Nellie Robin
Hallie Davis
Maggie Smith
Carrie Robin
Annie Hayes
Belle Brown
Lucy Hawkins

Jennie Coombs
Mary McKenna
Elsie Brown
Nellie Kelloway
Mary Smith
Mary Mills
Faith Robin
Lillian Adams
Lottie Allen

ILLUSTRATIONS

Columbian College Hospital

Figure 1 - Courtesy Library of Congress

Lincoln White House — Second Floor

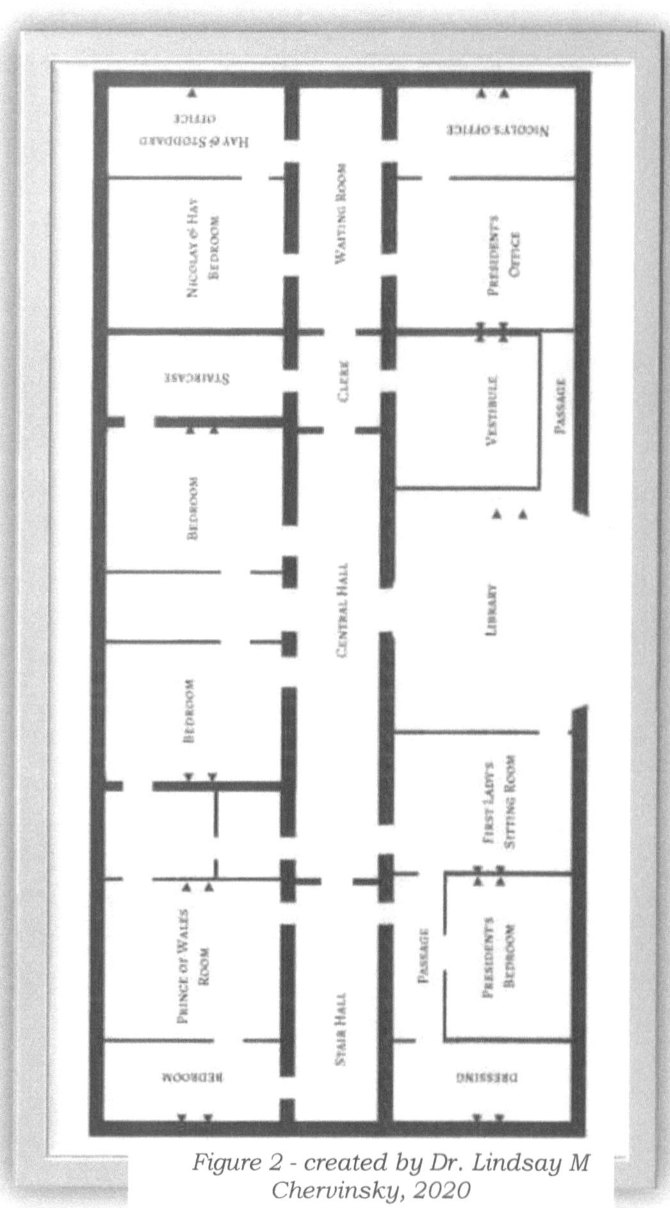

Figure 2 - created by Dr. Lindsay M Chervinsky, 2020

The Lincoln Cottage — Front View (North)

Figure 3 - Courtesy Library of Congress

Father Taylor's Seamen's Bethel

Figure 4 - Photo by Josiah Johnson Hawes ca. 1860

AUTHOR NOTES

Why is Rebecca Pomroy important?

According to President Lincoln, the nation owed her a great debt for holding up his hands in time of trouble.

Lincoln's language in praising Rebecca Pomroy draws on an image from Old Testament canon—a device he often employed. The allegory refers to an event during Israel's exodus out of slavery in Egypt when the Israelites' high priest, Aaron who was also Moses' brother, held up Moses' hands during a key battle against Amalek. It appeared that when Moses held up "the rod of God," the tide of battle went in the Israelites' favor, but when he tired and dropped his hands, their fortunes reversed. Aaron and another man, Hur, rushed forward and held up Moses' hands until victory was won.

Unknown artist's depiction of Hur holding up Moses' hands in time of trouble—courtesy Wikimedia Commons

By invoking that image, Lincoln underscored the critical role he believed Rebecca Pomroy played in saving the nation. He was making a comparison—if he was America's Moses, Rebecca was his high priest. She rescued him from despair and self-doubt when the Union could least afford for him to become debilitated by personal tragedy, battlefield losses, political turmoil, scandal, or a combination of all of them.

Based on Lincoln's commendation, we should explore her nexus to the first family—how those relationships came about and what she did to earn their esteem.

Why present her story as fiction?

There is a dearth of primary materials regarding Rebecca Pomroy's life, so some speculation is necessary to initiate serious discourse on her significance to history. Perhaps, there are documents, letters, family narratives, or the like that will surface once people awaken to the significance of her life. I suppose I could have chosen a different instrument, but I am a storyteller—that's the craft I have used. If *Lincoln's Angel* serves no other purpose, I hope it offers a launching pad for more research into Rebecca Pomroy's contribution to history.

How much of *Lincoln's Angel* is fictional?

Named characters were real people. I changed the spelling of the character named Elmyra Slade. Her real name was Almira Slade, but I changed the spelling to avoid confusion with two other Almira's who were connected to Rebecca Pomroy. Her relationships with all characters in the novel—family members, neighbors, co-workers, patients, notable people, etc.—are accurate based on the principal sources listed below, as well as documentation from public records (e.g. federal and state censuses, city directories, birth, marriage, death registrations, or similar official documents).

In most cases, interactions between Pomroy and other characters have been fictionalized, due to the absence of corroborating evidence and for the purpose of demonstrating important aspects of each character's recorded life experiences. For example, there is no record of Rebecca attending a worship service at the Seamen's Bethel when Charles Dickens was present there. However, Dickens did attend a service at the church along with Waldo Emerson, Charles Sumner, and Henry Longfellow. Records indicate that the relationship between Pomroy and the Bethel's pastor, Reverend Edward Taylor, was such that the scene in question was plausible. The scene also underscores Pomory's lifelong desire to alleviate suffering, especially among children and the destitute.

In cases where it was impossible to know the precise details of interactions between Rebecca Pomroy and others, including the Lincoln family and members of Lincoln's inner circle, I have endeavored to constrain my imagination to fit what has been documented in the principal sources listed below.

In all cases, I have attempted to fairly represent the people, environment, prevailing medical knowledge, transportation methods, and circumstances which I found during deep dives into available historical records.

Lincoln's Angel should be taken as a portrait, rather than a photograph. A portrait is an artist's interpretation of reality, while a photograph is reality captured through a camera's lens. Hence, I have refrained from interrupting the flow of the interpretation with extensive citations and present the following description of principal sources as the factual foundation of *Lincoln's Angel*.

Principal Sources

There are reasons for the gaps in our knowledge about Rebecca Pomroy. She was viewed by people around the Lincolns as a household servant. Nurses of that day were generally considered to be merely changers of chamber pots and soiled linens and washers of mangled flesh.

The sparse record of her life paints her as a hard worker who shunned public attention. It wasn't until her last months of life that she agreed to cooperate with an author, Anna L. Boyden, to leave for posterity a record of her time in the White House. That record appears to be a compilation of journal entries, letters, and personal reminiscences of its subject. It is the only volume written about any part of Rebecca Pomroy's life. Anna L. Boyden book published *Echoes from Hospital and White House: a record of Mrs. Rebecca R. Pomroy's experience in wartimes*, days after Pomroy's death.

The Liljenquist Family Collection of Civil War Photographs in the Library of Congress includes six letters written by Pomroy to Almira. Some of them appear in this book as transcribed by the Library of Congress staff. Excerpts from letters to Almira and other letters are quoted in part by Boyden in her 1884 book. The Almira letters have presented somewhat of mystery in the past, since Pomroy never gave the recipient's last name. A deep dive I made into genealogical records proves the correct identity. Almira Cushing was a girl of twelve when she first met Pomroy who was twenty-five years older. Years later, Cushing married a local Chelsea man, eight years her senior, named Solomon Fuller. Their son, Georgy, was born in 1860, a year before Pomroy joined the Army Nurses Corps. In the Almira letters, Pomroy made affectionate reverences to Almira Cushing Fuller's son Georgy Fuller as well as references to her brother Frank, her sister, Eliza, and Frank's wife Clara.

Erika Holst, Curator of History at the Illinois State Museum—Springfield, made available to me a photocopy of a portion of a daily journal Pomroy kept during her service as a civil war nurse. The complete original has been lost. The first section of the journal, which covered the period from October 1861 up to the middle of September 1863, was stolen along with her satchel and watch, while she was on furlough in Boston during the war. The second portion of the original journal, which Ms. Holst had previously photocopied, disappeared from a collection at the Winthrop Massachusetts public library and has not resurfaced.

Portions of *Lincoln's Angel* consist of excepts or paraphrases from principal sources, all of which are in the Public Domain. The following table cross-references this book's pages to the appropriate source citations.

Table of Citations

Source	Pages
Anna L. Boyden, *Echoes from Hospital and White House: A record of Mrs. Rebecca R. Pomroy's Experience in War Times*, D. Lothrop and Company, Boston, Mass., 1884, p. 18	168-170
Boyden, *Echoes*, p 15-17	173-178
Boyden, *Echoes*, p 12-14	183
Boyden, *Echoes*, p 21-26	191-194
Boyden, *Echoes*, p 31	206
Boyden, *Echoes*, p 48-50	207-209
Boyden, *Echoes*, p 53-57	211-223
Ida M. Tarbell, *In the Footsteps of the Lincolns*, New York, London, Harper & Brothers, 1924, pp 307-308	220
Boyden, *Echoes*, p 57	234
Boyden, *Echoes*, p 94-97	256
Boyden, *Echoes*, p 98	258
Justin G. Turner and Linda Levitt Turner, *Mary Todd Lincoln: Her Life and Letters*, New York: Alfred A. Knopf, 1972), p 128	259
Boyden, *Echoes*, p 98-99	268
Boyden, *Echoes*, p 100	277
Boyden, *Echoes*, p 91-92	285

Pomroy, Rebecca, Letter from Rebecca Pomroy, Columbian College Hospital, Washington, D.C., to Almira. [Feb 1862], Photograph. Retrieved from the Library of Congress, <www.loc.gov/item/2023630332/>.	295
Pomroy, Rebecca, Letter from Rebecca Pomroy, Columbian College Hospital, Washington, D.C., to Almira. [March 7, 1863], Photograph. Retrieved from the Library of Congress, www.loc.gov/item/2023630334/>.	300
Boyden, *Echoes,* p154	303
Boyden, *Echoes,* p 154	316-318
Boyden, *Echoes,* p 173-177	330-332
Boyden, *Echoes,* p 184-187	332-334
Francis B. Carpenter, Six Months at the White House with Abraham Lincoln: The Story of a Picture, New York: Hurd and Houghton, 1867, 17.	338
Boyden, *Echoes,* p 203-212	341-344
Boyden, *Echoes,* p 213-215	345-346
Boyden, *Echoes,* p 217-220	348-350
Frederick Douglass, *Douglass' Monthly* - May 1862	350
Boyden, *Echoes,* p 228-231	351-353
Boyden, *Echoes,* p 148-154	353-355
Boyden, *Echoes,* p 239	356
Boyden, *Echoes,* p 233-236	356-358
Boyden, *Echoes,* p 236-238	358
Pomroy, Rebecca, Letter from Rebecca Pomroy, Columbian College Hospital, Washington, D.C., to Almira. [Feb 13, 1865], Photograph. Retrieved from the Library of Congress, <www.loc.gov/item/2023630333/>.	364
Boyden, *Echoes,* p 244	365

Boyden, Echoes, p 246	365
"President Lincoln Visits City Point and Petersburg," www. nps.gov.	365
John W. Starr, Jr., *Lincoln's Last Day*, Frederick A. Stokes Company, New York, 1922.	366-374
John W. Starr, Jr., *Lincoln's Last Day*, Frederick A. Stokes Company, New York, 1922.	369
John W. Starr, Jr., *Lincoln's Last Day*, Frederick A. Stokes Company, New York, 1922.	370-371
John W. Starr, Jr., *Lincoln's Last Day*, Frederick A. Stokes Company, New York, 1922.	372-373
Anson G. Henry. "A Letter from Dr. Anson G. Henry to his wife". Remembering Lincoln. Web. Accessed December 12, 2023. https://rememberinglincoln.fords.org/node/1175	374
Chicago Tribune, April 17, 1865.	374
Boyden, *Echoes*, p 249	381
A Guide to the History and Records of The Rebecca Pomroy Newton Home for Orphan and Destitute Girls	384
Letter from Gideon Welles to Rebecca Pomroy, 1874, Christopher Foard Collection	384

Letters to Mrs. F., which are quoted by Boyden in her work, appear to be written to either Mrs. Octavia Forsyth, wife of Dr. James Forsyth, or to Mrs. Rebecca Fay, wife of Chelsea's Mayor Frank Fay. The letter to Sister H., also quoted by Boyden, could have been written to Rebecca's neighbor Ann Haskell.

ACKNOWLEDGEMENTS

I owe a great debt to Cheryl Feeney, who edited the three novels in the *Abraham Lincoln Lost Stories Series* and has been an invaluable publishing partner and friend. She challenges me to do better, because, according to her, I am better. Without her persistence and encouragement, none of my published titles would be half as good as they are. That is especially true for *Lincoln's Angel.*

Beta readers—Gayle Smalley, board member of the Rebecca Pomroy Foundation, Don Pugnetti, Jr., retired journalist and author, EC Murray, author and educator, Diane Anton, RN, OCN, Andy Becker, author and retired attorney, David Martyn, author, Denise Frisino, author, and Jo Simms, RN—provided important feedback.

Erika Holst, Curator of History at Illinois State Museum—Springfield, made an invaluable contribution to *Lincoln's Angel* with a photocopy of the second part of Rebecca's journal. She had photocopied the original while conducting research for an article she published on Rebecca Pomroy's experiences in the White House.

Christoper Foard, MSN, RN has made vital contributions to our knowledge of Rebecca Pomroy's wartime service. Among the materials he shared with me are the letters to Almira, which are now curated at the Library of Congress. He also gave me several hours of time by telephone and email to discuss the letters and other materials.

Historical societies like the Asbury Grove Historical Society, Revere Society for Cultural and Historical Preservation, and Salem Historical Society provided important records to help me understand the locales where Rebecca Pomroy lived and worked. During my extensive travels to Lincoln historical sites, President Lincoln's Cottage in Washington DC, has provided special inspiration for scenes in *Lincoln's Angel.*

Without libraries and librarians, especially the Library of Congress, Gig Harbor Washington Public Library with its access to interlibrary loans and genealogical research aids, and Winthrop Massachusetts Public Library and Museum, many of the resources necessary to uncover important details of Rebecca Pomory's life would not have been accessible.

The Pacific Northwest Writers Association, led by Pam Binder, has been an invaluable resource for more than a dozen years—almost since I began my author's journey. Through conferences, workshops, and literary contests, the association has provided encouragement, inspiration, education on the craft of writing, and manuscript critiques.

My many author friends across Washington State's Pierce and Kitsap counties deserve a big thank you for their support of my writer's journey. A special nod goes to Jackie Casella and friends at Creative Colloquy, as well as to the Greater Gig Harbor Literary Society and Mark Miller's Kitsap Literary Artists and Writers.

My writing ventures might have crashed and burned with COVID had it not been for the support and hospitality of the crew at BBQ2U in Gig Harbor. The restaurant's owner, Gary Parker, and his marketing assistant, Lucy Rau, are among my best cheerleaders.

I am also indebted to authors and publishing professionals whose works challenge and inspire me to further refine my craft—most of whom are likely unaware of their influence. Among them are Robert Dugoni, Kurt

Vonnegut, Ruta Sepetys, Wallace Stegner, Susan Higginbotham, publishing guru Jane Friedman, and story doctor Christopher Vogler.

Last, but by no means the least, I am grateful to my wife, Judi—for her patience, support, encouragement, and for indulging me the time and space to bring Rebecca Pomroy's story to life.

ABOUT THE AUTHOR

DL Fowler is an explorer of lost stories, under-told stories, stories we've rarely heard, stories about common people of great significance. Lost stories often contain more truth pages of history texts. They challenge us to view history from fresh angles and with greater empathy for the people who brought us to where we are today.

He earned a BA in English at the University of Southern California and an MBA at California State University-San Bernardino. He graduated at the top of his class from the Defense Language Institute in Monterey, California. Before turning to writing full-time Fowler spent more than twenty years in the finance industry, honing his research skills.

Fowler lives in the Pacific Northwest with his wife and Sprollie pup. When he's not writing or conducting research, he spends his time in the kitchen practicing culinary, rather than literary, arts. His daughter and grandchildren live ten minutes away, and his son and daughter-in-law live in Lincoln Land.

Learn more at  http://dlfowler.com

MORE BY DL FOWLER

Lincoln Raw: a biographical novel
The Turn: a bond that shaped history
Lincoln & the Dead: a short story
The Lincoln Murders: short stories
Ripples: a novel of suspense
Bittersweet: Poems and Essays